I0783707

TWWIST

TACTICAL WRITING WITH IMPACTFUL STORYTELLING TECHNIQUES

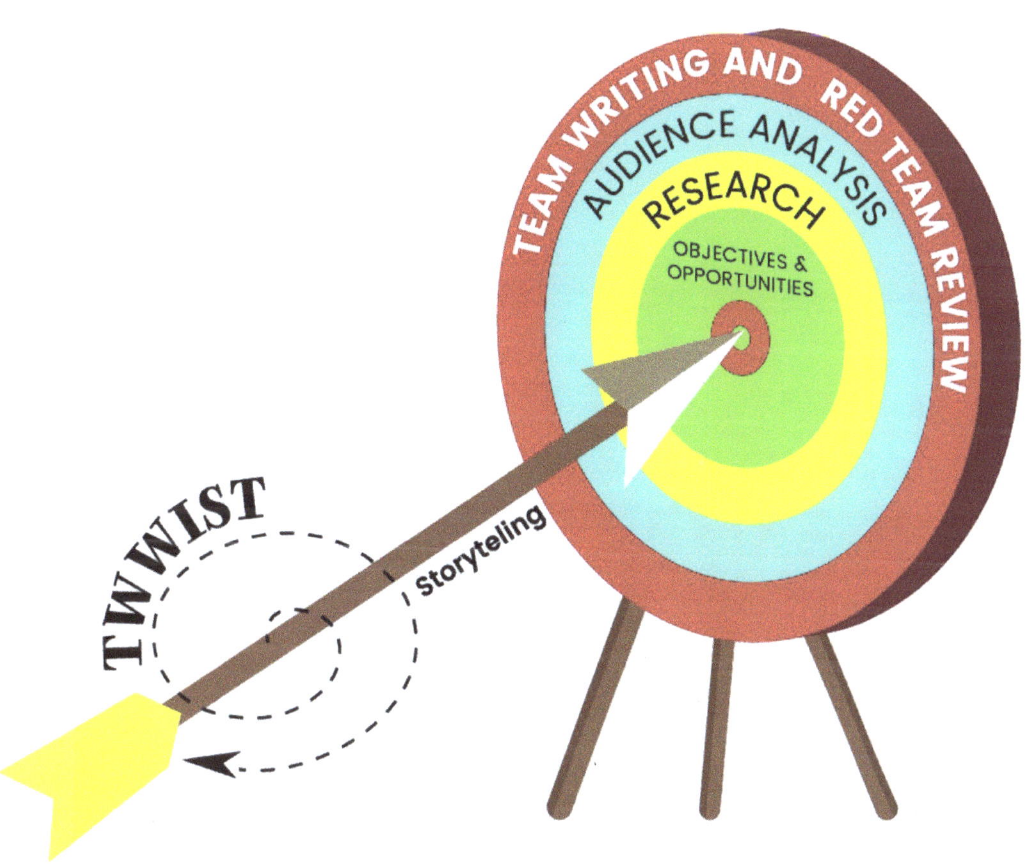

by Dr Terrance E. Boult

TWWIST

Published by Dr. Terrance E. Boult

© 2025 Dr. *Terrance E. Boult* All Rights Reserved.

https://www.innovation.uccs.edu

For more information about permission to reproduce selections from this book for academic/educational use, write to twwistbook@gmail.com.

PS: If you want to rate this book, please always add a short text comment. Did you like it? What can be improved? To whom would you recommend it? Without a text comment, your star rating will be invisible on the Amazon website.

Terrance E. Boult

eBook ISBN: 979-8-89795-457-5
Paperback ISBN: 979-8-89795-458-2
Hardcover ISBN: 979-8-89795-459-9

Dedication

To my wife Ginger. Thanks for loving me, sharing our lives together, and supporting my sometimes crazy endeavors – your love empowers me.   Without love, there is no purpose; without purpose, there is no impact.

"To all those who helped me learn, this book seeks to pay it forward; I ask my readers to pay it forward and ask others to pay it forward as a powerful way to create exponential growth. By helping someone else succeed, you impact their life and inspire them to do the same for others, creating a ripple effect of positivity and progress."

Epigraphs

I argue that the story is a basic human cognitive form; the artful creation and articulation of stories constitute fundamental parts of the leader's vacation. Stories speak to both parts of the human mind—its reason and emotion. Dr. Howard Gardner *Leading minds: An anatomy of leadership* [Gardner, 2011]

Stories are the most powerful delivery tool for information, more powerful and enduring than any other art form. Nancy Duarte *Resonate: Present visual stories that transform audiences.* [Duarte, 2013]

Contents

Foreword

Innovation is the transformation of ideas into impact. The innovation process starts with the communication of an idea in a way that inspires someone to act. The goal of this book is to help the reader to improve their Innovation is the transformation of ideas into impact.

Preface

Innovation is "the transformation of ideas into impact." The innovation process inherently starts with giving voice to an idea to inspire someone, possibly yourself, to act. This is followed by communicating more ideas to more people, ultimately producing more actions. Effective innovation requires multiple phases of tactical communication to influence different people to act to advance the idea. T.E.Boult

This free book aims to help the reader improve their tactical ability to write stories to influence others to help make an impact. As a writer, your communication strategy is the "what"—the impact you are trying to achieve, e.g., to inform, to persuade, or even to evoke a particular emotional response. The tactics, the focus of this book, are the "how" one achieves that strategy.

This book, like most of the curriculum in the Bachelor of Innovation™ curriculum, arose because I could not hire people with the skills I needed in my company – I could get computer scientists or business majors, but not the writing, teaming, or other soft skills I wanted. I realized that as a professor who taught only in my field, I was part of the "problem." I tried to make changes at Lehigh University, but they were too set in their ways. So I moved to the University of Colorado Colorado Springs (UCCS) to develop a new type of degree to address the issues I observed. We vetted the needs and curriculum with more than 50 companies before launching the degrees.

In the case of writing, the best new graduate hires at my company, consistent with our subsequent company interviews, showed that new graduates lacked writing skills and were poor at writing proposals. They should have been much stronger and faster at writing effective user manuals or sales sheets. They failed largely because they did not understand the power of stories. In addition, they also lacked instruction/experience in collaborative writing, which dominates most companies. They needed to improve their technology skills to enhance their writing speed/quality.

When I first proposed teaching a course on technical and proposal writ- ing, the comments I got ranged from confused to insulting. The confused would ask questions along the lines of "Why would a CS Ph.D. and internationally known researcher want to teach writing instead of teaching in their research area?" Or, "Why would I want to teach extra courses instead of doing research projects or lucrative consulting in my research areas?" The insulting comments were because, as a dyslexic, I often have low-level errors in my writing, especially in emails where I do not have someone proofread. To some faculty, my low-level errors were a sign of poor writing, and they argued that we should leave the writing courses to the English/writing faculty.

Figure 1: *Above is a QR code to take you to the BI giving site.   I hope the book has value for you and if you do find value in this free book, consider donating to the Boult't Family Innovationship Fund at the above QR or via the link on the Books website https://bit.ly/TWWIST-BOOK. If you want add a a "in honor/memory" note saying in memory of TWWIST so I know whereit came from*

Despite the opposition, I explained to the dean that if "those who can" are not the ones teaching a topic, then Shaw would be right that "Those that can, do; those who can't, teach." I argued that if the writing department had someone who had published hundreds of technical papers and brought in tens of millions in funded proposals, then I would concede they were more qualified and they should teach the course; I offered the first version of the new course the next year. Over the following two decades, I've transformed what I know works and my continual learning on this topic into tactics to address the most critical skills I observed that needed to be added to a tactical writing curriculum.

"Those who can, do. Those that have done should teach – Learn, Earn, Return!" — T.E. Boult

As someone who has authored 400+ papers and been part of hundreds of millions of dollars in proposals, including being a principal investigator on more than $40 million in R&D funding plus having been involved in three startups that did more than $7 million in revenue each, I have experienced time and time again the power of stories for academic, scientific, and business writing. I have been sharing these techniques in my courses and directly with my students for over 30 years. Since UCCS supported the launch of the Bachelor of Innovation programs, and as I approach retirement, I am focusing back on the BI and teaching. With that shift, I have the time and recognize the need to put these approaches into book form rather than just my lectures.

I was embarrassed when I was diagnosed in college with a learning/reading disability known as dyslexia. I now consider my dyslexia a "differentiability," not a disability. Because of it, I learned early on that working in teams is the best way to leverage different abilities while overcoming my limitations. I learned that effective writing was quite different from grammar and syntax (which should be fixed in the editing stage) and that mental imagery and stories were more important than syntax and grammar.

I have nearly 40 years of using technology and collaborators to improve my writing quality and productivity. Some of these tactics and tools may help you overcome your hurdles if you have struggled with writing. However, I also learned that few people learned as I did and that my undiagnosed struggles were because others expected me to learn/read like them. This experience made me a better teacher as I learned quickly to think explicitly about how different people learn and how to teach them.

A few of the lessons in this book are based on what I do, and I will try to be explicit when the techniques are better suited to those with differentiability. However, most of the lessons are things I have demonstrated to be effective for those with normal abilities. I have continued to learn more and refine how to help others with the writing processes and have adapted to newer technology.

Most of the chapters in this book are on timeless topics, e.g., on the importance of and process of storytelling, along with persuasive and collaborative writing. My use of these techniques has mostly stayed the same over the last decade; dozens of books and studies use these proven approaches.

Other topics, especially the chapters on technology/tools to enhance writing, may be quickly overshadowed by new technological advances; ChatGPT did not publicly exist until 2022. While I have used LLMs for many examples, including some in this book, and on successful proposals and in diverse collaborations, *caveat emptor still applies.* Although no one knows how quickly ChatGPT will be overshadowed by other ML-based tools, many of the lessons in that chapter are adapted from my long-standing interactions with human "collaborators" in writing, so I expect that the lessons/advice, albeit not the syntax, will continue to be useful as ML-models advance. Students should realize that these tools do not replace their role but can augment it. Teaching with such tools presents its own set of challenges, ensuring that students follow the TWWIST process even when using ML tools. The core idea is to use smaller assignments and track changes to see the actual edits and identify who made them – this is good for any team effort to allow non-uniform grades on the team.   I'll share other advice (via email) with other teachers.

You might be wondering why I've chosen to make this a free book. It is because I am focused on increasing my impact by helping more people make an impact. That can lead to exponential growth of impact. My focus on impact is also why I teach and why I moved from Tier 1 universities "down the academic ladder" to a school where I could have more impact. Financially, I could have retired more than a decade ago, but I keep teaching, often more than I am required to, and have developed this book because it's about helping others. So this free book is my gift to you, and as you grow, I hope you too will eventually give your time and skills to help others grow.

What you leave behind is not what is engraved in stone monuments, but what is woven into the lives of others. Pericles, 495 BC – 429 BC

Terrance E. Boult Colorado Springs, CO, USA

1 What Is Tactical Writing?

"First, have a definite, clear practical ideal; a goal, an objective. Second, have the necessary means to achieve your ends: wisdom, money, materials, and methods. Third, adjust all your means to that end."

-Aristotle

Technical Writing is a writing process that focuses on achieving a particular objective(s). Tactical Writing With Impactful Storytelling Techniques (TWWIST), as described in this book, takes the process a step further. Not only does TWWIST help the reader focus on the desired objective, it also inspires action through effective communication.

The ability to persuade, influence, and inspire action through writing has become crucial in our fast-paced, information- driven world. Tactical writing focuses on crafting messages that not only inform but also motivate readers to take specific actions that will help a writer's organization achieve its objectives. Whether the writer is a marketer, a business professional, a nonprofit advocate, a scientist writing research papers, or even a researcher or company seeking funding through proposals, mastering the art of tactical writing can be the key to achieving desired goals and making a significant impact in one's chosen field.

Toward this effort, we will explore the basics and nuances of tactical writing, providing practical tactics and techniques to help engage an audience and spur them into action. We will delve into the foundations of tactical writing, discovering its powerful application across various domains. We will examine real-world examples of tactical writing, illustrating its significance in everyday life.

1.1 Why Tactical Writing Matters

Effective communication is essential in the business world. Tactical communication skills can help us build strong relationships with clients, negotiate deals, and inspire teams to achieve their objectives. Tactical writing enables us to craft persuasive proposals, convincing presentations, and influential emails that leave a lasting impact on our audience. We can enhance our professional reputation, foster collaboration, and drive business growth by honing our tactical writing skills.

Within the realm of academia and research, scientific papers and funding proposals are prime opportunities to employ tactical writing. In scientific papers, researchers can use tactical writing techniques to not only present their findings but to persuade fellow scientists of the validity of their research and encourage further exploration of the subject matter. Proposal writers can use tactical writing to present a compelling case that convinces funding agencies of the importance and potential impact of a research project or social cause, thereby securing financial support for scientific endeavors.

In marketing, tactical writing is the driving force behind captivating advertisements, compelling sales copy, and engaging content. By understanding the principles of tactical writing, marketers can create persuasive campaigns that entice customers to purchase products or services. Effective communication of a company's unique value propositions and offerings will ultimately drive conversions and boost revenue.

Tactical writing plays a crucial role in advocating for social causes and driving positive societal change. Whether we are campaigning for environmental sustainability, raising awareness about social injustices, or promoting equality, the power to articulate our message in a way that motivates others to support our cause is vital. By studying and employing tactical writing, we can amplify our impact, mobilize communities, and create a meaningful difference in the world.

While we will not delve into the realm of literature, poetry, or fiction writing this book, it is important to note that there are strong ties between such storytelling and tactical writing techniques. Engaging narratives, compelling characters, and thought-provoking themes that captivate readers and immerse them in the world of the story will elicit emotional responses whether they appear in a novel, a proposal, or an advertisement. By studying and practicing tactical writing, we can refine our storytelling skills, master the art of engaging readers, and create written works that resonate powerfully with our audience.

1.2 Key Elements of the TWWIST Tactical Writing Process

Figure 1.1: *The core elements of the Tactical Writing With Impactful Storytelling Techniques writing process: analyzing objectives, analyzing the audience, researching the topic and review processes, and team writing processes, ideally combined using storytelling techniques. These core elements are summarized in this chapter, and each has one or more chapters in this book.*

The strategic approach of tactical writing focuses on achieving specific objectives. In order to facilitate the accomplishment of these objectives, the TWWIST (Tactical Writing With Impactful Storytelling Techniques) writing process [1] includes several core elements shown in Fig. 1.1 and summarized below:

➤ **Analyzing Objectives and Opportunities:** Tactical writing cannot happen unless we clearly define our goals—the outcome we need to achieve through our writing. We can then establish objectives to guide the

---

[1] Did you know that the fletching (e.g. feathers) on an arrow/dart is usually mounted at an angle to induce a spin or *twist* as the arrow/dart flies. The twisting along the shaft makes the arrow/dart fly much straighter on the path to the target. That mental image might help you remember the acronym/technique and its purpose—to key you on target while writing

writing process and ensure that analysis, research, reviews, and story help the final output effectively meet our goals. Identifying the available opportunities is a critical part of defining SMART objectives (as described in Chapter *LOOPS*) that ensure our goals are achievable.

➤ **Research:** Given the results of the objectives and opportunity analysis, considerable effort usually goes into researching the topic being addressed. Tactical writing requires the writer (and in team writing situations at least some team members) to have a reasonable understanding of the subject matter, any competing or potential solutions, and the audience review process. This understanding is achieved by gathering information from reliable sources, verifying facts, and exploring different perspectives on the topic.

➤ **Audience Analysis:** It is critical to the tactical writing process that we understand the target audience—who are they, what matters to them, what they know, and what they want. This knowledge helps tailor the language, tone, structure, story, and content of the writing to resonate with the audience and achieve the set objectives. This element of the process can also include an analysis of the audience's formal review process (see below).

➤ **Review Processes:** Two review processes need to be considered—the "audience reviews" and "internal reviews." Internal reviews are crucial in ensuring the quality and effectiveness of the writing. These review processes involve revising for clarity and coherence, proofreading for errors, and refining content based on feedback. Understanding the audience review process, if any, is often critical in ensuring that the writing complies with the required elements of the review criterion. This is distinct from understanding the "personality" issues of the audience and is particularly critical in proposals and scientific papers where the review may have required elements and/or unallowed elements.

➤ **Team Writing Processes:** Collaboration can significantly enhance the quality of writing and is often necessary for large writing efforts that require combinations of different skills/elements, e.g., different subgroups might contribute financial elements, technical elements, or graphics. Team writing processes may involve brainstorming ideas, assigning research, dividing writing tasks, reviewing each other's work, and collectively refining the document. Despite the diversity of team members, the final document must have a coherent structure and voice. However, sections intended for a different audience, e.g. the budget, can use different styles and voice variations to better match the anticipated audience.

➤ **Storytelling Techniques:** In tactical writing, storytelling plays a vital role in bridging the gap between achieving specific objectives and engaging readers on a human level. Stories capture attention, embedding a sense of curiosity and anticipation that keeps the audience engaged. Stories can also provide context to complex information, making it easier to understand and remember. They are a powerful tool for clarifying abstract concepts and can make dry data come alive. Beyond engaging the audience intellectually, stories tap into the reader's emotions, stimulating an emotional response that can significantly enhance the impact of the message. While providing details and memorable context, a story creates an emotional connection that fosters empathy and trust. By embedding a tactical message within a story's structure, a writer significantly enhances the likelihood that the audience will remember and act upon that message. In essence, storytelling is not just a literary technique; it is a strategic tool. By incorporating impactful storytelling in tactical writing, writers can captivate, clarify, evoke emotions, foster trust, and enhance memory, effectively boosting the impact of our message and the desired response from our audience.

These strategic elements of the TWWIST writing process are not purely sequential; they often are cyclical, revisited multiple times as new information is discovered and the story is refined. In particular, audience analysis and research are often reiterated as the team brainstorms the story based on their analysis and research findings. The audience analysis sets up the research agenda, which informs the story and becomes the basis for feedback for the next round of audience analysis, all in an effort to get through the audience's defenses and evoke a memorable connection with the audience.

In the context of tactical writing, communication, persuasion, and rhetoric, the term "audience defenses" typically refers to the barriers or objections that an audience may have when presented with a certain message or argument. In order to overcome the audience's defenses, one must anticipate potential objections and address them proactively using a mixture of facts/data and persuasive arguments. Correctly anticipating the audience's defenses or potential objections is crucial to formulating an effective story, argument, or message and even in setting up the research agenda.

1.3 Essential Phases of the TWWIST Writing Process

Successful writing, especially in a professional context, is not a simple outpouring of information onto a page. While every effort will be unique, successful tactical writing needs a well-structured approach to convey ideas effectively. Allocating appropriate time for each phase of the writing process is essential.

Adopting a 60-15-25 model — devoting 60% of the effort to pre-writing, 15% to the writing phase, and 25% to rewriting — can be a strategic way to apply the TWWIST approach and produce an impactful document. This time allocation is a good guide for most any significant writing endeavor, whether it is a report, an article, or a proposal. The only writing where we *a priori* expect a different allocation is in speech writing for oneself, where 5% to 15% percent of one's time is devoted to the practice of delivering the speech. The amount of time you allocate to practice will depend on your experience and the importance of your objective and your audience.

Tactical writing is as much about the journey as the destination. A formal, balanced writing process that emphasizes preparation as much or more than execution and revision is essential for producing high-quality content. Investing significant time in the pre-writing phase ensures the foundation is robust and makes the subsequent stages smoother and more effective. It is more efficient to research the story before spending time on the actual text than to have to go back and edit until it works. The TWWIST approach helps ensure the journey is both strategic and impactful.

1.3.1   Pre-Writing: Laying the Groundwork (60% of Effort)

➤ **Formalizing Objectives:** Before we pen a single word, it is essential that we define the purpose of our writing. What is our intent? What are we supposed to achieve? Whether we seek to inform, persuade, or call to action, our objectives must be explicit. It is not uncommon to have multiple simultaneous goals, so the formalization of our objectives provides a targeting scope throughout the writing process.

➤ **Discovering Opportunities:** Tactical writing often addresses a gap or an unmet need, so this phase involves understanding where the opportunities lie. Are we addressing a topic that has not been explored, presenting a unique perspective, or exploring an emerging trend in the industry? Our answers to these questions point us toward different opportunities. Proposals often require explicit processes for soliciting proposals and, hence, places to look for them.

➤ **Research:** No matter the expertise level of the writer, research is crucial. It involves collecting data, citing credible sources, and keeping up with the latest findings. Solid research is the backbone of content and the cornerstone of credibility. Research is essential in discovering opportunities and audience analysis. In Chapter *Research and Tools for Tactical Writing*, we touch on some tools for research, including web-searches, Google Scholar and recent advances like ChatGPT.

➤ **Audience Analysis:** Every piece of writing has a target audience. Whether writing to industry professionals, customers, or internal team members, understanding the needs, preferences, and level of understanding of our specific audience is paramount. We cannot ensure that our content will be relevant and engaging if we do not target our audience. In Chapter *Unlocking the Potential of Audience Analysis*, we will explore this stage in greater detail.

➤ **Formulating the Core Story:** A good tactical writer will have constructed a preliminary story idea before conducting the research and audience analysis. However, a good writer does not hold too tightly to that preliminary story. We should expect the story to morph as we go through the stages of the process and learn more about the opportunities, audience, and research. Storytelling in tactical writing is not just about the flow, but about the structure of the key messages and how to make the content more understandable, more relatable, more memorable, and more impactful. After gathering all the necessary information, the final story must be crafted using core storytelling techniques. We will cover some of these techniques in Chapters 5–6.

1.3.2   Writing: Constructing the Narrative (15% of Effort)

➤ **Team-based Textual Writing:** In collaborative environments, writing often involves multiple members who contribute their insights and expertise. Writing teams may involve a handful of people (3-5) to more than 100 people. While writing in teams can lead to richer, more well-rounded content, managing a team can be challenging. The team's roles and process for managing a team through a good writing process will be discussed in Chapter *A Team Approach to Tactical Writing*, but a few preliminary issues will be discussed in Chapter *LOOPS*.

➤ **Graphic Development:** The adage, "a picture is worth a thousand words," rings true here. Graphics, plots, infographics, or illustrations can support and enhance textual content. Graphics offer visual breaks and can present complex data succinctly. Well-done graphics allow readers to skim the document and grasp the overall story before they get into detailed reading. Due to the abundant resources on how to do good visuals/graphics, we will not devote much space to the subject, but we will explore their role in storytelling in Chapter *How to Create Tactical Stories*. Despite our shorter coverage and extensive use of references for this topic, do not underestimate the value of graphics nor the time it will take to create them—it is often 50% of the "writing" effort or about 7-8% of the total effort.

1.3.3   Rewriting: Polishing the Gem (25% of Effort)

➤ **Red Team Review:** The red team review process involves a subteam, ideally separate from the original writers, to review the document. Their aim is to identify any gaps, inaccuracies, or areas in need of improvement. Coming in with fresh eyes, the review team can spot issues that the writing team might have overlooked. If the overall team is small, the writers can switch roles and use formal checklists to do a review, but that is much less likely to provide the same level of performance that a red team review would provide. When working on very large proposals, a writing team will often use two review teams. The first team will conduct a smaller, high-level "pink team" review early in the process to assess the story and its alignment with company objectives and to identify missing elements and areas needing improvement. When the proposal is closer to completion, a more detailed "red team" review is done with eight to ten people. These reviews are an inherent part of good tactical team writing and will be covered in Chapter *A Team Approach to Tactical Writing*.

> **Editing:** Before sending a document for red team review, the writing team should conduct a grammar and style pass to find/fix as many small issues as possible. Grammar/style can benefit from automated tools, which will be discussed in Chapter *Research and Tools for Tactical Writing*. After the red team review, it is time for rigorous editing to check for grammatical errors and ensure that the content aligns with the objectives set during the pre-writing phase. This is also the time to refine the story narrative, ensure clarity, and ensure the document is as accurate and polished as possible.

1.4 Tactical Writing in the Realm of Nonfiction

There are many types of nonfiction writing depending on the domain and goals. Consider the following (partial) short list of some major types/styles:

1.4.1 Biographical Writing

> **Autobiography**: Unlike a biography, which can be written about any person, an autobiography is a self-written account of one's own life.

> **Biography**: A biography is a detailed description or account of someone's life. It involves more than the basic facts of education, work, relationships, and death; it portrays a person's experience through their life events.

> **Memoir**: A memoir is a type of nonfiction similar to an autobiography. However, instead of covering a person's entire life, memoirs typically focus on specific themes or periods from the author's life.

1.4.2 Persuasive Writing

> **Persuasive Writing**: In general, this type of writing can be on any subject and aims to convince the reader or listener of the writer's perspective or argument. It utilizes logic, reason, and emotion to show that one idea is more legitimate than another.

> **Business Pitches**: Business pitches are a specific form of persuasive writing, generally created with the aim of securing funding or investment. They briefly explain the company's product, business model, target market, competitive advantage, team, and financial projections.

> **Proposal Writing**: This type of writing is commonly used in academia, business, or nonprofits. It usually includes a problem or question to be addressed as well as outlining a method for study or solution. Proposal writing aims to persuade the reader to take action or approve a plan.

> **Company Proposals**: Company proposals are a specific type of proposal that is often drafted to propose a new business initiative, suggest a strategy for resolving a problem, or request funding for a project. They are usually addressed to decision-makers within an organization or to potential investors.

> **Copywriting**: This genre of writing may include advertising or other forms of marketing. Copywriting aims to increase brand awareness and ultimately persuade a person or group to take a particular action.

> **Essay**: An essay is a short piece of writing on a particular subject. It can be formal or informal and is often used to present an author's perspective or argument.

1.4.3 Informational Writing

> **Historical Writing**: This type of writing includes history books, academic articles, and encyclopedic

entries. It is used to inform readers about historical events, figures, or periods.

➤ **Instructional Writing**: Instructional writing (also known as a "how-to" or procedural writing) is written to explain a set of steps or a process. Examples include recipes, user manuals, textbooks, and educational guides.

➤ **Journalistic Writing**: This type of writing includes news reports, feature articles, and editorials found in newspapers, magazines, and online or broadcast news outlets. The main purpose is to inform readers about current events or issues.

➤ **Reports**: A report is a factual paper written with the specific intention of relaying information or recounting certain events in a presentable form. Reports often involve analysis of data or research findings but generally do not go through a review process.

➤ **Whitepapers**: A whitepaper is often viewed as a company report, but while it contains factual material, it is often written with the specific intention of enhancing the company brand or product placement. This type of writing often uses a fact-based approach but with the goal of selling the company or product.

➤ **Scientific Writing**: This type of writing is used to communicate scientific findings or theories. It includes research papers, laboratory reports, and articles in scientific journals. Scientific writing is a particular type of informational writing that is similar to a report, but it has two audiences: the peer reviewer and the eventual reader. This difference is important because scientific writing almost always goes through a peer-review process before it can go to press. So the authors must anticipate the reviewer as a hypercritical, often antagonistic, audience and must write to overcome reviewer objections that would otherwise "kill" the paper.

➤ **Speech Writing**: This refers to writing a script for a public address or some form of spoken presentation. Speeches can take many forms, including political speeches, ceremonial speeches, or motivational speeches. While a speech need not be written, we include it here because until a person is very experienced at speaking in public, speeches should be written first, then delivered. Also, the person writing the speech may not even be the person who delivers it. A speech must be crafted with the audience, the speaker, and the event's context in mind.

➤ **Technical Writing**: Technical writing is a specialized form of informational written communication that conveys complex information clearly, accurately, and succinctly to a specific audience. It is intended to inform, instruct, or explain something to the reader, typically in the fields of science, engineering, technology, and other technical domains.

➤ **Travel Writing**: This type of writing is used to describe places and experiences encountered while traveling. It includes travel guides, travel blogs, and feature articles in travel magazines.

1.4.4 The Relationship of Tactical Writing to Persuasive and Technical Writing

While you will be able to apply the tactical techniques discussed in this book for any of these types of writing, not all have an objective to persuade the reader to action.

From the list, persuasive writing is the type most related to tactical writing. While they may seem the same, it is significant that persuasive writing is about the writer's perspective or argument. In contrast, the set objective rather than the perspective or argument drives the content in tactical writing. Often, part of the goal of the tactical research phase is to "discover" and analyze alternatives to the perspectives or arguments.

While the techniques of persuasive writing are part of the tactical writing toolkit and will be discussed in this book, they are only a part of tactical writing.

Technical writing is the second type of writing that is highly related to tactical writing. Both types of writing require a deep understanding of the audience and a structured approach to delivering information to that audience, but each has distinct goals and methodologies. The key difference lies in their end goals and presentation style. Tactical writing is a strategic approach primarily used in fields to achieve a specific objective, whereas technical writing generally focuses on informing the reader.

The purpose of tactical writing is not just to inform but to engage, to resonate, and often to persuade a call to action. Tactical writing relies heavily on audience analysis, research, collaborative writing processes, storytelling techniques, and thorough review processes in order to achieve its specific objectives. It usually employs storytelling and emotional language to accomplish its goals, although it will employ technical writing when the analysis and research suggest the audience will respond positively to it.

In contrast, technical writing is used to clearly and accurately convey complex information related to scientific, technological, or other specialized fields. The focus is more on the content being precise, structured, and logical. The tone of technical writing is formal, objective, and impersonal, with the main aim being to instruct or inform rather than persuade. It is typically intended for an audience of professionals or individuals who seek to understand a complex concept, process, or product.

1.5 Focus on TWWIST Examples

To demonstrate the power of TWWIST tactical writing techniques, we will dive deeper into only a few of the types of writing we have explored.

➤ **Funding Proposals**: Proposals are among the most direct applications highlighting all aspects of the TWWIST processes. We will examine both finding and responding to three major types of them throughout the book:

➤ **Technical/Scientific Funding Proposals**, which require tactical writing to effectively research ideas, communicate past research findings, persuade peers and funding agencies, and secure support for further exploration of scientific ideas.

➤ A second, but often a quite different type of proposal, is the **Nonprofit Fundraising Appeal**. Nonprofit organizations rely heavily on tactical writing to raise funds for their causes. From heartfelt stories of individuals impacted by their work to compelling calls to action, tactical writing enables nonprofits to engage potential donors, create empathy, and inspire philanthropic support.

➤ A third type is a **Requests-for-Proposals** or **Requests-for-Quote**. When companies respond to requests-for- proposals (RFPs) from potential clients, tactical writing plays a crucial role. These responses require a persuasive approach to highlight the company's expertise, capabilities, and unique value proposition. Effective tactical writing in RFP responses can significantly increase the chances of winning contracts, securing business opportunities, and establishing fruitful partnerships.

➤ **Scientific Papers**: Scientific papers require tactical writing to effectively research ideas, communicate research findings, and persuade the reviewers to accept the paper. While it is often considered an area needing an impartial/objective approach, only the actual science itself needs to be objective. By employing tactical storytelling techniques, researchers can better connect with readers and convey the significance and potential impact of their work on their field, which helps the paper make it through the review process.

➤ **Copywriting**: Consider memorable marketing or advertising campaigns that have left a lasting impression on you. Companies like Nike, Coca-Cola, and Apple have mastered the art of tactical writing, crafting compelling taglines and messages that evoke emotion, instill brand loyalty, and drive consumers to take action. We will explore some aspects of this, including what makes advertising "stick."

➤ **Impactful Speeches**: Think of influential speeches by leaders like Martin Luther King Jr., John F. Kennedy, or Winston Churchill. Through their words, these iconic figures delivered messages that resonated with millions, mobilized communities, and inspired social change. Their speeches were meticulously crafted using tactical writing techniques to persuade and motivate audiences. To prepare ourselves for any public speaking opportunity, we will have a chapter on using tactical writing as a strong basis for speech preparation.

Personal Story: The Importance of Story Since a key strategy of tactical writing is storytelling, each chapter will have a personal tactical writing story. My first "personal" tactical writing story as a researcher comes from the summer when I was just starting as a faculty member at Columbia University. I had helped my advisors on previous grants but had done so as part of a team, so I was directed by others and wrote smaller parts of the proposal. Now that I was writing my first proposal on my own, I wanted to tell the story of my research and how I would approach the research for the problems I was proposing. I discussed this approach with my advisors, who had never seen a proposal like the one I was suggesting. However, as they always encouraged me to find my voice/path, they said I could try it.

I thought I had plenty of time, so I researched the topics and took my time writing it up. The proposal told my expected personal journey, including related problems I solved in my Ph.D. as well as those I failed to solve and why. I then described, in story form, how I attacked seven different problems. I explained why each was difficult yet important, considering the small amount of funding requested. I explained how I would attack each one and why I thought my approach might work despite the difficulties. When my advisors read it, they said it read like a collection of disconnected short stories. They said I provided too much motivation but not enough detail on how I would solve each problem. They said my proposal lacked a coherent connection between the problems. To top it off, they claimed that if they were a reviewer, they would probably not recommend it for funding!

By then, it was too late to rewrite the proposal in the traditional style. My advisor said I could wait until the next round but suggested I refine it and submit it. There was little to lose by submitting, and I could learn from the experience and feedback. So, with three days to the submission deadline, I expanded only the first story, cut it back to six problems, and added an introduction, explaining that in theoretical computer science, it's really hard to predict when things can be proven. I also added a few connections between the techniques, even if the problems were not connected.

My wife proofread it and suggested I add a flowchart to replace the textual timeline—the timeline was required, but those used the space more efficiently and allowed connections between ideas/items. With the flowchart, I could show more of the connections between the techniques used. It was a long weekend with 48 hours straight on the proposal to revise it by the deadline. I submitted it and waited for the reviews.

The reviews were very mixed. One reviewer strongly supported it, one weakly supported it, and one simply hated it. The negative review said it was the worst proposal in his review pile, lacked details, and I should have focused on only one or two problems. The positive reviewer said it was refreshing to see a proposal whose story reflected how most people actually did such research, not pretending that only one problem would be solved.

Although my proposal was funded, the negative review stung. I felt I just got lucky. For the next decade, I retreated back to more traditional proposal styles with less storytelling. For other reasons, I also refocused on more practical problems in vision and learning.

Then, while at a conference, I chatted about that proposal with the person who was my NSF program manager. He asked why he had not seen any more proposals from me. I told him the story of the proposal/review as well as why I switched to more practical problems. His reply surprised me. He said I won the grant because of the storytelling, not in spite of it. (He also applauded my switch to more impactful work, but that is a story for another day.)

That day, I learned three important lessons—the power of storytelling, the importance of getting feedback early in the process, and the importance of seeking formal review feedback whether one wins or loses. From that day onward, I went back to storytelling in my proposals and most of my science papers. Over time, I refined my writing process to the TWWIST approach of this book.

By studying these examples and diving deeper into the principles of tactical writing, you will understand how strategic and persuasive communication can shape opinions, drive action, and create meaningful impact in various domains. In upcoming chapters, we will explore the key elements of tactical writing including understanding audience psychology and aspects of audience review processes, crafting persuasive arguments and rhetorical devices, and employing storytelling techniques. Together, we will unlock the power of tactical writing, equipping you with the skills and knowledge to effectively communicate your ideas, inspire action, and achieve your desired outcomes.

So, let us embark on this journey of discovery and mastery of tactical writing, where you, too, can use TWWIST to become a powerful force for change and transformation.

1.6 Key Terms

1) **Tactical Writing:** *Refers to a writing process that focuses on achieving specific objectives, often through persuasive techniques and storytelling, in order to inspire action through effective communication.*

2) **Tactic:** *Tactic refers to the specific methods or techniques used to achieve an objective within the broader strategy of tactical writing to achieve the set objectives.*

3) **Objective:** *Refers to the specific goals or outcomes that the writing aims to achieve, which could range from informing to persuading or calling to action.*

4) **Persuasive Writing:** *A style of writing that aims to convince the reader or listener of the writer's perspective or argument.*

5) **Technical Writing:** *A specialized form of written communication that conveys complex information clearly, accurately, and succinctly to a specific audience.*

6) **Audience Analysis:** *The process of understanding the target audience's needs, preferences, and level of understanding to tailor the writing accordingly.*

7) **TWWIST:** *An acronym for Tactical Writing With Impactful Storytelling Techniques, which serves as a framework for effective tactical writing.*

8) **60-15-25 Model:** *Refers to the suggested distribution of effort in the tactical writing process: 60% for pre-writing, 15% for writing, and 25% for reviewing.*

9) **Red Team Review:** *The process by which an independent group reviews a written document to identify gaps, inaccuracies, or areas of improvement.*

10) **Graphics:** *Visual elements such as charts, graphs, and images are used in tactical writing to support*

and enhance the textual content.

2 LOOPS: Looping Over Objectives, Opportunities, and Preliminary Stories

"Don't wait for the right opportunity: create it."

-George Bernard Shaw

The TWWIST process begins with a substantial effort to lay the groundwork before the writing actually begins. The initial "Loop" of pre-writing activities focuses on formalizing objectives, searching for and analyzing opportunities, and developing preliminary stories. These activities are iterated because each impacts the other and should be repeated until the objectives are clarified and achievable.

2.1 Formalizing and Socializing Objectives

Individuals and organizations all have objectives and goals. Formalizing and socializing these objectives is a crucial process that paves the way for successful tactical writing. It involves identifying the desired outcomes and clarifying how they will be achieved. This process is complicated because individuals and organizations often have not one but many objectives— some of which are conflicting! Given that many diverse objectives may exist, how does one begin the process?

Start with a brainstorming session through which the team develops a comprehensive list of possible objectives. The process continues by looping over (i.e., iterating) the other stages to formalize and refine the objectives. Once the objectives are formalized, it is important to socialize them among the team/organization to ensure that everyone is on target and understands the priorities across multiple objectives. It is very annoying and wasteful to spend a lot of effort on a writing project only to discover that the team was not addressing the right objectives or did not share the same understanding of the objectives.

2.2 Using the SMART Framework to Formalize Your Objectives

One of the most effective methodologies for setting strong, functional objectives is the SMART framework, which stands for Specific, Measurable, Achievable, Relevant, and Time-bound. This framework is a powerful tool that transforms vague ambitions into clear, actionable objectives. The requirements for SMART objectives are:

- **Specific:** An objective must be clear, detailed, and unambiguous. A generic goal like "improve customer service" is vague. It lacks focus and leads to misunderstanding. It cannot produce cohesive, effective action. In contrast, a specific goal like "reduce customer complaint response time by 30% within the next two months" can produce a transformational outcome. This objective provides clear direction about what needs to be achieved, making it easier for employees to focus their efforts effectively. The clarity of detailed, specific objectives eradicates misunderstanding and guides team members toward the goal.

- **Measurable:** A good objective must have a tangible, quantifiable outcome. It must provide a clear metric that can be tracked over time. If a company is keen on expanding its market footprint, for example, it might set an objective like "increase the company's market share by 3% during the next quarter." This objective provides a specific numeric target, allowing the company to track its progress.

- **(Aggressively) Achievable:** Objectives must be realistic and attainable in light of the team's resources, skills, and capabilities. Unrealistic objectives may demotivate team members due to the perceived impossibility of the goal. If a company's current email marketing campaign is garncring 50 new subscriptions per week, an achievable objective might be to "increase weekly email subscriptions to 75 within two months." To insist on an immediate tenfold increase in subscriptions may be unrealistic, but if the current level is only one person/subscription, then a 10-fold increase may not be aggressive enough. While "achievable" is normally used alone for this part of the SMART objectives, students often interpret the term way too conservatively. Hence, adding "aggressive" as a modifier emphasizes that in nearly every setting, objectives should be aggressive as well as achievable.

The greater danger for most of us lies not in setting our aim too high and falling short; but in setting our aim too low, and achieving our mark. Michelangelo, 1475-1564

➤ **Relevant:** In order to ensure that the team's efforts contribute meaningfully toward the company's strategic plan, objectives must align with the company's mission, vision, and long-term goals. For example, if a software development company aims to broaden its digital footprint, a relevant objective could be to "launch a mobile application for our primary service in the next three months."

➤ **Time-bound:** Every objective must be tied to a specific timeline. A timeline conveys a sense of urgency and focus that helps facilitate effective time management. A time-bound objective could be to "increase social media followers by 20% within the next 90 days."

SMART objectives are integral components of strategic planning that establish a clear path toward long-term goals and foster synergy within the team. It is imperative to continuously revisit and reassess these objectives, measuring progress and making adjustments as required. Employing the SMART methodology makes the planning process more efficient and contributes to improved performance, productivity, and long-term success.

2.2.1   Understanding the Difference Between SMART Objectives and Vague Goals

Although we may frequently use "goals" and "objectives" as synonyms in our conversations and even in our writing, we must not confuse SMART objectives with vague goals. A goal can be viewed as a broad primary outcome or achievement, while an objective is a measurable step to achieve a goal. Without specifics, a goal can be vague, lacking the essential elements to guide the pursuit of its achievement. For instance, a vague goal could be, "I want our company to grow." This statement is clear. However, it does not provide any discernible direction or concrete measure for success.

To transform a vague goal such as this statement into a SMART objective, we must research to understand the context, determine the possibilities, and identify potential measures for success. This research might involve discovering/analyzing opportunities, understanding market trends, analyzing internal capabilities, and studying competitors.

After conducting our research, we might refine the vague goal to a SMART objective: "Increase our quarterly sales by 15% by the end of the fiscal year." This objective is Specific (increase quarterly sales), Measurable (by 15%), Achievable (given resources and market conditions), Relevant (to the overall growth of the company), and Time-bound (by the end of the fiscal year). This provides a clear path forward with milestones for success that everyone can understand and work toward.

Personal Story: The Origin of My Formal Writing Processes

You might wonder why I developed such formalized processes and spent time detailing each step if I were writing the proposals myself. The detailed process, however, was not intended for my personal benefit. In my second company, I worked to help our employees understand the practical aspects of writing proposals because proposals were critical to the success of our customers and to our business model.

The timing was right after the 9/11 tragedy when the government pushed for various ports and other major infrastructures to acquire the security systems we were developing. Our security products sold for between $250,000 and $1,000,000 dollars and most of our customers had to apply for government grants or loans to acquire them. However, most organizations lacked experience in developing or writing proposals. So, part of the sales team's effort was to help our customers understand not only our product and how it could improve their security but also how they could apply for government funding to acquire it.

Unfortunately, none of our sales teams had experience in government proposal writing, so I had to help them learn how to assist our potential customers in doing the research, writing the grants, and telling the stories necessary to acquire our products. Formalizing a process that they could follow and succeed in was essential to our success. I developed many of the techniques in this book during that time as I taught others how to use storytelling and tactical writing to achieve their objectives.

The tactical process steps described in this chapter are based on the formalizing of objectives that went into that effort. It was further refined when I started teaching this process to students in the Bachelor of Innovation degree at UCCS. As I learned more about the science of storytelling, I continued to adapt and refine the process, resulting in the LOOPS methodology explored in this and subsequent chapters. My students and I have used it with many companies as I help them go through the process of getting government-funded research, such as via an SBIR/STTR grant.

2.2.2   Team Objective Setting Facilitates the TWWIST Process

Team objective setting is vital to successful collaborative efforts. It is at times, a challenging process, but it also offers unique advantages. Once accomplished, the objectives set the stage for effective teamwork and ensure that the team's collective efforts are aligned with achieving a common goal. The key to successful team objective setting lies in transparency, communication, and mutual understanding.

One significant advantage of team collaboration in setting objectives is the diversity of perspectives that can result. Each member brings unique experiences and insights to the table that contribute to a more comprehensive view of the objectives. The team blend of different approaches and ideas allows for a more balanced and robust set of objectives.

When working on a team, it can be helpful to do some self-assessment and personal goal analysis before the first meeting. Individual self-assessment allows you to identify your strengths, weaknesses, and areas of interest. It is a powerful tool for personal development and goal setting. It can help you better relate to your team members and objectives when working on a collaborative effort.

By understanding your skills and tendencies, you can set more realistic and relevant personal objectives and become a more productive and effective team member. Techniques such as the SWOT analysis (Strengths, Weaknesses, Opportunities, Threats) or a reflective journal can assist in this self-assessment. Both techniques encourage introspection and help identify areas for improvement as well as opportunities to capitalize on your strengths. For example, if your personal objectives and skills are suited to managing others, then volunteering to lead a part of the writing effort can be satisfying and helpful to your team. If your personal objectives are more technical, volunteering to help with the research could be an excellent fit.

Once the team gathers, the first step in setting objectives is a team workshop or brainstorming session. Brainstorming allows for the free flow of ideas and helps the team to innovate and think outside the box. During these sessions, it is crucial to establish an open and non-judgmental environment in which each member feels comfortable sharing their ideas. The objective the team is seeking should be clearly defined and understood by all.

After the brainstorming session, it is time to refine and finalize the objectives. This process involves narrowing down the ideas, merging similar ones, and discarding those that do not align with the team's broader goals. The Affinity Diagram is a tool that can help with this step. This resource is free online. It can help the team organize similar ideas and concepts, which enables them to identify themes and visualize how different ideas connect.

Once the team has a list of potential objectives, the next step is to ensure they are SMART: Specific, Measurable, Achievable, Relevant, and Time-bound. The SMART framework ensures that the team's objectives are well-defined and trackable. Objectives should be specific enough to guide the team's actions, measurable to track progress, achievable to maintain motivation, relevant to the team's larger goals, and time-bound to provide a clear timeline for completion.

However, setting objectives is not a one-time activity; it is an ongoing process. The team must revisit their objectives regularly to verify progress, adjust strategies, and stay focused. Regular team meetings or check-ins facilitate this process, allowing the team to discuss challenges, celebrate achievements, and ensure everyone is on the same page.

Another essential aspect to consider during team objective setting is the distribution of tasks. It is crucial to ensure that tasks are allocated based on each team member's skills and capabilities. This increases efficiency and helps to ensure that the "achievable" aspects of the SMART framework match the team and its resources. The team can use techniques like the Responsibility Assignment Matrix (RAM), also called the Responsible, Accountable, Consulted, and Informed (RACI) Matrix, to track the responsibilities, assignments, and roles for each task. This helps to ensure that resources are identified and every team member knows what they are supposed to do, who is accountable, and who is accountable to whom.

The four roles are broken down as follows:

Responsible: The person(s) completing the task

Accountable: The team member coordinating the actions, making decisions, and delegating to those responsible for the task

Consulted: The person(s) who, as part of decision-making processes, will be interactively communicated with regarding decisions and tasks

Informed: The person(s) who will be (passively) updated during the project and upon its completion

The RACI matrix will be discussed in more detail in Chapter *A Team Approach to Tactical Writing,* when we discuss detailed team processes.

Team objective setting is about far more than setting goals. It is about creating a collaborative and supportive environment in which each team member contributes toward a shared vision. By using techniques such as brainstorming, Affinity Diagrams, the SMART framework, regular team check-ins, and the RAM/RACI matrix, teams can set clear, achievable, and meaningful objectives that lead to long-term goals.

2.3 Connecting Short-Term Objectives with Long-Term Vision

Short-term objectives are the stepping stones that, when methodically aligned, lead to realizing an organization's long-term vision. Short-term objectives offer a tangible direction, helping teams prioritize tasks for the present and set the pace for upcoming actions. While they serve immediate needs and present quick wins, their ultimate significance is gauged by how well they set the stage for the future.

As we seek objectives that will accomplish this task, we must not overlook the SMART requirement that objectives be *achievable.* In many writing efforts, this may not be clear at the beginning. When this occurs, the recommended TWWIST approach is to explicitly document objectives that require any prerequisite(s), such as "we must have X," in order to make the objective achievable. If this *a priori* requirement is not addressed early in the effort (e.g., by research or teaming), the effort is likely to fail. For example, in many proposal efforts, we quickly determined that a partner was needed to provide access to specific hardware or certain expertise that would enable the effort to succeed. Long before any "writing" would happen, identifying and securing those resources was critical to establishing the objective as potentially achievable.

The satisfaction derived from achieving short-term objectives, called Momentum Builders, can significantly boost morale. They act like a catalyst that propels teams to take further actions with renewed vigor. Each short-term goal, visualized as a foundational layer of the long-term vision, plays a pivotal role in preparing the way for long-term objectives that reflect the organization's larger vision and ambition.

While short-term objectives provide direction, long-term objectives provide a road map for achieving the long-term vision, the ultimate destination. Like short-term objectives, long-term objectives should be inspiring and motivating, challenging yet achievable. Long-term objectives are essential in setting future-focused targets that are aligned with long-term success. Techniques such as visualization, long-range planning, and scenario analysis can be used to develop meaningful long-term objectives that provide a broader perspective and more comprehensive vision.

Be aware that on the journey from the immediate to the ultimate, overlaps and conflicts between short-term tasks and long-term aspirations are inevitable. Recognizing areas where short-term objectives intersect with long-term vision helps to ensure that the former feeds into the latter. It is also necessary to gauge which short-term objectives have significant potential to shape or influence the envisioned long-term goals. Most importantly, while short-term objectives provide immediate direction and benefit, it is imperative to ensure that they align with the long-term vision if sustained growth toward the goal is to occur.

Maintaining alignment between immediate tasks and the future vision requires employing strategic techniques. Goal Mapping Workshops are interactive sessions aimed at visualizing and understanding the interplay between immediate tasks and overarching aspirations. Regular check-ins, which are essential for consistent monitoring, ensure that teams remain aligned and address deviations early. Priority-setting sessions, focused on addressing conflicts that may arise, help to guarantee that the team's energy is channeled toward tasks that are paramount in the larger scheme of things.

2.4 Opportunity Hunting — Often Looping Back for More Research

Once the long-term vision and the objectives that will advance it are in place, the tactical writing team must recognize and seize the opportunities that will make the ultimate destination achievable. A timely, identified opportunity and the articulate expression of it can act like a fulcrum for success in varied arenas—academia, business, or non-profit initiatives. However, opportunity hunting may not be as straightforward or simple as we might like. To help in this process, consider a few strategies for researching and identifying these pivotal opportunities and the subsequent additional research they will require.

2.4.1 Search for Call-for-Proposals (CFPs)

A great way to find opportunities is by finding someone who is looking for something that matches your objectives. We'll refer to these options as Call-for-Proposals (CFPs). Organizations, whether academic journals, business consortiums, or funding agencies, regularly disseminate CFPs that, in essence, invite potential contributors to share their expertise. So, CFPs are goldmines for professionals seeking structured opportunities if they understand the language. There are a number of specific names for types of CFPs that organizations use to make a public "call" (request) for people to submit proposals. Writers should be familiar with them so they can do web searches for the CFP plus (+) terms related to your objectives. Here are some effective synonyms and how they normally are used:

➤ **Request for Proposals (RFP):** Widely used in many industries, especially in business and government sectors, this term is common in the U.S.

➤ **Invitation to Tender (ITT):** Common in the U.K. and other Commonwealth countries, these are typically used to procure goods and services.

➤ **Request for Quotation (RFQ):** RFQs are used when the requester knows precisely what they want and seeks companies that will provide detailed pricing for a specific list of items.

➤ **Request for Information (RFI):** This request is often a preliminary step to an RFP, RFQ, or ITT and is used to gather information about supplier capabilities.

➤ **Call for Papers (CFP):** Specific to academic, research, or professional conferences, this is a solicitation for papers or presentations on particular topics.

➤ **Expression of Interest (EOI):** A preliminary document indicating interest in a project is used across industries and regions.

➤ **Call for Bids (CFB):** Used primarily in construction and real estate.

➤ **Request for Application (RFA):** Associated with grants to announce funding opportunities.

➤ **Notice Inviting Tender (NIT):** This invitation for product or service proposals is used in India and some other countries.

➤ **Request for Offer (RFO):** Used in business contexts for seeking offers or proposals for potential contracts.

➤ **Request for Expression of Interest (REOI):** This preliminary step to shortlist potential suppliers or contractors is used in Australia and New Zealand.

➤ **Broad-Agency-Announcement (BAA):** Used primarily by U.S. government agencies, this "standing" call for proposals allows organizations to submit on broadly described topics covered by the BAA. These are essentially contracting mechanisms that allow agencies to accept proposals on a topic without an explicit call for it.

Searching for one or more of these terms and a few terms of interest specific to your objectives can be an effective first step in finding relevant opportunities. Although some of the above are not actual CFPs, they still are useful for opportunity hunting. The Request for Information and interest-type calls, for example, allow organizations to provide information to the requester that the requester may use to decide if there is sufficient interest to issue a CFP. These often are longer-term opportunities whereby you can build relationships, network, and potentially influence the final CFP.

Other good options to explore include single-issue websites and aggregators that collect copies of CFPs/RFPs on relevant topics. Government agencies run many such sites, i.e., sam.gov, sbir.gov, and grants.gov, which are free services that list many government CFPs. Signing up on these or other websites can provide CFP email alerts directly to your inbox. Many commercial aggregators offer free access for applicants, some offer additional services, and a few require paid memberships. In addition, most academic conferences have formal CFPs to attract research papers. Regular monitoring of domain-specific websites, specialized forums like *WikiCFP*, and dedicated mailing lists can ensure you never miss out on potential opportunities.

Deciphering a CFP for rules and clues can often make the difference between acceptance and rejection, and this is one example where opportunity hunting requires looping back to do more research. We'll explore these in more detail in Chapter 8 on proposals, but here we just show how they relate to to more research. The primary goal of the CFP is to delineate the underlying objectives set by the issuer and specify review/evaluation criteria. However, the writing of the CFP can also provide insights into the "audience."

For instance, a CFP from the "National Endowment for the Humanities" might prioritize interdisciplinary approaches. By researching the organization's past winning proposals your team may find insights into what worked, giving an edge to proposals combining literature and technology, over art and music – or just the reverse. Another CFP might list requirements for complex budget/spending plans, suggesting a critical role for researching the type of details used in successful proposals or simply the tools used in that organization.

Ensuring alignment with guidelines from the submission format to the thematic approach is crucial. Many CFPs will link to formal websites for instructions and even for submission. In the tactical writing process, someone on the team often takes the details in a CFP and creates a proposal template that effectively generates a compliant document regarding structure, section order, and fonts. They then copy instructions for each section into that template to help text writers develop a compliant proposal.

2.4.2   Search For Less Traditional Funding Sources

CFP sites are a great option for opportunity hunting, but there are a myriad of opportunities to be found in less formalized or traditional places. Formal CFP sites often focus on the respective organization's contracts and grants, but many national and international organizations have a primary mission other than grant-making. They may have a philanthropic office or a related organization that offers grants related to their mission. For example, many large corporations may have a philanthropic mission to give grants in locations where they have large workforces.

In addition, local governments may offer grants for community-based projects. State and local organizations may offer a variety of grants to local or regional non-profits. For instance, if the objective is related to environmental issues, one might find a local environmental group to fund a project on community-based waste management or provide a grant for trees to improve a neighborhood. Because these opportunities are so varied, finding them can be a challenge, but an hour or so of research will turn up many options. The more unique the opportunity you seek, the more searching may be required.

Beyond internet searching, your own networking is essential. By attending industry gatherings, webinars, or seminars you can open up many unforeseen avenues. Digital platforms like LinkedIn can provide a way to connect and digitally network well beyond your local venues. Professionals on these platforms often share niche opportunities in a variety of fields. Entrepreneurs with an established network may consider crowdfunding platforms such as *Kickstarter, Indiegogo* or even *Patreon*, which offer alternate funding routes. A word of caution about networking is in order, however. Build solid relationships before asking about funding—to paraphrase a well-known adage, *"If you ask for money, you'll get advice. If you want money, ask for advice."*

2.5 Funder Alignment

Aligning your writing with the expectations and priorities of potential funders is crucial for proposal success. There are several early strategies you can use to align your objectives and proposals with funders' interests, thereby enhancing the likelihood of securing support. Remember, funders are not giving money to accomplish your mission, they are funding their mission. So you are likely to be successful only if you find a funder that is aligned with your objectives, or if you change objectives to become aligned with theirs.

2.5.1 Understanding Funder Priorities

To align your objectives with the funder's priorities, start with thorough research on the funder's mission, vision, and strategic goals. Understanding these priorities helps to tailor your proposal to address the funder's key interests, or reveals that they don't align with your objectives.

➤ **Research Funder's Mission:** Review the funder's website, reports, and funding announcements.

➤ **Analyze Past Funded Projects:** Identify common themes and successful strategies.

➤ **Identity Key Personnel:** Learn about the decision-makers' interests and preferences.

2.5.2 Aligning Your Proposal

Tailor your proposal to align with the funder's interests by framing your objectives, narrative, and outcomes to resonate with their goals.

➤ **Align Objectives:** Clearly articulate how your project's objectives align with the funder's goals.

➤ **Highlight Mutual Benefits:** Show how the funder's support advances their mission.

➤ **Use Relevant Metrics:** Adopt the funder's preferred metrics and evaluation criteria.

➤ **Be Specific:** Provide detailed plans, timelines, and measurable outcomes.

➤ **Use their language:** Reuse their lexicon and style rather than your own; to adapt your writing to fit their preferred style.

2.5.3 Building Relationships

Part of analyzing the opportunity and doing research on the funder often involves building relationships with potential funders. These relationships can advance your understanding and enhance the proposal's chance of success.

➤ **Attend Funders' Events:** Network at conferences, workshops, and webinars.

➤ **Engage in Dialogue:** Reach out to program officers or grant managers for feedback.

➤ **Follow Up:** Express continued interest after submitting your proposal.

➤ **Maintain Communication:** Keep funders updated on your project's progress.

Funder alignment is a strategic process requiring research and relationship building, leading to tailored writing. By understanding funder priorities, demonstrating mutual benefits, and maintaining communication, you can demonstrate alignment. By aligning your writing with the foundation's priorities and maintaining communication, it enhances your chances of securing funding and building a lasting partnership.

2.6 Formulating Preliminary Stories

In this chapter, we have focused on several processes that a writing team often needs to loop over multiple times in order to achieve their TWWIST goal. Once a team has engaged in the process of formalizing SMART objectives and researching related opportunities, it is time to begin assessing whether or not the objectives are achievable. At this point in the process, it may be too early to make that assessment with confidence, but that is why the TWWIST technique is an iterative process. Each stage works in connection with the others. If one part of the process isn't working, then revisiting, reassessing, and revising other parts of the process can help advance the whole process.

Consider, for instance, how the step of identifying achievable objectives can be enhanced by the process of formulating the core preliminary story. We will go into detail on story building in later chapters building on the work of Kendal Haven Haven [2007, 2014], but for now, start by summarizing your "story" using his one-sentence story template:

<table>
<tr><td colspan="2" align="center">Template for a One-Sentence Preliminary Story</td></tr>
<tr><td></td><td>________________________________(CHARACTER ALIGNED WITH FUNDER)</td></tr>
<tr><td colspan="2">NEEDS________________________________</td></tr>
<tr><td colspan="2">BECAUSE________________________________</td></tr>
<tr><td colspan="2">BUT________________________________</td></tr>
<tr><td colspan="2">SO,________________________________</td></tr>
<tr><td colspan="2">FINALLY ________________________________</td></tr>
</table>

This one sentence addresses six of the eight main elements of a good story! It provides a clear, foundational storyline. Equally important in the TWWIST process, writing this sentence will flag areas that likely need further research, analysis, and development.

To create a preliminary story, you start with a main CHARACTER that the audience can relate to and visualize. The CHARACTER must have NEEDS—and if you have an objective, it is ideal for the NEEDS to be something your objective will supply. (Note that the story is almost never about your needs.) You then must justify the NEED with a BECAUSE statement and reveal the reason the need is not currently met with a BUT statement. In the resolution portion of the story, your organization addresses the need SO that the customer FINALLY gains a solution.

Note that in many situations, the "customer" (the person who pays) is not the main character and may not even be in the story—it's critical that they relate to the character but not that they are the character. Unless you know you are writing for an audience of one person, the character is almost never the customer since there will be many customers with many differences but only one main character. Focus on a character with whom almost everyone in the customer organization can relate.

Preliminary story from a recent proposal

➤ **Space Vehicles** (Our main character)

- **NEED** provably stable controllers

- **BECAUSE** instability leads to unexpected outcomes such as crashes

- **BUT** most modern machine learning (ML) approaches have an unbounded space of errors

- **SO** we will use our probably bounded open-set ML algorithms to make new controllers

- **FINALLY** combining the advantages of ML with provable stability for next-generation controllers

The main character is a vehicle, not even a person. In this case, the "customer/funder" is the US Space Force, where a proposal review committee will be looking at the story. We could have made the main character some operator controlling the satellite, but others might care about fully autonomous systems, so they would not relate as well to human operators having problems. We can expect that every Space Force personnel will resonate with the vehicle as the character. So, our story aligns with the funder without explicitly having any of them as a character.

Here's where writing the preliminary story gets interesting and powerful. If you cannot fill in any of the six main elements, you probably need to LOOP back and do more analysis and research to refine the objectives and opportunity. For example, suppose your objectives and opportunity are tied to a specific solution, but you need to figure out its application. In that case, you may have to go back, validate the need, and verify that no one else is delivering it. If you can write many different complete preliminary stories, that is great progress. But you might need to loop back and do more research to help prioritize between them, especially using techniques from subsequent chapters.

When "shopping" for ideas and topics, LOOPS are part of the process. This is one of the reasons opportunity hunting by looking through CFPs can be so productive. In CFPs, we can find opportunities related to vague objectives. When we review customer requirement lists, e.g., SBIR topics, we can look for (and often find) a problem that fits our solution. If the CFP says there is a documented need, then we do not have to continue looking for one. That said, we may need to LOOP back and reconsider whether delivery of our solution is possible or if we need additional resources or partners to make it achievable. For instance, a small company with vital technology might face an end solution that requires large-scale system deployment. In that case, the company may need to integrate its technology into a partner company's existing systems for delivery and follow-through.

So, before digging deep into research and long before writing anything you expect to use, the tactical writing process expects a team to brainstorm and generate at least four to five preliminary stories for each tactical objective. Then, these stories will each be researched to discover which one has the best potential for further development. There is always more than one story for any tactical writing endeavor—there has to be because they need to be matched and adapted to the audience. A team will repeatedly LOOP back and validate the preliminary story to ensure the objectives are SMART and that the story fits with the identified opportunities.

2.7 Key Terms

1) **Tactical Objective:** *The primary objective(s) of the tactical writing process, which is focused on* *achieving specific objectives within a set time frame.*

2) **Personal Objective:** *A specific personal goal that the writer aims to achieve while taking part in the tactical writing project. It may be quite different from the Tactical Objective(s).*

3) **SMART Framework:** *A set of criteria (Specific, Measurable, Achievable, Relevant, Time-bound) used for setting objectives.*

4) **Alignment:** *The degree to which the writing matches the objectives and expectations of the audience or funder.*

5) **Preliminary Story:** *An initial narrative that outlines the basic elements of a project or proposal.*

6) **Opportunity Hunting:** *The process of actively searching for new opportunities, often through CFPs, that align with one's objectives.*

7) **SWOT Analysis:** *A technique for individual self-assessment and personal goal setting that involves the identification of Strengths, Weaknesses, Opportunities, and Threats.*

8) **Responsibility Assignment Matrix (RAM) / RACI Matrix:** *A matrix to track responsibilities, assignments, and roles within a team, including Responsible, Accountable, Consulted, and Informed roles.*

9) **Call-for-Proposals (CFPs):** *Public invitations for individuals or organizations to submit proposals or ideas that align with specific objectives.*

10) **Request for Proposals (RFP):** *A widely used term, especially in the business and government sectors, for formal calls requesting proposals.*

11) **Request for Quotation (RFQ):** *A term used when a requester knows precisely what they want and seeks detailed pricing proposals.*

2.8 Other Terms

1) **Momentum Builders:** *Short-term objectives that help to build confidence and momentum toward long-term goals.*

2) **Loop of Activities:** *The iterative process involves formalizing Objectives, analyzing Opportunities, and Preliminary Stories until achievable tactical writing objectives are defined.*

3) **Specific:** *In the SMART framework, an objective must be clear, detailed, and unambiguous, providing a precise direction for achievement.*

4) **Measurable:** *In the SMART framework, an objective should have a quantifiable outcome that can be tracked over time.*

5) **(Aggressively) Achievable:** *In the SMART framework, objectives must be realistic and aggressively attainable, given available resources and capabilities. We recommend aggressively achievable ones, so you push to achieve more.*

6) **Relevant:** *In the SMART framework, an objective must align with the organization's mission, vision, and long-term goals.*

7) **Time-bound:** *In the SMART framework, every objective must be tied to a specific timeline to create a*

sense of urgency and focus.

8) **Vague Goal:** *A broad and undefined primary outcome, lacking clear direction or measures for success.*

9) **Scenario Analysis:** *A technique for setting long-term objectives by considering various potential future scenarios and their implications.*

10) **Goal Mapping Workshops:** *Interactive sessions aimed at visualizing and understanding the interplay between immediate tasks and overarching aspirations.*

11) **Brainstorming:** *A technique during team workshops to encourage the free flow of ideas and innovative thinking.*

12) **Funder:** *The organization or individual providing the financial resources for a project.*

13) **Affinity Diagram:** *A tool for refining and organizing ideas, grouping similar concepts, and identifying themes.*

14) **Short-Term Objectives:** *Immediate outcomes serve as stepping stones toward longer-term goals, often following the SMART framework.*

15) **Long-Term Objectives:** *Objectives reflect an organization's larger vision, roadmap for the future, and alignment with long-term success.*

16) **Visualization:** *A technique for developing long-term objectives is creating a mental image of the desired future state.*

17) **Expression of Interest (EOI):** *A preliminary document indicating interest in a project used across various industries and regions.*

18) **Request for Information (RFI):** *A preliminary step to gather information about supplier capabilities, often preceding formal proposal requests.*

19) **Call for Papers (CFP):** *Specific to academic, research, or professional conferences, soliciting papers or presentations on particular topics – often confused with CFP Call for proposals.*

20) **Invitation to Tender (ITT):** *A term commonly used in the U.K. and other Commonwealth countries for procurement- related proposals.*

21) **Broad-Agency-Announcement (BAA):** *A government agency's standing call for proposals, which allows them to accept submissions on broadly described topics.*

22) **Crowdfunding:** *A funding method where individuals or organizations raise money for projects or initiatives from a large number of people.*

3 Research and Tools for Tactical Writing

"Nothing has such power to broaden the mind as the ability to investigate systematically and truly all that comes under thy observation in life."

-Marcus Aurelius 121-180AD

Research is imperative! It is the linchpin of tactical writing. It shapes the content, guides audience analysis, and frames how an idea is conveyed. Drawing from my experience in reviewing numerous papers and grant proposals, I have discerned a recurring pitfall in tactical writing submissions: credibility can be swiftly eroded by factual inaccuracies or a lack of comprehensive research on the competition or the state-of-the-art. No riveting narrative or impeccable prose can compensate for these foundational lapses. I have been privy to review panel remarks such as "If they can't get this basic fact right, how can we entrust them with our funds?" Once this question is voiced, there is no recovery.

We cannot deny the imperative nature of meticulous research. The bedrock of tactical writing, and occasionally the genesis of innovative ideas is contingent on grasping the known, discerning competitors' moves, fathoming what is feasible, and understanding our audience's knowledge and aspirations. We cannot take on these challenges without research and analysis that leads toward pivotal content and stylistic choices.

This chapter provides an overview of various tools that can help us in our research and tactical writing. The tools for researching, managing citations, spelling and grammar correction, and text generation are advancing rapidly and will continue to change and evolve. Emerging Large Language Models (LLM) such as ChatGPT were not widely available even a year before this book was started, yet they have evolved considerably in that time. While some details of what we explore in this chapter will quickly become outdated, the concepts and processes of research and our use of the tools and the cautions that go with them will likely be viable for decades.

3.1 Web Searches: More Than Just a Preliminary Step

For a majority of tactical writing projects, the research odyssey commences with web searches. Web searches shine when researching business proposals, especially if the primary quest is to unearth competing products or concepts. However, before we traverse the academic search landscape, we need to refine our familiar web search techniques. It is natural to search using familiar jargon, but this can inadvertently perpetuate existing biases. When initiating even a rudimentary web search, we must be cognizant of the specialized avenues that lead to deeper insights. Our initial searches may point us toward more authoritative research, especially when we grapple with the lexicon for citation searches. So while many people might boast of their web search acumen, I have tailored strategies that will hone Google search skills specifically for tactical writing.

Googling,' as many terms it, is akin to angling for trout in a landfill. The odds of landing a trout are slender. More likely, you'll reel in a multitude of beer cans. The term 'Google' is derived from 'googol-plex,' which represents ten raised to the power of 100, mirroring the myriad of irrelevant entries one typically encounters. Ruth Harrison, Reference Librarian, on "Prairie Home Companion"

When searching the web for tactical writing purposes, adopting the lens of the audience is paramount. We do this by grasping their lexicon and steering our searches accordingly. If our audience's profile is nebulous, then we can deploy different terminology for identical search goals so that we acquire diverse answers. For instance, when we scout for competition, we can do so in light of how varied customers might perceive it.

Persona models help in this effort. Envisioning a friend or kin as a quintessential persona model can help us consider diverse perspectives, potentially unlocking new information. When we can envision and describe a concept in myriad ways, ideally with minimal overlap, we gain a broader and more holistic view.

It is most prudent to chronicle the pages we stumble upon during web searches. The vast expanse of the web can easily overwhelm one's memory, resulting in a hazy idea with no trail to the links that led there. Tactical writing generally requires strong supporting references, so tools that record and organize the information are essential. The browser bookmark tool allows the creation of a bookmark folder that is dedicated exclusively to the links for research on a given project. This facilitates swift bookmarking, obviating the need to retrace steps. Bookmarking is typically adequate for conventional Google searches. In addition, reference management tools such as Zotero, Mandely, and EndNote will be discussed later in this chapter.

When conducting competition analysis, merely possessing the websites and the monikers of the products and rival firms might suffice for certain tactical writing tasks. However, more formal writing endeavors such as grant proposals or technical dossiers demand intricate details and credible citations. This need nudges us toward specialized research materials.

3.2 The Tools of More Formal Research

For tactical writing destined for a formal review, it is essential to cite the primary sources of information, which sidesteps diluted or misconstrued renditions. Given the surge in misinformation concerns, it is judicious to circumvent potential pitfalls by referencing sources. This requirement limits the use of some sources as authoritative resources.

Platforms like the New York Times, for example, are generally perceived as credible but they do not undertake firsthand research so they are not truly authoritative. Similarly, while Wikipedia provides a cursory overview of a topic, it is never an authoritative source. Its editable nature can lead to biases or inaccuracies. This doesn't mean these resources have no value to the researcher. In fact, the true value of Wikipedia lies in its reference lists that reveal what can be authoritative sources. Consider also the following resources that help in directly locating and researching authoritative resources.

3.2.1   Engaging With Libraries

If you are venturing into research for the first time or exploring a novel topic, reference librarians can furnish basic materials to kickstart your journey. Until you have garnered a foundational understanding of the field you are researching and its lexicon, employing the appropriate vocabulary, even for Google searches, is often challenging. Reference librarians can be very beneficial in this endeavor. They can guide you to pertinent materials, steer you in the right direction, and often direct you to specialized databases.

3.2.2   Accessing Specialized Databases

Do not rely solely on websites for your research. Most libraries grant access to specialized databases that are pivotal for academic and business research. Databases encompassing market segmentation data, for example, are invaluable for business pitches in which you aim to elucidate the market's magnitude. Some government databases provide statistics such as census data or Bureau of Labor and Standards data. These databases are often subscription-based, but libraries, especially university ones, typically subscribe to many of them. By accessing these databases through the library, you can tap into authoritative and specialized information.

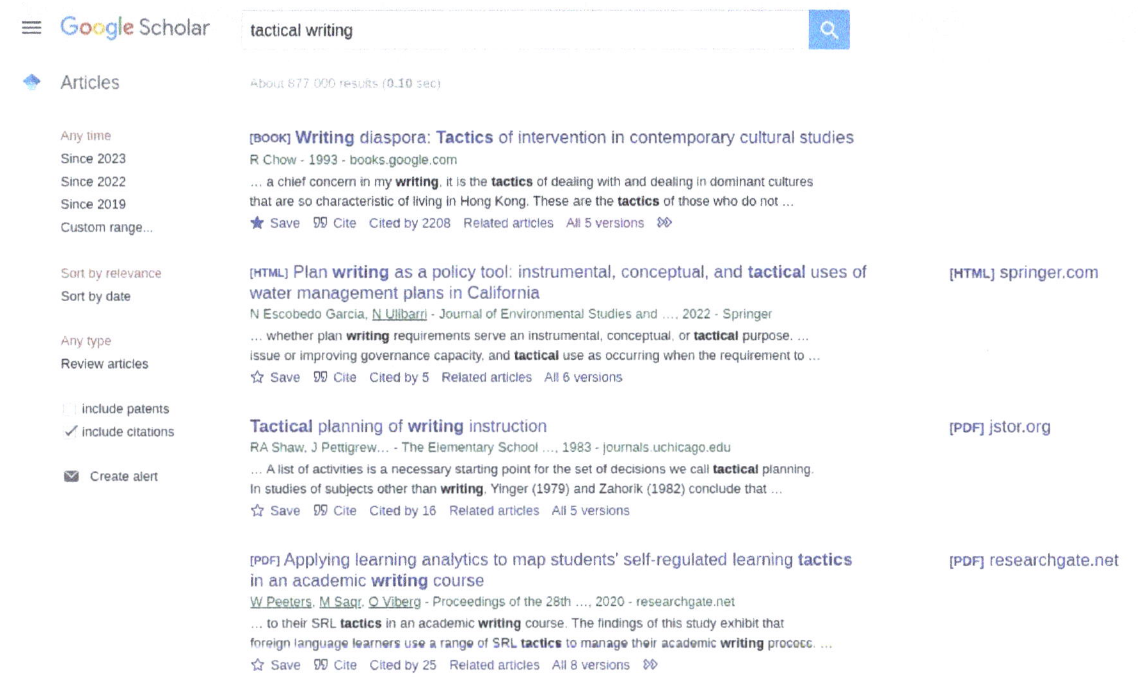

Figure 3.1: *Google Scholar search results/interface. For each found source, it is easy to get to the paper's different formats of citations, the papers cite it, different versions of the paper, and related articles, and if there is an accessible version, a link to the actual content. Users can save to a "library," or reference tools like Zotero can save the results.*

3.2.3 Discovering Google Scholar

Some tactical writing research can be done using traditional web searches such as Google or Bing, but you must be careful when you are doing research that requires content from more than just websites and needs proper citations. Fortunately, there is a special part of Google called Google Scholar (GS) where you can easily perform more academic searches. GS is an academic's answer to the vastness of the Internet. It also provides the familiar and undeniable comfort of the Google interface.

Why choose GS over Google? When it comes to academic research, GS offers a more tailored, refined experience. Instead of sifting through endless web pages for references, GS narrows the search to scholarly articles, theses, books, conference papers, and patents. Its automated process finds more and different content than the specialized academic databases. GS results are predominantly reliable scholarly sources, however, it is typically less stringent about its inclusions than more curated, subscription-based academic databases like Scopus and Web of Science. So a discerning eye is essential to assess the credibility of resources linked through GS.

Beyond the familiar search bar, the GS results page offers more refined information that is tailored for academic research. For instance, searching for "machine learning" will display core bibliographic details, direct links to full-text versions, and citation counts. The "cited by" feature is particularly useful as it showcases the impact of an article by listing subsequent works that have been cited.

GS also provides tools to copy formatted citations in styles like MLA and APA, export bibliographic data, explore citation chains, and locate full-text versions of articles. While GS is free, not all content it indexes is. However, GS does its best to find open-access versions of restricted articles. For those who are affiliated with academic institutions, library connections can be set up to access institutional subscriptions.

3.3 Navigating Google Scholar

Now that you know how GS compares to Google and understand some of its special features, let's learn more about how to use it effectively. As we explore the features, fire up a browser, go to scholar.google.com, and try some of the exercises or ideas as we go.

3.3.1   Efficient Searching: Advanced Search and Customization

Although GS can display up to 1,000 results, sifting through them is not feasible. So those who desire more control and fewer, more specific results can use the GS advanced search feature. Accessible via the hamburger menu, this tool offers refined search parameters. The settings menu also allows for customization such as choosing collections to search and setting up library links for institutional access. Consider also the following pro tips for effective searching:

➤ **Case Sensitivity:** GS searches are not case-sensitive. "Machine Learning" and "machine learning" will yield the same results.

➤ **Keywords vs. Sentences:** Instead of using full sentences in the search bar, use concise keywords to acquire more relevant results.

➤ **Advanced Search Menu:** Use this menu to refine and then learn the syntax.

➤ **Exact Matches:** Use quotes to search for exact word combinations.

➤ **Search Options:** You can search for items via titles or authors.

➤ **Year-Specific Searches:** Add the publication year to narrow down results.

➤ **Boolean Operators:** Use AND, NOT, and OR for more controlled searches.

You can access these features via the advanced search web interface (menu under the hamburger/triple bar menu on the left) or enter them with special Google syntax. You can learn the syntax by using the advanced search using the menu and then looking at the resulting search query to learn the syntax of shortcuts. You can then enter the shortcuts directly into the search window.

3.3.2   Leveraging GS "Cited by" and "Related articles"

Academic research often extends beyond the discovery of a single, pivotal paper. Harnessing the web of scholarly articles that a search can provide offers a plethora of insights to be unraveled. Discovering just a few key articles can significantly broaden one's scope of research and ensure a comprehensive understanding of one's topic. Two of the most potent GS tools in this endeavor are the "Cited by" and "Related articles" features.

"Cited By": Traces the Impact and Evolution of Research.

Every scholarly article stands on the shoulders of its predecessors, drawing inspiration, challenging theories, or building upon established knowledge. The "Cited By" feature in GS provides a window into this lineage.

➤ *Understanding Influence*: An article's impact on its field is related to the number of times it is cited in other works. A high citation count suggests that the research has resonated with the academic community and perhaps influenced subsequent studies. New papers with fewer citations are not necessarily less valued;

they may just need more time to be cited.

 Discovering Subsequent Research: By exploring articles that cite a particular work, one can trace the evolution of ideas, methodologies, and findings. This is especially valuable for staying up to date with the latest advancements in the field.

 Identifying Collaborations and Debates: Cited articles can reveal collaborations between researchers or matters of debate and counter-arguments regarding the original research. Such insights enrich one's understanding of the academic discourse surrounding a topic.

Figure 3.2: *Google Scholar advanced search: Fine-tuning your academic exploration.*

"Related Articles": Broaden the Research Spectrum.

While "Cited By" references reveal the descendants of a paper, "Related Articles" references offer a lateral view of works that share thematic or methodological similarities with the chosen article.

 Unearthing Hidden Gems: Not all relevant articles cite each other. The "Related Articles" feature may reveal lesser-known, but equally valuable, papers that otherwise would be easy to overlook.

 Diverse Perspectives: Exploring related articles can introduce researchers to diverse perspectives that foster a more holistic understanding of a selected topic.

 Cross-Disciplinary Insights: Often, breakthroughs occur at the intersection of disciplines. The "Related Articles" feature can lead to papers from other fields that offer fresh, cross-disciplinary insights.

Conducting research for scientific papers and proposals is akin to searching a vast ocean for information. While one paper might set the course, tools like "Cited By" and "Related Articles" act as the compass and map, guiding researchers through uncharted territory to discover hidden treasures. By effectively leveraging these GS features, we can ensure a thorough and enriched exploration of nearly any research topic.

3.4 Harnessing Google Scholar for Content Ideation

Even in the vast expanse and opportunities of the digital age, content remains a cornerstone for effective communication. Whether our purpose in writing is for marketing, blogging, or personal exploration, the quality and relevance of our content can make or break the impact of what we write. While the strength of GS for formal research is widely recognized, it also emerges as a potent tool for content ideation. This section delves into strategies to harness its potential for generating content ideas.

3.4.1 The Potential of Google Scholar for Generating Content

While it is traditionally viewed as an academic search engine, GS offers a treasure trove of scholarly literature that holds untapped potential for tactical content creators. By adeptly navigating its features and inputting keywords pertinent to one's industry or topic, GS becomes a gateway to high-quality, relevant content ideas. By harnessing the vast repository of GS, we can generate content that is not only informative but resonates with our target audience and can help us achieve our tactical writing objectives. Whether we need insight on digital marketing trends in healthcare or the latest in quantum computing, GS stands ready to assist.

We will delve into generating content in more depth in Section 3.8 but for now, suffice it to say that the credibility of our content is essential. Adding formal citations to tactical academic writing can make the difference between content that comes across as unsubstantiated opinions and falls flat vs. on-target, credible content that makes a memorable impact. Combining actual papers from Google Scholar with your content generation can ensure greater precision/correctness and credibility. In today's ever-evolving digital landscape, tools like GS can be the linchpin that sets content apart.

3.4.2 Strategies for Content Ideation

☞ **Search by Year for Trending Topics**: Leveraging Google Scholar's advanced search can unearth the most pertinent research papers by year. This is especially helpful for capturing the *zeitgeist* of current trends in any domain.

☞ **Explore Related Articles**: The "Related Articles" feature provides a lateral exploration, suggesting articles that share thematic or methodological ties with a selected paper. This can be a goldmine for diversifying content.

☞ **Dive Into Popular Articles and Publications**: By browsing the top 100 publications, one can discern which topics resonate most with the academic community. This can be a beacon for content that strikes a chord with a wider audience.

☞ **Follow the Citations**: The "Cited By" feature offers a breadcrumb trail to other relevant works, enriching the depth and breadth of one's research.

☞ **Narrow Results by Field**: For those seeking precision, the Advanced Search option can filter results to specific fields of study, ensuring content relevance.

☞ **Keyword Research for Richer Content**: Many articles list keywords upfront. These can be harnessed for content enrichment or to discover related concepts.

➤ **Scout Industry and Competitor Topics**: Keeping an eye on competitors and industry leaders can provide a pulse on current discussions, debates, and innovations.

➤ **Expand Your Customer Base With Google Scholar**: Beyond content ideation, GS can be a tool for business expansion, identifying potential customers, partners, or competitors.

Personal Story: Yes, There Can Be Too Much Research

Research is essential for most writing endeavors, but there can be such a thing as too much research. Some of us have a tendency to prefer reading what other people write over generating our own stories. It is easy for us to get sucked down the rabbit hole of spending too much time on research and failing to achieve other aspects of the writing process. This cautionary personal story mirrors the behavior I frequently see in my students.

My experience occurred in 1986 when doing research was much more difficult and time-consuming than it is today. Research required going to the library to get physical journals and articles. Even with the excellent library at Columbia University, we didn't have everything in-house. While researching a particular paper, I made an inter-library loan request for two papers that I thought were relevant. While waiting for them, I wrote up the story and felt it was in good shape. I had good experimental results, but I didn't consider my paper to be finished until I had addressed the new papers I requested.

Murphy's Law, the papers arrived on the day my paper needed to be submitted to the conference. I went to the library thinking I had plenty of time to read them and incorporate the related paragraphs into my story. Once the writing was completed, I planned to print it out, physically prepare the submission, and get it to FedEx in time to meet the deadline for delivery by 10:00 a.m. the next morning.

Caught up in my excitement as I read the papers, I lost track of time slightly. When I realized my oversight, there wasn't time to thoroughly edit the story to address the new material. Instead, I quickly incorporated two sentences and the citations into the paper. When I went to print it out, the printer jammed, and fixing it took longer than I wanted. I missed the FedEx deadline.

The paper was not submitted, and the publication opportunity died— all because I was too excited about ensuring I had done all the relevant research. To make a paper happen, we must find the right balance between saying, "I have done all the relevant research," and "Enough is enough; even if I'm missing something, I have done the best research for the story given the time I have." If our tactical writing projects are to make an impact, we must hit those deadlines.

While many of my students and I continue to work on our papers until the last possible minute— our work can almost always be improved— I've now set personal deadlines that all of the research, all of the related papers, all of that part of the paper/story has to be done a week ahead of time. I have learned that finding that "one more thing" and taking the time to incorporate it and change your story takes too long. Whatever research we have a week ahead of the deadline is it. Research is important, but a consistent, impactful story that hits the deadlines is far more important.

3.5 Image Searches: Say It with Pictures

Tactical writing is often improved by using good graphics to help tell the story. While there are many commercial vendors of graphics and images, Google offers Google Image Search, a valuable tool for finding figures or inspiring ideas for illustrations. The usability of Google Image Search is commendable; simply enter textual prompts, example images, or even upload sketches, and the platform will provide relevant image results. In addition, the tool offers filters to refine the search and restrict the size, color, image type, posting time, and usage/licensing rights.

Image licensing rights are a crucial consideration when utilizing Google Image Search. Not all images sourced from the platform can be freely used, given copyright restrictions. Fortunately, Google Image Search features a filter that allows users to sift through images based on their licensing terms. For instance, users can limit their search to images under the Creative Commons license, which typically does not require financial remuneration for usage. Conversely, certain images may fall under commercial licenses and necessitate due diligence on the user's part to comply with the associated terms.

It's imperative to note that the mere accessibility of images on the Internet doesn't grant unrestricted usage rights. In the realm of copyright law internal usage may be permissible, but utilizing copyrighted images in external documents such as proposals can lead to complications. If one chooses to invoke the "fair use" doctrine when using an image, it's essential to provide proper attribution, typically in the form of a URL citation detailing the source and the date of access. Such attributions are generally deemed acceptable for non-commercial applications such as internal reports. However, if the objective is to publish the content or use the image for commercial benefit, it is paramount to ensure that the image falls under the Creative Commons license—used with proper citation—or that the requisite commercial licenses have been procured. Thankfully, Google Image Search simplifies identifying freely usable images that require attribution only. When the figures from your search are under a Creative Commons license, they can be directly incorporated into tactical writing — but always adhere to the citation rules for the figure.

3.6 Reference Support Tools: Their Importance and Key Players

Managing, tracking, and formatting references is essential in tactical writing and traditionally has required a lot of work. With myriad academic literature and research materials readily available in digital form today, the usefulness of powerful reference management tools for tactical writing cannot be overlooked. These tools streamline the research process, ensuring accurate collection, organization, and citation of vast data, which reinforces solid research practices. While Zotero, Mendeley, EndNote and Ref Works are among the frontrunners in reference management, they represent a broader and evolving ecosystem that is dedicated to simplifying and elevating the research and citation management experience.

The most widely used reference support tools generally provide the following benefits:

➤ *Organization*: They efficiently manage growing volumes of papers, articles, and web resources, enabling researchers to quickly locate and utilize sources.

➤ *Efficiency*: The tedious task of manually tracking and citing each source is significantly alleviated, allowing researchers to direct their focus on content development.

➤ *Collaboration*: Modern research is often collaborative and interdisciplinary. Reference tools support collaboration by enabling resource sharing and collective annotations.

➤ *Simplicity*: Proper citation formatting can be tedious, and the need to restructure if one changes formats is error-prone. Reference tools can insert citations in documents, properly format both the citation and the bibliography, and switch to a different format in seconds.

3.6.1 Zotero

Created by the Roy Rosenzweig Center for History and New Media, Zotero stands out with its desktop application and browser extension. A free tool, Zotero provides a suite of features to ease the collection, organization, and annotation of research materials:

➤ *Word Processor Integration*: Zotero offers plugins for Microsoft Word, LibreOffice, and Google Docs, enabling easy insertion and formatting of citations and bibliographies.

➤ *Dynamic Bibliography Generation*: As users add or remove citations in a document, the Zotero plugin automatically updates and formats the bibliography according to a chosen style, such as APA, MLA, or Chicago.

➤ *Automatic Citation Detection*: Whenever a user navigates to a web page with citable content, Zotero can automatically recognize and add it to the user's library. It can save citation information plus the URL, HTML, PDF files, and your notes regarding the referenced item. It can rapidly import multiple citations from Google Scholar.

Figure 3.3: *Zotero is a free reference management tool with good word-processor integration and web-based support for integration with Google Scholar. The interface allows one to add/edit citations, insert/edit bibliographies, and set properties such as citation style. The underlying database for references can be local or shared via a web-based library to facilitate multi-user tactical writing efforts.*

➤ *Integrated Web Browser Connector*: This feature permits the direct saving of sources from multiple browsers, including Chrome, Firefox, and Safari, to one's Zotero library.

➤ *PDF Metadata Retrieval*: Zotero can automatically find and attach metadata to PDFs, turning them into citable items.

➤ *Advanced Organization*: With collections, tags, and a powerful search feature, Zotero ensures that users can organize and locate any material with ease.

➤ *Sync and Backup*: Zotero can synchronize libraries across devices and offers cloud backup, ensuring that a researcher's materials are always accessible and safe.

➤ *Collaboration Tool*: Zotero supports collaboration using cloud-based, shared collections of references.

3.6.2 Mendeley

An offspring of a startup that was acquired by the publisher Elsevier, Mendeley serves as both a reference manager and an academic social network.

➤ *Citation Plugin*: Mendeley offers seamless citation in Word and LibreOffice.

➤ *Research Network*: Connect easily with peers, share publications, and stay updated with research trends. This tool is useful for finding emerging research before it is formally published.

➤ *PDF Reader*: A built-in viewer allows streamlined reading and annotations.

3.6.3　EndNote

This premium reference management tool is recognized for its advanced features and integration with Microsoft Word.

➤ *Research Smarter*: This tool enables users to efficiently organize references and create bibliographies.

➤ *Collaboration*: Allows users to share libraries with up to 100 people.

➤ *Integration*: EndNote directly integrates with Microsoft Word for effortless citation.

3.6.4　Ref Works

A product of ProQuest, Ref Works offers a robust online reference management solution suitable for researchers at all levels.

➤ *Web-Based*: Ref Works provides the convenience of accessing references from any device.

➤ *Collaboration*: By enabling users to share libraries or specific folders with colleagues, this tool provides a unified platform for team research.

➤ *Write-N-Cite*: A convenient plugin that lets users quickly insert references into papers, ensuring consistent formatting.

3.7 Employing Grammar and Spelling Tools in Tactical Writing

Tactical writing is focused on achieving its objective and is often used in contexts where the stakes are high and errors can be costly. Whether we are drafting a critical memo or developing company guidelines, the clarity, accuracy, and correctness of the message are paramount. When the written work goes through a formal review, as for a proposal or scientific paper, any errors or lack of clarity and accuracy can lead to rejection. To this end, grammar and spelling tools have become indispensable allies for professionals who engage in tactical writing. Consider the prominent features and key benefits of grammar and spelling tools:

➤ *Accuracy Enhancement*: Even seasoned writers occasionally miss a typo or a subtle grammatical error. Grammar and spelling tools continuously scan the text to identify and rectify these slip-ups, ensuring the content remains error-free.

➤ *Clarity and Conciseness*: These tools often provide suggestions to rephrase sentences, eliminate redundancy, or choose more direct words, all of which contribute to the clarity and brevity essential in tactical writing.

➤ *Style and Tone Consistency*: Some advanced grammar tools can detect writing style or tone inconsistencies, allowing for a uniform and consistent document befitting the seriousness of tactical contexts.

➤ *Multilingual Support*: For operations or scenarios involving multilingual communication, many grammar tools support multiple languages, ensuring correctness across varied linguistic landscapes.

➤ *Customizability*: Certain tools allow users to input custom rules or guidelines specific to their field or organization. This helps to ensure that the writing adheres to specialized standards of tactical writing.

➤ *Educational Feedback*: Beyond mere corrections, some tools explain the rationale behind their suggestions, enabling writers to learn and avoid similar mistakes in the future.

Take note, however, that these tools offer valuable support but do not replace the tactical writer's expertise and judgment in terms of the story, style, and word choice. Relying solely on automated tools can sometimes lead to oversights or misunderstood nuances that—like some examples of auto corrections— are potentially embarrassing. While more modern tools like Grammarly use advanced models that have a model of context, they can still take a document off course. The optimal approach is to use these tools as a supplement, combining their computational efficiency with human expertise to produce clear, precise, and effective tactical content.

Another recommendation is to avoid using real-time correction and visual feedback when writing your first drafts. For most people, real-time feedback, e.g., the red underline, interrupt the writer's thinking and flow. Story and flow are so critical to the tactical writing process that it is better to focus on clear thinking as you write and return later to fix the spelling/grammar issues. The visual distraction of real-time feedback can derail one's writing progress, especially if the writer already has attention issues.

Although it is not their primary purpose, these tools also provide a valuable learning experience. When you make a grammar pass over a document, don't automatically accept the tool's suggestions. Instead, think about why the tool is making the change. Learn from your errors. Correct your mistakes, but make sure the correction fits your overall story/style.

"Any sufficiently advanced technology is indistinguishable from magic? Arthur C. Clarke, Third Law from *Profiles of the Future: An Inquiry into the Limits of the Possible"*

3.8 Using Deep Learninin, Large Language Models and ChatGPT

Conversations about machine learning models (often called "AI") and the potential generative capacity and usefulness of Large Language Models (LLM) are common today in academia, business, and industry. One of the most widely known LLMs is ChatGPT, or "Chat Generative Pre-trained Transformer." It is built on the groundbreaking "transformer" architecture and its operational dynamics are underpinned by a multifaceted linguistic capability accrued from vast and diverse datasets from the internet. For our purposes, we will focus our exploration of LLMs on the design, functionality, and inherent limitations of ChatGPT. Note that ChatGPT and LLMs are evolving rapidly so some of the issues raised here may be resolved by the time you use them, but it is always good to be aware and check.

The power of ChatGPT lies in its ability to model and aggregate information. It mines data, then processes and structures it to allow predictive contextual responses. It has the capacity to build a model that, given a short history, predicts what should come next. This is no simple echo of stored data; it is a generative process that produces outputs based on learned patterns. A hallmark of LLMs design are there adeptness at crafting well-structured sentences. Their outputs are grammatically correct, and adherence to syntactical norms ensures clarity, readability, and coherence.

3.8.1   Navigating the World of Generative AI: Language, Image, Multimodal Models, and Web

Navigating the World of Generative AI: Language, Image, Multimodal Models, and Web Research Bots

In the ever-evolving landscape of artificial intelligence, generative models have become indispensable tools for both personal and professional use. These models, which include language, image, and multimodal capabilities, offer a wide array of functionalities that can transform the way we work and create. As the field continues to advance, it's crucial to stay informed and adaptable. Regular web searches and exploration of resources will keep you updated on the latest developments. I encourage readers to regularly perform web searches to stay abreast of the latest advancements and explore resources like this Wikipedia page for a comprehensive list of notable LLMs whch is likely to keep being updated.

3.8.2 Large Language Models

Language models are the backbone of conversational AI, providing the ability to understand and generate human-like text. Here's a look at some of the top language models available through BoodleBox:

- **ChatGPT-4o**
    - **Advantage**: Known for its remarkable ability to understand context and generate human-like text across a wide range of topics.
    - **Disadvantage**: Limited to the knowledge it was trained with, which may have a data cut-off.
    - **Use Case**: Ideal for analysis, second opinions, and generating well-formatted content.
- **OpenAI's GPT-3 Free Tier**
    - **Advantage:** Offers a robust set of features for text generation and understanding.
    - **Disadvantage:** Limited usage and access compared to paid versions.
    - **Use Case:** Suitable for casual use and experimentation with AI-driven text generation.
- **Claude-3.5-Sonnet**
    - **Advantage**: Excels in ethical reasoning and maintaining coherent long-form conversations.
    - **Disadvantage**: May require more nuanced prompts to fully leverage its capabilities.
    - **Use Case**: Perfect for generating ideas and first drafts of content.
- **LLAMA-3.1**
    - **Advantage**: Offers efficiency, accessibility, and adaptability, hosted on a BoodleBox-controlled server for privacy.
    - **Disadvantage**: May not integrate as seamlessly with other ecosystems.
    - **Use Case**: Use when privacy is a concern or when you want a unique flair.
- **Gemini-1.5-Pro**
    - **Advantage**: Capable of processing and producing large amounts of content efficiently.
    - **Disadvantage**: Its extensive capabilities might be overwhelming for smaller tasks.
    - **Use Case**: Best used when dealing with large volumes of information.
- **Pi**
    - **Advantage**: Designed to be friendly and personal, offering a supportive AI experience.
    - **Disadvantage**: May not be as robust for technical or complex queries.
    - **Use Case**: Ideal for when you need a supportive AI that feels like a friend.
- **DeepSeek**
    - **Advantage**: Excels in providing precise, structured answers, particularly for complex mathematical problems and research tasks.
    - **Disadvantage**: Raises privacy concerns due to its Chinese origin and extensive data collection practices.
    - **Use Case**: Ideal for tasks requiring strong reasoning and math capabilities.

- **Grok**
    - **Advantage:** Incorporates real-time information from X (Twitter), offering dynamic and engaging responses with citations.
    - **Disadvantage**: May struggle with information accuracy due to reliance on X data.
    - **Use Case:** Best for tasks requiring real-time information integration with X and engaging, creative responses.

3.8.3 Deep-learning based Image Generators

Another Popular generative type of model is immage generation models which transform textual descriptions into visual content, offering creative possibilities: These can be very useful fo rgenreation of figures to help illustrate your wrting and stories.

- **DALLE3**
    - o **Advantage**: Excels in rendering complex scenes and artistic styles from textual descriptions.
    - o **Disadvantage**: Requires detailed and specific descriptions for optimal results.
    - o **Use Case**: Best for projects where you have a clear vision of the desired outcome.
- **Midjourney**
    - o **Advantage:** Generates images from natural language descriptions, offering a unique artistic style and flexibility.
    - o **Disadvantage:** Currently in open beta, which may mean ongoing changes and updates.
    - o **Use Case**: Ideal for creating artwork using Discord bot commands or the official website, especially when exploring new artistic styles.
- **Flux**
    - o **Advantage**: Known for high-quality image generation with precise control over visual elements.
    - o **Disadvantage**: Requires detailed prompts to achieve the best results.
    - o **Use Case**: Use when you need rapid, high-quality images with specific visual elements.
- **SD3**
    - o **Advantage**: Offers speed and efficiency, suitable for those new to GenAI image tools.
    - o **Disadvantage**: May not provide as much detail or style diversity as other models.
    - o **Use Case**: Ideal for iterative creation when you're exploring possibilities.

3.8.4 LLM Web Research Bots

Web research bots are essential for finding relevant, real-time information from the internet. They enhance your research capabilities by providing detailed, citation-backed answers:

- **Perplexity**
    - o **Advantage**: Provides fast, detailed, citation-backed answers synthesized from multiple sources.
    - o **Disadvantage**: May require verification of sources for accuracy.
    - o **Use Case**: Ideal for real-time information or research and fact-checking.
- **Bing**
    - o **Advantage**: Leverages Microsoft's Bing search engine for up-to-date information and a comprehensive search experience.
    - o **Disadvantage**: Results can be broad, requiring more time to sift through.
    - o **Use Case**: Use when you have time and want more detailed web search results.
- **Google**
    - o **Advantage**: Taps into Google's vast index of the web to provide highly relevant and diverse results.
    - o **Disadvantage**: The breadth of results can be overwhelming.
    - o **Use Case**: Best for when you want to see diverse search results.

As you explore these tools, remember that the AI landscape is constantly changing. Embrace the TWWIST mindset of continuous learning and strategic application to maximize your impact in this dynamic field.

LLM Capabilities

Consider some of the noteworthy features of ChatGPT and other LLM models:

➢ **Grammatical Proficiency**: Responses are almost always grammatically accurate, demonstrating the strength of its training.

➢ **Syntactic Accuracy**: Beyond grammar, the sentences structured by LLM, like ChatGPT, adhere to correct syntactical constructs, enhancing readability and comprehension.

➢ **Data Mining**: LLMs can mine and extract vast amounts of data that serve as a foundation for their knowledge base.

➢ **Modeling Information**: Post data extraction, modeling ensues. The acquired data is processed and structured to be readily deployable.

➢ **Aggregation**: Data is compiled coherently to ensure that the responses produced are pertinent and contextual.

➢ **Recollection of Previous User Interactions:** One of the primary capabilities of modern conversational agents is the ability to recall what a user mentioned earlier in a conversation. This capacity enables the system to maintain context throughout the interaction, thereby offering a coherent and dynamic response structure. While this feature does not imply long-term memory or the ability to remember personal details, it aids in providing real-time conversational flow that mimics a natural interaction between two human beings.

➢ **Provision For User-Led Corrections:** Another essential feature is the ability for users to make follow-up corrections. As in human-to-human conversations in which misunderstandings occur, conversational agents can sometimes misinterpret user input. Recognizing this, the capability to accept and adapt to user-led corrections is invaluable. This flexibility not only rectifies immediate misunderstandings but can also improve the system's accuracy over time. In part, good output from ChatGPT is the result of the user learning better "prompting" to get ChatGPT to provide the desired output and style. Feedback further improves the user's understanding and the system's "learning" based on the user's response.

3.8.5   LLM Limitations

Despite its strengths, ChatGPT and all modern LLMs have areas where they currently underperform. They struggle with sustained analysis of long texts, discerning recent events outside their training, and sometimes their idea generation can be hit-or-miss. Some of these limitations are addressed in GPT-4 through plugins, allowing for the reading of larger documents and even PDFs. However, it is crucial to remember the adage "Garbage-in-Garbage-out" when feeding information to ChatGPT. Since it was trained on the internet, it was trained with plenty of garbage. So, while ChatGPT is an impressive tool it also has many limitations. Users should be aware of the following constraints:

➢ **Potential For Fictitious Outputs**: ChatGPT may generate information that, while plausible, is entirely fictitious. It does not "know" the truth but produces outputs based on its training data.

➢ **Knowledge Cutoff (203 version limited to pre-2021)**: Its training data extends only up to September 2021. This means it might not have information on events, advancements, or developments after this date.

➤ **Possible Harmful Outputs**: Even with safeguards in place, there is a chance ChatGPT might produce harmful, offensive, or biased information.

➤ **Lack of Deep Understanding**: ChatGPT does not "understand" topics in the way humans do. It generates responses based on patterns from data, not genuine comprehension.

➤ **Sensitivity to Input Phrasing**: The phrasing of a question influences the response. Slight changes in how a question is posed may lead to different answers.

➤ **Uniqueness and Originality:** ChatGPT's outputs, while distinct, are derived from vast internet datasets. As such, while it does not plagiarize in the traditional sense, there may be strong resemblances to existing content. This potential conflict demands a user's discretion, especially in formal contexts where originality is paramount.

➤ **Handling Inappropriate Requests**: Safety and respect are paramount in all forms of interaction. Modern conversational agents are trained rigorously to decline or refrain from responding to inappropriate or potentially harmful requests. Chat GPT3.5 (the free version in 2023) has some guardrails and is relatively safe, but it still generates many inappropriate responses.

➤ **Continuing Improvement in Commercial Systems** ChatGPT4 and ChatGPT4o are both much better than ChatGPT3.5 but at the time of this writing are not free. I've found the $20/month current price worth it for the improvements it gives me in correcting my writing, but both still have many of the problems above.

3.8.6   What ChatGPT Currently Does Well

As a result of its advanced machine learning architecture, ChatGPT excels in many linguistic and content generation tasks. Here are some of the areas where ChatGPT particularly shines:

➤ **Summarizes**: ChatGPT can distill vast amounts of information into concise summaries. This feature is especially useful when users need background or overview information on a specific topic. Its ability to provide this context allows users to grasp the essence of intricate subjects quickly, albeit with a risk of errors in the summary.

➤ **Mimics**: Beyond answering queries, ChatGPT can generate text in a style mimicking specific authors or genres. This mimicry function has been used in various applications from creative writing projects to replicating specific writing styles for content generation. Its versatility in this area underscores its prowess in understanding and generating diverse linguistic patterns.

➤ **Outlines**: For those in the initial stages of a project, ChatGPT and the other LLMs can be instrumental in brainstorming and outlining. It swiftly generates and organizes ideas coherently, serving as a preliminary draft or a blueprint for further elaboration. It is like having a collaborative partner that can create a structure on demand.

➤ **Fixing Writing Versus Thinking**: While ChatGPT and other LLMs are adept at rectifying many writing issues, such as grammar, structure, and coherence, it is essential to differentiate between "writing" problems and "thinking" problems. The model can polish the language and make a text more readable, but it does not necessarily enhance the depth or originality of the underlying thought. Users should approach the tool with a clear distinction between refining their expression and improving the substance of their ideas.

While ChatGPT boasts impressive linguistic abilities, it is essential to recognize where its shortcomings lie. It does not perform well, for example, when used in contexts that demand intricate understanding, deep reasoning, and personal experiences. These limitations stem from the inherent challenges of machine learning models and the vast, but sometimes inconsistent, data on which they are trained. Consider the areas in which ChatGPT might not perform optimally:

➤ **Provide a Line of Reasoning Supporting a Claim**: While ChatGPT can produce highly probable sequences, it does not truly understand human logic. As a result, it may present reasoning that appears superficial, lacks depth, or is logically incorrect.

➤ **Nuanced Relationships Among Ideas**: Grasping the intricate interconnections between various ideas is challenging for the model. It might overlook subtleties or miss out on deeper connections that a human thinker would naturally discern.

➤ **Writing Process and Revision**: ChatGPT delivers content in a one-shot manner. It does not have a true iterative writing and revision process, making its content susceptible to inconsistencies or a lack of coherence.

➤ **Rhetorical Context (Audience Awareness)**: The model does not inherently consider who the audience is, so tailoring content to specific audiences with unique needs and contexts can be hit-or-miss.

➤ **Self-reflection**: ChatGPT is a program. It has no self-awareness or the ability to self-reflect, so its responses cannot reflect genuine introspection or personal growth.

➤ **Personal Experience (Authentic Voice)**: ChatGPT does not have personal experiences or emotions. Its "voice" is a composite of its training data, so it lacks the authenticity of lived experiences.

➤ **Verifiable Sources and Quotations**: The model often does not cite sources or provide verifiable quotes, making it challenging to trace the origin or verify the accuracy of certain statements.

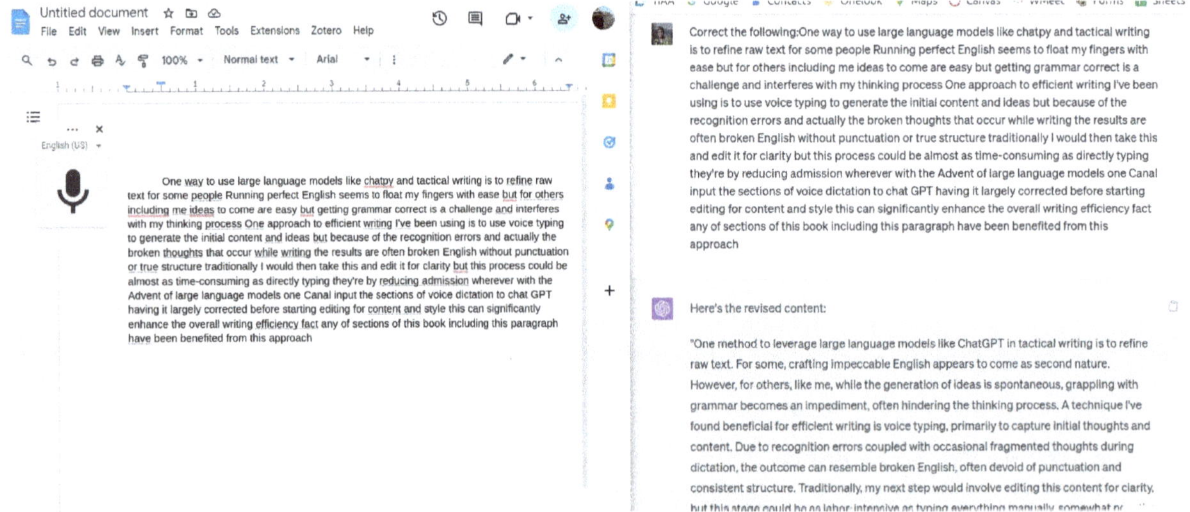

Figure 3.4: *Combining voice-typing with correction via ChatGPT may improve your writing efficiency. Variations of this usage include correcting any written material and rewriting, e.g., to make your writing*

fit in a submission of limited length, e.g., 2000 characters.

- **Analysis of Visuals, Video, and Other Multimedia**: ChatGPT is primarily text-based. It does not analyze multimedia elements directly, so its understanding of such content is limited to textual descriptions.

- **Sustained Analysis/Generation of Long Text**: While recent versions of the model can handle larger documents, a deep, sustained analysis of extensive texts remains a challenge. Similarly, getting it to generate a long and consistent output is difficult.

- **Idea Generation**: Although it can generate a myriad of ideas, the quality and feasibility of these ideas can be inconsistent. The age-old principle of "garbage-in-garbage-out" applies. The output quality depends on the clarity and precision of the input. Since ChatGPT was trained on a mix of "qualities" including total fiction, it is capable of generating "impossible" ideas.

Many current limitations of ChatGPT are intrinsic to the current state of artificial intelligence. However, ongoing research and iterative improvements, like plugins in GPT-4 that allow for the reading of larger documents, lead toward addressing these challenges. We can expect improvements, especially those related to operation, to evolve quickly. Improvements related to "understanding," for example, will develop at a slower pace.

To mitigate the risk of hallucinations, users can employ web-connected bots like Perplexity, which integrate real-time data from the internet to provide more accurate and up-to-date insights. These bots enhance the reliability of information by offering detailed, citation-backed answers synthesized from multiple sources, thus addressing the factual limitations of static LLMs. By combining the strengths of ChatGPT with the dynamic capabilities of web-connected bots, users can achieve a more comprehensive and accurate understanding of their topics of interest. This approach not only reduces the risk of misinformation but also enhances the overall quality and credibility of the information obtained.

It is worth noting that while some limitations might be addressed in various LLMs and will likely get better with furture iterations or through plugins, the principle of "garbage-in-garbage-out" always holds true. LLM based generation can sometimes be hit-or-miss, with some responses being incorrect or even impossible due to the inability of LLMs to discern fact from fiction in training data. It is up to the tactical writer to use a generative language model to validate its output in terms of the desired content and style. Users must approach outputs from ChatGPT critically, verifying information from trusted sources and not relying on it without due diligence.

3.8.8 Examples of ChatGPT in Tactical Writing and Research

ChatGPT can be leveraged as a writing assistant, offering services like polishing abstracts and rephrasing content. For instance, when provided with an abstract, ChatGPT can generate a rephrased version that maintains the essence while potentially enhancing clarity and coherence. Consider the following examples of ChatGPT assistance that show both effective use and cautionary examples of failure.

Refining raw text is one method to leverage large language models like ChatGPT in tactical writing. For some, crafting impeccable English appears to come as second nature. For others like me, generating ideas is spontaneous, and grappling with grammar is an impediment that hinders my thinking process. A technique that I've found beneficial for efficient writing is voice typing. I use it primarily to capture initial thoughts and content. Due to recognition errors coupled with occasional fragmented thoughts during dictation, the outcome can resemble broken English that often is devoid of punctuation and consistent structure.

Traditionally my next step would involve editing this output for clarity, but this can be as labor-intensive as typing everything manually, which negates the advantages of voice typing. The rise of large language models, however, has changed the game. Now, I can feed these voice-typed sections into ChatGPT and the bulk of errors will be rectified before I delve into nuanced content and stylistic editing. This strategy boosts my writing efficiency considerably. In fact, several sections of this book, including the current paragraph, have been improved using this very approach.

While it is not evident in the example of Fig. 3.4, maintaining a consistent voice is essential in tactical writing. Often the corrections via ChatGPT sound quite different from other writing in the document, so it will be necessary to edit the output personally. It is possible to have ChatGPT try to mimic your style, but that is somewhat weak because it only uses 4,000 characters, making it hard to capture much of your style or ensure consistency in a large document. The recommended process for using any ChatGPT-like system output is to always edit by hand for style, content, voice, and word choice. Then use more traditional grammar/spelling tools to address any errors in the editing.

ChatGPT can also be used in tactical writing to generate outlines and summaries of larger documents. However, it may not always include the items most relevant to the story you want to tell—its predictions are based on the "most likely" output given its training. In tactical writing, we are often trying to find unique/novel approaches to increase our competitive advantage, and the most probable idea is often not the most effective.

Can you check and correct my grammar?
Of course, I'd be happy to help! Please provide the text you would like me to check.

Certainly! Here is a corrected version of your text:

While some tactical writing research can be conducted using traditional web searches, such as Google or Bing, you must exercise caution when undertaking research that requires proper citations. Many proposals should include valid citations, not just content from websites. There's a specialized section of Google known as Google Scholar, which caters to the more academic side of searching. We'll begin this chapter by discussing how to effectively use Google Scholar, ensuring you're familiar with its unique features and how it compares to standard Google searches. As we delve into the examples discussed in this section, I strongly recommend that you open a browser, visit scholar.google.com, and try out some of the exercises or ideas presented in this chapter.

Can you reduce the length of that by 25%

Certainly! Here's a more concise version of your text:

While traditional web searches like Google or Bing are useful, research requiring proper citations demands caution. Many proposals need valid citations beyond website content. Google Scholar offers a more academic search approach. In this chapter, we'll explore its unique features and its advantages over standard Google searches. I recommend visiting scholar.google.com and trying out the exercises as we discuss them.

Figure 3.5: *Demonstration of ChatGPT's capability as a writing assistant, correcting grammar (input not shown), then reducing the length.*

3.8.9   Leveraging ChatGPT for Idea Generation in Tactical Proposal Writing

ChatGPT can be a valuable asset for generating research ideas, particularly when one is not deeply acquainted with a specific topic. It can provide terms that subsequently can be used to obtain more reliable information using the aforementioned search techniques on specialized databases, Google, or Google Scholar (GS). Using prompts such as "generate

ideas for [topic of your proposal]" or "list issues that must be considered when proposing [your topic]" can be a good starting point for finding ideas. Subsequent queries can be posed to delve deeper.

For those who are navigating the complexities of tactical proposal writing, ChatGPT can offer unique insights to bolster your proposal's strength. Here are example prompts for ChatGPT, its potential outputs, and subsequent actions using GS to validate and strengthen these ideas:

Prompt for ChatGPT:

"What are key factors to consider when proposing a project on urban sustainability?"

ChatGPT Output:

"Urban green spaces, sustainable public transport systems, low-carbon buildings, waste reduction strategies, and community engagement initiatives."

Follow-up on GS:

Research each of the terms provided by ChatGPT to find case studies or evidence of effective strategies that can be included in the proposal, e.g "successful community engagement initiatives in urban sustainability."

Prompt for ChatGPT:

"List potential challenges for implementing AI in healthcare."

ChatGPT Output:

"Data privacy concerns, integration with existing systems, training medical personnel, ensuring model interpretability, and handling diverse patient data."

Follow-up on Google GS:

Search by combining the prompt plus the responses, e.g. "Data privacy concerns integration challenges of AI in healthcare systems" to glean insights on how other projects tackled these issues and to anticipate potential roadblocks in the proposal.

Prompt for ChatGPT:

"What are the main hurdles for securing funding in the game development industry?"

ChatGPT Output:

"Intense competition in the market, high development costs, proving unique game concepts, securing intellectual property rights, and ensuring a return on investment for stakeholders."

Follow-up on Google/GS:

This topic is less academic so searches should explore both Google and GS, e.g. start with "successful strategies for securing game development funding", then follow up with queries like "proving unique game concepts to secure game development funding." This type of search chain will help uncover academic and industry insights on methods or approaches that have worked in the past, which can then be tailored and incorporated into the proposal.

Example: Using ChatGPT ChatGPT and other generative AI tools can be very effective in aiding the research process for tactical writing. I use such tools and encourage my students to use them. However, it's crucial to be aware of ChatGPT limitations when deploying it for research purposes. Be extremely careful to verify its research results because of its propensity for hallucination. Allow me to share a personal example of what can happen when we rely on it too heavily for research without proper verification.

I asked ChatGPT 3.5 (the free version in 2023) to do a " literature review of open-set recognition with citations ." It replied: Certainly, here's a literature review on open-set recognition with citations:

Open-set recognition, a challenging problem in machine learning and pattern recognition, deals with the classification of unseen data instances that do not belong to any known classes. Over the years, researchers have proposed various methods to address this issue.

Li et al. (2015) introduced OpenMax, a method that extends traditional softmax-based classifiers to estimate the probability of an instance being from an unknown class. They achieved promising results on open-set recognition tasks by modeling the discrepancy between known and unknown class activations \citeOpenMax.

Scheirer et al. (2013) proposed a principled framework named Classifier Rejection for open-set recognition. Their approach involves developing reject option classifiers that explicitly label instances as unknown if the confidence of a class prediction is below a certain threshold \citeScheirer2013.

Bendale and Boult (2016) introduced the concept of Negative Data Augmentation (NDA) for open-set recognition. NDA generates additional examples that are similar to known classes but not in the training set, effectively enhancing the classifier's ability to distinguish unknown from known classes \citeBendale2016. ....

Since this is my research area, I realized that every one of its statements was factually incorrect. To push it farther I asked for the citations, to which it replied

Certainly, here are the citations for the papers: Ge, W., Huang, Z., Li, X., & Lu, T. (2017). Generative openmax: Open set classification with adversarial generative networks. IEEE International Conference on Computer Vision (ICCV), 1930-1938. DOI: 10.1109/ICCV.2017.211.

Li, W., Wang, R., Liu, W., & Hou, J. (2015). Openmax: A novel softmax loss-based open set classification. IEEE International Conference on Computer Vision (ICCV), 9-16. DOI: 10.1109/ICCV.2015.9. ....

It is a nice response, except not one of these papers exists! The summary of the papers was inaccurate; multiple references and their descriptions, while plausible, were wrong. All of the formal citations were wrong in at least one important aspect. If I were to use these research results in a paper or proposal, it would likely lead to instant rejection, independent of the rules around the use of LLM in submissions.

OpenAI, the creators of ChatGPT, faced many complaints and news articles about hallucinations. ChatGPT-4 (the paid version) responds differently, stating, "I'm sorry for any confusion, but I'm unable to provide specific citations as I don't have real-time access to external sources beyond September 2021. However, I can help you structure a literature review on open-set recognition. You can replace the placeholder citations with actual references from relevant papers and articles." This response is better as it warns about the limitation. However, when asked differently, it does provide "content" but adds a disclaimer at the end.

My story is cautionary, and while we can expect these systems to improve, tactical writers should not trust LLMs to provide correct facts. By nature, LLMs generate highly probable outputs but don't store or reason about facts and cannot verify them. Thus, ChatGPT's limitations are inherent in all LLMs and existing conversational "AI" designs. I used to say we don't have artificial intelligence, but with these systems, we have reached artificial stupidity—they get lots of the "words" right and sound good enough to fool many people, but they get lots of the details wrong. This situation may improve in a few years, but as a tactical writer, it will always be your job to research and check the facts. When leveraging LLMs for tactical proposal writing, it's crucial to corroborate responses with in-depth research on platforms like GS that provide rigorous validation and evidence.

Leveraging BoodleBox: **MultiBot Tools**

While most of the examples above are from ChatGPT, there are many LLMs and GenAI tools you can use. Choosing just one can seem daunting. But there is one that Dr. Boul't highly redomments for its enhanced productivity and collaboration. BoodleBox.ai is a versatile AI platform designed to integrate mu.tiple Generative AI tools into workflows, offering a unique multi-bot experience that enhances productivity and creativity, at a very good price. Here's how BoodleBox stands out, especially in the realms of writing and proposal research:

- **Free Access and Paid Pro Queries**
  - o **Free Access**: Explore BoodleBox's features without any initial investment, perfect for newcomers to AI.
  - o **Paid Pro Queries**: Experience advanced features with five complimentary pro queries, allowing users to delve deeper into the platform's capabilities. For team with limited funds this can allow them to compete with the current state of the art tools, albeit with more planning. At the time of writing, BoodleBox.ai's full unlimited licenses were still cheaper than any of the other paid individual LLM tools, and for that price you get access to more than a dozen.
- **Diverse Range of Bots and Stacking Bots for Enhanced Analysis**
  - o **Variety**: Access a wide array of commercial bots tailored to specific tasks, ensuring effective handling of diverse topics.
  - o **Specialized AI Helpers**: Over 1,000 specialized bots collaborate to provide comprehensive solutions, making BoodleBox a one-stop-shop for AI-driven productivity.
  - o **Synergistic Effect**: Stack different bots to analyze each other's output, enhancing the quality and accuracy of results.
  - o **Refined Outputs**: Ensure outputs are thoroughly vetted and refined, leading to more reliable and insightful conclusions.
- **Idea Generation and Drafting**
  - o **Creative Assistance**: Use AI tools to generate ideas and draft content, maintaining creativity and coherence.
  - o **Diverse Perspectives**: Leverage multiple bots for varied suggestions, enriching content and expanding creative horizons.
- **Proposal Research and Writing**
  - o **Comprehensive Research**: Utilize BoodleBox for in-depth proposal research, accessing real-time data and diverse insights. But you still want to verify sources.
  - o **Strategic Writing**: Apply the TWWIST approach to craft proposals that are not only informative but also persuasive and impactful and then use multiple different bots to give you feedback on your proposal including comparisons with chechlists and requirement.,
- **Seamless Collaboration**
  - o **GroupChat Feature**: Facilitate interaction among multiple users, AI assistants, and knowledge sources within a single conversation.
  - o **Hybrid and Remote Teams**: Bridge the gap between physical and virtual workspaces, promoting a collaborative environment.
- **Secure Data Handling**

- o **Improved Privacy**: Robust data handling protocols ensure user data protection, allowing teams to collaborate with confidence and their IP terms assure your data is not used for training.
  - o **Knowledge Integration**: Integrate existing team knowledge into AI processes, enhancing insights and expertise; their knowdge bank makes it easy to add knowledge sources then combine them with chats while technique while not providing full documents to the end LLM.

BoodleBox offers a comprehensive platform for integrating Generative AI into writing and proposal research workflows. With its free access, paid pro queries, diverse range of commercial bots, and the ability to stack bots for enhanced analysis, BoodleBox provides users with the tools they need to maximize productivity and creativity. Its focus on collaboration, security, and knowledge integration makes it an ideal choice for teams looking to harness the power of AI to achieve their goals. Whether you're a writer, a business professional, or part of a large organization, BoodleBox is equipped to support your journey into the world of AI-driven innovation.

And if you are an instructor using this book,, there are many advantages to using BoodleBox in your course, which I did when using this book. The team/collaboration is very useful and there are ways you can use it to give your students more rapid feedback, e.g., I use it to show students how to get their own feedback on their proposals following the TWWIST methodology and the requirements of the particular grant they were pursuing. This will be described in a later chapter on reviewing.

3.9 Key Terms

1) **Audience Analysis:** *The process of understanding the needs, expectations, and preferences of the audience for whom the writing is intended.*

2) **Authentic Voice:** *The unique style or tone that comes from personal experience and emotion, which language models do not possess.*

3) **Citation:** *A formal reference to a source of information used in research or academic writing.*

4) **Copyright Law:** *The legal right granted to an author, composer, playwright, publisher, or distributor to exclusive publication, production, sale, or distribution of a literary, musical, or artistic work.*

5) **Google Scholar:** *A freely accessible search engine that indexes scholarly articles, theses, books, and conference papers.*

6) **Hallucination:** *The tendency of a language model to generate information that is incorrect.*

7) **Image Searches:** *The act of querying a search engine to find specific images on the internet.*

8) **Large Language Model (LLM):** *A machine learning model trained on a vast dataset for various natural language processing tasks.*

9) **Reference Management:** *The practice of collecting, organizing, and citing sources of information, potentially supported with tools like Zotero, Mendely, EndNote, or RefWorks.*

10) **Research:** *The systematic investigation into and study of materials and sources to establish facts and reach new conclusions.*

11) **Verifiable Sources:** *Sources that can be checked for the accuracy of their information.*

1) **Brainstorming:** *A technique during team workshops to encourage the free flow of ideas and innovative thinking.*

2) **Fictitious Outputs:** *Generated information that may sound plausible but is entirely made-up, see Hallucination.*

3) **Idea Generation:** *The process of creating, developing, and communicating new ideas.*

4) **Knowledge Cutoff:** *The date until which the training data for a language model extends.*

5) **ChatGPT:** *A Large Language Model built on the transformer architecture, designed for generating human-like text based on the data it was trained on.*

6) **Clarity and Conciseness:** *The quality of being clear and straightforward in expression and using only as many words as necessary.*

7) **Collaboration:** *The act of working with someone to produce or create something.*

8) **Content Generation:** *The process of creating material for publications, websites, or other platforms.*

9) **Data Mining:** *The process of extracting and processing large amounts of data to generate new information or predictions.*

10) **EndNote:** *A commercial reference management software package used to manage bibliographies and references when writing essays and articles.*

11) **Garbage-in-Garbage-out:** *A principle stating that the quality of output is determined by the quality of the input.*

12) **Grammar and Spelling Tools:** *Software or applications designed to check and correct grammatical and spelling errors in a text.*

13) **Grammatical Proficiency:** *The ability of a language model to generate text that is grammatically correct.*

14) **Mendeley:** *A reference manager and academic social network that helps organize research, collaborate with others online, and discover the latest research.*

15) **Multilingual Support:** *The capability of software or other systems to operate effectively with multiple languages.*

16) **RefWorks:** *A web-based reference management tool designed to help researchers at all levels gather, organize, store, and share all types of information and generate citations and bibliographies.*

17) **Specialized Databases:** *Databases that focus on a specific subject area or field of study.*

18) **Style and Tone Consistency:** *The uniformity in the writing style and tone throughout a document or set of documents.*

19) **Syntactic Accuracy:** *The adherence to rules of sentence structure in the generated text.*

20) **Transformer Architecture:** *The underlying neural network structure upon which models like*

ChatGPT are built.

21) **User-led Corrections:** *The feature that allows users to correct a model's output or interpretation.*

22) **Voice Typing:** *The use of speech recognition technology to convert spoken language into written text.*

23) **Web Searches:** *The act of querying a search engine to find specific information on the internet.*

24) **Zotero:** *A free, open-source reference management software to manage bibliographic data and related research materials.*

4 Unlocking the Potential of Audience Analysis

"Estimating your audience is not just a chapter in the story of successful writing, it's the first TWWIST process that transforms simple words into resonating messages, turning readers into active participants in your story who help you reach your objectives."

-T. E. Boult

In any form of writing, it is important to develop a well-grounded understanding of your audience. In tactical writing, it is absolutely essential. Understanding an audience is an easy thing to say, but how does one actually do it? The process starts by estimating your audience's reactions, then you work to improve the impact of your writing based on your analysis of audience feedback. It sounds simple, but there are many facets to the process.

Audience estimation is more of an artful skill you develop through practice than a cookbook recipe you follow. It is important that you not only practice predicting your audience but that you seek feedback and analyze how well you estimate their response. What didn't you know about your audience that perhaps you should have? What new information did their response reveal? On the basis of your audience analysis, you then can consider how you might more effectively communicate with that audience the next time. As you pursue this estimation and analysis process, you may well benefit by augmenting your writing team with someone who has more experience. However, do not just ask them for their answer. Make your own estimation first, ask for the expert's opinion and rationale, and then follow up to improve your estimation skills.

4.1 Ten Techniques for Audience Analysis Research

This section provides an overview of ten techniques for audience analysis, listed in alphabetical order, plus examples of how they are commonly used. Be aware that many audience analysis techniques depend on access to a sample audience, which can be a major challenge. Furthermore, if an "audience sample" is not representative of the whole, then the analysis results will be skewed. So, a few of the techniques covered – competitor analysis, context analysis, demographic analysis, and psychographic analysis – do not require an audience sample. These approaches are based on estimations from passively observable data. We will delve more deeply into context analysis and psychographic analysis, which are among the most useful techniques in audience analysis for proposals and papers.

4.1.1 Audience Interviews and Persona Models

Audience interviews offer an in-depth understanding of your audience's needs and expectations. Conducted one-on-one or in groups, these interviews provide immediate feedback that can greatly influence your content development. One advantage of this technique is the interaction between the interviewer and the audience and the interviewer's ability to ask follow-up questions or clarify ambiguous responses.

The disadvantage to this technique is that face-to-face interviews are time-consuming and may not be feasible if your audience is widely dispersed geographically. Also, interviewer bias can potentially affect data reliability. Despite these potential pitfalls, audience interviews are instrumental in many areas of writing, particularly in speech writing, where understanding the audience's perspective and expectations is critical.

Companies and organizations frequently conduct audience interviews to gather insights into customers, clients, donors, and other stakeholder perspectives so they might tailor their messages accordingly.

Companies such as Coca-Cola invest time and resources to meet customers face-to-face, understand their experiences, and gain insights used to enhance their products and marketing strategies. Similarly, TED Talk organizers use audience interviews to understand their listeners' interests and expectations. They conduct interviews to ask which topics interest them, which speakers they admire, and which presentation styles engage them the most. This understanding helps the organizers to curate presentations that captivate and educate their audience.

To help a writing team have a more concrete view of the data, audience interviews are often condensed into persona models that capture the data in a few idealized caricatures of people. These persona models embody specific reported characteristics, needs, motivations, and potential behaviors of the interviewed audience. This is particularly common in the customer discovery phase of entrepreneurial startups where they try to understand their potential market and communicate it in a business pitch.

4.1.2   Audience Surveys

Audience surveys are a direct and effective method for gathering data about your audience's needs, expectations, and preferences. Surveys can be distributed to a large and diverse group of people, often with little effort or cost. With the capacity to collect both quantitative and qualitative data, surveys can provide a comprehensive understanding of your audience's perspective.

However, surveys also present challenges. The quality of output data depends in large part on the quality of survey questions: poorly designed questions lead to misleading or unreliable data. Furthermore, low response rates and respondent selection bias can skew your results.

Despite these potential pitfalls, surveys are a valuable tool in audience analysis. They are particularly beneficial for copywriting and technical proposal writing. For instance, Google often uses audience surveys to understand its users better and improve its products and services. They gather feedback about user experiences, feature requests, and issues, which allows them to make user-centric decisions in their product development process. Similarly, Netflix uses surveys to understand audience preferences and viewing habits. This data is instrumental in the content creation process, helping them to create shows and movies that their audience will love enough to continue subscribing.

4.1.3   Competitor Analysis

Competitor analysis entails evaluating the successes and failures of similar messages from competitors or other sources. This technique helps identify strategies that work, areas that need improvement, and opportunities that have not been exploited. By understanding how competitors communicate with their audience, tactical writers can glean insights into how their target audience may respond and use this knowledge to enhance their own communication strategy.

One challenge with competitor analysis is that it requires a deep understanding of the writer's particular industry and its competitors. A thorough analysis can also be time-consuming. Despite these challenges, competitor analysis is a vital tool in audience analysis. It is especially helpful in copywriting and technical proposal writing where understanding the competitive landscape is crucial.

For example, Samsung often analyzes how Apple communicates with its audience. They study Apple's marketing messages, customer interactions, product announcements, and customer feedback to identify opportunities for their own marketing strategy. By understanding what Apple's audience responds to, Samsung can craft messages that appeal to similar audience segments. Microsoft also conducts competitor analysis to understand how other software companies, like Adobe or Oracle, interact with their audience.

This analysis helps them better understand the needs and preferences of their audience so that they can improve their software offerings and create more effective marketing campaigns.

4.1.4   Context Analysis and Review Requirements

Context analysis involves understanding the environment in which your audience will receive your message. This includes the physical context (where they will read or hear your message), the social context (the cultural, societal, or personal factors that may influence their interpretation of your message), and the temporal context (which external events may impact their reception of your message such as how much time they will allocate for reading/decision making). In some cases, context analysis needs to consider if there are formal review criteria as is common in scientific writing and proposal reviews (see section 4.3.) Understanding these factors can help tailor the message to ensure it is received as intended.

However, context analysis can be complex and time-consuming. It requires a deep understanding of the audience's environment. Despite these challenges, context analysis is a crucial aspect of audience analysis, particularly for speech writing. TED Talks organizers, for example, consider the context in which their speeches will be given and the audience's reaction to speakers' previous talks. They think about where their audience will be watching (e.g., at home, at a TED event, or just listening on their commute), which societal or cultural factors may influence their interpretation of the talk, and how current events may make the talk more or less relevant. Consideration of these factors helps speakers craft more impactful and engaging talks and helps TED select speakers who are likely to grow their audience.

Similarly, political speechwriters must consider the context when crafting speeches. The immediate cultural, societal, and political climate can greatly influence how a speech is received. A speech given during a national crisis, for example, may need to be more comforting and uniting while a speech given during an election campaign may need to be more persuasive and policy-focused. By understanding the context, speechwriters can write more appropriate and effective speeches.

4.1.5   Demographic Analysis and Persona Modeling

Demographic analysis involves learning the basic characteristics of your audience such as their age, gender, location, education level, occupation, and income level. This information helps in understanding who an audience is and what their needs, preferences, and challenges are. For instance, a younger audience may prefer more modern, digital communication methods while an older audience may prefer direct mail or more traditional methods.

Demographic analysis is a fundamental step in audience analysis. It provides essential information for audience segmentation and targeted communication strategies. However, it is important to remember that while demographics can provide useful insights, they do not tell the whole story. People are more than their demographic characteristics, and it is important to consider additional factors, such as psychographics and behavior when analyzing an audience.

Companies across all sectors use demographic analysis. Facebook uses demographic analysis to deliver tailored ads to its users. By understanding their users' age, location, and interests, Facebook can show ads that are relevant and interesting to various users, increasing the likelihood of engagement. Similarly, the New York Times uses demographic analysis to understand its readership. Factors like age, location, education level, and occupation help them to understand who their readers are, the topics they likely are interested in, and how they prefer to consume news. This information helps the New York Times tailor content and distribution strategies to their audience's needs.

Demographic data can be used to create audience persona models, which are detailed, hypothetical representations of different target audience segments. Persona models embody specific demographic characteristics, needs, motivations, and potential behaviors of typical audience members. The persona models can provide a more tangible and relatable understanding of the audience that guides writers in creating content that resonates effectively with different audience segments.

Not all persona models are developed in the same way, and they can be used for different purposes. For example, demographic-based generic persona models are inherently weaker than interview-based persona models because more assumptions are made in their development. However, both types of models are used relatively interchangeably during the writing process. Customer persona models are commonly used in formulating early business pitches and in responding to RFPs when there is minimal access to actual data. As we will see in later chapters, persona models are also used directly in the storytelling process.

4.1.6   Feedback Analysis

Feedback analysis involves examining responses from past communication with similar audiences. This process may include analysis of customer reviews, survey responses, social media comments, email responses, or any other feedback received. Feedback can provide valuable insights into what an audience likes and dislikes about your current communication methods. It also can point toward what changes they would like to see.

This type of feedback is generally more open-ended than what can be gained through a survey. The feedback analysis process can be challenging because it can involve sifting through large amounts of unstructured data and interpreting qualitative feedback, which can be diverse and subjective. Despite the difficulties, the insights gained through feedback analysis can be extremely valuable for improving communication strategies.

Non-profit organizations and scientific paper publishers often use feedback analysis. Almost all good publishers consider reviewer/user feedback from readers and authors to improve the quality and impact of their scientific articles. They consider feedback on the clarity of the writing, the relevance of the content, the rigor of the research, and the impact of the findings. This feedback informs their editorial decisions and helps them ensure their content meets the needs and expectations of their audience.

Similarly, non-profit organizations such as UNICEF analyze feedback from donors, beneficiaries, and volunteers to improve their communications. They evaluate feedback on their donation process, their communication frequency and methods, the clarity of their mission and its impact, and the transparency of their operations. Feedback helps them understand what their audiences value and how to meet their needs with greater precision.

4.1.7   Ethnography: Direct Observation and Participation

Ethnography involves immersing oneself in the audience's environment. This may mean attending events or meetings that the audience attends, following online forums or social media groups where your audience interacts, or experiencing firsthand the challenges or needs your audience faces. Firsthand experience can provide insights into your audience's needs, preferences, and behaviors that may not be evident through other analysis methods.

Direct observation and participation can be time-consuming and may not be feasible for all audiences or all communicators. Using this method requires a balance between observation and participation. Too much participation can bias your observations and too little can prevent you from gaining the deep understanding of your audience that you desire.

Despite these potential pitfalls, this method is particularly useful for non-profit organizations that work closely with the communities they serve. Organizations like the Bill and Melinda Gates Foundation and Doctors Without Borders often immerse themselves in the communities they serve. They participate in community activities, observe community interactions, and engage in conversations with community members. This firsthand experience helps them understand the challenges, needs, and culture of these communities, which in turn informs program development as well as communication strategies.

4.1.8   Psychographic Analysis

Psychographic analysis involves studying the psychological attributes of your audience including their attitudes, values, behaviors, interests, and lifestyles, e.g., using the Myers-Briggs Type Indicator discussed in more detail in Sec 4.2. Knowing the psychological attributes of your audience can help you understand how to communicate in a way that aligns with their apparent motivation and values. This understanding is particularly useful when crafting messages intended to resonate deeply with your audience.

Psychographic analysis is also challenging because it requires collecting and interpreting complex data. It is often difficult to segment audiences based on psychographic characteristics, as these characteristics are often subjective and can vary widely within a demographic group. Despite these challenges, psychographic analysis provides insights that assist in tailoring communication strategies.

When connecting with the audience on a deeper, more personal level can enhance the effectiveness of the message, psychographic analysis is particularly useful. Thus it is an effective technique when copywriting and when preparing proposals or technical papers for which a small number of decision makers are involved in the review process. Companies like Nike and Apple use psychographic analysis to understand their customers' lifestyles, values, and personality traits. They analyze customer behaviors, attitudes, and feedback to understand what motivates their customers and what drives their values. This understanding helps them craft marketing messages that resonate with their audience and build a strong emotional connection with their brand.

4.1.9   Social Media Analysis

Social media analysis involves examining audience interactions on social media platforms in order to understand their needs, preferences, attitudes, and behaviors. The data analyzed includes social media comments, likes, shares, and follows, as well as broader trends and conversations. As we might imagine, social media platforms provide a wealth of data and insights to be gained.

However, social media analysis is challenging due to the sheer volume of data and the rapid pace of social media. It also can be difficult to accurately interpret social media data due to the informal and varied nature of social media interactions. Despite these challenges, social media analysis is a valuable tool for audience analysis, particularly in copywriting and non-profit proposal writing.

Coca-Cola and other companies use social media analysis to understand their audience's needs and tailor their content and campaigns accordingly. They analyze social media trends, customer comments, and shares to understand what content resonates with their audience, which product features are popular, and what customer concerns or issues need to be addressed.

Similarly, non-profit organizations like the American Red Cross use social media analysis to understand their audience's needs and tailor their fundraising campaigns. They analyze social media trends, donor comments, and shares to understand what resonates with their donors, what donation methods are preferred, and what donor concerns or issues need to be addressed.

4.1.10   User Testing

The user testing method allows a sample of your audience to interact with your content before it is finalized. This could involve having users read your draft content and provide feedback, complete tasks using your content and discuss their experience, or observe users interacting with your content and note any issues or difficulties. User testing can be time-consuming and may require specialized knowledge to plan, conduct, and analyze. However, it can provide valuable insights

into how your audience will receive and use your content in the real world, which can inform your revisions and enhance the effectiveness of your content.

This technique is particularly useful in technical proposal writing and scientific paper writing. For example, red-team feedback, discussed in Chap.7, can help improve the clarity, relevance, and impact of the content. Companies like Adobe utilize user testing to understand how well their software tutorials and guides meet their users' needs. They conduct user tests in which users attempt to complete tasks using their guides and collect feedback on the clarity, usability, and helpfulness of the guides. This feedback informs their revisions and helps them improve the effectiveness of their guides.

Similarly, scientific publishers like IEEE and Nature Publishing Group use peer review, which is a type of user testing, to understand how well their articles meet the needs of their readers. The peer review process will reject a large number of submissions, often the majority, to help select the best and most relevant papers. The review process, effectively, is a user test where readers attempt to understand a scientific concept using their articles and collect feedback on the articles' clarity, relevance, and comprehensibility. This feedback is provided to the authors to inform their revisions and help them improve their articles.

Personal Story: Analyze the Audience for *Every* Proposal; They May Surprise You.

Throughout my company's history, I have witnessed and participated in many examples of trying to understand the audience. One of the critical things I have learned is that audience analysis is imperative every time. No matter how experienced you are, no matter how long you've been working in this space, no matter how many proposals you have submitted, you can easily misunderstand your audience.

In this story, one of my engineers was particularly interested in ecology, the environment, major animals, and whatever. He found an SBIR topic on detecting, counting, and managing endangered species for the Air Force. By this time, I thought I had a good handle on the SBIR process. We had done 30 or 40 over my career by this point, so I thought I understood the audience. I even had a good persona model that included the importance of talking about dual-use technology and the value of a system from multiple different uses. Our traditional approach and story would have been to feature a system that could not only detect and track endangered species but could also track other targets for military and commercial applications.

My engineer, however, started by looking up papers associated with the topic. He was intrigued because the papers had very little traditional military jargon or application. They were focused entirely on endangered species. My engineer wanted to dig a little further into his audience research, so we directly called the technical point of contact. As is often the case, we ended up leaving a voicemail about our questions and focus.

To our surprise, the technical point of contact called us back within 10 minutes! He was excited by our interest and the questions we asked. We had an hour-long call discussing why he wrote this topic, what the goals were, and – much to our surprise – how he would prefer a system that focused entirely on the biological

---

sciences and endangered species questions rather than trying to find a balance between endangered species and dual-use technology. He thought the problem was different enough and important enough to focus solely on that and did not want us to spend too much of our effort on the other applications.

Since he was a key part of our audience, we followed his advice and wrote our proposal focusing entirely on the biological services aspect. We had to dig deep into our research literature to ensure we were addressing the key problems that were typically outside our primary expertise, but our proposal was successful. Not only that, our follow-on proposals were successful, working with them was successful, and it led to a million dollars in revenue. We delivered multiple systems that they used in the field, software that they used for years afterward, and also developed joint papers.

If we had not taken the time to deeply understand our audience, and if we had not reached out to interview the primary contact, we would have written the wrong proposal. We would have written a proposal focused on dual-use technology with other military and commercial applications, and our efforts would not have been rewarded. In the end, understanding the audience was the first step in our success.

4.2 Using Myers-Briggs Type Indicator for Audience Analysis

Many audience analysis techniques require direct access to the audience. Some audience awareness can be inferred from public information and discussions with other experienced players. At times even a single phone call with one or more key decision-makers can provide essential insights into the characteristics of a particular audience. In addition, the use of the Meyers-Briggs Type Indicator (MBTI) and the 16 MBTI persona models can be very helpful in audience estimation and analysis for proposals. By understanding these personality types and how people identified as a certain type tend to process information, it is possible to write in a manner that resonates effectively with that audience. So let's dig deeper into how the MBTI audience analysis process works.

The MBTI categorizes individuals according to 16 personality types based on four dichotomous pairs: Extraversion (E) vs. Introversion (I), Sensing (S) vs. Intuition (N), Thinking (T) vs. Feeling (F), and Judging (J) vs. Perceiving (P), Myers et al. [1985]. Some of these characteristics are summarized in Figure 4.1 The columns in the rows combine two dimensions related to how people tend to take in information (S vs. N) and how they prefer to make decisions (T vs. F) which roughly describes shared characteristics within the column. The S vs. N and T vs. F are the two dimensions most important for writing to the audience. The J vs. P dimension is important in some writing, and the E vs. I dimension, while generally less important for written information, can be very important for speeches and small-scale, direct presentations.

The figure also shows the groupings associated with the four "temperaments" that are widely used for simplified modeling. Estimating which of the four temperaments are in the expected decision-making pool can often be a good starting point for a writer in determining a communication style appropriate for the audience. Knowledge of the audience types can also be useful for writing team formation. By covering as many dimensions as possible within a writing team, the team can better estimate how that dimension will impact the writing and can address the need appropriately.

Be aware that MBTI is not the only tool for assessing audience personality types. The Big-5 theory of personality is often considered to have better scientific underpinnings than MBTI and is more predictive for things like employee performance, McCrae and Costa Jr [1989]. In contrast, the simpler MBTI provides a smaller number of "persona" to use in estimating the audience. Furthermore, the MBTI dimensions are more of a trait (as in the Big 5) than an actual personality type.

While personality type tools are helpful in audience analysis, they are not perfect. When using such tools be aware that people may change their behavior. They may respond in ways that are not consistent with how they would be rated on an MBTI self-assessment.

4.2.1 Estimating MBTI Types Through Observation

Estimating an individual's MBTI type through observation requires careful attention to their behavior, preferences, and communication style. There are multiple papers on using modern machine learning to estimate these factors based on public data, and some companies will analyze the data for a fee. If you have access to a lot of customer data or even their social media feeds, these can be automatically analyzed for audience estimation. The following guidelines provide an overview of how audience data can provide direction for impactful writing according to MBTI categories.

➤ For *Extraversion vs. Introversion*, observe whether the individual appears to gain energy from social interaction and outward activity (Extraversion) or from solitary, inward activity (Introversion).

➤ For *Sensing vs. Intuition*, consider if the individual focuses more on concrete facts and details (Sensing) or on interpreting and adding meaning (Intuition).

➤ When distinguishing *Thinking vs. Feeling*, observe if decisions are made based on logic and objectivity (Thinking) or on personal values and the potential impact on others (Feeling).

➤ Finally, to differentiate *Judging vs. Perceiving*, consider whether the individual prefers a planned, organized approach to life (Judging) or a more flexible, spontaneous approach (Perceiving).

4.2.2 Applying MBTI Types to Writing

Once you have estimated your audience according to MBTI types, you can apply this knowledge to the writing process.

➤ *Extraverts* may appreciate direct, action-oriented language and content that encourages interaction, but *Introverts* may prefer detailed, reflective content.

CHARACTERISTICS OF EACH OF THE 16 MBTI and their PROCESSING STYLES

	Sensing Types		Intuitive Types	
Introverts	**ISTJ** Focused, diligent, success-driven. Practical, logical, and dependable. Responsible, organized, and in charge. goal-oriented, resilient, committed.	**ISFJ** Friendly, responsible, and diligent. Devotedly meets obligations, lends stability to projects or groups. Thorough, accurate, patient with details. Loyal, considerate, perceptive, empathetic towards others.	**INFJ** Succeed through persistence, originality, and adaptability. Devote strong efforts to work. Quietly determined, and empathetic. Likely lead in serving the common good.	**INTJ** Possess original minds and strong drive for personal ideas. Excel in organizing tasks of interst. Skeptical, determined, occasionally stubborn. Compromises on lesser matters to secure greater victories.
Introverts	**ISTP** Calm observers. Quiet, reserved, detached curiosity with original humor. Interested in cause and effect, mechanics, logical organization of facts.	**ISFP** Reserved, kind, and modest. Avoid conflicts, don't impose opinions. Prefer to follow and be loyal. Relaxed approach to tasks, value the moment over haste.	**INFP** Enthusiastic and loyal, share openly with familiarity. Value learning, ideas, and independent projects. Less focused on possessions or surroundings.	**INTP** Reserved, drawn to theoretical and scientific pursuits. Problem-solvers with logic and analysis. Interested in ideas, less in socializing. Have specific, defined interests and in purposeful work.
Extroverts	**ESTP** Skilled at spontaneous problem-solving. Embrace the present without worry. Interested in mechanics, sports, and socializing. Adaptable, tolerant, value conservatism. Prefer practical tasks	**ESFP** Outgoing and enthusiastic, make things enjoyable for others. Active in sports and events. Eager participants recall facts well. Practical, people-oriented, thrive in diverse situations.	**ENFP** Enthusiastic, imaginative, versatile. Quick problem-solvers, always ready to assist. Rely on improvisation over preparation. Skillful at persuasion and finding solutions.	**ENTP** Innovative, versatile, engaging, outspoken, and often argumentative. Thrive on tackling novel challenges but may overlook routine tasks. Proficient at justifying preferences.
Extroverts	**ESTJ** Practical, business- minded, adept at mechanics. Focus on useful subjects, adapt when needed. Enjoy organizing and leading. Potential for effective administration.	**ESFJ** Warm, talkative, cooperative, conscientious. Skilled in teamwork and committees and fostering harmony. Supportive and kind. Flourish with encouragement. Primarily interested in practical ways to help others.	**ENFJ** Responsive, considerate, and responsible. Attuned to others' thoughts and feelings. Skilled in presenting ideas and leading discussions. Sociable, sympathetic, and well-liked. Open to feedback and praise.	**ENTJ** Hearty, candid, decisive leaders. Excel in reasoning and intelligent communication, including public speaking. Informed and curious learners. Sometimes exude more confidence than their experience suggests.
	Directing	Relating	Valuing	Visioning

Temperament	Description
Guardian (SJ)	Practical and responsible individuals who value stability, tradition, and order

Artisan (SP)	Spontaneous and adaptable individuals who seek excitement, enjoy hands-on experiences and value freedom and creativity.
Idealist (NF)	Compassionate and imaginative individuals driven by a strong sense of purpose, valuing personal growth and harmony.
Rational (NT)	Analytical and strategic thinkers who prioritize intellect, logic, and problem-solving, aiming for innovation and mastery.

Figure 4.1: *Summary of some characteristics of 16 MBTI types and the processing styles as well as the four temperaments. Descriptio5n1s adapted from Myers et al. [1985].*

➢ *Sensing* types may value clear, factual, and practical information with concrete examples, while *Intuitive* types may prefer a focus on concepts, ideas, the big picture, and implications.

➢ *Thinking* types may appreciate clear logic, objectivity, and factual information, and *Feeling* types may respond well to empathetic language that encompasses values and personal or social implications.

➢ *Judging* types may appreciate content focused on structure, clear plans, and decisiveness, while *Perceiving* types may prefer options, flexibility, and content that encourages exploration.

Remember, MBTI types are a tool, not a definitive guide to understanding individuals or audiences. MBTI analysis does not replace direct audience research when it is feasible. It always should be used in conjunction with other audience analysis techniques.

A man really writes for an audience of about ten persons. Of course, if others like it, that is a clear gain. But if those ten are satisfied, he is content.

-Alfred North Whitehead

4.2.3   Writing for a Mixed Audience

In most situations, an audience will comprise individuals with different MBTI types. This presents the challenge of writing in a manner that resonates with a diverse range of personality types. The methodology for writing to a mixed audience also applies if you do not have any real audience data. Several approaches can cover most of the bases when writing to a mixed audience and do so with minimal risk.

One approach is to incorporate elements that appeal to each of the MBTI dichotomies in your writing. For example, you might use a blend of concrete examples and big-picture concepts to cater to both sensing and intuitive types. You could also strive for a balance between factual information (for thinking types) and considerations of values and impact on people (for feeling types).

Another approach is to segment your content to cater to different personality types. For instance, you might include big-picture and strong conclusions in an executive summary for intuitive and judging types who prefer to see conclusions upfront. In the same document you can provide detailed appendices or exploration opportunities for introverts and perceiving types who prefer to delve deeper.

An important consideration is the context of your communication and the dominant personality types for that context. For instance, when writing a scientific report, it is reasonable to focus on the preferences of an audience of thinking and judging types. Conversely, in a piece designed for a community advocacy group, you might focus more on the preferences of an audience of feeling and perceiving types. You can also use temperaments, which are groupings of multiple subtypes, as a starting point for mixed audiences.

The goal of considering MBTI types is not to stereotype people or make assumptions about individuals. Rather, it is to gain a useful tool for understanding and writing appropriately to different behavior preferences and communication styles within your audience. It is common for people in organizations to "exhibit" an apparent MBTI type that is not their actual personal preference, e.g., management may act as a judging type even if they prefer thinking. By using MBTI as an audience analysis tool, you are not making judgments about your audience as people but about their apparent communication preferences.

4.3 Context Analysis and Review Requirements

Understanding the context in which your audience receives and interprets your message is an integral part of effective communication. When preparing to write, whether for a proposal submission or a scientific paper, knowing your audience's expectations and criteria for success is paramount. Let's delve deeper into these processes and explore some practical examples of how context analysis can be used effectively.

Any writing being submitted to a formal review process **must** meet all the requirements specified. It does not matter if you tug on the heartstrings of an emotional reviewer; if you violate a review requirement, you will not reach the objective. Review committees are inflexible when it comes to specified requirements.

I have seen a proposal returned without review because it lacked a "required section" on past work even though there was no relevant past work. Other parts of the proposal explicitly said there was no relevant past work. If we had "completed" the required section, it would simply have said "not applicable." As some review processes have both "required" and "optional" elements, it is strongly advised to have a checklist that lists everything that is required and what is optional. Include detailed information on each to be used later by the internal review team.

4.3.1   Understanding the Formal Proposal Review Process

In a formal proposal review process, such as those undertaken by organizations, government bodies, or corporations, understanding the context is key to achieving a favorable outcome. Reviewers typically adhere to a strict set of criteria. They carefully assess the relevance, feasibility, cost-effectiveness, and potential impact of each proposal.

For instance, the National Science Foundation (NSF) in the United States employs a well-defined review process. It scrutinizes proposals for their intellectual merit, their potential to advance knowledge and broader impacts, and the proposal's capacity to benefit society. Intellectual merit involves factors such as the innovativeness of the methodology, the proposal team's qualifications, the novelty of the concept, and the appropriateness of available resources. Broader impacts may be demonstrated through societal relevance, contributions to research and education infrastructure, or the potential to increase diversity in STEM fields. Tailoring a proposal to meet these expectations can significantly increase its chances of success. To uncover these criteria and their respective sub-components, writers should review the NSF's publicly available Grant Proposal Guide. They should also study successful proposals and attend NSF-run workshops or webinars.

However, not all proposals are submitted to grant-awarding bodies like the NSF. Often, businesses respond to Request for Proposals (RFPs) issued by corporations looking to procure goods or services. A technology firm such as IBM may issue an RFP for a new data management system. Respondents would need to analyze the RFP's context. They would need to consider IBM's unique needs, the expected timeline, the proposed budget, and any technological or regulatory constraints. A successful proposal would demonstrate a deep understanding of the required elements, offering solutions uniquely tailored to IBM's context.

In scientific academia, formal paper reviews hold great significance. They determine whether research findings get published and how they are presented to the global community. In this setting, the audience comprises peer reviewers who are experts in the subject matter. They assess the research's validity, novelty, and significance alongside other factors like the robustness of the methodology and the relevance of the data presented.

Leading journals like "Nature" and IEEE, as well as leading conferences, outline clear criteria for their reviews. Papers must be original, significant to the specific research field, of interest to researchers in other disciplines, and carry potential public interest. Originality implies novel ideas or findings, while significance indicates the paper's potential impact on its field of study. Interest in other disciplines suggests the research has broader relevance or interdisciplinary value. Expected public interest may be catered to by highlighting the societal implications of the research. Journals and conferences may also have explicit criteria for "reproducibility" or sharing of data.

Understanding and catering to the specific criteria and expectations of reviewing organizations increases the chance of acceptance. However, understanding these criteria involves more than simply reading the journal's "Guide for Authors" or the conference's call for papers. Authors can usually request the review criterion, study previously published papers, and read editorials or blog posts on the publication process. A particularly effective method of understanding the context of the review process could be to discuss the experiences of colleagues and authors who have had successful submissions. Attending conferences and networking with professionals, including journal editors, can provide invaluable insights into the publication process for different journals. This kind of interaction provides firsthand knowledge, often shedding light on the unspoken expectations of the review process.

One of the best ways to gain insights into the reviewing criterion and audience is by reviewing past submissions and their reviews. Most companies keep a long history of past projects and reviews, and some venues publish past reviews, which indicates the criteria and how they are interpreted. In academic venues, you can normally request submissions and review them from colleges.

In conclusion, context analysis and review requirement analysis are crucial in preparing a proposal or scientific paper. It requires studying the formal criteria and going beyond understanding the unique circumstances and expectations of the audience. While laborious, this preparation can greatly increase the chances of acceptance, making your message heard, respected, and appreciated. As the adage goes, "It is not just about what you say but how and when you say it." Understanding your audience's context is the key to mastering the 'how' and 'when.' It is the first "research" stage of a tactical writing process and should not be skimped on or taken lightly.

4.4 Key Terms

1) **Audience Analysis:** *The process of studying and understanding the characteristics, needs, preferences, and behaviors of a specific audience.*

2) **Audience Interviews:** *In-depth interactions with the audience to gain insights into their needs, expectations, and perspectives.*

3) **Audience Surveys:** *Direct methods of gathering data about the audience's preferences, needs, and expectations using questionnaires.*

4) **Competitor Analysis:** *Evaluating the communication strategies and messages used by competitors to gain insights into what works and what needs improvement.*

5) **Context Analysis:** *Understanding the physical, social, and temporal context in which the audience will receive your message.*

6) **Demographic Analysis:** *Examining the basic characteristics of the audience, such as age, gender, location, education, and income.*

7) **Ethnography:** *Immersing in the audience's environment to gain firsthand experience and insights into their needs and challenges.*

8) **Feedback Analysis:** *Analyzing responses and feedback from past communications with similar audiences to improve communication strategies.*

9) **MBTI:** *MBTI refers to the Myers-Briggs Type Indicator, a psychology theory of personality with 16 "persona" that can be used for basic audience analysis*

10) **Persona Models:** *Idealized caricatures of audience segments embodying specific characteristics, needs, motivations, and behaviors of typical audience members.*

11) **Psychographic Analysis:** *Studying the psychological attributes of the audience, including attitudes, values, behaviors, interests, and lifestyles.*

12) **Social Media Analysis:** *Examining audience interactions and behaviors on social media platforms to understand preferences and attitudes.*

13) **User Testing:** *A method where a sample of your audience interacts with your content before it is finalized to gather feedback and insights.*

4.5 Other Terms

1) **Ambiguous Responses:** *Instances when interviewees provide unclear or vague answers, requiring further clarification.*

2) **Content Development:** *The process of creating and refining written material or messages for a specific audience.*

3) **Idealized Caricatures:** *Abstract personas that capture the essence of different audience segments from interviews.*

4) **Interviewer Bias:** *The potential for the interviewer's perspectives or assumptions to affect the data collected during interviews.*

5) **Tailored Messages:** *Messages customized to resonate with a specific audience based on their characteristics and preferences.*

6) **Targeted Communication:** *Communication strategies directed at specific audience segments to address their unique needs and interests.*

5 Why Does Storytelling Matter in Tactical Writing?

It's not what you SAY that matters. It's what forms inside their minds. Kendall Haven

There is no shortage of people who have something to say about story and storytelling. With seemingly little thought, they use the term "story" in diverse contexts that lead to different understandings— and misunderstandings. So what is a story? What distinguishes a story from a narrative, an essay, or who knows what?

An obvious place to start our inquiry is the dictionary. One definition describes a story as "a narrative account of a real or imagined event or events." This definition is concise and simple, but is it adequate?

Dr. Kendall Haven, a senior research scientist, award-winning author, and master storyteller would say "no." In his assessment, the dictionary definition lacks depth and is misleading. It focuses too much on the "event" or the plot and fails to capture the essence of what a story truly is—a complex interplay of characters, motives, conflicts, and resolutions.

Having researched extensively the science of story and storytelling, Dr. Haven offers a deeper, more nuanced understanding of what a story is. He defines it as "a detailed, character-based narration of a character's struggles to overcome obstacles and reach an important goal." This definition takes the concept of a story far beyond a mere sequence of events. Through this lens, Dr. Haven emphasizes that stories are not just about what happens but why it happens and what it means for the characters involved.

Dr. Haven's insights provide a more comprehensive understanding of what constitutes a story than simplistic and misleading definitions allow. He invites us to understand the essence of a story as being a complex interplay of the character's motives, struggles, transformations, and ultimate objectives that engage the audience on multiple levels. This concept of story and the elements required to create an effective story are significant for our purposes because they are essential to the tactical writing process.

5.1 Common Myths About Story

One way to clarify and expand our understanding of the essence of a story is to explore what a story is not. In his book, *Story Proof*, Haven [2007], Dr. Haven identifies several myths about stories that are commonly held but are fundamentally misleading. Let's consider his insights that debunk the myths that confuse our understanding of the concept of story.

- **All Narratives Are Stories:** This myth stems from confusion between the terms "narrative" and "story." Dr. Haven uses the example of a historical account, which can be a narrative but often lacks the character-based focus that would make it a story.

- **A Story Is Just a Sequence of Events:** This myth is problematic because it reduces a story to its plot. Dr. Haven counters this misunderstanding by explaining how a character's internal struggles and transformations are crucial story elements. For example, he points out how the story of Cinderella is not just about a girl going to a ball but about her transformation in learning to overcome her difficult circumstances.

- **Factual Accounts Cannot Be Stories:** The belief that only fictional accounts can be stories is also a myth. Dr. Haven uses real-life examples, like the story of Rosa Parks, to show that real events can be structured as stories if they focus on character development, goals, struggles, visual details, and transformation.

5.2 The History and Science of Storytelling

Storytelling is an ancient art form that predates written language. It has been a cornerstone of human development and culture for thousands of years. In contrast, the science behind storytelling that seeks to understand why stories can be so compelling and how they can be crafted for maximum impact is a relatively new field of study. Dr. Haven is a leader in this field. He builds his history and support for story impact on human brain research work from Nelson and Fivush [2004], Donald [1991], Rochat [1995], and Bruner [1990]. A brief overview of the history and science of storytelling will set the landscape for further exploration. Then we will delve into the history of storytelling—tracing its evolution from oral traditions to the written word and beyond and its science—exploring its physiological and psychological underpinnings.

➣ **The Dawn of Storytelling:** The roots of storytelling can be traced back more than 100,000 years when humans began using storytelling as a means of communication and archiving learning, wisdom, facts, knowledge, values, beliefs, and history. The long-standing practice of telling stories has profoundly impacted human interaction and, some say, even led to evolutionary changes in the brain. The human brain seemingly has been rewired to think in specific story terms, either because storytelling evolved to match how humans think and remember or, more likely, the human brain is predisposed to think in story terms to facilitate making sense, understanding, and remembering.

➣ **The Written Word and Logical Forms:** Approximately 7,000 years ago the advent of writing marked a significant milestone in storytelling history. This was followed by the development of logic and argumentative forms about 3,200 years ago. These advancements enabled more complex stories to be told, archived, and shared across generations. However, it was a mere 200 years ago that most people learned to read, further democratizing access to stories and knowledge.

➣ **The Modern Era and Beyond:** In the modern era, storytelling is taking on new forms and mediums, evolving from books to films and podcasts to interactive video games, for example. However, the core elements that make stories compelling remain largely unchanged. According to Dr. Haven's presentation in Haven [2007], the human brain is still predisposed to think in story terms. Our "Neural Story Net," a fixed, connected set of subconscious brain sub-regions, continues to process specific story concepts and informational elements. This neural predisposition ensures that storytelling will likely remain a dominant form of human communication for the foreseeable future.

So storytelling is more than an art. Being one of the oldest forms of communication, storytelling is a fundamental part of human history and cognition. As we have evolved, so has the art of storytelling. Our communication methodology may adapt to new technologies and mediums, but it always retains its core elements. Understanding the history and science of storytelling enriches our appreciation of this ancient practice and sheds light on the cognitive processes that make us uniquely human.

5.3 Why Humans Think in Terms of Stories

Storytelling is not merely a form of communication. Thinking in terms of story is a fundamental way our brains are structured to perceive and make sense of the world. In fact, the human brain is wired to love stories! Dr. Haven argues human brains have evolved to have what he called a "Neural Story Net." Let's now consider the scientific and psychological dimensions of how humans inherently think in terms of stories, drawing upon the insights provided by Dr. Haven in his book *"Story Proof,"* Haven [2007].

The propensity of the human brain to think in terms of stories is not a random occurrence but results from evolutionary processes that shape human cognition. Dr. Haven points out that the human mind employs story concepts as frameworks by which it creates narratives from virtually every sensory and experiential event. Our predisposition to story thinking has been crucial for our survival, as it enables us to quickly understand complex situations, predict outcomes, and make decisions. Dr. Haven uses the example of how early humans used storytelling to pass down crucial survival information such as locations of food and water or how to avoid predators.

Pattern Recognition, Goal Anticipation

Recognizable patterns of events and relationships are a fundamental element in storytelling. So it should not surprise us that pattern recognition is one of the first cognitive skills babies learn. As babies develop, they are keenly attuned to recognizing patterns and relating them to their goals. For instance, they quickly learn the sequence of events that leads to feeding or sleeping and associate specific caregiver actions with anticipated activities. Babies learn the pattern of parents' voices as the source of resolution for their discomfort long before they understand the actual meaning of words.

A more advanced pattern recognition skill is understanding cause and effect, which is crucial to establishing a coherent narrative in storytelling. Babies start to grasp this concept at a very early age. Long before they can talk, they learn that crying leads to attention from caregivers, which demonstrates their understanding of the cause-and-effect relationship between their actions and the responses they elicit. They quickly learn that crying not only gets attention but rewards them with what they want: being fed or changed.

Babies are being primed for storytelling even before they can articulate words. Their cognitive and emotional development is closely aligned with the fundamental elements of storytelling, underscoring their innate human connection to this ancient form of communication. The essence of many stories is a journey or quest driven by curiosity and the need for discovery. Babies exhibit this trait by being naturally curious and explorative. They seem driven to touch, taste, and manipulate objects in order to understand their properties, much like characters in a story are driven to pursue a quest to discover something significant.

Young children learn patterns of behavior by imitation. They often imitate the actions and sounds they observe, which is a rudimentary form of role-playing. These behaviors are not just mimicry. Rather, they are an early form of understanding characters and their roles, which is foundational to character development in storytelling. When they imitate, children are learning behaviors and inventing roles, taking the first steps toward telling their own stories.

Pattern Recognition and Goal Anticipation in Other Animals

While *Story Proof*, Haven [2007] focuses on pattern recognition in humans, it is worth noting that pattern recognition is well-known in the animal kingdom. Pavlov's iconic experiments with dogs, Pavlov [1927] have become a cornerstone in the study of behavioral psychology, specifically in conditioned responses, which can be considered a form of pattern recognition and anticipation. In these experiments, Ivan Pavlov rang a bell before presenting food to dogs. Initially, the food naturally triggered salivation. After repeated pairing of the bell and the food, the dogs began to salivate merely at the sound of the bell, even when no food was presented.

This behavioral change indicated that the dogs had learned to associate the bell with the arrival of food, demonstrating their ability to recognize patterns and anticipate outcomes. This phenomenon, termed "classical conditioning," is a powerful example of how organisms can learn to associate one stimulus with another, revealing the inherent capability to identify patterns and make predictions based on past experiences.

More recently, research has shown that many animals are "born imitators," including apes, monkeys, dogs, corvids (crows/ravens), parrots, and dolphins, De Waal [2016]. Some animals can learn new behaviors and anticipate the outcomes by watching other animals perform a task. While we once believed that humans were the only tool makers, it is now well established that animals not only make tools but communicate how to make them to other animals, Shumaker et al. [2011], Bandini et al. [2020]. Making and using tools suggests deeper mental models of recognition and use of patterns in anticipation of reward (food) and is seen in many evolutionary branches.

Lest we think that recognizing and using patterns in anticipation of a reward is just a function of advanced animals and higher-level minds, even honey bees have strong pattern recognition and anticipation abilities. If we put food in one location and then in another based on a pattern, the bees will be waiting at the next likely location after three to four successful locations. This is true even when somewhat complex topological spacing is used Chen et al. [2003]. The bees can learn that certain patterns, such as horizontal or vertical lines, are signals for food.

Thus pattern recognition, goals, and anticipation, key elements of story structure, are recognized traits in a wide range of animal brains. It is then reasonable to conclude that these established biological mechanisms are evolutionary in nature because they are useful for species' survival, including that of the human species.

5.3.2 Cells That Fire Together Wire Together

The principle that "cells that fire together wire together" is well-known in neuroscience Yuste [1992], Shamay-Tsoory [2022]. The low-level neuron connections in a growing brain have the property that concurrent activation (firing) leads to new synaptic connections. Once connected, activation in one neuron increases the potential for activation in the connected neuron—allowing us to have associations from sensory data and emotions to memories. In the story context, this neural mechanism means that the more frequently a child or adult engages their neural story network to interpret incoming sensory input, the more likely they are to do the same in the future.

The activation of this neural process is a cornerstone in understanding how humans think in stories. We learn and anticipate patterns naturally, and our upbringing reinforces the neural connections that in turn, reinforce the cognitive process of interpreting our experience in terms of story. Dr. Haven demonstrates how this principle is reinforced by the ubiquitous presence of stories throughout childhood when they hear stories, see stories, have stories read to them, and read stories themselves. This constant exposure to stories strengthens the neural pathways to story thinking, making it a dominant cognitive process. Even if we share with animals a predisposition toward some aspects of storytelling—pattern recognition, goals, and anticipation— the unique social and educational process by which human children are immersed in stories further wires their brains to think in story terms.

Another key aspect of the story is emotional resonance. Even infants are highly sensitive to the emotional tones in their environment. They can sense the mood of their caregivers and react accordingly, which is a rudimentary reflection of the emotional engagement that stories aim to achieve. The impact of our social interactions with our emotions impacts brain development Shamay-Tsoory [2022] throughout our lives. Emotionally laden interactions implicitly activate the fire-together-wire-together mechanism. In *Story Proof*, Haven [2007], Dr. Haven points out that this emotional tuning is a precursor to the more complex emotional understanding and response that stories often evoke.

5.3.3   The Role of Story in Human Perception and Learning

Jerome Bruner, a renowned developmental psychologist, boldly states that "stories are not innocent: they always have a message." Research concurs, showing that stories align with how humans naturally perceive, process, think, and learn. Dr. Haven further notes that life often follows a story form and format, making it possible to relate real-life experiences to stories. This is particularly important in educational settings where stories can be effective tools for teaching complex concepts without actually risking life and limb. If there were an evolutionary advantage to early humans for developing storytelling, the ability to use stories to teach toolmaking and hunting techniques safely would be a likely application.

5.3.4   Flipping It Around—Did Stories Evolve to Match How Human Brains Work?

Story Proof, Haven [2007] presents a compelling narrative about how the human brain evolved to align with storytelling. We already mentioned that some aspects of neurological functioning, such as pattern recognition and anticipation, are shared across many species and, hence, are likely biologically driven to evolve. This makes sense as patterns and anticipation regarding where to find food, water, or shelter, would have a major impact on survival.

But the story is more than pattern recognition and anticipation. The temporal correlation between story and advances in human communication, as well as the correlation in brain function/imaging and story, are well-established. However, correlation is not causation and human evolution is a very slow process. Genes, the core of human evolution, "evolve" primarily through procreation and become evident in new generations. Moreover, it is unclear how long it would take for "story" understanding to provide a survival advantage and lead to evolutionary pressures to change brain functioning. So what might be the process whereby brain functioning aligned with storytelling?

Consider the possibilities if we view the association and evolution from a different angle. Instead of saying the human brain evolved to think in terms of stories, what if it is more likely that we learned to evolve stories to better match how the human brain works? In this scenario, individuals could be evolving their understanding of how well different story structures work on a weekly or even daily basis. Once improvements were recognized, they could be disseminated quickly to many people. Story evolution would be much faster than genetic evolution, and it would still yield the observed correlation between story and brain function.

Independent of which direction we consider the evolution happening, the data showing the relationship between the brain and story is overwhelming.

AT TIB MAP

PLET WI TTE RMI

CR OSO FT

Figure 5.1: *As an example of the power of prior knowledge and grouping of data, read in 15 seconds, and try to remember the sequence of characters. After trying, look at figure 5.2 to see the discussion of power, prior knowledge, and grouping.*

5.4 Ways to Make Meaningful Connections in Stories

Published research provides solid evidence behind the power of a story, but we need to move on and consider examples of how we convert a story into a memorable experience. Dr. Haven argues that certain dimensions of knowledge and experience are critical to creating effective stories because they help the brain fill the gap between the words and statements of a story and its meaning and impact on the reader. Let's consider how prior knowledge, cultural context, goals, and details have an impact on how we interpret, evaluate, and remember stories. These examples will help us see why storytelling can have such an impact and is so important in tactical writing.

5.4.1   The Role of Prior Knowledge

Prior knowledge plays a significant role in how a story is received. Audiences bring their own experiences, beliefs, and cultural backgrounds into their interpretation of a story. As an example of the power of prior knowledge and how contextual grouping of related items matters to our comprehension and memory, see figure 5.1. There is strong scientific support for the critical role of prior knowledge in memory and understanding. Some key issues and terms include:

➢ **Schema Theory:** Thorndyke and Yekovich [1980] This cognitive framework proposed mechanisms that help people organize and interpret new information based on their knowledge.

➢ **Confirmation Bias:** Klayman [1995] People are more likely to engage with stories that confirm their existing beliefs.

➢ **Surprisal:** Kagan [2002] In story-based presentations, something often builds on prior knowledge but then deviates in a surprising way. This surprise prompts better attention and leads to better retention.

AT TIB MAP

PLET WI TTE RMI

CR OSO FT

ATT IBM APPLE

TWITTER MICROSOFT

Figure 5.2: *Continuing the example of the power of prior knowledge and context to grouping information, the top part of the figure shows the same letters with regrouping, and now it should be trivial for you to remember.*

➢ **Cultural Context:** The impact of a story can vary greatly depending on the audience's cultural background. Stories with cultural context can exploit a wealth of knowledge and emotion tied to the context of previous stories.

➢ **Intertextuality:** This refers to how a story references or draws upon other stories, adding layers of meaning for those who are familiar with the referenced material.

➢ **Audience Expectations:** Knowing your audience's expectations can help in crafting stories that resonate with them—it can drive any of the above impacts of prior knowledge if you know enough about the audience's knowledge to use it.

Being able to exploit cultural context is a powerful element in making memorable stories. Consider each of the following one-sentence "action sequences:"

- John walked on the roof.

- Bill picked up the eggs.

- Pete hid the ax.

- Sam sat in the chair.

- Jim flew the kite.

- Frank built the boat.

- Harvey flipped the electric switch.

- Ted wrote the play.

Without looking back, how many of the sentences can you remember? Who hid the ax? Who picked up the eggs?

Let's see what happens when we exploit cultural context, at least for an American audience. How much better do you remember these action sequences:

- Kris Kringle walked on the roof.

- The Easter bunny picked up the eggs.

- George Washington hid the ax.

- Goldilocks sat in the chair.

- Ben Franklin flew the kite.

- Noah built the boat.

- Thomas Edison flipped the electric switch.

- William Shakespeare wrote the play.

Remembering these sentences is trivial if you know the stories behind them—all you have to do is index your memory bank of stories and recall the connection. But it is not easy for everyone. For example, I used this set of sentences in one of my graduate classes attended by many international students who had been in the U.S. for only a few weeks. For them, some of the references meant nothing more than random names. Without a cultural context, how does one see the relationship between an Easter bunny and eggs? Those who could remember that one without prior context likely did so because they were surprised at the unlikely juxtaposition, which helped them learn it. We shall see later that surprise is part of what makes a sticky story, as a surprise is another element of stories that can improve memory, Kagan [2002].

5.4.3 Goals and Details Help Stories Make Sense

Characters, actions, and events are not enough to make a story memorable. But when we add goals for the character, sensory details for the actions, and perspective for the events, the reader gains the cognitive data to make sense of the story and engage with the experience. Goals and details are essential for understanding a story and remembering it.

To experience how this works, consider the following one-sentence examples of characters and actions from Bransford and Stein [1993]. Read them once, then look away or cover them up and see how many you can remember:

- The fat one bought the padlock.

- The skinny one purchased the scissors.

- The toothless one plugged in the cord.

- The barefoot one climbed the steps.

- The bald one cut out the coupon.

- The kind one opened the milk.

- The poor one entered the museum.

Can you recall who climbed the steps or purchased the scissors? Despite having some aspects of a story— descriptions of characters and events— these one-sentence sequences are hard to remember. They make little sense without context or reasons for the action.

To make the importance of goals more apparent, consider what happens when we expand the sentences to provide goals that are meaningfully associated with the character and action. Now read them once, then look away or cover them up and see how many you remember:

- The fat one bought the padlock *to place on the refrigerator door.*

- The skinny one purchased the scissors *to use when taking in her clothes after losing weight.*

- The toothless one plugged in the cord *to the food blender.*

- The barefoot one climbed the steps *leading to the vat of grapes.*

- The bald one cut out the coupon *for a hair restoration clinic.*

- The kind one opened the milk *to give to a hungry child.*

- The poor one entered the museum *to find shelter from the snowstorm.*

Although we added more information and detail to remember, the whole sentence is easier to remember because a goal connects the sequence. When reading this extended version, most of us developed mental images and maybe added more details and context to our neural story net.

Multiple works have assessed the effectiveness of different text structures to create accessible memories

Armbruster [1984], Barnett [1984], Armbruster et al. [1987], Meyer et al. [2014], and concluded that story-based problem/solution structures that use character/goal/problem/resolution were the most successful. Character-based story structures with goals rate significantly higher than expository structures. In addition, they have shown that teaching the structural schema of stories significantly improved the delayed recall of scientific texts for both college and ninth-grade students. Apparently story is not good for fiction only!

5.4.4 Filling in Gaps

The human brain wants to connect things. Years of evolution have taught us that temporal sequence generally has meaning, so given a sequence of events, our minds struggle to connect them in some coherent story. When we take in a story as listeners or readers, we use story structure and prior banks of knowledge to fill in gaps that are not stated so that what we hear or read makes sense in our worldview. Haven argues that any sequence, two or three random sentences in order, will force people to make connections and assumptions so they can make sense of the input.

From a tactical writing point of view, it is important to be aware that readers not only fill in the gaps but that different readers may fill in the gaps very differently. Consider the following two-line example adapted from Haven [2007]. Read the block two or three times, then pause for 10 seconds before reading on.

<table>
<tr><td colspan="2" align="center">Example story</td></tr>
<tr><td>Person #1: "Where's Donald?"
Person #2: "Well….I didn't want to say anything. ...</td><td>But ... I saw a black limo parked in front of Karen's."</td></tr>
</table>

Did you think this story does not make sense? Or did you make assumptions to fill in the gaps? Did you presume a relationship between Donald and Karen? Who did you fill in for Person #1 and #2? Did you fill in all four characters with people you know, well-known people from the news, or some generic role? Did you infer something illicit going on or something innocuous? The relationships you envisioned are your imagination, created by your own mind to satisfy your inherent demand for meaning.

Multiple researchers, including Bransford et al. [2000], Clough [2011], Crossley [2000], and Anderson et al. [2004], have argued that the human mind uses story structure to organize and interpret experiences and that cognitive skills impose order on sensory input. We generate mental models from inputs and remember the mental models we form from a text, rather than remembering the text itself. Our mental model is a mixture of the inputs plus our assumptions. As stated on page 39 of Haven [2007]:

Possible combinations of meanings based on these assumptions are pre-coded and pre-connected in the brain before cognitive processing. Only the possible meanings that are consistent with our assumptions and neural models and maps are allowed in for cognitive consideration. That is, we only initially consider meanings and interpretations that we expected to find, that we are predisposed to find. We instantly assess based on preconceived stereotypes and other base cues.

5.4.5 Stories and Memory

In a fascinating variation on traditional memory studies, Joshua Foer's research, Foer [2012], explored the specialized memory techniques employed by competitive memory champions. Foer's research found that concrete information is easier to remember than abstract information, suggesting that we should leverage our strong visual and spatial memories to improve the retention of material. Many of the memory champions have a unique approach to memorizing new sequences of random information. Their most prevalent technique involves crafting a character, an action, and an object for each specific item that needs to be remembered. For instance, if they are trying to remember the order of a deck of cards, they would assign these elements to each card. These pre-memorized images are then organized along a temporal pathway, essentially forming a plot. Intriguingly, these are all elements commonly found in storytelling. By constructing a story, memory champions can provide both context and relevance to what would otherwise be considered meaningless or random information.

Let's see how well that memory idea worked for you. Who used the padlock and why? You are half right if you said the fat man, so he would not eat. It was the fat one (not the fat man), but we never said why they padlocked the refrigerator door; you just imagined the reason. Memory champions must be precise in their use of story and visualization, but it still takes practice.

The idea of visual stories as a memory aid is ancient. Foer notes that memory-enhancing techniques have documentation on their use back to Greek and Roman antiquity, originally designed for remembering speeches as part of oratory and rhetoric. Cicero, a renowned Roman orator, advised creating mental images for each topic rather than writing everything down and imagining them in particular locations. When giving the speech, one mentally strolls through the "memory palace" to recall what comes next. Did you ever wonder where the phrase "on the other hand" comes from? Cicero often used it when giving speeches because the next item in his memory palace was, in his mental image, his other hand.

5.5   The Importance of Story in Organizations

"Every organization has critically important stories they need to tell to internal and external audiences— stories about values, attitudes, a future vision, purpose, history, people, services, brands, or about the organization itself."

-Kendall Haven

Organizations are made up of people, and stories resonate with people. Research by SarbinSarbin [1998] and Crossley Crossley [2000] has shown that human beings think, perceive, imagine, interact, and make moral choices according to narrative story structures. Dr. Haven elaborates on why organizations, consciously or unconsciously, rely on stories to convey their values, missions, and objectives. Stories are a powerful tool for organizational communication, helping build a shared understanding and foster a sense of community among employees. Dr. Haven provides case studies where organizations successfully used storytelling techniques to improve employee engagement and productivity.

An extensive review of more than 125 peer-reviewed research studies on the organizational use of stories, Boyce [1996] concluded:

Stories create a sense of community, effectively share values and attitudes, build camaraderie, build culture, promote interaction, communicate management priorities and philosophy, share knowledge and information, etc. Research explicitly shows that, within organizations, stories are useful for new member socialization and generating commitment; stories are an effective vehicle for social control; stories provide and define meaning within the organization's culture and structure, and familiarity with dominant organizational stories is an indicator of adaptation.

A more recent survey by Beigi et al. [2019] examines the progression of organizational storytelling research over four decades, based on 165 papers from 1975 to 2015. The authors argue that this field has gained a solid place alongside traditional organization studies. It also highlights the rise of critical storytelling, affirming and expanding five key themes: sensemaking, communication, change, power, and identity. The review underscores the increasing impact of critical management studies, focusing on how stories challenge conventional narratives and enrich organizational understanding.

As Dr. Haven puts it in Haven [2007], "Understanding the science of story is crucial for anyone interested in influencing others, whether it be in the field of education, business, or any other domain requiring human interaction." He contends the human brain is hardwired to think in terms of stories. This is not an evolutionary accident but a result of how our brains have been shaped to perceive, process, and understand the world around us. Story pathways serve as express routes into the human mind, facilitating rapid comprehension and decision-making.

So, why does storytelling matter? Because story structure helps us remember, connect, and convey ideas. For millennia, storytelling has been how we passed down knowledge and grew the knowledge banks of the human species. It is how we form connections and build societies. *Story Proof*, Haven [2007], makes the case that storytelling is innately tied to how the human brain works and that *"Humans are truly homo narratus, story animals."*

Moreover, because of that hardwiring plus the natural pressures to process inputs in real-time so that the human mind can make it make sense, any input, spoken or read, is filtered, and the listeners/readers routinely:

- change (even reverse) factual information

- make assumptions

- create new information

- ignore parts of your presentation

- infer connections and information

- infer motive, intent, significance

- misinterpret

- ignore/forget

Thus, if we want our stories to be effective in tactical writing and help us reach our objectives, we need to learn to use the key elements of stories. We need to use the characters, goals, details, emotions, as well as anticipation of the audience's prior knowledge and cultural context, in a manner that will facilitate keeping our message on target.

5.6 Key Terms

1) **Story:** *Refers to the essence of narration that explores character-based struggles and objectives. Dr. Haven's definition is a story involving character struggles and goals.*

2) **Narrative vs. Story:** *The distinction between a narrative and a story, clarified by Dr. Haven.*

3) **Character-Based Focus:** *The emphasis on character development in Dr. Haven's definition of a story.*

4) **Plot vs. Story:** *The differentiation between a plot and a story, as explained by Dr. Haven.*

5) **Factual Accounts as Stories:** *The concept that real-life events can be structured as stories if they focus*

on character development, goals, and transformations.

6) **Evolution of Storytelling:** *The historical progression of storytelling from oral traditions to written language and modern media.*

7) **Pattern Recognition:** *The ability to recognize patterns, a fundamental element in storytelling and cognitive development.*

8) **Cause and Effect:** *Understanding cause-and-effect relationships, important for establishing coherent narratives.*

9) **Journey and Quest:** *The essence of many stories involving curiosity, exploration, and discovery.*

10) **Neural Story Net:** *Dr. Haven's concept of a neural network specialized for processing story concepts.*

11) **Emotional Resonance:** *The emotional engagement that stories aim to achieve, starting from infancy.*

12) **Impact of Social Interactions:** *How emotion-laden interactions impact brain development and emotional understanding.*

13) **Memory Techniques:** *Memory champions' use of storytelling elements like characters, actions, and objects.*

14) **Memory Palace:** *The concept of a memory palace is used to aid memory by associating information with specific locations.*

6 How to Create Tactical Stories

"I believe everybody has a story worth telling, but precious few know how to get it down on paper."

-Oprah Winfrey, in "O here we go!" O Magazine, August 2007

In previous chapters, we explored the concept and significance of storytelling. We introduced tactical writing as an essential tool for communicating with impact. In this chapter, we will learn the fundamentals of creating tactical stories. We will focus on the main elements of a story, explaining what they are and how to use them effectively. We also will explore classic storytelling frameworks and delve into the actual structuring of a story. But before we get into the details of how to construct tactical stories, let's begin by distinguishing between traditional and tactical storytelling.

6.1 From Storytelling Triangle to Tactical Tetrahedron

The storytelling triangle is a foundational model that identifies the three core elements of any narrative structure: story, audience, and author. These elements are interconnected, so each influences and is influenced by the others. The storytelling triangle serves as a conceptual guide that identifies and demonstrates the intricate relationship between the three vertices: author, audience, and story. This framework elucidates the role and interaction of each vertex as each influences and is influenced by the others in a dynamic system that facilitates the storytelling process. Consider the specific role of each of the elements:

➣ **You (The Storyteller/Author):** The author is the originator of the story, the creative force that brings an idea to life. However, the storyteller/author's role is not just to write; it is to actively engage with the other vertices. In order to craft a story that resonates, the storyteller must interact with the audience's needs, expectations, and cultural background. Similarly, the author must connect with the story, ensuring it aligns with the themes and messages it is intended to convey.

➣ **The Audience:** The audience is the recipient of the story, but it is far from passive in this role. An engaged audience adds layers of meaning to the story by bringing their own interpretations, emotions, and experiences to the mix. The author must anticipate and consider audience input when crafting the narrative. The audience's reaction provides necessary feedback that enables the author to refine future storytelling endeavors.

➣ **The Story:** The story is the medium through which the author and audience interact, and the story evolves as it moves from the author to the audience. The story carries the author's original intent, but it gains additional dimensions as the audience engages with it. The author must ensure that the story is robust enough to withstand this input, evolution, and distortion while still delivering the intended message.

The storytelling tetrahedron is my extension of the foundational model. It builds upon the traditional storytelling triangle by introducing a fourth vertex: the tactical objective. The framework of four vertices provides a more nuanced understanding of the storytelling process. It captures the dynamic interplay between the author, audience, and story, as well as the tactical objective.

➣ **The Tactical Objective:** The tactical objective is the intended outcome or goal the author aims to achieve through the story. Whether it is to inform, entertain, persuade, or inspire, the objective is the guiding light that informs every aspect of storytelling. It is not an afterthought; it is the lens through which the entire storytelling process must be viewed. The tactical objective influences the author's approach, shapes the story's structure, and sets the criteria for its success with the audience. At times, the objective can be clearly seen by the audience, but at other times it may be subtle or almost invisible to the audience.

The idea of a story having an objective is not new; it is as old as storytelling. While many stories are created for entertainment purposes, our earliest ancestors likely told stories for the purpose of teaching or influencing others. Today, tactical objectives are hidden in many stories. By our emphasis on tactical writing, we simply are making our objectives a more explicit element of our storytelling.

➤ **Interactions with the Other Vertices:** The tactical objective vertex interacts dynamically with the other three vertices. It guides the author in crafting a narrative that aligns with the intended outcome. It shapes the story, ensuring that each element, from plot twists to character development, serves the overarching goal. It also sets the stage for audience engagement, as a clear objective helps the audience comprehend the story's relevance and importance and respond to it.

6.2 Navigating Audience Engagement with the Storytelling Triangle and Tetrahedron

The storytelling triangle and the tetrahedron serve as useful frameworks for understanding the storytelling process. Their utility, however, extends beyond the mere conceptualization of the story. These models can also guide the author in navigating audience engagement and immersion in the story.

6.2.1   Engagement in the Triangle

In the storytelling triangle, the initial focus is often on the story vertex, where the author crafts a narrative designed to capture the audience's attention. Once the audience is engaged, the story then immerses the audience, effectively pulling their focus inward, toward the story itself. Once that point of immersion is achieved, a skilled storyteller can then direct the audience's attention back to themselves, prompting self-reflection, or into a deeper understanding of the story's themes. The author then may choose to make themselves an integral part of the story or draw the audience's attention to the storytelling process, e.g., if it is a personal story and the author is relating directly to the audience. As writers, understanding where in the triangle we want to lead our audience greatly impacts how we tell a story.

6.2.2   Engagement in the Tetrahedron

In the storytelling tetrahedron, the tactical objective vertex adds another layer of complexity to the model. After defining the objective, the author focuses on crafting a story that does not simply engage the audience but also achieves the desired outcome. The audience is drawn into the story and becomes immersed in the narrative. The author then may introduce elements into the story that align with the tactical objective and subtly guide the audience toward the intended outcome. At this point, the audience's attention may be directed back to themselves, prompting self-reflection, or toward action that aligns with the objective. As in the story triangle, the author may choose to reveal themselves, either subtly or explicitly, to reinforce the objective, add credibility, or a personal element. The writer must always be aware of how the other three vertices of the storytelling tetrahedron are influencing and being influenced by the tactical objective.

6.2.3   Dynamic Navigation

By understanding and actively navigating the storytelling triangle and tetrahedron, storytellers can create narratives that engage, immerse, and ultimately achieve specific objectives. As they actively engage with each vertex, storytellers can better understand and navigate the complex relationships of tactical storytelling and create narratives that are compelling, resonant, and aligned with a clear objective. This dynamic approach to storytelling offers a richer, more impactful experience for both the author and the audience.

Navigating these frameworks is not a linear process but a dynamic one. The storyteller must be attuned to the audience's reactions, ready to adjust the narrative to maintain engagement, deepen immersion, or refocus attention as needed. This dynamic navigation allows for a storytelling experience that is not only engaging but also purposeful, fulfilling both the author's and the audience's objectives.

6.3 Essential Story Elements

Before we identify the essential elements of a story, it will help if we first make sure we understand how the human brain processes stories and what makes stories engaging. Dr. Haven's work is most helpful in this understanding. If you recall, we reviewed what a story is and how humans process stories in Chapter 5.

6.3.1   The Magnificent Seven

Now, we will consider the "Magnificent Seven," a set of cognitive principles that guide how stories are processed, which Dr. Haven unveils in *Story Proof*, Haven [2007]. These concepts are not merely academic constructs; they are the cognitive underpinning for understanding effective stories. They offer a window into the intricate workings of the human mind as it processes stories, providing both theoretical insights and practical applications. The "Magnificent Seven" are the mental scaffolding for how we understand stories and as such help drive the process of writing effective stories. We will briefly review the general concept and give an example of each principle so they can become simple, concrete mechanisms to use in developing effective stories.

➤ *Experience: Play It Again, Sam.* Our experiences modify the brain's physical structures and create mental frameworks. This principle underscores the mind's use of these frameworks for understanding new narratives and input. It is a form of cognitive shorthand, and it shapes how we interpret and respond to new stories. If you are familiar with detective novels, for example, that framework helps you grasp a new story in the same genre.

➤ *Structure: Order in the Court.* This concept emphasizes the mind's craving for organization in narratives. A well-structured story fits neatly into our mental frameworks, making it easier to digest and more engaging. This is why we like stories that follow a logical sequence. A narrative structure that starts with a mysterious event, for instance, and is followed by an investigation and a resolution satisfies the need for order.

➤ *Meaning: Get My Meanin'?* Our minds naturally seek the "why" and "how." This principle focuses on the mind's active quest to find meaning in narratives. Whether a story conveys a moral lesson or a deeper emotional truth, we are always searching for the underlying message. So, stories with strong, meaningful themes have a greater impact.

➤ *Intent: Intent Drives the Car.* This concept zeroes in on the role of intent and motive. Understanding intent adds depth and complexity to the narrative. Discovering a character's motives, for example, can provide insights into their actions that make the narrative more engaging and relatable.

➤ *Gaps: Mad About What's Missing.* This principle highlights the mind's inclination to fill narrative gaps. This practice is a form of cognitive efficiency, allowing us to understand the narrative without needing every detail to be explicitly stated. If a narrative mentions a sad character but does not reveal the reason why, our minds might fill in a reason based on other contextual clues.

➤ *Characters: Every Story Is Somebody's Story.* Narratives revolve around characters, and characters are not just vehicles for plot events. Characters are the emotional and thematic core of the story. As such, characters carry much of the weight in stories that make an impact.

➤ *Conflict: Such a Struggle.* This principle focuses on the role of conflict, the engine that drives narratives. Conflict provides the high stakes and tension that keep an audience engaged. Conflict in a story can be as subtle as a character's internal moral dilemma or as grand as a fight to save the world.

In "These Are All Signs of the Magnificent Seven Concepts at Work" [Haven, 2007, p. 43], there is a clear relationship between certain of these principles and the eight essential elements of an effective story. In contrast, other principles are related to the details that enrich the storytelling process.

6.3.2   The Essential Story Elements

The "Magnificent Seven" naturally leads into eight essential story elements. The essential elements of every story or narrative are:

➤ CHARACTER(s): Who is the main character? Who are the other characters? What are their relationships with one another?

➤ CHARACTER TRAITS: Which character traits make the characters interesting and/or relatable?

➤ GOAL: What do the characters need to do or get? What is the goal they seek to achieve or acquire?

➤ MOTIVE: Why is the goal important to the characters? What is their motive?

➤ CONFLICTS & PROBLEMS: What conflicts/problems block the characters from achieving their goal?

➤ RISK & DANGER: How do the conflicts/problems create risk and danger for the characters?

➤ STRUGGLES/ACTIONS: What do the characters do to reach the goal? What are their actions and struggles?

➤ IMAGERY: What sensory details make the story seem real?

Introspective Exercise

When we introduced the one-sentence version of a story in Chapter 2, we had only six items, and now we are saying there are eight. What did we add as essential, and why do you think they are "essential" but not in the six items in the one-sentence story?

These eight elements are necessary for a good story and can be used effectively in many different ways. However, on their own, these elements are not sufficient to create an effective story. If we consider the essential eight in conjunction with the "Magnificent Seven," we find some clear alignments: characters, goals/motives, and struggles. But other principles, such as experience, structure, meaning, and gaps, are captured only indirectly in the essential eight. By developing a good story process and structure, we can ensure the "Magnificent Seven" works well with the essential eight to deliver an effective tactical story.

It isn't difficult to recognize the way in which many classic fiction stories fit these elements, but the way these elements might apply to nonfiction and tactical writing may be less obvious. So before we get into the actual story process, take some time to study how these eight elements might be used in different tactical writing applications. Figures 6.2-6.5 show some brief examples of how these eight elements might be applied in different tactical writing examples: proposals, marketing material, and two examples of science/technology.

The experience of the magnificent seven is useful when trying to exploit a well-known structure plus the audience's experience/knowledge. The story structure and details need to address the question of meaning. While the gaps can be used to engage the audience, we also work on the story structure and details to try to ensure the audience does not fill in gaps in ways we do not want.

6.4 Major Steps in Tactical Story Creation

A compelling, tactical story is best written through a structured process. Kendall Haven's, Haven [2014], presents an excellent seven-step process that ensures a story will not only capture the reader's attention but also convey the intended message effectively. For our purposes, we have adapted and expanded a version of that process to specifically address tactical story generation. Be aware that this is a brief introduction to these steps, and we highly recommend reading Story.

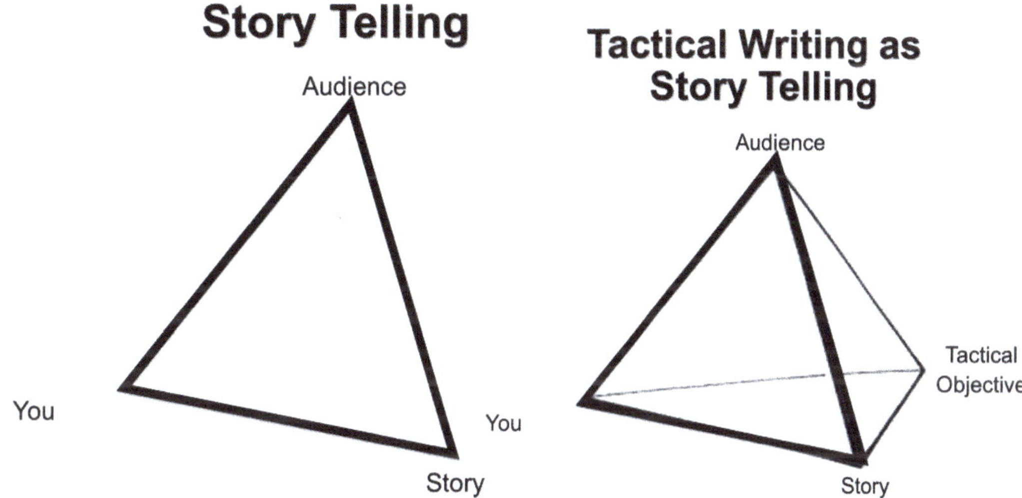

Figure 6.1: *The Storytelling Triangle and the Story Tetrahedron.*

Proposal story

1. WHO IS THE MAIN CHARACTER?
Someone with whom the Funder will emotionally connect
2. WHAT CHARACTER TRAITS MAKE THEM INTERESTING?
What helps the reader visualize and remember WHY they care about them
3. WHAT DOES THE CHARACTER NEED TO DO OR GET (GOAL)?
How will the world/science be better given the proposed work is done
4. WHY IS THAT GOAL IMPORTANT (MOTIVE)?
Why is that measure/property important
5. WHAT CONFLICTS/PROBLEMS BLOCK THE CHARACTER?
What makes them hard to do
6. HOW DO THEY CREATE RISK & DANGER?
What are the risks/danger if not successful
7. WHAT DOES THE CHARACTER DO (STRUGGLE) TO REACH GOAL?
What are you proposing that will help the character to reach the goal
8. WHAT SENSORY DETAILS MAKE THE STORY SEEM *REAL*?
Metaphor for examples of proposed idea to make it seem real

Figure 6.2: *One way a proposal story might be mapped to the eight essential story elements.*

A Marketing Story

1. WHO IS THE MAIN CHARACTER?
The reader or a person with generic title similar to the reader's
2. WHAT CHARACTER TRAITS MAKE THEM INTERESTING?
Traits similar to what is expected of the reader
3. WHAT DOES THE CHARACTER NEED TO DO OR GET (GOAL)?
What do you think is the goal of the reader
4. WHY IS THAT GOAL IMPORTANT (MOTIVE)?
Why is that goal important/desired
5. WHAT CONFLICTS/PROBLEMS BLOCK THE CHARACTER?
What makes them hard to do
6. HOW DO THEY CREATE RISK & DANGER?
What are the risks/danger if not successful
7. WHAT DOES THE CHARACTER DO (STRUGGLE) TO REACH GOAL?
What are you proposing/offering that will help the reader to the goal
8. WHAT SENSORY DETAILS MAKE THE STORY SEEM *REAL*?
Show examples of benefits of proposed idea to make it seem real

Figure 6.3: *One way a marketing story might be mapped to the eight essential story elements.*

Science/Tech Story V1

1. **WHO IS THE MAIN CHARACTER?**
   Science/tech/algorithm/system/theory of the paper
2. **WHAT CHARACTER TRAITS MAKE THEM INTERESTING?**
   What helps the reader remember WHY it works/is better
3. **WHAT DOES THE CHARACTER NEED TO DO OR GET (GOAL)?**
   What is the measure by which you beat state-of-the-art
4. **WHY IS THAT GOAL IMPORTANT (MOTIVE)?**
   Why is that measure/property important
5. **WHAT CONFLICTS/PROBLEMS BLOCK THE CHARACTER?**
   What makes it hard to do
6. **HOW DO THEY CREATE RISK & DANGER?**
   What are the risks/dangers if not successful
7. **WHAT DOES THE CHARACTER DO (STRUGGLE) TO REACH GOAL?**
   Ablation study or experiments on parts of what make it work (related to traits)
8. **WHAT SENSORY DETAILS MAKE THE STORY SEEM *REAL*?**
   Analogy + examples of success + show some failure cases

Figure 6.4: *One way a science/tech story might be mapped to the eight essential story elements, with greater emphasis on the actual science/tech. This is well suited to many traditional scientific publication styles.*

SmartHaven [2014] for further details and many good examples and stories. Let's consider the eleven steps to creating an effective tactical story and see where they lead us.

6.4.1   Define the Target Audience

Understanding your audience goes beyond mere demographics. It is not just about age, gender, or geographical location; it involves a multi-faceted approach that delves into the psychographics, values, cultural nuances, and even the unspoken needs and wants of your audience. It is about lifestyles, beliefs, and emotional triggers. Understanding your audience is about getting into the collective psyche of the people you are trying to reach and resonate with as you share your message.

So, defining the target audience is not just a preliminary step; it is the bedrock upon which your entire tactical story is built. It is akin to setting the GPS before embarking on a journey. Before you write one word, you need to know where you are going in order to make sure you take the best route. The tone, language, and content of your story should be tailored so meticulously that your audience feels you are speaking directly to them. A well-defined audience is the first step toward a targeted approach that can make the difference between a story that is merely heard and a story that truly lands and sticks.

Key Point: A multi-faceted understanding of the audience goes beyond demographics to include psychographics, values, lifestyle, and cultural nuances.

Takeaway: Tailoring your story to your audience is essential for creating resonance and impact.

6.4.2   Crafting a Theme and Message

Think of the theme as the DNA of your story—it is what makes it unique and identifiable. The message, on the other hand, is the takeaway, the lesson or insight that you want your audience to walk away with. It is the "so what?" factor that gives your story its *raison d'être*. The theme and message are the soul and essence of your story. They are the invisible threads that weave through every word, sentence, paragraph, and chapter, giving a sense of unity and purpose to your narrative.

Crafting a compelling theme and message begins with brainstorming core ideas. But the magic happens once you refine and distill those ideas into a clear, concise, and impactful message. Careful crafting of the theme and message ensures that every element of your story, from the characters to the plot twists, serves that central theme. We list it as the second step, but it is an iterative process, not a one-time task. Because crafting the theme and message requires consistency throughout the narrative, it will need revision as the story changes. Brainstorming is recommended to get multiple possible themes to match the messages aligned with the tactical objectives.

➤ **Key Point:** The theme and message are the soul and essence of the story and deserve the effort of careful crafting. This may include brainstorming, refining, and distilling core ideas.

➤ **Takeaway:** A consistent theme and message give your story unity, purpose, and impact.

6.4.3　Identifying Core Metaphors, Imagery, and Figurative Language

In the simplest terms, a metaphor is a figure of speech that describes an object or action as something other than what it actually is. It is not just a decorative element; it is a powerful tool that can encapsulate complex ideas in an easily digestible form. Analogies and similes are close relatives of metaphors. While a metaphor might say, "Time is a thief," a simile would say, "Time is like a thief," and an analogy might elaborate on how time stealing moments is similar to a thief stealing valuables.

The core metaphor and imagery in a story serve as its intellectual and emotional visual anchor. These forms of figurative language serve as the conceptual lens through which your audience will interpret and remember your narrative. They are the visual or conceptual shorthand that encapsulates the essence of what you are trying to convey. Identifying these metaphors and imagery are not about picking a random symbol or image. It is about choosing one that aligns seamlessly with your theme and message. It is about selecting a metaphor, simile, or analogy that not only aids in recall but also reinforces and enriches your central message.

Often, a metaphor becomes a recurring story motif, a thread that you weave throughout your narrative to add layers of meaning and depth. It can make your story not just memorable but intellectually and emotionally resonant. When a tactical story has multiple objectives, multiple metaphors or analogies can be used. When considering a possible metaphor, remember that there may be an emotional connotation that can be exploited or needs to be avoided, e.g., the thief above generally has a negative connotation, whereas "time flows like a river" is a simile that may have a more positive connotation.

➤ **Key Point:** The core metaphor may also be a simile, analogy, or image. It is the story's intellectual and emotional anchor and aligns with the theme. It aids in recall and reinforces the message of the story.

➤ **Takeaway:** A well-chosen metaphor or image, along with other forms of figurative language, adds layers of meaning and connection with emotions that make the story resonate with the audience.

6.4.4　Creating Relevance and Context

Relevance and context are foundational pillars of storytelling. Dr. Haven's, *Story Proof*, Haven [2007] underscores the cognitive resonance of storytelling when the story is both relevant and contextual to the audience. "To the audience" is the key phrase. Writers often succumb to the assumption that what is relevant and contextual to them will automatically be so for their audience. This is a critical mistake. The story must resonate with the lived experiences, aspirations, or challenges of the audience, not just the writer.

Setting the scene or providing background information is not just about your own understanding of the narrative; it is about giving your audience a road map into the world you have created. Highlighting the story's importance must be done in terms that are meaningful to the audience, making the narrative not just engaging but deeply impactful. Using familiar settings or scenarios is akin to speaking your audience's dialect; it makes the narrative instantly relatable. These elements work in concert to ensure the story is not only heard but felt and remembered.

➣ **Key Point:** Relevance and context must be audience-centric. This is accomplished by providing audience-relevant background; emphasizing the story's importance in terms meaningful to the audience; using familiar settings for audience relatability.

➣ **Takeaway:** A story tailored to the audience's context and relevance is not only heard but deeply felt and remembered.

6.4.5   Character Development in Tactical Stories

Characters are the lifeblood of the narrative. This is especially true in tactical storytelling, where the story aims to achieve a specific outcome or takeaway. To achieve this goal, characters must be meticulously crafted, not just thrown into the mix. Character choices are not about aesthetic appeal, they are about strategy. Characters drive the story forward so they must be intrinsically tied to the takeaway message. They need depth, goals, and a trajectory for growth. They should be relatable not only to the writer but to the audience as well.

How does one create such characters? The first step is to develop a detailed profile for each one. The profiles should outline the character's backstory, motivations, and traits. The characters must align with the tactical story's theme and resonate with the audience's knowledge and context.

The next step is to work the character subtly as the story unfolds. Do not dump all the information about the character on the audience at once! Do not forget to refine the characters based on feedback. Test the characters for credibility to ensure they act in ways that are consistent with their profiles.

➣ **Key Point:** Characters are the lifeblood of a tactical story. Create detailed profiles that include the character's backstory, motivations, and traits. Ensure characters have depth, goals, and a trajectory for growth; making them relatable and credible; use characters to drive the story; refine characters based on feedback.

➣ **Takeaway:** Meticulously crafted characters make a tactical story not just compelling but relatable and memorable.

6.4.6   Build the Story Elements

Once the groundwork is laid with your characters, theme, constraints, and audience, it is time to actually build your story. This is where the rubber meets the road. This is when you select a story structure that aligns with your objectives and begin to weave all these elements into a coherent narrative. This step may take longer than you anticipate, as you may need to experiment with multiple structures to find what fits best.

Every story needs a clear beginning, middle, and end from which to draft an appropriate skeletal framework. Next, identify where your story begins, what and when you want the struggle to be, and how the climax and resolution of your story will tie back to your takeaway message. These are the muscles that give your story its movement and tension. Then comes the iterative process of revising and refining your story to ensure flow and consistency. This is the skin that covers the muscles and bones, making your story not just functional but also aesthetically pleasing. Building the story may require multiple drafts, but it is crucial for creating a story that is not just compelling but also deeply resonant.

➤ **Key Point:** Building a story involves more than stringing events together. A good story has a clear beginning, middle, and end identifying key moments like struggle, climax, and resolution.

➤ **Takeaway:** A well-constructed story is a harmonious blend of various elements that have been thoughtfully arranged (often through many drafts) to achieve a specific impact.

6.4.7 Planning with Storyboarding and Figures

Planning is not just a preliminary step in tactical storytelling; it is an integral part of the creative process and storyboarding is one of the most effective planning techniques. Much like an architectural blueprint helps us visualize the final building, storyboarding allows us to visualize the structure, flow, and even emotional peaks and valleys of a story. Always prioritize creating the story in your mind before putting pen to paper. The iterative mental process of storyboarding enables you to see the big picture and understand how each element fits into the whole. Then you will be able to enrich the story with vivid details, making it more compelling when finally written.

Remember, too, that storyboarding is not just about the text. It is also about the visuals. Figures and visuals are not mere embellishments; they are narrative tools that can significantly enhance the presentation of your ideas. They can make complex concepts more accessible, add layers of meaning to your narrative, and even serve as mnemonic devices for your audience. The key to success is to incorporate these figures strategically. They should support, never overshadow, your narrative.

➤ **Key Point:** Storyboarding and figures are integral parts of effective storytelling. Storyboarding helps in the critical process of creating structure and flow; incorporating figures and visuals can strategically support the narrative and enhance presentation.

➤ **Takeaway:** Proper planning and strategic use of visuals can make your story more compelling and impactful.

6.4.8 Adjust for Constraints

In the real world, storytelling does not happen in a vacuum, it happens within a set of constraints. Constraints can be time limits, medium-specific limitations, or even audience-related restrictions. Ignoring constraints is a recipe for failure. For instance, a story that runs too long risks losing its audience's attention, and one that does not fit the medium can lose its impact.

A story that does not consider its audience's constraints can miss the mark entirely. The key is to identify these constraints upfront and adjust your narrative accordingly. Ask the questions: How long will the audience have to read? What is their reading level? Will the audience be comparing different submissions to make a selection?

Adapting to constraints is not about watering down your story but about refining it to fit the parameters and making strategic choices to ensure your core message remains clear and impactful. This might mean cutting down on certain elements, rethinking the pace, or even rephrasing the core message to better suit the medium or the audience. Although we may not like dealing with them, constraints are not necessarily a bad thing. Constraints often serve as a catalyst for developing creative solutions and innovations in storytelling.

➢ **Key Point:** Every story operates within constraints such as time, medium, and audience. By refining the narrative to fit these constraints we ensure the core message remains clear.

➢ **Takeaway:** Skillful adjustment to constraints can lead to more creative and impactful storytelling.

6.4.9 Writing a Persuasive Story

In the realm of tactical storytelling, persuasion is often the name of the game. Tactical stories are not just about sharing information. They are about trying to move the audience to action. But how do you do that? How do you turn a narrative into a catalyst?

The answer lies in a combination of elements that build energy, focus on what's in it for your audience, use structure to facilitate easy scanning and craft a narrative that builds emotion and energy.

➢ building energy,

➢ focusing on "What's in it for them,"

➢ using structural elements for easy scanning, and

➢ crafting a narrative that builds emotion and energy.

Let's consider each of these critical components in greater detail. Together, these four components serve as a brief guide to crafting stories that not only inform but inspire action.

➢ *Build Energy:* Energy in storytelling is like momentum in physics; it propels the narrative forward. It keeps your audience engaged and makes them want to know what happens next. Energy can be built through pacing, tension, and stakes. Pacing controls the speed of your narrative, tension adds to the drama of conflict and challenge, and stakes give your audience something to care about. Together, they create a compelling force that drives your story.

➢ **Key Point:** Energy is the momentum that propels your story forward. Pacing, tension, and stakes build energy.

➢ **Takeaway:** A story with energy is a story that engages and retains the audience.

➢ *What's in it for them (WIIFT):* No matter what your story is about, your audience is always viewing it from their view and you must anticipate: "What's in it for them?" You must address this unspoken question directly. Show the benefits, outcomes, and transformations that your story promises. Most importantly, this is not about listing features or facts; it is about translating those into advantages and benefits that resonate with your audience's needs and desires. When you design your story to answer the WIIFT question convincingly, passive observers become active participants.

➢ **Key Point:** Clearly address the question that lurks in the audience's mind: "What's in it for me?" by demonstrating the benefits and outcomes.

➤ **Takeaway:** A story that speaks to the audience's self-interest is a story that persuades.

➤ *Structural Elements for Scanning:* In today's fast-paced world, not everyone reads every word. When you make your story scannable, you increase its reach and impact, allowing even those who skim rather than read to grasp its essence. Headers, bullets, and other structural elements help to make your story scannable. This is not about diluting your message but about making it accessible.

➤ **Key Point:** Make your story easy to scan by using headers, bullets, and other structural elements.

➤ **Takeaway:** A scannable story is a more accessible story.

➤ *Build Emotion and Energy: Hook, Lede, Proof, Bullets:* Start your story with a hook that grabs attention. Follow it with a lede that sets the stage. Offer proof to build credibility. Use bullets for easy consumption. All of these elements build toward a climax and a call to action. Each component of this simple but powerful formula serves a purpose: the hook captures attention, the lede provides context, the proof offers substantiation, and the bullets make the information digestible. Together, they build emotion and energy that culminate in a compelling climax and a persuasive call to action.

➤ **Key Point:** Use the specific storytelling techniques of hook, lede, proof, and bullets to build emotion and energy.

➤ **Takeaway:** A well-crafted narrative leads to a compelling core message and a persuasive call to action.

6.4.10 Crafting Sticky Stories: Insights from *Made to Stick*

In the world of tactical storytelling, the goal is often to create narratives that "stick," stories that are not just heard but are remembered and acted upon. The book *Made to Stick* by Chip and Dan Heath, Heath and Heath [2007], offers a treasure trove of insights into how to accomplish this. According to the Heaths, "stickiness" is achieved through six key principles: Simplicity, Unexpectedness, Concreteness, Credibility, Emotions, and Stories (SUCCESs). We will discuss these principles in more detail later, but we introduce them briefly because they are essential elements of good tactical storytelling.

➤ **Simplicity:** Complexity is the enemy of stickiness. The idea should be stripped down to its essential meaning and core messages should be both simple and profound.

➤ **Unexpectedness:** Surprise is a powerful tool for grabbing attention. Use the unexpected to keep your audience engaged. Breaking patterns makes your idea memorable.

➤ **Concreteness:** Abstract theories are easily forgotten. Use concrete images and examples to make your point. Tangibility enhances memory retention.

➤ **Credibility:** For an idea to stick, it has to be believable. Bolster credibility by citing authorities or anti-authorities. Trustworthiness enhances the stickiness of an idea.

➤ **Emotions:** People are more likely to remember how they felt than what you actually said. Tap into emotions to make your idea resonate. Emotional impact equals memorability.

➤ **Stories:** Sticky narratives have the power to drive action. They provide a framework that aids memory and influence. A well-crafted story makes your idea unforgettable.

Crafting ideas that stick is an art. The SUCCESs model provides a comprehensive framework for developing ideas that not only capture attention but also inspire action. When you begin filling in that framework with the details and images of your story, the six key principles of the SUCCESs model can serve as a checklist to ensure your story will stick.

➤ **Key Point:** Stickiness in storytelling can be achieved through the six key SUCCESs principles. By simplifying the core message, incorporating unexpected elements, ensuring concreteness and credibility, leveraging emotions, and using the power of stories your message can be unforgettable.

➤ **Takeaway:** Crafting a sticky story involves a strategic blend of these elements that will not only capture attention but hold it, not only inform but inspire action.

6.4.11   Start Writing the First Draft

We have outlined the foundational elements and advanced techniques for crafting a compelling, tactical story. Now it is time to put pen to paper or fingers to keyboard. Remember, the first draft is just that—a draft, a starting point. It is the raw material from which your final masterpiece will be sculpted. It is where you start to breathe life into the skeletal framework you have constructed. It is where your characters start to speak, where your metaphors find their home, and where your theme begins to resonate.

Here, we must offer a word of caution: do not aim for perfection in the first draft, that is not its purpose. For a tactical story, it is not only okay but good to start with what Anne Lamott, in her seminal book *Bird by Bird*, refers to as the "shitty first draft." Lamott argues that almost all good writing begins with a terrible first effort, a draft that is an affront to the craft of storytelling. But that's okay.

In fact, it is more than okay; it is necessary. The shitty first draft is liberating. It frees you from the paralyzing grip of perfectionism and the unrealistic expectation that you should be able to churn out a masterpiece in one go. It gives you permission to make mistakes, to explore dead-ends, to write sentences that you will later look back on and cringe.

The beauty of the shitty first draft is that it is a beginning, not an end. It is a way to start the conversation with your story, to get to know your characters and to understand the nuances of your theme. It is a way to silence the inner critic, at least temporarily, so that your creative voice can be heard.

Most importantly, the first draft is something that can be fixed, shaped, and improved upon. Allow that to happen. For instance, many people are distracted and find that their flow is disrupted by spelling/proofing markers and the red underline in text editors. So turn it off if that helps you focus.[2] And for other people it

---

[2] To turn off Proofing in Word: Click File > Options > Proofing, clear the Check spelling as you type box, and click OK. To turn spell check back on, repeat the process and select the Check spelling

is even more practical to use voice typing for that first draft so you can think rather than worry about the errors you make when typing.

So, as you embark on writing your first draft, give yourself the freedom to write badly. The first draft is not about perfection; it is about initiation into the world you are creating. The shitty first draft is your ticket to that world. Take it.[3]

➤ **Key Point:** The "shitty first draft" is an essential, liberating step in the writing process. It allows you to break free from the paralysis of perfectionism, make mistakes, and explore your story's potential.

➤ **Takeaway:** Embrace the shitty first draft as your initial step into the world of your story. It is a rite of passage every writer must go through. It is the raw material from which your final, polished narrative will be crafted.

6.5 Choosing the Right Writing Structure

In the labyrinthine world of storytelling, the path you choose makes all the difference. Writing structures are not just containers for words. As the architectural blueprint for your narrative, the structure shapes the experience of your reader: guiding their attention, building tension, and delivering revelations. But not all structures are created equally, nor are they universally applicable. Your choice of structure can amplify or dampen your story's impact. It can make your narrative memorable or render it forgettable.

So, how do you choose the right structure? The answer is both art and science, intuition and analysis. The process begins with understanding your objectives and your audience. Are you aiming to inform, persuade, entertain, or inspire? Who are you speaking to, and what are their preferences, cultural nuances, and pain points? Once you have a handle on these, you can start to match your story to the strengths of different structures. Do you need a structure that excels at simplifying complex topics, one that builds suspense, or one that creates emotional resonance? Different structures can help accomplish these needs and much more.

Let's now explore various writing structures. We will dissect their mechanics, evaluate their strengths, and consider their ideal use. When we are done, you'll have a tactical toolkit of structures, each with its unique capabilities, ready to be deployed in the service of your narrative.

6.5.1   Narrative Arc, the Hero's Journey

The narrative arc is not just a structure; it is the backbone of countless stories from ancient myths to modern blockbusters. The structure of the hero's journey is as old as storytelling itself. It provides a framework that has captivated audiences for centuries.

The journey starts with an exposition, a gentle introduction to the world and its characters. But lest the reader get too comfortable, the rising action is just around the corner. Conflicts and obstacles ratchet up the tension. Then comes the climax, the moment of highest tension, where everything is at stake. But the journey is not yet over. The falling action provides a space for the story to resolve itself, tie up loose ends, and set the stage for the denouement, which provides a final sense of closure.

---

as you type box. To check spelling manually, click Review > Spelling & Grammar.

[3] To turn off Proofing in Word: Click File > Options > Proofing, clear the Check spelling as you type box, and click OK. To turn spell check back on, repeat the process and select the Check spelling as you type box. To check spelling manually, click Review > Spelling & Grammar.

This structure is a powerful tool for writers. It offers a tried-and-true framework for creating compelling stories that engage the reader from start to finish. It can be tricky to do a full hero's journey in nonfiction tactical writing, but simpler forms of the narrative arc are quite common.

⊱ **Key Point:** The narrative arc is a storytelling journey of conflict, obstacle, and climax from exposition to denouement.

⊱ **Takeaway:** Provides a framework for tension and resolution best recognized in fiction.

6.5.2 OSCAR: A Five-Element Structure

What I refer to as the OSCAR structure is also known as a hamburger or sandwich structure. It is the bread and butter of academic writing, especially for students. It is an effective, straightforward structure that provides a clear, linear path through an introduction, three body paragraphs/sections, and a conclusion.

The structure says, "Here is my argument, here is my evidence, and here is my conclusion." It is particularly useful for beginners or in academic writing, where it can help to hone the skills of argumentation and evidence presentation. Its utility extends beyond academia, however, as it is also effective in opinion pieces and business reports.

I like to call this OSCAR because the five sections are:

⊱ **Opening:** Creating a broad hook to engage readers

⊱ **Setting:** Narrowing down to the specific story and problem

⊱ **Challenge:** Presenting the problem or challenge to be addressed

⊱ **Action:** Describing experiments, algorithms, and actions taken

⊱ **Resolution:** Tying back to the opening and highlighting the contributions

Visually, by opening with a hook for a broad audience, then narrowing to the middle sections, and then tying the end back to the opening to make it more broadly appealing—the image is a bit like the Oscar statue itself, see Figure 6.7. Note how the five sections differ from the 5-acts of a Freytag pyramid but have some of the same overall structure.

While not required, one feature of the OSCAR structure is the ability to use it at multiple levels. For example, at the section level, each section may use all five elements. OSCAR can be applied recursively within paragraphs in the section, with at least an opening, challenge, or action and resolution. Within a sentence, parts of the OSCAR structure may reoccur.

⊱ **Key Point:** Structured and straightforward, OSCAR is versatile in application and is useful for beginners who are honing their argumentation skills.

⊱ **Takeaway:** Effective for clear, concise arguments, especially in academic writing and opinion pieces.

6.5.3 Inverted Pyramid or Bottom-Line-on-Top

The inverted pyramid is a journalistic marvel, a structure designed for a fast-paced world where attention is a scarce commodity. This structure is not just a way to write; it is a way to think. The story starts with the most crucial information, the crux of the story, right at the top. This is the hook that grabs the reader and says, "This is important; pay attention." From there, the details taper off, becoming less and less critical as you move down the pyramid.

This structure respects the reader's time and attention, delivering the essential facts first and allowing a deeper dive if the reader desires. It is not only confined to journalism as it is effective in any writing where brevity and clarity are paramount. In a world drowning in information, the inverted pyramid guides the reader quickly to what matters most. In business writing, this structure is often called bottom-line-on-top, which is an implicit reference to the "bottom-line" of a classic profit-loss statement.

➢ **Key Point:** Front-loaded with the most important information first followed by tapering details, this structure focuses on immediate attention and quick news delivery.

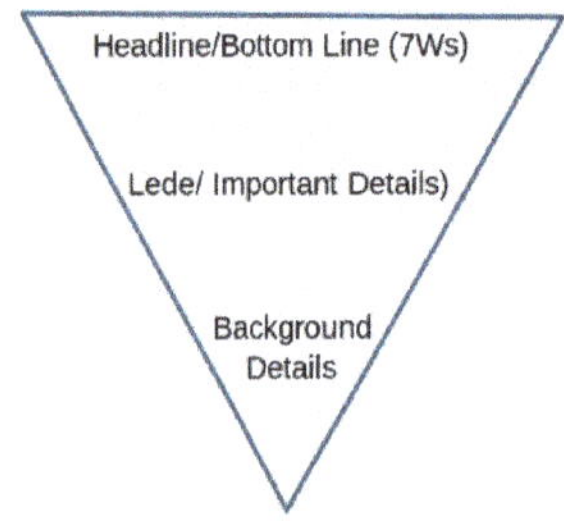

Figure 6.8: *Key elements of an Inverted Pyramid Structure*

➢ **Takeaway:** Effective in journalism and business writing due to its brevity and clarity.

6.5.4   Compare and Contrast

The Swiss Army knife of academic writing this structure is a versatile tool that allows you to dissect, analyze, and restructure subjects or ideas in a new light. Whether used when examining literature, historical events, or scientific concepts, compare and contrast provides the framework for a deep dive. It is not just about listing similarities and differences but takes the

Science/Tech Story V2

1. WHO IS THE MAIN CHARACTER?
Someone impacted by the results of the science/tech
2. WHAT CHARACTER TRAITS MAKE THEM INTERESTING?
Traits that make the character relatable to the reader
3. WHAT DOES THE CHARACTER NEED TO DO OR GET (GOAL)?
What is the end result and measure by which you beat state of the art
4. WHY IS THAT GOAL IMPORTANT (MOTIVE)?
Why is the end-result or science property important
5. WHAT CONFLICTS/PROBLEMS BLOCK THE CHARACTER?
What makes it hard to do
6. HOW DO THEY CREATE RISK & DANGER?
What are the risks/dangers if not successful
7. WHAT DOES THE CHARACTER DO (STRUGGLE) TO REACH GOAL?
Ablation study or experiments on parts of what make it work (related to traits)
8. WHAT SENSORY DETAILS MAKE THE STORY SEEM REAL?
Analogy + examples of success + show some failure cases

Figure 6.5: *A second way a science/tech story might be mapped to the eight essential story elements, with greater emphasis on the actual impact. This mapping is well suited to mainstream media and can make a more memorable scientific publication.*

OSCAR

Integral elements in order:

Opening (Broad hook)

Setting the Stage

Challenge

Action

Resolution (Must tie back to opening)

Figure 6.7: *The core steps in OSCAR and their relation to the basic one-sentence story structure.*

next step is to draw meaningful conclusions from them. It is about highlighting strengths and weaknesses and then arguing for or against a particular point of view.

This structure encourages critical thinking that invites the reader to engage with the material on a deeper level. Its usefulness is not confined to academic writing. In persuasive writing, it is a powerful tool for presenting evidence that supports one side over the other. In essence, this structure allows for a nuanced, multi-dimensional analysis of complex subjects.

➤ **Key Point:** This structure highlights similarities and differences for the purpose of analysis and contrast to gain a deeper understanding. It is helpful for arguing for or against a point.

➤ **Takeaway:** A versatile tool for complex analysis required in academic and persuasive writing.

6.5.5 Problem-Solution

In a world full of challenges, the problem-solution structure serves as a blueprint for change. A structure that is as pragmatic as it is persuasive, this approach not only presents facts that convince the reader to understand a problem but frames them in a way that drives action. This is the go-to framework when you are not simply identifying issues but are offering actionable remedies.

The problem-solution structure says, "Here is the challenge we face, and here is how we can overcome it." This structure is particularly effective in persuasive writing where the goal is to convince the reader to take a particular course of action. Its utility does not stop there, however. It is also widely used in academic papers, marketing copy, and policy documents.

➤ **Key Point:** As its name implies, this structure identifies problems and offers solutions that drive action. Applicable across multiple genres, it is a persuasive blueprint for change.

➤ **Takeaway:** An effective tool for driving change through persuasive writing, academic papers, and marketing.

6.5.6 Cause and Effect

Cause and effect are the detectives of writing structures. It does not merely describe events, it digs deeper to uncover the underlying causes and their subsequent effects. It addresses the question, "Why did this happen, and what were the consequences?"

This structure is a powerful tool for writers who want to explore the intricacies of complex systems, whether they are social, scientific, or personal. It is particularly effective in persuasive writing, where it can demonstrate the impact of a particular course of action. However, its utility is not confined to persuasive writing; it is widely used in academic papers, policy documents, and narrative journalism. In a world that is increasingly complex, the cause-and-effect structure serves as a lens through which we can better understand the myriad forces that shape events that impact the reader.

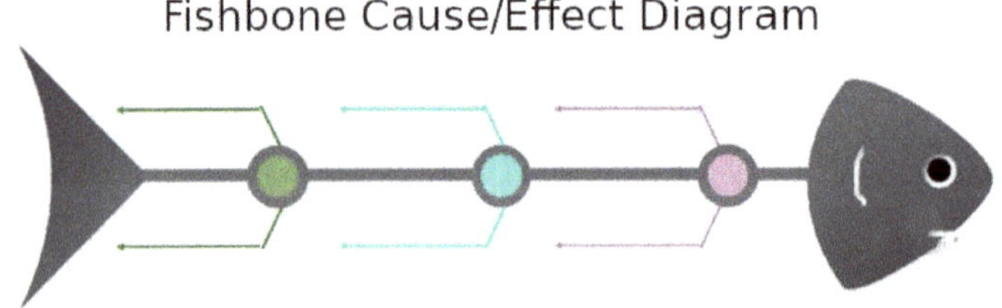

Figure 6.9: *Example of a FishBone diagram for the Cause and Effect Structure*

When using the cause-and-effect structure, it is important to recognize that correlation is not causation. Even so, the human mind will often assume that correlation does imply cause and effect, which can lead the audience to jump to a conclusion or, if a reader detects abuse of correlation instead of the cause, reduce your credibility and lead to rejection of your tactical story. Thus, you must be clear on whether your intent is causal or correlated only.

You can verify your understanding of the cause-and-effect sequence with a fishbone diagram; see Figure 6.9. In the diagram, each line represents an object, action, or an event that causes something that is then combined with another intermate state, which can then lead to the final effect.

➤ **Key Point:** Useful for deep exploration of complex systems and unveiling underlying causes and effects in multiple genres.

➤ **Takeaway:** Effective for understanding complexity in persuasive writing, academic papers, and policy documents.

6.5.7   Chronological Order

The time traveler of writing structures and chronological order takes the reader on a journey through time from the earliest events to the most recent. The structure is as straightforward as it is effective, providing a clear, linear path through a series of events or developments. Whether recounting a historical event, telling a story, or explaining the evolution of an idea, this structure allows the writer to convey a sense of progression and sequence: "This happened, then this, then this." The structure can use explicit timing, sequences, or a mix of the two.

The chronological order allows the reader to understand not just the events themselves but their context and significance. The writer also has the option to skip items in the sequence, which often leads to the reader filling the gap. If the writer can estimate the audience's context and assumptions, such omissions can be used strategically to enhance the reader's engagement with the narrative. This technique is less risky than a misleading correlation as an effect, in which the reader just fills in the gaps.

This structure is particularly useful in business and academic writing as it can be used to trace the development of business events, ideas, or academic theories and experiments over time. But its utility extends beyond academia. It is also effective in general storytelling, journalism, and technical reports.

➤ **Key Point:** This straightforward time-based sequence conveys progression and provides context that is useful in multiple genres.

➤ **Takeaway:** It is effective for conveying history and progress in academic writing, storytelling, and journalism.

6.5.8   Braided Essay or Interwoven Stories

The braided essay, a.k.a. interwoven stories, is an easy-to-use literary structure that defies the conventional linear narrative. It is like a complex tapestry woven from multiple threads of narrative, each distinct yet interconnected. Imagine a braid made of strands of personal anecdotes, historical events, and philosophical musings. These strands are not just laid side-by-side; they are intricately woven to create a complex and nuanced narrative.

This structure can be well suited to team writing and allows writers to explore complex ideas and themes in a way that is both captivating and intellectually stimulating. It is like a playground for the mind, a space where the writer can dance between different worlds, perspectives, and voices, all while maintaining an overarching theme or question that ties everything together. This structure invites the reader to engage deeply with the text and follow the writer on a journey that is as unpredictable as it is enlightening. It can use different substructures per "braid" yet allows the narrative to be interconnected.

➤ **Key Point:** The braided essay is a non-linear, interwoven narrative that mixes anecdotes, history, and philosophy in distinct yet interconnected strands.

➤ **Takeaway:** This structure enables intricate exploration and works well for creative nonfiction.

6.5.9 Listicle

In a world where attention spans are shrinking and information overload is the norm, the listicle serves as a quick and effective way to communicate key points. This quality makes this structure the darling of digital media. It is designed for the scrolling, skimming, and sharing habits of the modern reader.

The listicle is as accessible as it is engaging and breaks down complex information into easily digestible chunks. It is the structure that says, "Here are the key points in a format you can quickly understand and easily share." While some people criticize listicles for being superficial, they are an effective way to present information in a concise and engaging manner. This structure is particularly effective in online articles, blog posts, and even educational content such as this book.

➤ **Key Point:** In an easily digestible format, the listicle breaks down complex information into quick-to-read, shareable points.

➤ **Takeaway:** Effective for quick communication, especially for online articles and educational content.

6.5.10 How-To Guide

The how-to guide is the handyman's writing structure, a bit like an expanded listicle. It is practical and instructional, providing a step-by-step guide to accomplishing a specific task or solving a particular problem. This structure breaks down complex tasks into manageable steps and says, "Here is how you do it." It is particularly useful in instructional manuals, blog posts, and educational content.

➤ **Key Point:** The How-to Guide structure breaks down complex tasks into practical, step-by-step instruction.

➤ **Takeaway:** Effective for teaching and guiding, this structure is best used for instructional manuals and educational content.

6.5.11 Process Analysis

The engineer of nonfiction writing structures, the process analysis structure outlines a process in a sequential manner and explains each step in detail. It is similar to the how-to guide structure in that it breaks down complex procedures into understandable steps, but its focus is on *why* it works rather than *how* to do it. The structure's "Here's how it works" approach is particularly useful in technical manuals and scientific papers.

➤ **Key Point:** Sequential and detailed in breaking down complex procedures to show the how and why.

➤ **Takeaway:** Very effective for explaining processes in technical manuals and scientific papers.

6.5.12 FAQ

The FAQ (Frequently Asked Questions) is the problem-solver of writing structures. It is a structure designed to address common questions or concerns in a straightforward and organized manner. It is the structure that says, "You have questions, we have answers." This structure is particularly useful in customer service documents, product manuals, and informational websites.

➤ **Key Point:** Addresses common questions in a straightforward, organized manner.

➤ **Takeaway:** Effective for quick information retrieval in customer service and informational websites.

6.5.13   Circular Narrative

The circular narrative is the philosopher among writing structures. Focusing on themes of repetition, closure, and the cyclical nature of life, the structure concludes, "We have come full circle." By exploring relevant themes and returning to the beginning, this structure provides a sense of resolution or closure.

In a world that often feels chaotic and disjointed, the circular narrative offers a sense of unity and wholeness. It reminds us that every ending is also a new beginning. It invites the reader to ponder deeper themes to engage with the material emotionally and intellectually. Commonly used in literary fiction, this structure is also effective in genres such as memoirs or creative nonfiction.

➤ **Key Point:** A cyclical structure, the circular narrative explores themes of repetition and closure that invite deeper engagement.

➤ **Takeaway:** Offering a sense of unity and wholeness, this structure is often used in literary fiction, memoirs, and creative nonfiction.

6.5.14   Vignette

The vignette structure can be viewed as the impressionist painter of writing structures. The structure focuses on brief, evocative descriptions, episodes, or impressions that do not necessarily have to connect directly with each other. It is the "snapshot" structure that provides a glimpse into a scene, character, or idea. It is particularly useful in creative nonfiction, poetry, and certain types of fiction. It is often used as a structure within another structure, e.g., to tell a sub-story of a character.

➤ **Key Point:** Uses brief, evocative snapshot-like descriptions to create episodes or impressions.

➤ **Takeaway:** Effective for creating mood and atmosphere this structure is best for creative nonfiction, poetry, and fiction.

6.5.15   Descriptive

The descriptive structure is the painter of nonfiction writing. It focuses on providing a detailed account of a person, place, thing, or event. It is the structure that says, "Let me paint you a picture," and offers vivid descriptions that appeal to the senses. This structure is particularly useful in travel writing, profiles, and feature articles.

➤ **Key Point:** This structure paints a vivid and detailed picture with a strong appeal to the senses.

➤ **Takeaway:** Effective for creating a vivid impression, the descriptive structure is used in travel writing, profiles, and feature articles.

6.5.16   Case Study

The case study is the detective of nonfiction writing structures. It dives deep into a specific subject, situation, or individual in order to provide a comprehensive understanding. The approach says, "Let's dissect this," and proceeds with a detailed analysis backed by research and real-world examples that generally abstracts away non-relevant details.

One of the case study structure's powers for tactical writing is the ability for the authors to decide which facts to present, in what order and—as well as what to delete. This allows the audience to draw a conclusion from the facts that are presented (filtered by the authors). The temporal order of the presentation plus skipped items leads to the audience filling in the gap, which can be used strategically if the authors correctly estimate the audience context and assumptions. This structure is particularly useful in academic papers, business reports, journalistic pieces, and in some educational settings.

➢ **Key Point:** Provides a research-backed, in-depth analysis focusing on a specific subject.

➢ **Takeaway:** Effective for enabling a deeper understanding of a subject, but it can be used to lead an audience down a particular path. Useful for academic papers, business reports, and journalism.

6.5.17   Epistolary

The epistolary structure is the intimate confidant of writing structures that involves telling a story or conveying information through a series of letters or written correspondence between characters. This structure can create a sense of intimacy and immediacy in the writing because the reader feels as if they are reading private correspondence between characters. The structure allows for a nuanced, multi-dimensional analysis of complex subjects. It is often used in novels but can be effectively used in memoirs or personal essays. In a world that is increasingly digital and impersonal, the epistolary structure serves as a charming and unique way to convey information and tell a story.

➢ **Key Point:** Intimate and immediate, the epistolary uses letters or correspondence to reveal a character's actions, thoughts, and traits.

➢ **Takeaway:** Used effectively for conveying intimacy in novels, memoirs, and personal essays.

6.6 How to Approach Tactical Storytelling

We have covered many foundational concepts and how-tos in this chapter. To be sure, tactical storytelling is not a task to be taken lightly. It requires a deep understanding of various elements—audience, theme, characters, structure, and even constraints—and how they interact to create a compelling, impactful narrative. Tactical writing is an art that combines creativity with strategy, and this chapter has provided you with the tools to master it. Use it as a reference, a how-to guide, as you put what you have learned into practice. Whether you are a seasoned writer or a novice, the guidelines and insights offered here will equip you to craft stories that are not just compelling but also deeply resonant, memorable, and impactful.

6.7 Key Terms

1) **Storytelling Triangle:** *The foundational model identifying narrative elements.*

2) **Storytelling Tetrahedron/Tactical Tetrahedron:** *An extended model of the storytelling triangle that introduces the objective.*

3) **Audience:** *The recipient of the story in the storytelling triangle.*

4) **Author:** *The creator of the story in the storytelling triangle.*

5) **Audience Engagement:** *Active participation of the audience.*

6) **Tactical Objective:** *The intended outcome in tactical writing and a vertex in the tactical tetrahedron.*

7) **Cognitive Resonance:** *How storytelling affects the mind.*

8) **Narrative Arc:** *A structure for storytelling involving exposition, rising action, climax, falling action, and denouement.*

9) **Inverted Pyramid:** *A journalistic structure that presents the most important information first, followed by details.*

10) **Compare and Contrast:** *A structure for analyzing subjects by highlighting their similarities and differences.*

11) **Problem-Solution Structure:** *A framework that identifies a problem and provides actionable solutions.*

12) **Cause and Effect Structure:** *A structure that explores the causes and consequences of events or actions.*

13) **Chronological Order:** *A time-based structure that presents events in a sequential manner.*

14) **SUCCESs Model:** *Stickiness in storytelling can be achieved through six key principles: Simplicity, Unexpectedness, Concreteness, Credibility, Emotions, and Stories (SUCCESs), from the book Made to Stick.*

6.8 Other Terms

1) **Brainstorming:** *A technique during team workshops to encourage the free flow of ideas and innovative thinking.*

2) **OSCAR Structure:** *A five-element writing structure, common in academic writing, including Opening, Setting, Challenge, Action, and Resolution.*

3) **Relevance and Context:** *Making the story meaningful to the audience.*

4) **Character Development:** *Crafting relatable story characters.*

5) **Structural Elements:** *The use of headings and bullets for accessibility.*

6) **Braided Essay:** *A literary structure that interweaves distinct yet interconnected narratives.*

7) **Listicle:** *A format that breaks down information into easily digestible lists or points.*

8) **Circular Narrative:** *A narrative structure that explores themes of repetition and closure.*

9) **Vignette:** *A structure focusing on brief, evocative descriptions or impressions.*

10) **Descriptive Structure:** *A format that provides vivid and detailed descriptions.*

11) **Unexpectedness:** *Surprise is a powerful tool for grabbing attention in storytelling and an important part of SUCCESs*

12) **Concreteness:** *Using concrete images and examples to make a point in SUCCESSful storytelling.*

13) **Emotions:** *Tapping into emotions to make a story resonate with the audience in important for sticky Stories.*

7 A Team Approach to Tactical Writing

"My model for business is The Beatles. They were four guys who kept each other's kind of negative tendencies in check. They balanced each other, and the total was greater than the sum of the parts. That's how I see business: great things in business are never done by one person, they're done by a team of people."

-Steve Jobs

Teams have become a critical element in how modern businesses function. Druskat et al. Druskat and Wheeler [2004] report "a survey of Fortune 1000 companies reveals that 79 percent already rely on self-managing teams and 91 percent on various forms of employee work groups." Also pertinent to our exploration, another survey of 120 major U.S. companies Skripak et al. [2018], found that writing is a "threshold skill" for employment and promotion. They report that "writing ability could be your ticket in— or your ticket out." Applicants and employees who cannot write and communicate clearly will not be hired and are unlikely to last long enough to be considered for promotion. Thus, a critical business skill today is the ability to work in self-managed, multi-disciplinary teams for tactical writing projects.

In a world where the pace of change is accelerating, where the information we must consider is increasingly diverse, and its volume is overwhelming, the act of writing is no longer a solitary endeavor. More often than not, team writing is how communication is done. In this chapter, we will delve into the complexities, benefits, and challenges of tactical writing as a team.

7.1 Welcome to Team Writing

In the realm of team writing, a group's collective intelligence is harnessed to produce work that is greater than the sum of its parts. However, team writing is not about creating a document by consensus, nor is it a bunch of people writing independently and sticking their work into a single document. While we may hear phrases such as "collaborative writing," "group writing," "team writing," and "distributed writing" used to refer to such processes, the terms are not synonymous. Each term has its own meaning and nuance. Our focus and discussion will use the term "team writing" to describe the collective efforts of individuals working together on a written project with the objective of producing the best possible work for an organization's benefit by leveraging the skills and ideas of multiple contributors.

To further clarify our terminology, note the difference between "teams" and "groups." These terms are often used interchangeably but are not synonymous, especially when it comes to writing. Understanding the distinction can help us identify the dynamics and expectations involved in team writing.

A "group" is a collection of individuals who may work together, but they have a less structured relationship than a team. They may work on different aspects of a project independently, with each member responsible for a specific task. In group writing, the focus is often on individual accountability, and the project's success is the sum of the individual contributions. In contrast, a "team" is a more integrated unit with a shared goal and collective accountability. Team members work closely, often cross-functionally, to produce a unified output. The project's success hinges on the team's collective performance, not the individual contributions. Team members are interdependent, meaning one person's work affects the work of others. This interdependence requires higher coordination, communication, and trust among all team members.

In team writing, the distinction between teams and groups is crucial. A writing team's end document is truly a collective effort. It is not a patchwork of individual pieces but a cohesive, unified work that reflects the team's shared vision and voice. Team writing requires a specific approach to planning, drafting, and

99

revising as well as a commitment to open and honest communication and constructive feedback. It often involves a more complex decision-making and conflict-resolution process because team members need to negotiate different ideas, perspectives, and writing styles to arrive at a consensus. Team writing requires true collaboration.

7.1.1 Benefits of Team Writing

Team writing is not just about putting words on paper. From a task perspective, it is more about improving ideas and stories than about a division of labor. From an organizational perspective, collaborative team writing has a mindset that values the collective over the individual. When people work together in the team writing process, they consciously choose to set aside their personal ambitions for the greater good of the team and, by extension, the organization they represent. As a result, team writing can play a role that has powerful and positive benefits for an organization. This benefit, which is articulated in *"The Collaboration Imperative"* Nidumolu et al. [2014] identifies an organization's true potential by its people's collective skills, experiences, and energies. In the book, *Collaboration Begins with You: Be a Silo Buster*. Blanchard et al. [2015], the authors argue that collaboration transcends team dynamics, and effective collaboration needs to be embedded in the DNA of the company culture.

The unified, collaborative effort of team writing offers a plethora of advantages that make it a preferred approach for many organizations. Consider some of its key benefits:

➤ **Quality of Output**: When executed correctly, team writing can produce a superior end product because it draws on the collective skills and commitment of the team and aims for a result that benefits not just individual members but the entire organization.

➤ **Diversity of Ideas and Viewpoints**: A well-thought-out team often includes members from diverse backgrounds, genders, and cultures, providing intellectual diversity that enables the creation of documents that are sensitive to a wide array of audiences. This is something that a single writer or even some writing groups might find challenging to achieve.

➤ **Technological Advantages**: The rise of various collaboration tools such as video calls, automatic transcription, e-mail, instant messaging, and shared document workspaces has made an efficient team writing process possible. While some team members may be more facile with technology and address specific issues better than others, these technologies enable team members to engage more effectively and complete projects in a more streamlined manner.

➤ **Leadership and Team Skills**: Team writing allows team members to explore different roles, from leadership to subordinate positions. It also allows for role rotation, giving employees experience in various capacities such as team lead, recorder, researcher, and editor. These options can be beneficial for career growth as they provide a holistic understanding of the project and its challenges.

➤ **Active Learning and Skill Development**: The collaborative process is an active form of learning. Team members can hone their existing skills or acquire new ones by working alongside colleagues with different areas of expertise. Embracing the learning potential of team writing sometimes means letting team members work in areas where they are less skilled and then having a more skilled team member review their work.

➤ **Fosters a Positive Work Environment**: Team writing often necessitates verbal, electronic, and sometimes virtual communication. This multifaceted interaction fosters a collegial atmosphere that contributes to a more enjoyable and productive work environment.

➢ **Organizational Growth**: When team members recognize their contributions as crucial to the project's success, they are more likely to contribute proactively, which positively affects the organization's bottom line. This sense of ownership among employees contributes significantly to their personal satisfaction, and to the company's longevity.

7.1.2　　Types of Team Writing

As we have seen, a truly collaborative environment fosters communication, learning, innovation, and, ultimately, profitability. While such collaborative environments are ideal, there is always room for improvement. Every writing team can work toward leveraging their collaborative mindset by learning when to apply the following six types of team writing and the four styles of collaboration that are loosely adapted from Ede and Lunsford [1992], Lingard [2021], Bingham and Conner [2010].

➢ **One-for-All Team Writing**: In this approach, one person writes on behalf of the entire team. It is often used for tasks that are relatively simple and straightforward. The advantage is stylistic consistency and efficiency, but it may limit the diversity of ideas and perspectives. It can be improved by a one-for-all and all-for-one approach in which a single author produces a first or second draft that the full team reviews (all-for-one). The reviewers may then edit the draft directly or give feedback for the original author to revise for a subsequent review.

➢ **Each-in-Sequence or Each-in-Turn Team Writing**: In this type, one person starts the writing, completes their task, and then passes it on to the next person. This is particularly useful for teams who work asynchronously and meet infrequently. It allows for straightforward coordination, but minimal social interaction and potential bottlenecks may be drawbacks. This mode starts after the pieces are identified, i.e., after the tactical story generation process is at or beyond the first draft stage.

➢ **All-in-Parallel Team Writing**: In this model, the writing work is divided into discrete units, and all writers work simultaneously. This is effective for easily divided writing tasks when the sections are not mutually dependent. It offers more process efficiency and writer autonomy than in-sequence writing. However, it can be effectively used after the first steps of the tactical writing process are complete, a basic outline of the story has been fleshed out, and it is time to draft the text and graphics.

➢ **All-in-Reaction or Real-time Team Writing**: In this approach, team members create a document together in real-time, adjusting for each other's changes and additions. This can support consensus through fluid and creative expression, but the process may lead to chaotic development and difficulties with version control. This style can be very effective in the early stages of the tactical writing process, but it could be more convenient and efficient for larger groups if used when it is time to generate text and graphics.

➢ **Multi-Mode or Hybrid Team Writing**: This hybrid approach combines all the elements of the above styles. For example, combining one-for-all writing with all-for-one editing/reviewing is a hybrid. Hybrids are often used for larger writing projects to leverage the advantages of each style while mitigating the disadvantages. A common approach would be to use a larger team for the story generation phase and red-team reviewing, then use a mix of the other approaches depending on the project and the team.

➢ **Team Reviewing/Red-Team Review**: Editing is where the game is often won or lost, so having formal reviews as part of the collaborative tactical writing process is essential. Even a single round of peer review from someone who is truly collaborating will improve the outcomes. These reviews can be done as part of any approach and can be done by one peer, by a team in sequence, or by a parallel team. While reviews can be used in all types of team writing, we call them out separately, as reviews should be on the project schedule, and the style of review should be the best fit for the project.

7.1.3   Styles of Collaboration

Once a writing team is established, it must determine how it will work together. This decision depends on the type, size, and skills of the team as well as the focus and objectives of the writing project. Consider the differences between and benefits of the following collaboration styles.

➤ **Communication-Oriented Collaboration**: This style emphasizes effective communication among team members. It is most useful for one-for-all writing and each-in-sequence writing, where clear communication is key for coordinating tasks and ensuring everyone is on the same page.

➤ **Task-Oriented Collaboration**: This style is all about achieving specific tasks, goals, or projects. It is most useful for each-in-sequence writing and all-in-parallel writing where the focus is on completing specific sections or tasks within a larger project.

➤ **Network-Oriented Collaboration**: This style leverages the network of skills and expertise among team members. It is most useful for all-in-parallel writing, where the division of labor is planned according to each writer's core expertise.

➤ **Community-Oriented Collaboration**: This style aims to build a sense of community and shared purpose among team members. It is most useful for all-in-reaction writing and multi-mode writing, where the collaborative environment is fluid and focuses on building consensus and shared understanding. It is most beneficial for red-team review because it provides diverse views and helps others learn from the review process, which enhances the organization's long-term value.

7.1.4   Ten Tips for Effective Interpersonal Interactions in Team Writing

Communication and interpersonal interaction in team writing presents great potential for exceptional success and great potential for disaster. The following ten tips can help prevent and manage problematic communication and interaction within the writing team. Team leaders need to be attuned to team dynamics and actively practice these tips to keep the team on track and happy. Effective team interaction is *not just* the responsibility of the leaders; it is every team member's responsibility.

1) **Build Trust**: To foster open communication and collaboration, establish a foundation of trust among team members. For example, sharing past experiences and writing samples can help team members to understand each other's strengths and weaknesses.

2) **Active Listening:** Listen actively to validate team members' contributions, ideas, and concerns. During meetings, summarize what you have heard to ensure everyone is on the same page.

3) **Be Mindful of Team Dynamics:** Pay close attention to group dynamics. If one member is dominating discussions, make an effort to solicit input from the quieter members and, if necessary, adjust roles or processes.

4) **Conflict Resolution:** If two team members disagree, address the conflict directly and constructively, aiming for a resolution that benefits the project. Facilitate a discussion to find a compromise.

5) **Celebrate Small Wins:** To boost team morale and motivation, celebrate small milestones.

6) **Be Open to Diverse Perspectives:** Encourage diversity of thought by actively seeking input from team members with different backgrounds or expertise. Be open to ideas that differ from yours.

7) **Show Empathy:** Be aware and considerate of team members' feelings and perspectives. When a team member struggles with a section, offer support rather than criticism.

8) **Be Transparent:** Maintain transparency about project status, challenges, and changes. If you need to adjust a deadline, for example, communicate to the team as soon as possible.

9) **Share Credit:** Acknowledge and celebrate each team member's contributions. During a team meeting or in the final document, give credit to individuals for their specific contributions.

10) **Maintain a Positive Attitude:** When faced with setbacks, focus on solutions rather than dwelling on the problems. A positive attitude can be contagious and help the team overcome its challenges.

> Personal Story: My Introduction to Formal Team Writing
>
> As a Ph.D. student and later as a faculty member, I worked on collaborative papers and proposals with multiple authors. These projects involved teams, but they were largely done using a divide-and-conquer approach. Team members were assigned their particular sections, and there was little collaborative pre-work, actual group writing, or review. I didn't experience or understand the power of multidisciplinary team writing until I started consulting with Siemens Corporation on a large proposal to NIH on a new MRI technology.
>
> I was part of a team that included medical doctors from another state, business people from Siemens, and other scientists. We had to develop a coherent story, and most of our sections had to be co-written with the technologists and medical professionals to ensure our project addressed both sides well and used harmonized terminology. This was crucial because the review panel included experts in three areas: medicine, MRI technology, and business.
>
> This experience introduced me to very formal review processes that demanded early deadlines for drafts. The many deadlines and the multiple different colored reviews that each raised different points of view initially annoyed me. The process was painfully slow, but as they had a long history of success I just worked through it. The process turned out to be extremely educational.
>
> I learned to improve my own processes, realizing that reviews were not just about expecting feedback but actually valuing it. It took me a while to appreciate the perspectives of others, which were often very different from mine. I spent lots of time trying to understand what they were asking and why they were pushing me to change things. My lexicon and mindset were often confusing to them, just as their terms confused me. I learned to appreciate the viewpoints of business people and grant specialists at the hospital because they had extensive experience with multi-million dollar NIH proposals.
>
> Our first attempt at this funding was unsuccessful. However, the scoring of our NIH proposal was enlightening. The review reflected many points that had been brought up during the gold and red team reviews— points I had initially dismissed while arguing for my own perspective. The review showed that the other internal reviewers were generally correct and that some of my views led to our proposal being unsuccessful. We revised and resubmitted, and I learned my lesson.
>
> This experience with interdisciplinary collaboration has influenced the rest of my career. It affected how my startup companies functioned and was a fundamental element in the design of my approach to innovation teaming. True team writing is probably the single most important thing I learned from working with a big company.

7.2 Team Writing Leadership and Project Management

Effective team leadership and project management are crucial for the success of any team writing project, so leadership selection is key. In many organizations team leads are appointed, and in self-managing groups the leads are often self-selected. Team leads for tactical writing projects may be assigned to a special role in the organization, such as a project manager, with cross-domain people assigned or added to the project. There may also be a "visionary" for the project who helps define the key elements of the story but may be involved only a few times a week.

Writing a story, you understand, is not done by consensus. But we do learn from each other, and we remind ourselves how important this work we're doing is.

-John Dufresne

The project manager is the backbone of a team writing project, ensuring that tasks are allocated efficiently and that the deadlines are met. They are the central point for communication and coordination to facilitate streamlining the writing process. For example, in a multi-author research paper, the project manager coordinates between subject matter experts, writers, and editors. Take note of the following key components on which a project manager should focus:

Task Schedules: Publicize Deadlines and Responsibilities

A well-defined task schedule helps in setting clear deadlines and responsibilities. It ensures that every team member knows what is expected of them and by whom. For instance, in a grant writing project, a task schedule might specify the date by which the literature review must be completed.

Meeting Minutes: Build Accountability and Consensus

Documenting meeting minutes is essential for building accountability and consensus among team members. It serves as a written record of what was discussed, what decisions were made, and who is responsible for what. For example, if a decision is made to change the direction of a chapter, the meeting minutes would document the change and note who is responsible for its implementation.

Meeting Agenda: Keep Discussions on Track

A pre-defined meeting agenda ensures that team discussions remain focused and productive and that all the important points are addressed within the stipulated time. An agenda for a project kickoff meeting, for instance, might include items such as a project overview, role assignments, and timeline discussion.

Email Reminders & Notifications: Step in When Problems Occur

Timely email reminders and notifications act as safety nets, helping to keep the project on track. They serve as nudges for team members who might be lagging. For example, an automated email reminder could be sent two days before a deadline.

Other Project Management Documents

Apart from the above, a project manager might produce other documents such as risk assessment reports, progress reports, or even project closure reports. A risk assessment report, for instance, could outline potential challenges like the unavailability of key team members and propose mitigation strategies.

7.2.1 Use a Team Charter

A team charter can serve as a road map and agreement for any project, including larger tactical writing projects. The charter outlines the team's goals, individual commitments, and conflict resolution guidelines. This is especially helpful for teams with little history working together or for teams that have failed in the past. The key elements in a charter include:

Team Objectives: What constitutes success?

Projects need SMART objectives and agreement on what success looks like. For a tactical writing project, this could mean completing a proposal within a set time frame. It should have all the SMART characteristics but start with "success" to get overall buy-in from the team. A team objective might be to complete the proposal one week before its due date in October.

Personal Goals: What do individuals want from the project?

Individual team members may have personal learning or career objectives. For example, junior writers might aim to improve their technical writing skills.

Individual Commitment: How much effort will each individual invest?

Each member should define their responsibilities clearly and commit to a specific number of hours—20, for example— per week.

Individual Information: What other individual factors might affect performance?

Team members should disclose any factors that might affect their performance, including possible conflicting commitments, such as involvement in another high-priority project.

Irreconcilable Differences: How will the team resolve impasses?

The charter should outline the conflict resolution mechanisms that will be used. For example, using a majority vote to resolve minor decisions and escalating major issues to the project manager.

Late Work: How will the team handle missed deadlines?

The charter should specify the consequences of missing deadlines, which may result in a redistribution of tasks among team members.

Unacceptable Work: How will the team handle poor-quality contributions?

Clear guidelines should be set for maintaining quality such as addressing poor quality work with specific feedback and a time frame for revision.

Put It All Together

Once all the elements are defined, all team members should agree upon the team charter. It is a living document that can be updated throughout the project. It should be shared via a collaborative platform where all team members can access and review it.

Experienced or large corporate teams may have standard operating procedures that address some of these team charter elements, i.e., handling irreconcilable differences and unacceptable work. However, discussing and formalizing the SMART objectives, personal goals, and individual commitments are still good practices for tactical writing teams.

 Using the RACI Matrix for Project Management

One way to manage the many activities and tasks of a tactical writing project is to use a project management tool like the Responsibility Assignment Matrix (RAM), also called the Responsible, Accountable, Consulted, and Informed (RACI) matrix. The RACI matrix helps to clarify roles and responsibilities within a tactical writing team and facilitates communication with the people involved. This tool is well suited for larger writing projects such as proposals and books. Each of these designations serves a specific function for the project:

➤ **Responsible**: These are the "doers" of the project, the individuals who are actively working on completing writing tasks. Examples include content writers, editors, reviewers, copywriters, budget analysts, and graphic designers.

➤ **Accountable**: These individuals are responsible for the overall success and completion of the writing project. They are often also part of the "informed" group. Examples include the project lead, budget office/signature authorities, and editorial manager.

➤ **Consulted**: These are the experts whose opinions are sought; their feedback is crucial for the project. Examples may include subject matter experts, government relations staff, information security and cybersecurity experts, and legal advisors for content compliance.

➤ **Informed**: These individuals need to be kept in the loop but are not directly involved in decision-making. Examples include external stakeholders, marketing teams, and business owners.

A RACI chart is important for larger projects or new teams. It provides a structured approach to project roles that reduces scope creep and budget overruns and ensures that everyone knows their responsibilities. It also enhances communication among team members, which is crucial for success. Granted, formality takes effort and is not always needed. One can skip the RACI if:

➤ A small team already communicates well.

Task / Stakeholders	Project Lead Anne	Eng. John	Business Dev. Natasha	Art Steven	External Sarah	Visionary CEO Allison
Task 1: Opening & Setting Stage	A	C	R	C	R	A
Task 2: Big picture Picture	A	C	I	R	C	R
Task 3: Challenge Section	A	R	R	C	I	C
Task 4: Action (Technical Solution)	I	A	C	C	I	C
Task 4: Action (Business Solution)	I	C	A	I	I	C
Task 5: Resolution/Conclusion	A	C	C	C	R	I
Task 6: 7Budget and Justification	A	I	R	I	I	I
Task 7: Review applications	R	C	C	C	C	A

RACI

R - Responsible
The people who take action to get the task done. They are responsible for the work or making the decision. You can have more than one person responsible for a task, but to make the decision-making process effective, try having one person responsible for a single task.

A - Accountable
The person who owns the task or deliverable. They might not get the work done themselves, but they are responsible for making sure it is finalized. To avoid confusion and the diffusion of responsibility, it's better to have one accountable person per project or task.

C - Consulted
The person, role, or group who will help complete the task. They will have two-way communication with the people responsible for the task by providing input and feedback over the task completion.

I - Informed
The people, roles, or groups that need to be up to date on the task's progress. They will not have two-way communication, but it's essential to keep them informed since they will be affected by the final outcome of the task/project.

Figure 7.1: *Example Tactical Story RACI Matrix in a spreadsheet using a template from https://www.aihr.com/blog/ raci-template/. A more advanced version would have task completion dates and might be used in parallel with a GANTT chart for very large tactical writing efforts to show the timing and dependencies.*

➤ All individuals stay on top of their work.

➤ The project is small enough that going through the steps outlined in the RACI matrix template would waste more time than the project; e.g., a project making two web pages for new departments may be too simple for RACI.

➤ The project team uses an agile framework/Scrum for writing with clear assignments in their processes.

Presuming you want to use RACI, there are many free tools to help structure it, see Figure 7.1, although any spreadsheet tool would be sufficient.

7.2.3 How to Build a RACI Matrix

The RACI matrix should be a simple-to-use document that provides a snapshot of the project and everyone's roles and responsibilities. Creating a RACI matrix for a tactical writing project involves several steps aimed at ensuring a well-defined project scope and clear roles for all team members:

➤ **Plan Ahead**: Before diving into the RACI matrix, understand the project's demands by communicating with key stakeholders and decision-makers.

➤ **Determine the Scope**: Identify the project's key activities, tasks, and deliverables, usually in consultation with the editorial manager or project lead. Identify and fill in the first column ('A' in a spreadsheet) with those items, i.e., one row per task that needs to be completed, including milestones for checkoff and red-team review.

➤ **Identify Involved Parties**: List all individuals and groups who need to be part of the writing project and fill them in the first row as column headers (row 1 in a spreadsheet).

➤ **Outline Project Roles**: For each activity and deliverable, identify who is responsible, accountable, consulted, and informed, putting an "R" "A" "C" or "I" in the appropriate cell.

➤ **Group Review**: Hold sessions with key team members (ideally as a single group) to align everyone on their roles. If the project has already started, it is not too late to implement a RACI matrix. Host a kickoff meeting to unveil the proposed matrix, answer questions, and ensure everyone is on the same page. As in any teamwork, getting everyone's buy-in and agreement to their assignments is critical.

➤ **Ongoing Review**: Periodically review the RACI matrix to ensure it remains relevant, especially if there are changes in project scope or team members.

By following these steps, you can create a RACI matrix and manage a proposal process that provides clarity, enhances communication, and sets up your tactical writing project for success.

An alternate RACI form is a set of lines at the beginning of a document with section assignments with the R (first) and then A, C, I, and associated names. Putting this data in the same shared document rather than in a separate matrix is often more convenient for shorter efforts. This can be combined with dates and page allocations in the kickoff meeting so that people know what they are responsible for and how much space and time they have to complete their tasks. Combining the information with some color coding of "risks" and "status," e.g., red for a high risk that it might not make the deadline, yellow for some risk, and green for completed tasks, can make the document itself a simple way to "inform" upper management of the things they most need to do—putting the RACI bottom line on top during development.

7.2.4   Scheduling in the Context of RACI

Scheduling is integral to project management, especially when using a RACI chart for a tactical writing project. Here are the key elements to consider:

➤ **Identify Major Tasks**

The first shared step in RACI and scheduling is identifying the major tasks, such as drafting, editing, and proofreading a technical manual, that must be completed.

➤ **Identify the Roles for Individuals: Motivation vs. Experience**

When "assigning" roles, consider team members' motivation and experience. It is generally more effective to create buy-in by including them in the decision process and the schedule by which they can complete the task. For example, a highly motivated junior writer can be assigned to draft a section by COB next Monday that will be reviewed by an experienced editor by COB Tuesday.

➤ **Schedule the Tasks**

Once roles are assigned, schedule the tasks with specific deadlines. Drafting, for example, could be scheduled for completion in two weeks, followed by a red-team review, leaving one week for editing.

➤ **Balance the Workload**

Ensure that the workload is evenly distributed among team members, but consider their other assignments when determining the balance. If one writer is responsible for three chapters, ensure they have more time or help than the writer who is assigned one chapter.

➤ **Technology and Tools for Task Schedules**

For larger projects, utilize project management software or other tools to keep track of tasks and deadlines. Even if these tools are not essential for the project at hand, they make self-feedback on missed deadlines easier to use in improving future scheduling estimates. Use tools like Asana or Jira to set tasks, assign roles, and track progress.

- **Plan for Slippage and Reassess Progress Regularly**

Schedules are rarely completed early, so you should probably include some slack for slippage. But regularly assess where the project stands relative to the schedule. Set a policy that if a writer thinks they will miss a deadline, they notify you three days in advance so you can reassess where the others are and potentially get them help.

7.3 Team Review and Constructive Feedback

Team review and providing constructive feedback are critical steps in the writing process, especially for tactical writing projects that require precision and clarity. Team reviewing encompasses many elements, and in larger organizations, there may be multiple levels of review. It is important to remember that review is not just about finding issues. A good review also requires communicating constructive feedback so that the writers/editors can understand and act on the issues. Done well, constructive feedback not only improves the quality of the work but fosters a culture of continuous improvement and learning. Done poorly, feedback often leads to resentment and issues being ignored.

7.3.1　Guidelines for Providing Feedback

How team leaders and members view the review process matters. Team reviewing is always about the objective and the writing; it is not personal. The goal is to offer constructive feedback that encourages a collaborative and respectful work environment that, in turn, leads to an exceptional end product. Here are some general points to consider when reviewing any team writing project:

- **Be Specific**

General comments like "good job" or "needs improvement" are not very helpful. Be specific about what you liked or what needs to be changed. Instead of saying, "This section is unclear," point out which sentences or phrases are confusing and suggest alternatives.

- **Focus on the Work Product, Not the Person**

Ensure your feedback is about the work product itself and not a critique of the individual. Avoid saying "you" or "your" in the review. Say, "This argument could be strengthened by including more evidence," instead of "You did not make a strong argument."

- **Be Timely**

Feedback is most useful when given promptly. Do not wait for weeks to review a piece of writing, especially just before the deadline. Try to review and provide feedback within a few days of receiving the draft.

- **Use the "Bad News Sandwich" Method**

Start with something positive, follow with the critique, and end with another positive comment. For example, "The introduction is very engaging, but the conclusion could summarize the key points more effectively. Overall, it is a well-researched piece."

- **Encourage Dialogue**

Feedback should be a two-way street. If something is not clear, encourage the writer to ask questions or clarify comments. After providing feedback, ask, "Do you have any questions about my comments?"

7.3.2   Critical Elements of the Review Process

The review process must include an evaluation of the critical elements of storytelling as well as compliance with submission requirements in the document.

➣ **Story**

Verify that the document's story and theme are aligned with the tactical objectives. Consider the audience knowledge, audience context, story inconsistencies, and omissions. For instance, compare audience research and the writing team's preliminary story and theme for alignment.

➣ **Content**

Verify that the document's content and data are accurate, complete, and relevant to the document's purpose. Look for errors, inconsistencies, and omissions.

➣ **Format**

Ensure that the document's formatting—font size, spacing, margins, and page numbering—is uniform, properly aligned, and easy to read.

➣ **Structure**

Assess the document's structure for organization and flow. Check headings, subheadings, and the sequence of information. Make sure the introduction, body, and conclusion flow logically.

➣ **Language**

Review the language for clarity, conciseness, and appropriateness for the audience. Check for spelling and grammar errors. Flag overly technical language that the intended audience might not understand.

➣ **Compliance**

Confirm that the document complies with applicable regulations, standards, and guidelines. For example, ensure that any safety procedures mentioned comply with relevant safety standards.

➣ **References**

Check that all references are accurate, timely, relevant, and correctly formatted.

➣ **Consistency**

Review for consistency in terminology, formatting, capitalization, abbreviations, and other style requirements.

➣ **Usability**

Ensure the document is user-friendly and easy to navigate. Verify that instructions are clear and tables and figures are well-labeled.

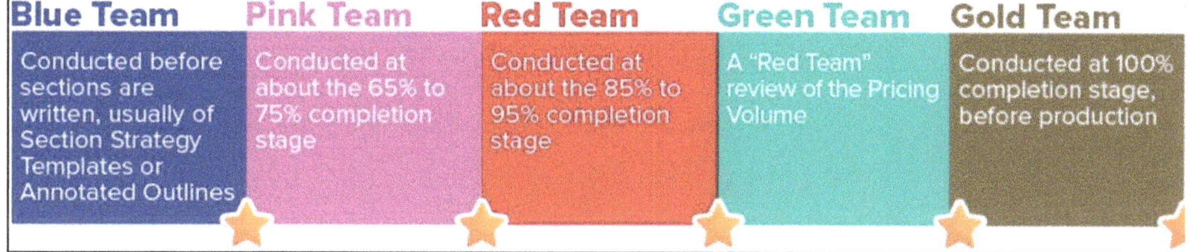

Figure 7.2: *Different stages of major writing project reviews with somewhat standard color naming*

7.3.3   The Color-Coded Review Process

Multi-stage reviews are important, and the more significant the tactical objective or document, the greater the level of reviews that will be required. Reviews need to be done while there is still time to fix any issues and before time is invested in polishing a document that does not work. Each level of review serves specific purposes in the proposal development process and contributes to making the proposal compliant, compelling, and complete.

Since color-coded names for team reviews are widely used in academia and the workplace, we present the reviews with those common names. The standard color reviews are blue, pink, red, green, and gold. A few organizations use additional or other colors. Each color team review has a specific purpose, and the results of the review and future actions to be taken are recorded and tracked through final disposition.

Earlier in this book, I used the term "red team review" because, for many projects, there is only one major review that includes people outside of the writing team. Thus, I often use the term "red team review" generically to mean a critical review of the document. It is important to note that the actual terms for a particular review are not as critical as understanding the requirements for different levels of reviews. A red team review is an independent group that takes the customer's perspective to identify weaknesses and gaps in the final draft of the proposal.

The practice of naming reviews after colors is a convention widely adopted in various industries, particularly for proposal development, project management, and government contracting. The color-coded system serves as a structured, disciplined approach to guide the development and assessment of proposals or projects through various stages of maturity. Each color represents a different level of review, with specific objectives and criteria to be met before moving on to the next stage. The series of colors (blue to gold) reflects the increasing maturity of the proposal document(s). It is a way to quickly identify where a project or proposal stands and what needs to be done to move it to the next level.

Using colors adds a visual element that can make the process more engaging and easier to manage. Overall, the color-coded system aims to improve team members' clarity, focus, and coordination. A description of the purpose and process for each of the "colors" of review follows.

➣ **Blue Team Review:**

Purpose: The blue team review is the starting point of the proposal development process and its focus is on establishing a strong foundation. The review ensures that the proposal template/outline is correct and complete, assigning writers to specific sections and identifying gaps in information, data, or themes. The blue team review sets the stage for all subsequent development and reviews, so the team's feedback is crucial for steering the proposal in the right direction. It should provide a critical review of the preliminary story, or if there is not a preliminary story, it directs the audience analysis and generation of the story.

Review Details: The review should last about one to two hours. Feedback should be concise but comprehensive, ideally within a two- to three-page document. Proposal managers, section leads, and subject matter experts should be involved. *Example:* In a proposal for a tactical writing project on cybersecurity, the blue team ensures that sections like "Threat Assessment," "Solution Architecture," and "Implementation Plan" are outlined and assigned to specific writers.

➤ Pink Team Review:

Purpose: The pink team review takes place after content assigned during the blue team review is added and the proposal is about 65-70% complete. The pink team focuses on adding narrative and detail, ensuring that no section is left blank. While the emphasis is on content rather than form, the document should show stylistic consistency.

Review Details: The review team should include proposal managers, writers, subject matter experts, and initial reviewers from the blue team. The review should last about two to three hours, and feedback should be detailed, ideally within a three- to five-page document.

Who Should Be Involved: In a proposal for creating a technical manual, the pink team ensures that all sections have substantial content and preliminary graphics.

➤ Red Team Review:

Purpose: The red team review is where the tactical writing effort, e.g., the proposal, should start looking like a finished product. The document should be nearly complete, incorporating all changes and feedback from the pink team review. The red team focuses on compliance with the RFP and clarity of content. They act as the customer's evaluators, ensuring that the proposal meets the requirements and tells a compelling story aligned with the tactical objective.

Review Details: The review should last about three to four hours and involve senior managers, proposal managers, and key stakeholders. Feedback should be extensive, ideally within a two- to seven-page document.

Example: In a proposal for a training program, the red team scrutinizes whether the training modules align with the client's requirements and whether the pricing is justified.

➤ Green Team Review:

Purpose: The green team—green for the color of money— review focuses solely on the proposal's pricing aspect to ensure that the pricing information is accurate, competitive, and follows the myriad rules required by the CFP. Some reviewers validate that the technical solution proposed can be realistically delivered within the budget. This review is crucial for assessing the financial viability of the project. Another aspect is checking for compliance, which is often done by a separate group that ignores the technical aspects.

Review Details: The review by financial analysts, proposal managers and technical leads should last about one to two hours. Feedback should be focused on pricing, ideally within a two- to three-page document.

Example: In a proposal for software development, the green team ensures that the cost estimates for software licenses, development hours, and post-launch support are accurate and competitive.

➤ Gold Team Review:

Purpose: The gold team review is the final checkpoint before the proposal is submitted. Conducted by senior executives or managers, this review focuses on high-level themes and discriminators. The gold team ensures that the proposal is compliant and complete and also compelling enough to win the contract. They ensure the proposal is priced to win, providing the final seal of approval.

Review Details: The review team of senior executives, business unit leaders, and key stakeholders should spend about one to two hours on the review. Feedback should be executive-level, ideally within a one- to two-page document.

Example: In a proposal for a research project, the gold team ensures that the research methodology is sound, the team is qualified, and the budget is realistic.

For clarification, please note that in the descriptions, the time and length are estimated for a 20- to 40-page proposal. While one might expect the time to scale with length, experience shows it does not – a 5-page proposal sometimes takes longer than 15 pages as it takes a lot of work to make the story fit into limited space. Also, the "time" does not include the time required to read the documents before the review. The length includes a summary of major issues and the length of comments that are directly embedded in the document (if any). With modern shared editing tools, such comments are an effective way to capture issues and assign them to someone to correct and follow up as they are resolved.

The team lead or project manager will select different groups of people according to the level of the team review. For example, a pink team starts with the basics: content and format. The red team builds on this by adding considerations for structure and language. Finally, the gold team brings in the big guns: compliance and executive oversight to ensure that the document is well-crafted and aligned with broader organizational goals.

7.3.4   Tips for an Effective Review

Reviewing a tactical writing document is a critical task that requires meticulous attention to detail and a structured approach. Here are tips to make the review process more effective and efficient.

➤ **Determine Review Stages and Reviewer Team:** Break down the review process into stages, focusing on different aspects such as content, formatting, and compliance for each stage. For instance, the first stage could focus on content accuracy, the second on formatting, and the third on compliance with industry standards. Select the team of reviewers for each stage based on their expertise.

➤ **Understand the Purpose of the Document:** Before diving into the review, reviewers should be familiar with the document's objectives and target audience. This understanding will serve as a lens through which to evaluate the document's effectiveness. When reviewing a technical manual, for example, understand that its purpose is to guide users in performing specific tasks. Within that context, evaluate whether the manual is user-friendly and provides clear instructions.

➤ **Collaborate and Communicate:** Effective review is not a solitary activity. It often requires collaboration and open communication among team members. As a reviewer, make sure to discuss your findings and seek clarification on any ambiguous points. This ensures that everyone is on the same page and contributes to a more thorough review. If a section in a technical manual is unclear, discuss it with the writer and other reviewers. Perhaps a subject matter expert can provide insights that will make the section more understandable.

➤ **Seek Input from Subject Matter Experts:** If the document covers topics outside your expertise, consult with subject matter experts to ensure the content's accuracy and completeness. For a document on cybersecurity protocols, for instance, consult with cybersecurity experts to verify the accuracy of the information.

➤ **Use a Checklist:** Create a checklist of key elements to review such as accuracy, completeness, and formatting. This ensures that you do not overlook any critical aspects. Also, maintain a checklist for the reviewers to ensure that the right people review the right sections. A checklist might include items like "verify factual accuracy," "check for grammatical errors," and "ensure compliance with style guide."

➤ **Use a Style Guide:** Utilize your organization's style guide to ensure consistent terminology, tone, and formatting. This makes the review process more efficient as both the writer and reviewer are aligned. Refer to the style guide to verify that the document uses correct abbreviations, technical jargon, and citation style.

➤ **Proofread:** Beyond checking for grammatical errors, proofreading ensures that the document effectively serves its purpose. Allocate the right team to review specific types of documents. For a user manual, ensure that the steps are easy to follow and that no ambiguities could confuse the reader.

➤ **Proof-Listening:** Sometimes hearing the document read aloud reveals issues that may not otherwise be apparent. This technique is particularly useful for catching awkward phrasing, run-on sentences, or inconsistencies in the flow of the document. Many modern text editors offer a "read aloud" feature that can be used for this purpose. If you are reviewing a complex technical guide, use this feature to listen to the document. It can help you identify areas where the language may be too complex or jargon-heavy for the intended audience. If you are reviewing a marketing brochure, listening to the text can help ensure the tone is consistent and engaging throughout the document.

➤ **Review for Accessibility:** In today's diverse environment, ensuring your document is accessible to people with disabilities is crucial. This includes checking for proper alt text for images, ensuring the document is navigable by screen readers, and checking that color schemes are legible for those with color-related vision deficiencies. Use automated tools to check if the PDF version of your document is accessible.

➤ **Verify References and Usability:** Ensure all cited references are current and accurate. Also, check for the 4 C's—Clear, Concise, Correct, Complete—to improve the document's usability. Verify that all hyperlinks are functional and lead to the correct sources. Ensure that the document is easy to navigate and understand.

➤ **Automate:** To make the review process more efficient, consider using automated tools for technical documentation. These tools can help customize checklists, notify reviewers, and inform everyone about the review status. For instance, a documentation platform can send automated email reminders to writers based on feedback in the document and allow writers to reply or approve changes with a single click.

7.3.5   What to Avoid During the Review Process

➤ **Never Rush Through the Review Process:** A hurried review can lead to overlooked errors and missed opportunities for improvement. Allocate sufficient time for a thorough review. Do not try to rush through the review of a 50-page technical document in an hour. Plan ahead and allocate enough time to scrutinize each section.

➤ **Avoid Unconstructive or Personal Criticism:** Criticism should be constructive and aimed at improving the document, not commenting about people. Provide specific suggestions for improvement. Instead of saying, "This section is unclear," suggest how it could become clearer.

➤ **Never Ignore Inconsistencies:** Consistency in terminology, formatting, and style is crucial for readability and professionalism. If abbreviations are introduced, make sure they are defined first and used consistently throughout the document.

➤ **Do not Assume Accuracy or that Others Checked It:** Unless told otherwise, always verify the information presented in the document. Assumptions can lead to the propagation of errors. If a technical specification is cited, double-check its accuracy from the original source.

➤ **Do not Overlook Compliance and Legal Requirements:** Always ensure the document adheres to relevant laws,

regulations, and guidelines. If the document discusses data handling, for instance, ensure it complies with data protection laws like GDPR.

➤ **Do not Make Unilateral Changes:** Consult the author or stakeholders before making significant changes to the document. If you think a section should be rewritten, discuss it with the author first rather than rewriting it.

➤ **Do not Ignore User Feedback:** User feedback can provide valuable insights into how the document can be improved. If multiple users point out that a certain instruction is hard to follow, it likely needs to be revised.

➤ **Do not Forget to Follow Up:** Verify that suggested changes have been implemented. Ideally, an automated check can make that easy. If you have suggested that certain technical terms be defined, check the final version to ensure these definitions have been included.

➤ **Do not Rely Solely on Automated Tools:** While automated tools can be helpful, they are not a substitute for human judgment. Always manually review the document in addition to using any automated checks. Spellcheck might not catch homophones or words used in the wrong context, so a manual review is essential for catching such errors.

➤ **Never Skip the Final Review:** The final review is crucial for catching any last-minute errors or inconsistencies. Skipping this step can result in a less-than-perfect document. Even if the document has gone through multiple rounds of review, always perform a final check before considering it complete.

7.4 Selecting Team Members for a Tactical Writing Team

Selecting team members with the right background is crucial for the success of a tactical writing project. Furthermore, it is crucial to consider both background skills and personality types when selecting potential team members. Team members should have a mix of expertise in the subject matter, technical writing skills, project management experience, and interpersonal communication skills. A well-balanced team will have a mix of skills and personality types to ensure that all aspects of the project are handled well in light of the range of skills and personalities in the expected audience.

Example: Team Selection Based on Skill Set:
- ➤ A subject matter expert in cybersecurity to ensure the content's accuracy.
- ➤ A technical writer with experience in creating user manuals.
- ➤ A project manager to keep the team on schedule.
- ➤ A graphic designer for visual elements such as charts and infographics.
- ➤ A legal advisor for compliance and intellectual property issues.

Although it is essential to have skilled, subject-based team members to ensure accuracy and appropriate understanding and communication of technical information, do not ignore personality types in the team selection process. A well-balanced team will have a mix of skills and personality types to ensure that all aspects of the project are well-handled. In chapter four we explored the use of MBTI (Meyers-Briggs Type Indicator) as a tool for audience analysis. There is also a significant amount of literature on using MBTI and temperaments in team formation, Gladis [1993], Bradley and Hebert [1997], Gorla and Lam [2004], Wilde [2008]. Let's now consider how the MBTI can help us build efficient and highly effective tactical writing teams.

7.4.1   Using the Four Temperaments for Team Organization

The four temperaments identified by the MBTI—Guardians (SJ), Artisans (SP), Idealists (NF), and Rationals (NT)—provide a layer of personality categorization that can be useful for team organization. Each temperament has its own set of characteristics that can complement the skills and knowledge needed by a tactical writing team. Let's briefly review the four temperaments, the MBTI types associated with each temperament, and a summary of the characteristics commonly associated with each type so we can understand how they apply to team assignments.

The Four Temperaments

Guardians (SJ) Guardians are practical, detail-oriented, and focused on duty and responsibility. They value tradition and are often seen as the stabilizers in a group.

MBTI Types: ISTJ, ISFJ, ESTJ, ESFJ

Artisans (SP) Artisans are spontaneous, creative, and focused on the here and now. They are adaptable and usually excel in solving immediate problems.

MBTI Types: ISTP, ISFP, ESTP, ESFP

Idealists (NF) Idealists are intuitive, empathetic, and focused on personal growth and the growth of others. They are often drawn to opportunities to help and inspire people.

MBTI Types: INFJ, INFP, ENFJ, ENFP

Rationals (NT) Rationals are logical, analytical, and focused on acquiring knowledge and competence. They enjoy dealing with complex problems and abstract thinking.

MBTI Types: INTJ, INTP, ENTJ, ENTP

7.4.2   WriteTypes Based on MBTI

The concept of "WriteType" categorizes writers based on their MBTI profiles. In this variation of MBTI use, types are mapped to "WriteType" Gladis [1993] to define four major writer subtypes:

- **Corresponders (SF - Sensor/Feelers):** Corresponders excel at interpersonal communication and are often found in public relations, customer service, and human resources roles. Their strength is in writing heartfelt customer emails, empathetic HR policies, or community outreach materials.

- **Technical Writers (ST - Sensors/Thinkers):** These detail-oriented writers excel in logical, structured environments. They are often found in roles that require technical expertise such as creating user manuals, technical guides, or process documentation.

- **Creative Writers (NF - Intuitive Feelers):** Imaginative and driven by a sense of purpose, creative writers excel in crafting narratives, storytelling, writing ad copy.

- **Analytic Writers (NT - Intuitive Thinkers):** Often found in roles that require strategic thinking, these writers are logical and analytical. They enjoy complex problem-solving and excel in writing research papers, analytical essays, and strategic plans.

7.4.3   WriteTypes vs. Temperaments

The WriteTypes are not exactly the same as temperaments but they can roughly be mapped to the four temperaments as follows:

- **Corresponders (SF):** Align with the *Artisans (SP)* temperament, which is spontaneous, sensory-oriented, and focused on the here and now.

- **Technical Writers (ST):** Resemble the *Guardians (SJ)* temperament, focused on duty, responsibility, and upholding tradition.

- **Creative Writers (NF):** Align with the *Idealists (NF)* temperament, which is enthusiastic, creative, and driven by a sense of purpose.

- **Analytic Writers (NT):** Similar to the *Rationals (NT)* temperament, which is logical and analytical, and focused on problem-solving.

Understanding both the WriteTypes and temperaments can provide a more nuanced approach to team composition and dynamics. While WriteTypes focuses on writing style and strengths, temperaments give insights into how a person interacts with others, manages stress, and approaches problem-solving.

Team 1:

Example: Team Selection Based on Combining Skills/Knowledge with Temperament

- Project Manager (ENTJ, Rational): Provides decisive leadership and direction.

- Creative Writer (ENFP, Idealist): Adds flair and creativity to the content.

- Compliance Officer (ISTJ, Guardian): Ensures all guidelines are followed.

- Editor (ESFP, Artisan): Keeps the content engaging and well-structured.

Team 2:

- Technical Writer (INTP, Rational): Ensures all data and facts are accurate.

- Project Manager (ESTJ, Guardian): Keeps the project on schedule and within budget.

- Quality Assurance (ISFP, Artisan): Checks for consistency and reliability.

- Market Analyst (ENFJ, Idealist): Keeps the project aligned with market needs.

Team 3:

- Ethical Advisor (INFJ, Idealist): Ensures the project aligns with ethical standards.

- Team Facilitator (ESFJ, Guardian): Keeps the team motivated and on track.

- Technical Writer (ISTP, Artisan): Handles the technical aspects of the content.

- Business Strategist (ENTP, Rational): Aligns the project with business goals.

7.5 Using Temperaments in Review Teams as a Balance to Writing Teams

In most cases, the composition of a writing team is largely constrained by specific skills, time requirements, and the availability of personnel, which can limit the diversity of temperaments. In such scenarios, review teams can be strategically composed to fill in the gaps and provide a more balanced approach to the project. By assigning reviewers based on their temperaments, a project lead can ensure that the review process covers a wide range of perspectives. It can also enhance skills that may be missing in the writing team. Having review team temperaments that include the expected audience temperaments is also useful.

Here are some of the Benefits of Temperament-based Review Teams:

- **Comprehensive Review**: Different temperaments focus on different aspects, ensuring a thorough review.

- **Balanced Feedback**: A review team with varied temperaments can provide feedback that is both detail-oriented and

big-picture, analytical and creative.

- **Enhanced Collaboration**: A diverse review team can stimulate better discussions and more innovative solutions.

- **Audience Alignment**: A review team is composed to better align with audience persona models to help ensure the tactical story resonates.

Color-Based Review Teams Based on Temperament and Roles

While combining temperaments with the different levels of review teams may seem overly formalized, the core idea of mixing personality types and skills for teams is what is really important. Different roles can effectively use more than one temperament when doing multi-level reviews for larger projects. Assuming we can get the right technical skills within the temperament, we might use something like the following role and temperament examples to build teams for pink, red, and gold reviews: Benefits of Temperament-based Review Teams

Pink Team Review

Content Reviewer (Guardians: ISTJ, ISFJ, ESTJ, ESFJ) focuses on the factual accuracy and completeness of thedocument.

Format Specialist (Artisans: ISTP, ISFP, ESTP, ESFP) checks the document's layout, font, and overall visual presentation.

Red Team Review

Content Reviewer (Guardians: ISTJ, ISFJ, ESTJ, ESFJ) recheck

Format Specialist (Artisans: ISTP, ISFP, ESTP, ESFP) recheck

Structure Analyst (Rationals: INTJ, INTP, ENTJ, ENTP) reviews the logical flow and organization of the document.**Language Editor** (Idealists: INFJ, INFP, ENFJ, ENFP) focuses on the document's clarity, tone, and grammatical accuracy.

Gold Team Review

Content Reviewer (Guardians: ISTJ, ISFJ, ESTJ, ESFJ) recheck **Format Specialist** (Artisans: ISTP, ISFP, ESTP, ESFP) recheck **Structure Analyst** (Rationals: INTJ, INTP, ENTJ, ENTP) recheck**Language Editor** (Idealists: INFJ, INFP, ENFJ, ENFP) Recheck

Compliance Officer (Guardians: ISTJ, ISFJ, ESTJ, ESFJ) ensures the document meets all legal and regulatory requirements.

Executive Reviewer (Rationals: INTJ, INTP, ENTJ, ENTP) provides a high-level review focusing on alignment withbusiness goals and objectives.

These examples are meant to serve as a starting point for thinking about what is needed and to give those who lack sufficient management experience a starting point on what is desirable. While some organizations may not formally discuss MBTI types in relation to team assignments, it is common to discuss what "type" of person to add to a review team to gain a greater diversity of views and better match the expected audience.

A seasoned manager with keen observational skills can often approximate the essence of temperaments without resorting to formal MBTI assessments. These managers have a knack for recognizing their team members' natural inclinations, strengths, and weaknesses. They can identify who is detail-oriented, who thrives in brainstorming sessions, who is the go-to person for ensuring compliance, and who can paint the big picture. A manager can effectively assemble a balanced team with diverse viewpoints by aligning these informal observations with the core traits of the four temperaments—Guardians, Artisans, Rationals, and Idealists. This intuitive approach, rooted in experience and observation, can often yield teams that are cohesive and effective without resorting to formal personality assessments. When they are missing something, they can then reach out to the organization for help in locating the skills and temperament needed. The key lies in the manager's ability to not only see but to understand their team members and leverage their natural tendencies for the collective good.

Four-Temperament Model for Tactical Writing Review

Our final use of temperaments in the tactical writing review process is to build off the expected audience persona model. Or, if you are not using a persona model, try to review in light of all four temperaments. If each of the temperaments is represented on your review team, the audience persona review can naturally be accomplished by the team's personal knowledge. Even so, it is worth asking each reviewer to at least run through a mental checklist of each temperament and review the document from each temperament's perspective.

By employing a four-pass model based on the four primary temperaments—Guardian, Artisan, Rational, and Idealist—a team can achieve a comprehensive and nuanced evaluation of the document. This approach helps the review team to step away from their own perspective and ensures the content is well-rounded and caters to a diverse audience with varying needs and preferences.

➤ **Guardian Pass:** This first pass focuses on reliability, factual accuracy, and thoroughness. Guardians value tradition and authority, so this review ensures that all claims are substantiated and that the document adheres to established guidelines or standards. This review will check for proper citations, factual consistency, and whether the document meets industry-specific compliance requirements.

➤ **Artisan Pass:** Artisans value experience and engagement, so this pass focuses on the document's readability, flow, and whether it engages the reader effectively. This review will evaluate the use of graphics, narrative flow, and the inclusion of engaging anecdotes or examples.

➤ **Rational Pass:** Rationals seek logic and efficiency. This pass reviews the document for logical coherence, clarity, and whether the arguments presented are well-reasoned and logically structured. The review also must verify that the data presented supports the conclusions.

➤ **Idealist Pass:** Idealists are concerned with personal growth and the greater good. This pass evaluates whether the document speaks to values, ethical considerations, or broader societal impacts related to the topic.

7.6 Expanding your "team" with GenAI/LLM-Based Bots

Incorporating a bot into your team can revolutionize the way you approach proposal development and review. While these AI tools are not truly intelligent in the human sense, they excel at language tasks, making them invaluable assets in enhancing productivity and accuracy. By leveraging Generative AI and Large Language Models (LLMs), teams can streamline their workflow, ensure compliance with guidelines, and improve the overall quality of their proposals.

A single user, equipped with a few well-chosen bots, can form a preliminary team that, while not as effective as a full team of human collaborators, can significantly enhance the initial stages of proposal development. This setup allows for a thorough preliminary review, cleaning up errors and refining content before engaging more formal review teams. By reducing the number of errors and improving the clarity of the proposal, these AI tools ensure that formal review teams can focus on higher-level feedback and strategic improvements, rather than basic corrections.

This section explores how to effectively utilize GenAI/LLM-based tools for project review using proposal reviews as the examples. The same concepts can be used in any TWWIST writing effort. The following focuses on the use of LLMs including uploading background documents, example prompts for reviews, and the strategic application of multiple bots.

7.6.1   Using Background Documents for Comprehensive Reviews

To maximize the effectiveness of GenAI/LLM-based reviewing, it is crucial to provide the AI with comprehensive background documents. These documents serve as a foundation for the AI to understand the context, requirements, and expectations of the proposal. Here's how to effectively use background documents:

- **Identifying Background Documents**: Clearly distinguish between background documents and the proposal itself. Background documents typically include:

    o   Official Call for Proposals: Outlines objectives, requirements, and evaluation criteria.

    o   Proposal Formatting Guidelines: Ensures adherence to required structure, style, and formatting rules.

    o   Past Reviews and Related Reviews: Provides insights into previous feedback, highlighting areas of strength and improvement.

    o   Any Additional Reference Materials: Such as industry reports, research papers, or organizational guidelines.

- **Loading Documents into BoodleBox**: Use BoodleBox's knowledge bank to upload and organize these documents. Label each document appropriately to ensure clarity. For instance, use tags like "Background" or "Proposal" to differentiate between types of documents.

- **Example of Specifying Documents in a Prompt:**

    o   Prompt: "Using the 'Call for Proposals' and 'Formatting Guidelines' as background, review the attached proposal draft. Focus on compliance with the outlined objectives and formatting requirements."

- **Refining Prompts with PromptBot**:

    o   Use BoodleBox's PromptBot to refine prompts for specific situations. PromptBot can help tailor prompts to ensure they are clear, specific, and aligned with the desired outcomes.

    o   Example: "PromptBot, refine this prompt for a compliance review to ensure it covers all necessary formatting and submission criteria."

By equipping the AI with these documents, teams can ensure that the reviewing process is thorough, contextually informed, and aligned with the proposal's objectives.

7.6.2   Example Prompts for Different Levels of Reviews

Utilizing example prompts tailored to different levels of reviews can enhance the feedback provided by GenAI/LLM tools. By defining specific roles and employing multiple bots, teams can obtain diverse perspectives and comprehensive evaluations. Here's how to implement this approach:

Initial Review Prompts:

- **Role**: Content Reviewer

- **Prompt::** "As an Initial Reviewer, conduct a preliminary assessment of the proposal using the attached knowledge documents to ensure foundational elements are in place. Please:

    o   Verify that all required sections are present and complete, referencing the 'Proposal

Formatting Guidelines' document.
  - Assess the clarity and coherence of the proposal's main objectives, using insights from the 'TWWIST Tactical Writing' document.
  - Identify any major gaps or inconsistencies in the content, considering past feedback from the 'Using AI to Help Students Find Their Authentic Voice' document.
  - Ensure that the proposal aligns with the basic requirements outlined in the 'Call for Proposals' document.
  - Provide feedback on the overall structure and suggest areas for improvement to enhance clarity and focus."

Mid-Level Review Prompts:

- **Role**: Compliance Specialist

- **Prompt**: "As a compliance specialist, perform a detailed evaluation of the proposal, focusing on content depth and compliance, with reference to the attached documents. Please:

  - Analyze the proposal's alignment with the funder's objectives,
  - Evaluate the logical flow and progression of arguments and evidence,
  - Check for adherence to formatting guidelines and submission requirements, referencing the 'Proposal Formatting Guidelines'.
  - Identify any sections that require further elaboration or clarification, or issues raised in using past reviews that are not addressed
  - Provide constructive feedback on how to strengthen the proposal's narrative and compliance with guidelines."

Final Review Prompts:

- **Role**: Strategic Advisor

- **Prompt**: "As a strategic advisor, evaluate the proposal for its alignment with the funder's objectives. Please:

  - Analyze how well the proposal's goals and objectives match those of the funding agency.
  - Assess the clarity and relevance of the proposed methods and outcomes in achieving these objectives.
  - Identify any gaps or misalignments between the proposal's aims and the funder's priorities.
  - Suggest improvements to enhance the proposal's strategic alignment with the funder's mission and goals.
  - Ensure that the proposal effectively communicates its potential impact and significance in the context of the funder's objectives."

Some proposal have specialized requirements, e.g. a commercalizatoin plan, which can call for a sepcalized review pass like this:

Prompt: "As a Commercialization Analyst, review the proposal to assess its commercial potential and competitive positioning. Please:

  - Evaluate the proposed idea's market potential and identify any unique selling points.
  - Analyze the competitive landscape and assess how the proposal differentiates itself from existing solutions.
  - Identify potential barriers to market entry and suggest strategies to overcome them.
  - Assess the feasibility of the commercialization plan, including timelines and resource

requirements.

- o Provide recommendations to strengthen the proposal's commercial appeal and competitive advantage."

These prompts are designed to guide reviewers in conducting thorough and focused evaluations of proposals, ensuring they meet compliance standards, align with funder objectives, and demonstrate strong commercial potential.

- **Using Multiple Bots**:

  - o Deploy different bots for each role to leverage their unique capabilities. For instance, use a bot specialized in content analysis for the initial review, a compliance-focused bot for the mid-level review, and a strategic analysis bot for the final review.

  - o Encourage collaboration between bots by having them analyze each other's feedback, ensuring a well-rounded and comprehensive evaluation.

By employing these example prompts and strategically using multiple bots, teams can enhance the depth and quality of their proposal reviews, leading to more polished and competitive submissions.

7.6.3. Evaluating Improvements from Past Reviews

To continuously improve the quality of proposals, it's essential to evaluate how current submissions have improved from past reviews. Here's how to incorporate this evaluation into the review process:

- **Comparative Analysis**:

  - o Use past reviews as a benchmark to assess current proposals. Identify areas where improvements have been made and areas that still require attention.

  - o Example Prompt: "Based on past reviews, evaluate how this proposal has improved in terms of clarity, coherence, and compliance. Highlight any persistent issues."

- **Feedback Loop**:

  - o Create a feedback loop where reviewers can provide insights on how well the proposal has addressed previous critiques. This encourages a culture of continuous improvement and learning.

  - o Example Prompt: "Reviewers, please provide feedback on how well this proposal addresses past critiques. Are there areas that still need improvement?"

- **Incorporating Reviewer Insights**:

  - o Use insights from reviewers to refine future proposals. Encourage reviewers to suggest actionable steps for improvement based on their analysis.

  - o Example Prompt: "Based on your review, what specific steps can be taken to further enhance the proposal's quality and competitiveness?"

By systematically evaluating improvements from past reviews, teams can ensure that their proposals are continuously evolving and meeting the highest standards of quality and compliance.

7.7 Troubleshooting Team Writing Issues

Team writing introduces complex writing issues that do not arise when one is working alone. Team dynamics can be complex, and problems are almost inevitable. But the challenges of team writing are nothing new and there are tried and true solutions to these challenges. The following guide to troubleshooting common issues that may arise during the tactical writing process can help a team work efficiently, effectively, and harmoniously.

7.7.1 Dealing with Changing "Voice" in Team Efforts

Maintaining a consistent "voice" can be particularly challenging in all-in-parallel writing collaborations. Sometimes, a change in voice is expected or even desired, e.g., the budget section could be quite different from the technical section. However, overall changes in voice that are not tactically considered should be avoided. Here are some strategies to ensure uniformity in tone and style across different sections written by different team members.

➤ **Establish a Style Guide:** Create a style guide that outlines the desired tone, style, and voice for the project. Share this guide with all team members. Many companies have official style guides or may use past successful work as a template, which is an unofficial style guide. If the project requires a formal tone or special terminology, specify this in the style guide and provide examples.

➤ **Regular Check-ins:** Schedule regular meetings to review the work and ensure alignment with the established voice. Use these meetings to read excerpts aloud to see if they meet the team's expectations.

➤ **Peer Reviews:** Create a peer review checklist that includes a point on voice consistency and encourage team members to review each other's sections for voice consistency.

➤ **Voice Editor Role:** Assign one person the role of "voice editor" with the responsibility to ensure that the entire document has a consistent voice. The voice editor generally does not need the technical expertise to have written the document but must have enough understanding to edit for consistency and have a good grasp of the desired tone and style.

➤ **Voice in Reviews:** In the red and gold reviews, ask for explicit feedback on changes in voice and, if needed, conduct a final review focusing solely on voice consistency across all sections. It can be helpful to use text-to-speech software to listen to the document, as inconsistencies in voice are often more noticeable when heard aloud.

7.7.2 Problems with Revision/Editing

Some people are good writers as individuals but struggle with a team. This can lead to less obvious problems that take good communication to resolve. Here are some issues/suggestions.

➤ **People not Open to Revisions:** Foster a culture of constructive feedback and continuous improvement. Explaining how you understand it, or asking questions can prompt the writer to see the need.

➤ **My Work Is Being Destroyed:** Discuss the changes and seek to understand their rationale. This is one place where version control can allow one to quickly recover work.

➤ **Inadequate Feedback:** Ask for specific, constructive feedback.

➤ **Unsure How to Give Good Feedback:** Use guidelines or templates for providing constructive feedback.

7.7.3 Problems with Showing Up and Turning in Work

Team members can be overworked or not motivated, resulting in a range of problems. Here are some classics and ideas on how to address them:

➤ **A Teammate Misses a Meeting:** Address the absence directly but diplomatically. Check if the absence was due to an emergency and briefly recap what was discussed during the meeting.

➤ **A Teammate Misses a Deadline:** Discuss the reasons for the delay and re-evaluate the timeline. Make sure the team is aligned on the importance of deadlines.

➤ **A Teammate Turns in Incomplete Work:** Identify the gaps and assign them as action items. Revisit the project scope to ensure everyone understands their responsibilities.

➤ **A Teammate Turns in Poor Quality Work:** Address the issue openly and constructively. Consider additional training or resources.

➤ **A Teammate Disappears Completely:** Try to contact them through multiple channels. If unresponsive, redistribute their tasks among the team.

7.7.4   Problems with Personal Interactions

Personalities don't always get along. Here are some common problems and some suggestions:

➤ **My Team Does not Trust Me to Do Good Work:** Openly discuss any concerns and take steps to rebuild trust, such as by consistently delivering quality work.

➤ **My Team Is Not Listening to Me:** Assert your points clearly and ask for feedback. Ensure that team meetings provide a forum for all voices.

➤ **Other Team Members Are not Committed:** Address the issue directly and discuss the importance of commitment to the project's success.

➤ **Disturbing or Demeaning Behavior:** Report the issue to higher-ups or human resources and address it directly if appropriate.

➤ **Excessive Criticism:** Seek to understand the root of the criticism and address it constructively.

7.8 Final Tips for Effective Tactical Team Writing

Much of this chapter was about the team, its roles, assignments, and reviews. However, teams are made up of individuals working together for a common goal. This means that each member of a tactical writing team— not just the team lead—has responsibilities to the team and to its individual members. The following guidelines, when practiced by each team member, will facilitate a satisfying and successful team effort:

➤ **Be Clear on Objectives:** Understand the writing project's goals, objectives, and processes. Knowing what the team aims to achieve will help you contribute more effectively. If the project is to write a research paper, for example, ensure you understand the thesis statement and the key arguments to be presented.

➤ **Communicate Regularly:** Maintain open and regular communication among team members. This means active listening and proactively addressing potential issues. Hold regular meetings (daily/weekly, depending on schedule) to discuss progress and address any issues. But remember, you do not have to wait for a meeting to bring up a potential issue; if a meeting is needed to resolve it, suggest one.

➣ **Communicate Openly:** Open and honest communication is crucial for resolving conflicts, brainstorming ideas, and keeping everyone on the same page. Use team meetings to discuss progress, share ideas, and clarify any misunderstandings. If you see something, say something.

➣ **Be Open to Feedback:** Constructive criticism helps improve work quality. Be open to receiving feedback and willing to revise your contributions. Help create an environment where constructive feedback is encouraged by providing it to others and thanking those who give it. During peer reviews, listen carefully to feedback and ask clarifying questions if you do not understand a point. Think deeply about the feedback you get to improve the document and to improve your involvement in the team-writing process. Make it clear you are using the feedback given. Use comments and track changes for transparent and constructive feedback.

➣ **Contribute Fairly:** Every team member should contribute to the writing, research, and editing processes. Don't leave all the work to a few individuals. If you are strong in research but weak in writing, offer to take on more research tasks while collaborating with a stronger writer for the write-up.

➣ **Show Empathy:** Empathy can go a long way in building a cohesive team. Understand that every team member has their own strengths, weaknesses, and circumstances. If a team member is struggling with a particular task, offer your assistance or work together to find a solution.

➣ **Maintain Professionalism:** Always maintain a professional attitude. This includes being respectful, punctual and committed to the team's goals. Avoid negative or derogatory language and respect the opinions and contributions of all team members.

➣ **Stay Organized:** Keep all your research, drafts, and other materials well-organized. This helps you and makes it easier for team members to understand your work. Using a shared folder on Google Drive or Dropbox allows all team members to easily find and access project materials.

➣ **Revise and Edit:** Allocate time for multiple revisions and personal editing rounds. After the first draft is complete, schedule at least two rounds of revisions before finalizing the document.

➣ **Use Collaborative Tools:** Utilize collaborative writing tools that allow multiple people to work on the document simultaneously. There are many such tools, with more in development. While these tools may take a little time to learn, they have many powerful features and benefits that will save time in the long run. Use Google Docs, Office 365, or similar platforms for real-time collaboration with edits and comment tracking.

➣ **Leverage Version Control:** Use a version control system to manage different document versions. This ensures that everyone is working on the most recent version and allows for easy tracking of changes. Some, like Google Docs, allow formal versions built in, while others can track changes and merge versions so you can save many versions and merge parts. By having a version, you can be free to try changes and quickly revert to a previous version if it does not work. If nothing else, save the file with timestamps or version numbers in the file name. Use tools like Git to maintain a repository of document versions. If a controversial change is made, the team can easily revert to a previous version while the issue is discussed.

➣ **Ask Questions:** Do not hesitate to ask questions when you are uncertain about the project's objectives, the target audience, or specific tasks. Avoid making assumptions. Asking questions clarifies your understanding and prevents mistakes. For example, if you are unsure about the document's tone, ask the team for clarification and get it right the first time.

➢ **Be Adaptable:** Flexibility is key in team projects. Be prepared to adapt your role or approach based on the team's needs. If a team member is unable to complete a section on time due to unforeseen circumstances, be willing to step in and help.

➢ **Be Self-Aware:** Know your strengths and weaknesses as a writer and communicator. Leverage your strengths and work to improve in your areas of weakness. If you are good at research but weak in proofreading, for instance, consider pairing with a team member who complements your skills.

➢ **Be Reliable and Meet Deadlines:** Meet your deadlines and produce quality work. Use a personal or team calendar to keep track of deadlines for drafts, revisions, and final submissions. If you commit to finishing a section by a certain date, ensure you do so. Your reliability in meeting deadlines ensures that you are not holding up the team's progress and builds trust among team members.

➢ **Celebrate Small Wins:** Celebrating small achievements can boost team morale and motivation. It is not just about the end goal, the journey matters, too. After successfully completing a challenging section, take a moment in the next team meeting to acknowledge the hard work that went into it. It costs you nothing to tell others they did good work and offer small praises.

In tactical writing, the adage "two heads are better than one" takes on a new level of significance. As we conclude this chapter, it should be clear that writing teams are not a passing fad or a luxury; they are often necessary for tackling complex writing projects that require diverse skills, perspectives, and expertise. The collaborative synergy of a well-formed team can produce a final product that is accurate, comprehensive, and rich in quality and effectiveness.

Although tactical writing teams are generally formed according to the mix of skill sets needed for the project, forming a team is not just about technical skills; it is also about creating a balanced group dynamic. When forming a team an understanding of personality types, often categorized through frameworks like MBTI or the Four Temperaments, can be invaluable. Knowing each team member's natural inclinations and strengths assists in assigning roles that people are naturally suited for, thereby increasing efficiency and harmony within the team.

Once the team is formed, the work is far from over. The review process serves as the backbone of quality assurance.

Color-coded reviews, a standard practice in many industries, provide a structured approach to iterative improvement that ensures the document is compliant, compelling, and complete at each stage. Each color— blue, pink, red, green, and gold—serves as a milestone, guiding the team closer to a polished final product.

The team-based tactical writing experience is a multifaceted strategy designed to optimize both the process and the final product. It is a dynamic interplay of skills, personalities, structured reviews, and continuous improvement. When executed correctly, it results in work that is not just complete but exemplary—a testament to the collective intelligence and effort of the team.

The collaborative environment of tactical team writing is also fertile ground for learning—be it through asking questions, giving and receiving feedback, or simply observing the work styles of peers. Being part of a team writing process can facilitate each member's personal growth and improvement as it provides the opportunity to refine their skills, expand their knowledge base, and become a more effective communicator.

1) **Team Writing:** *Collective efforts of individuals working together on a written project for an organization's benefit.*

2) **Team Charter:** *A document outlining team goals, commitments, and conflict resolution guidelines.*

3) **Team Objectives:** *SMART objectives defining what constitutes success for a team.*

4) **Personal Goals/Objectives:** *Individual team members' personal learning or career objectives.*

5) **RACI Matrix:** *Approach for assigning elements of a project based using a Responsible, Accountable, Consulted, and Informed matrix for clarifying roles and responsibilities.*

6) **Scope Creep:** *Uncontrolled changes or growth in project scope.*

7) **Budget Overruns:** *Exceeding the planned budget for a project.*

8) **Milestones:** *Significant points or achievements within a project timeline.*

9) **Kickoff Meeting:** *A meeting to unveil and discuss project plans and assignments.*

10) **GANTT Chart:** *A visual representation of project tasks, their timing, and those responsible.*

11) **Stakeholders:** *Individuals or groups with an interest in the project's outcome.*

12) **Project Management Software:** *Tools for tracking tasks, deadlines, and project progress.*

13) **Slack:** *Additional time or flexibility built into a schedule to account for delays.*

14) **Constructive Feedback:** *Feedback aimed at improving the quality of a document while maintaining a positive tone.*

15) **Bad News Sandwich:** *A feedback technique that begins with positive feedback, followed by constructive criticism, and ends with positive feedback.*

16) **Blue Team Review:** *A blue team review is an early-stage internal review of a document or project. It typically involves members of the core team assessing the expected content's accuracy, completeness, and alignment with project goals.*

17) **Pink Team Review:** *A pink team review is a mid-stage internal review that focuses on evaluating the document's reliability, factual accuracy, visual presentation, and overall coherence. It ensures that the document is on target and suggests adjustments as necessary.*

18) **Red Team Review:** *A red team review is a comprehensive internal review aimed at assessing logical flow, argument coherence, clarity, tone, and grammatical accuracy. It serves as a critical evaluation to improve the document's quality.*

19) **Green Team Review:** *A green team review is a comprehensive internal review of the financial aspects of the proposal addressing both realism and compliance.*

20) **Gold Team Review:** *A gold team review is a final-stage internal review that rechecks all aspects of the document, including reliability, visual presentation, logical flow, clarity, compliance with legal requirements, and alignment with business goals. It ensures the document's readiness for external distribution.*

21) **Four Temperaments:** *A personality categorization of personality types into Guardians, Artisans, Idealists, and Rationals, which can be useful for assigning people to tactical writing and review teams*

7.10   Other Terms

1) **SMART Objective:** *A goal-setting framework that helps individuals or teams define and achieve clear and meaningful objectives. The term SMART is an acronym that stands for Specific, Measurable, Achievable, Relevant, and Time-bound.*

2) **Threshold Skill:** *Writing ability considered essential for employment and promotion.*

3) **Self-Managing Teams:** *Teams relying on their members to manage themselves and work independently.*

4) **Active Learning:** *Educational aspect of collaborative writing, where team members actively learn from each other's expertise.*

5) **Organizational Growth:** *Impact of team members' contributions and collaboration on an organization's growth.*

6) **Collaborative Writing:** *Practice of multiple individuals working together on a written project.*

7) **Scheduling:** *Planning and managing task schedules within the context of team writing.*

8) **Late Work:** *Handling missed project deadlines and potential consequences.*

9) **Unacceptable Work:** *Work that does not meet the guidelines for maintaining quality.*

10) **Workload Balancing:** *Ensuring that tasks are evenly distributed among team members.*

11) **Team Review:** *The collaborative evaluation of written documents to ensure quality and precision.*

12) **Review Levels/Colors:** *Different stages or levels of document review, often designated by colors such as red team review.*

13) **Responsible (R):** *Individuals actively working on completing writing tasks within a project.*

14) **Accountable (A):** *Individuals responsible for the overall success and completion of the writing project.*

15) **Consulted (C):** *Experts whose opinions are sought, and whose feedback is crucial for the project.*

16) **Informed (I):** *Individuals who need to be kept informed but are not directly involved in decision-making.*

17) **Personality Types:** *Individual characteristics and traits that influence how team members work together.*

18) **Subject Matter Expert (SME):** *A person with in-depth knowledge in a specific field or domain.*

19) **Legal Advisor:** *A person who provides guidance on compliance and legal matters.*

20) **Diversity of Ideas:** *Advantage of team writing with team members contributing diverse perspectives and ideas.*

21) **Technological Advantages:** *Benefits of modern collaboration tools and technologies in team writing.*

22) **Leadership and Team Skills:** *Opportunity for team members to develop skills and leadership roles within a writing team.*

23) **Scheduling:** *The process of creating a timeline for project tasks and deadlines.*

24) **Content Review:** *Verification of the document's accuracy, completeness, and relevance.*

25) **Inconsistencies:** *Discrepancies or variations in terminology, formatting, or style.*

26) **Accuracy Verification:** *The act of confirming the correctness of information presented in a document.*

27) **User Feedback:** *Insights and suggestions provided by users to enhance the document.*

28) **Team Members Selection:** *The process of choosing individuals with the right background and skills for a project.*

29) **Background Skills:** *Expertise and knowledge possessed by team members relevant to the project.*

30) **Technical Writer:** *Someone skilled in creating user manuals and technical documentation.*

31) **Project Manager:** *A role responsible for keeping the team on schedule and within budget.*

32) **Graphic Designer:** *An individual who specializes in creating visual elements like charts and infographics.*

33) **Culture of Continuous Improvement:** *A workplace environment that encourages ongoing learning and enhancement of skills.*

34) **Format Review:** *Ensuring consistency and readability in terms of fonts, spacing, margins, and page numbering.*

35) **Structure Review:** *Assessing the organization and logical flow of the document, including headings and subheadings.*

36) **Language Review:** *Reviewing the clarity, conciseness, and appropriateness of language for the target audience.*

37) **Compliance Review:** *Confirming that the document adheres to relevant regulations, standards, and guidelines.*

38) **References Review:** *Checking that all references are accurate and up-to-date.*

39) **Consistency Review:** *Ensuring uniformity in terminology, formatting, and style throughout the document.*

40) **Constructive Criticism:** *Feedback that aims to improve the quality of a document or work.*

41) **Compliance:** *Adherence to relevant laws, regulations, and guidelines.*

42) **Unilateral Changes:** *Making significant alterations to a document without consulting the author or stakeholders.*

8 Tactical Writing of a Winning Proposal

"Although a great proposal by itself seldom wins a deal, a bad proposal can definitely lose one."

-Tom Sant, Persuasive Business Proposals: Writing to Win More Customers, Clients, & Contracts (2012)

We will now shift gears from our exploration of the overall TWWIST process and focus on an application of tactical writing that is all but indispensable in the professional realm: developing a proposal. In the real world, a well-crafted proposal can be the deciding factor in securing funding, landing a client, or setting the stage for a groundbreaking project. While the TWWIST framework has illuminated the tactical approach to various forms of writing, including short examples for proposals, an effective proposal calls for a unique blend of these techniques and requires the addition of many specialized elements. This is not to downplay the core writing that is, by far, the most important aspect of proposal writing.

However, proposals generally require elements beyond the "story," such as creating a budget or schedule, that don't quite suit storytelling techniques. This does not mean that TWWIST is not applicable or helpful in developing these parts of the proposal. In fact, the foundational TWWIST mindset of audience analysis, opportunity discovery, well-defined objectives, and funder alignment is essential in adding non-story elements to a proposal with strategic precision. While these items are not likely to lead directly to a win, bad execution in adding these elements will quickly kill an otherwise well-written proposal.

For this reason, this chapter will hone in on adding the nuts and bolts that go into the additional elements of proposal writing. It will serve as an initial guide to the added complexities of proposal development. We will not just talk theory here. Expect actionable tips and real-world examples centered around setting clear objectives, crafting a detailed Statement of Work(SOW), establishing a realistic schedule, and formulating a transparent budget to guide you through the maze of these additional proposal requirements. Consider this your first step on the road to writing proposals that do not just meet the mark but truly make an impact.

8.1 TWWIST and Beyond: Adding Required Elements to the Proposal Story

When preparing any proposal, whether it is for a government grant or a business opportunity, the writer(s) must meet a unique set of guidelines and requirements. Understanding the particular demands and expectations of each kind of proposal is not merely a bureaucratic exercise but a critical aspect of your proposal strategy. Navigating the labyrinth of distinct (and often inflexible) guidelines and aligning your proposal to the specific agency's unique needs, expectations, and formal requirements is crucial for success. The following generalities provide an overview of what a proposal writer can expect to encounter, but one must dig into the particulars for the specific proposal you are preparing.

➤ The **National Science Foundation (NSF)** generally emphasizes scientific innovation and broader societal impacts, requiring proposers to articulate how their project will contribute to both. The NSF also requires many specialized forms for the proposal.

➤ The **National Institutes of Health (NIH)** focuses heavily on biomedical research, requiring detailed methodology sections, especially when human subjects are involved. Specialized forms and presentation styles are generally required.

➤ The **Department of Defense (DoD)** and its sub-agencies such as the **Defense Advanced Research Projects Agency (DARPA)** often have stringent proposal preparation requirements. They also use a lexicon focused on their mission, including rapid technology development and deployment considerations.

Many government economic development proposals, such as those from state agencies or the federal **Small Business Innovation Research(SBIR)**, require a detailed commercialization plan and/or measuring economic impact, with explicit guidelines for these proposal elements.

In a **Business-to-Business (B2B)** context, proposals must demonstrate a clear understanding of the client company's needs and offer customized solutions frequently focusing on scalability and integration with existing workflows.

Business loan proposals, typically submitted to banks or other financial institutions, require a strong emphasis on financial stability, profitability projections, and risk mitigation strategies.

Unlike the above types of funding, **philanthropic grants** often come from private foundations or individual donors focused on helping the receiving organization. This is a very broad and varied category of proposals as entities have unique criteria, priorities, and administrative structures, which makes them a different ball game altogether.

8.2 Clarity on What a Proposal Is Not!

At its core, a well-crafted proposal is a tactical story that aims to persuade the client that your organization is the best fit for solving their problem. It outlines how your organization can deliver value to the customer's organization and help them meet a specific need. It serves as a compelling argument for why your approach is the most effective and efficient way to meet that need. It should be a focused, strategic document that offers a comprehensive, compelling argument substantiated with facts, figures, and a clear alignment with the client's goals and needs.

However, there is a balance between a tactical story with required data—a proposal—and other types of project and business documents. It is imperative that we understand what a proposal *is not* in order to avoid common misconceptions that can lead to failure. A proposal is:

Not a Price Quote: Although a proposal often includes cost estimates, it is not merely a listing of prices for services or products. It provides context, justification, and a strategic overview that a simple price quote cannot offer.

Not a Contract: A proposal is a formal offer awaiting acceptance but should not be confused with a binding contract. It becomes a contract only when both parties agree to the terms outlined. However, because a proposal can quickly become a contract, many organizations have significant legal reviews and processes that can delay the proposal if not addressed early.

Not a Scope of Work (SOW): While a proposal may contain elements similar to a SOW, it goes beyond simply listing tasks. It argues for the *why*, *how*, and *what* behind those tasks.

Not a Project Plan: A proposal may lay the groundwork for a project plan but it is not a substitute for one. Project plans are more detailed and usually developed separately, often after a proposal has been accepted, to avoid wasting time on a plan that might change.

Not a Bill of Materials: Although a proposal may list resources or materials required, it is not merely an inventory or bill of materials. A proposal should show how these materials contribute to solving the client's problem.

Not a Company History: While background information can be useful, a proposal is not the place for an extensive history of your company. Keep the focus on the client's needs and how you can meet them. Include history only when requested or needed to establish credibility to deliver.

➤ **Not a Sales Sheet:** Although persuasive elements are essential, a proposal is not primarily a promotional document. It must be rooted in facts and research, clearly aligned with the client's objectives, and filled with compelling arguments supported by evidence.

Personal Story: A Tale of Two Proposals

Even before I launched the Best of Innovation program, I knew a class in proposal writing was a critical element. Based on my experience in my own companies, I also knew that many faculty would oppose it, saying, "They're not successful at grants, why should we think students could be?" I knew that students would resist it too, saying, "Oh no, we can't do that." But I am here to say, "Yes! Students, students like you, can be successful at proposal writing."

During my first year at the University of Colorado Colorado Springs (UCCS), I chose two undergraduate students who seemed reasonably talented—one junior and one freshman—and said, "We're going to write grant proposals together."

At first, as expected, felt they couldn't do this. I said, "We'll mentor you through the process." I found a local startup that needed proposal help (I didn't want to use my own companies due to conflict of interest concerns). This local company had a potential interest in some SBIR/STTR topics and wanted funding to build their technology. So we worked together. The company didn't have a strong direction or proposal process, so I mentored both the company and the students through it.

Along the way, I could see the students' confidence growing. Armed with what I was teaching them, they realized they could actually do this! We wrote two successful proposals that year, and I used that experience as part of the story for building up the Bachelor of Innovation (BI) degree program at UCCS. However, there were concerns raised by faculty, as I pushed the BI, that the students' success might have largely depended on the quality of the company.

While I disagreed, I took the argument to heart and developed a strategy to show that student-led startups could be successful at writing proposals to help fund their companies. Our very first BI graduate did exactly that. In his senior year, we came up with an idea for a company that he was passionate about. We wrote an NSF SBIR for which he would be the PI after graduating with his undergraduate degree. He was going to lead a company and the proposal effort to launch it. The company would develop technology to help improve compliance and recovery for people recovering from drug and alcohol abuse. I did not "lead" the proposal effort but challenged the student to follow the process he learned and lead his team through it.

Again, the proposal effort was successful. It showed that students could not only work on proposals but also lead a proposal and a company successfully. This was a student's first attempt at a company, and winning the grant proposal gave him $100,000 in funding to start and prove the idea. While the phase one experiment did not find the technology effective enough to proceed to product development, the team obtained the funding to develop/evaluate it and learned some great lessons. By following a good process, they were able to get started without taking on debt.

I have to temper this story with the fact that we've also seen many unsuccessful proposals, and I've seen students get discouraged. Proposals are a bit of a numbers game—you might need many to win. However, the fact that undergraduate students can not only participate but lead such a team effort successfully should give other students the confidence to step out of the shadows and onto the court. Proposals are a tactical writing effort that you can master. Tell yourself, "I can do this. I *will* do this." Then go for it.

8.3 Funder Goals: A Tactical Approach to Objectives and Alignment

Navigating the labyrinth of proposal writing begins with a crystal-clear understanding of your objectives and those of your potential funder. This dual-awareness is not just a nice-to-have; it is a must-have. The objectives you set function like the coordinates in a GPS, providing direction and defining success. Knowing the point to where the *funder* will arrive is critical in guiding *you* on the path to get them there.

8.3.1 Articulating Your Objectives

One of the first steps of the TWWIST framework is always setting your objectives. Your objectives are critical for the tactical process and also set the stage for a compelling proposal where you and the funder are protagonists in a story of success and impact. Also articulating your objectives can help in checking the alignment of your objectives with those of the funder.

➤ **SMART Framework:** Always formulate your objectives as SMART—Specific, Measurable, Achievable, Relevant, and Time-bound. This framework ensures that you are realistic and accountable in what you aim to accomplish.

➤ **Separate Specificity:** Before you put pen to paper or fingers to keyboard, articulate the specific impact you wish to make, assuming the project is funded. The specified impact is not the same as the proposal objectives. Having specific, separate objectives for the desired impact and for the proposal gives you a clearer pathway and allows for more effective measurement of outcomes.

➤ **Deciphering Funder Objectives:** At this point in the proposal process, the most critical objectives are not yours but the funder's:

1) **Funder Research:** The funder is now the audience so researching the funder is essential. Thoroughly investigate the funder's mission statement, prior projects they have supported, and any guidelines or criteria they have published. This research sets the foundation for your alignment strategy.

2) **Echoing Themes:** After understanding the funder's goals, identify themes and keywords that resonate with their objectives. For better alignment, echo these themes in your own objectives. Even if your company has its own terminology, use mostly the funder's terminology. It is good to have one section where you relate your terminology and theirs just in case they see other materials (with different terminology) from your company.

3) **Preliminary Outreach:** Direct contact with the funder is not always permitted, but it can provide invaluable insights if allowed. Consider sending a well-crafted email or making a phone call to clarify any ambiguous points in the funder's guidelines. This point of contact can set you apart and enhance your understanding of their objectives. Some funders expect you to try to contact them; if you do not, it can come across as not caring about their views.

4) **Investigating Previously Funded Proposals:** One highly effective way to align your objectives with those of the funder is to study proposals they have already funded. Many agencies make abstracts, sometimes even full proposals, publicly available for transparency. These can serve as invaluable resources to understand the kind of work the funder supports, the level of detail they expect in a proposal, and the key themes that resonate with them. Analyzing these documents can help you tailor your proposal's objectives, scope, and emphasis to better align with the funder's interests and priorities.

➤ **Resource Alignment:** After setting three sets of objectives—for the proposal, project, and funder—immediately consider whether they align with your available resources. A tactical objective must always be anchored to an actionable outcome—what do you hope to achieve that aligns with your capabilities and resources?

8.3.2 Adjusting Alignment for Tactical Precision

Your objectives are probably not the same as the funder's goals. Aligning your objectives with your funder's goals is not a linear, one-off task but a dynamic, iterative process. Again, the funder's objectives are what will drive their decision process, so understanding and alignment is critical. Tactical writing involves clarity, persuasiveness, and the agility to pivot and adapt as you gain more insights into how you might deliver what you think the funder seeks.

➤ **Gap Analysis:** Once you have drafted your objectives and understood the funder's objectives, perform a gap analysis. Are there areas where your aims and those of the funder diverge? Identify these and think of ways to bridge them. If your team has gaps in what it can provide, can you identify partners to help fill those gaps?

➤ **Objective Refinement:** Make fine-grained adjustments to your objectives to fit more snugly with the funder's aims. Always ensure these are genuine adjustments and not forced fits.

➤ **Iterative Review:** Alignment is not a set-and-forget task. It is an ongoing process. Continually revisit your objectives, especially as you develop other proposal sections, to ensure they remain aligned with the funder's goals.

8.4 Crafting a Tactical Budget: The Financial Roadmap of Your Proposal

Crafting a tactically sound budget involves much more than arithmetic. Like any tactical writing effort, it demands a keen understanding of the project's priorities and a pathway for achieving the project goals. It also requires alignment with the funder's objectives and a strategy to convey the value of the project to the funder. In this essential role, the budget serves as the financial roadmap for your proposal—a detailed and strategic plan that shows the funder how you will allocate resources to meet your objectives.

In a proposal, money not only talks—it shouts. A meticulously prepared budget serves as the financial embodiment, the financial narrative, if you will, of your proposal's ambitions and feasibility. As funding limits the scope of what can be done and who will be involved, the budget is one of the most critical added elements of the proposal. Thus it is important to start the budgeting process very early and ensure it is deeply integrated with the early story formulation.

You set the stage for a well-balanced, realistic, and compelling budget narrative by strategically estimating your budget limit and expenditures for key items. This approach ensures your tactical story aligns with your team's capabilities as well as the funding agency's expectations, which optimizes your chances of proposal success. We will now provide an overview of key practices for constructing a realistic and compelling budget and offer guidance on how to present your financial needs in a way that engenders trust and demonstrates your team's competency.

"The budget is not just a collection of numbers, but an expression of our values and aspirations."

-Jack Lew

8.4.1 High-level view of significant budget elements

Dealing with proposal budgets is an iterative process, so before diving into the details, let's start with a high-level overview of the core elements of a proposal budget. These elements may vary depending on the agency, but the primary components are generally consistent. Most parts are "direct costs," which are those things directly needed to do the project.

The most significant direct cost is typically personnel, which often includes associated fringe benefits, such as Social Security in the United States or health and medical benefits. Organizations usually apply a fringe benefit charge on top of personnel costs, making these two items the largest portion of the budget. Another major related budget element can be subcontracts. In some cases, subcontracts can exceed personnel costs because the subcontractor takes on the personnel expenses, receiving a substantial portion of the budget.

Next are smaller expenses like travel, materials, and supplies. These are distinct from equipment costs, which typically include higher-value items typically greater than $5,000.

Another significant expense category is indirect costs, sometimes referred to as general and administrative charges. These costs cover various organizational expenses that support the project indirectly, such as building use, electricity, operational accounting, and other overhead items. These costs are added to the budget to ensure the organization can sustain its operations while supporting the project.

Now that we have a high-level understanding of the budget components, let's delve into how to balance the items we can include in a budget with the project's scope of work.

8.4.2   Estimating Budget Funding Limits: Aligning Program Specifications with Team Scope

One of the pivotal initial steps in crafting a tactical budget involves estimating the total funding limits based on the program specifications provided by the funding agency. This estimate serves as a boundary within which your story must unfold, ensuring that the scope and ambitions of your project are well-matched with the available resources. Consider the key steps:

➤ **Analyzing Program Budget Guidelines:** Start by thoroughly reviewing any budget guidelines or financial constraints outlined in the Funding Opportunity Announcement (FOA). Agencies usually indicate a total program budget and sometimes even the expected number of awards. Divide the total program budget by the number of expected awards to get an average award size that will serve as a guiding limit.

➤ **Balancing Scope with Budget:** The estimated funding limit serves as a narrative constraint, requiring you to prioritize tasks and objectives that can realistically be achieved within that financial boundary. A more constrained budget might require a more focused set of objectives, while a larger budget might allow for greater scope and innovation.

➤ **Team Size and Experience:** The experience of your project team impacts not just the costs, it also impacts the credibility of your proposal. A team with a track record of completing projects within budget may have a strategic advantage in the review process. Highlighting your team's experience in the proposal can help justify a higher budget request. Balancing the budget with team size and experience is a nuanced endeavor. Your core team may lack some of the skills necessary to complete the project, or you may find that your initial team is either too small or too large to match the expected budget size.

➤ **Adding Partners:** If your initial estimate shows that the project budget will be substantially larger than what your core team would typically require, consider bringing in external partners. Collaborators can add value through specialized expertise, facilities, or geographic reach. However, additional partners also mean additional administrative overhead and complexity. Always weigh the potential benefits against the added complexity and articulate each partner's added value in your tactical story.

➢ **Leading vs Subcontracting:** Another strategic decision is whether to lead the proposal or to join as a subcontractor. Leading the project generally allows for greater control over the project narrative and budget but also comes with higher administrative responsibilities. Subcontracting can be a way to participate in larger projects that align with your objectives without taking on the mantle of leadership. Each role has different budgetary implications; being a subcontractor usually means preparing a budget that will be part of a larger proposal, while leading requires integrating subcontractor budgets into your own. Specify the role you are taking on and make sure your budget narrative accurately reflects it.

➢ **Assessing Expertise:** A team's expertise significantly impacts labor costs. A more experienced team, while commanding higher salaries, may offer efficiencies that make the higher labor cost justifiable. Be sure to present a balanced view, showcasing how the team's experience and capabilities offer value for money and how this aligns with your project's objectives.

➢ **Preliminary Cost Assessment:** Before delving into detailed budgeting, conduct a preliminary cost assessment involving key team members to ensure the project scope aligns well with the estimated funding limits. This early-stage reality check can save considerable time and effort later in the proposal process.

8.4.3 Task-Allocation Budgeting and Tactical Story Integration

Program managers are looking for projects that contribute to their program's success and will make their job easier. A well-prepared budget signals to the program manager that you have thoroughly thought through the project and, ideally, that you are well-equipped to deliver on it. Conversely, a sloppy, incomplete, or unrealistic budget could indicate that you are likely to encounter difficulties in meeting program objectives, thus reducing your chance of success and possibly making the program manager's job more challenging.

Despite the critical importance of realistic and well-prepared budgets to funding project managers, budget alignment and realism are among the most overlooked elements in proposal preparation. From a proposal success standpoint, far more proposals fail due to budget misalignment or a lack of compelling details rather than requests for excessive funding. Getting the budget right, while not directly part of the proposal narrative, is essential to presenting the whole proposal story. This section delves into how task allocation budgeting can seamlessly integrate your proposal's tactical story to create a compelling, realistic, and strategically aligned financial plan.

Often, the allocation of funds can convey priorities more effectively than the narrative text. Therefore, ensuring a high degree of alignment between the budget and proposal tasks is crucial. During the review process, while the "green team" is typically responsible for scrutinizing the budget, it is equally important for the "red" or "gold team" to verify that the budget accurately reflects and supports the tasks outlined in the proposal. Failure to ensure this alignment could send conflicting signals to the reviewers and compromise the proposal's credibility. By tightly weaving the task-allocation budgeting with the tactical story and audience objectives and verifying that alignment, you not only validate the feasibility of your proposal but also create a compelling argument for why the project should be funded.

➢ **Objective-Task Alignment:** The initial step in task allocation budgeting involves aligning each project objective with corresponding tasks. This alignment is essential not only for achieving project goals but also for portraying a well-organized tactical story. Connecting tasks with objectives establishes a purposeful narrative structure for which resources can be allocated. For instance, if an objective in your tactical story is to develop a new water purification system, the budget should allocate resources for the corresponding tasks of market research, prototype development, and field testing.

☞ **Role of Personnel in the Tactical Story:** An effective tactical story needs well-defined characters to bring it to life. Assessing the skill sets within your team and mapping them to specific project tasks demonstrates optimum efficiency and enhances the story you are telling. If your tactical story emphasizes the innovative aspect of your project, then your R&D team becomes the "innovators" in the narrative and their tasks should receive a higher budget allocation.

☞ **Task Prioritization and Tactical Focus:** Once you have aligned tasks with objectives and matched them with appropriate personnel, the next step is to prioritize them. These critical, high-priority points should be reflected in your budget by higher resource allocation. If your project is aimed at community health, for example, and your tactical story identifies an upcoming health fair as a critical milestone, then the associated tasks should be clearly identified in the budget.

☞ **Cost Realism and Tactical Feasibility:** A budget serves as a reality check for the ambitions laid out in your proposal story. Given the narrative scope and technical challenges, the numbers must reflect what is feasible. So if your tactical story outlines a goal of reducing manufacturing costs through automation, but the new equipment and software budget appears unrealistically low, it could undermine the story's credibility.

☞ **Budget Justification and Story Narration:** Documenting how each line in your budget serves the tactical story is important, but those who review the budget may not read the full proposal. The budget justification, in that case, can provide a narrative bridge that explains why each expenditure is necessary for realizing the story's objectives. The budget justification should elaborate on why certain roles are needed. For each role (e.g.,lead researcher, project manager, etc.), emphasize the contribution of the role to the tactical story, the necessary skills and level of effort to help justify the allocated amounts. In addition, this is a chance to add details and reinforce the key characters in your story of delivering for the funder.

8.4.4   Interplay of Budget, Personnel Costs, and Task Prioritization

Understanding the intricate relationship between your budget, the cost of personnel, and the tasks you aim to accomplish is pivotal for any tactical proposal. Every line item and personnel decision should map directly to a task or objective within the proposal. Striking the right balance between your budget and personnel costs can create a domino effect that positively influences task accomplishment and ultimately helps you meet or exceed your objectives. This balance not only helps you allocate funds effectively but also aids in aligning your objectives with achievable outcomes.

☞ **Objective-Task Alignment:** Before diving into the budget, each project objective should have corresponding tasks. The task identification creates a direct pathway to achieving each goal, which is vital when resources are limited.

☞ **Personnel Skill Mapping:** Assess the skill sets within your team and map them to the tasks at hand. This helps assign the right personnel to each task, ensuring efficiency while controlling labor costs.

☞ **Task Prioritization:** Not all tasks are created equal. The most critical tasks may necessitate a larger budget share, while less critical tasks might have to be scaled down or executed more economically. Prioritize tasks based on their impact on achieving the project's objectives.

☞ **Cost-Efficiency Analysis:** Examine the cost-benefit ratio of assigning specific team members to tasks. Sometimes, a higher-skilled yet more expensive, team member can accomplish a task more efficiently and effectively than a less skilled but less expensive team member.

➤ **Flexibility and Adaptability:** Always prepare for uncertainties. Establish a tactical balance between your budget and personnel allocation so that you may adjust for unexpected cost increases without derailing the project.

8.4.5   Core Sections of a Proposal Budget

The budget is not merely a financial plan but a strategic document that delineates how resources will be allocated to achieve the project objectives effectively. Let us delve into the core sections that make up a comprehensive proposal budget.

➤ **Personnel:** This is a comprehensive listing of all individuals contributing to the project. it is often divided into multiple classes such as principal investigators, co-investigators, research assistants, and administrative staff. Different organizations will have different models, e.g., monthly salaries and percent efforts, which are common for universities, while per-employee hourly rates and hours on projects are common in government contracts and company proposals.

➤ **Fringe Benefits:** These are the benefits, in addition to salaries, provided to employees. Common examples of these benefits include health insurance, retirement contributions, and social security taxes. Most companies lump them together into a single factor that is usually a set percentage of salary:

$$\text{Fringe Benefits} = \text{Total Salaries} \times \text{Fringe Rate} \tag{8.1}$$

➤ **Travel:** Include funds for all necessary travel. Separate domestic and international trips. Include airfare, accommodation, per diem, and other incidental costs. Most organizations require justification for the travel and actual estimates, not rough guesses.

➤ **Material and Supplies:** List the cost of all materials and supplies that are indispensable for the project. To justify the necessity, be as specific as possible.

➤ **Subcontracts:** If portions of the work are to be subcontracted, detail the costs associated with those contracts.

➤ **Participant Costs:** Include any stipends or other reimbursements for participants in the project, such as study subjects.

➤ **Modified Total Direct Costs (MTDC):** This is the base for calculating indirect costs, usually total direct costs minus exceptions like equipment, participant costs, and subcontracts above a certain amount.

$$MTDC = Total\ Direct\ Costs - Excluded\ Costs \tag{8.2}$$

➤ **Indirect Costs:** These are the costs that are not directly linked to the project but are necessary for its completion, such as overhead. A common model looks like this:

$$Indirect\ Costs = Modified\ Total\ Direct\ Costs \times Indirect\ Cost\ Rate \tag{8.3}$$

Some organizations have multiple indirect cost rates with different levels for different locations and categories, so verify what is needed.

8.4.6   Calculating Fringe, Indirect Costs, and Modified Total Direct Costs

The calculations for fringe benefits, indirect costs, and Modified Total Direct Costs (MTDC) are vital as they provide a complete picture of the budget. Indirect costs, also known as Facilities and Administrative or F&A costs or overhead, are usually calculated as a percentage of the MTDC. MTDC includes all direct costs except specific items that are exempted, e.g., tuition, capital equipment, and large subcontracts.

$$Fringe\ Benefits = Total\ Salaries \times \frac{Fringe\ Rate}{100} \tag{8.4}$$

$$MTDC = Total\ Direct\ Costs - (Equipment\ Costs + Participant\ Costs + Subcontracts\ above\ X) \tag{8.5}$$

$$Indirect\ Costs = MTDC \times \frac{Indirect\ Cost\ Rate}{100} \tag{8.6}$$

In a well-thought-out budget, each dollar has a tactical purpose. So the budget is not merely a financial obligation; it is a testament to your project's planning and feasibility. Understanding these essential budgetary sections and their interactions can help better align your budget with your project objectives and the funder's expectations. Crafting the budget with the same care you invest in the rest of your proposal is crucial for a convincing pitch. Different types of salaries can have different fringe rates; for example, universities often have higher rates for faculty than students, and companies may have different rates depending on the state in which the employee works.

8.4.7   The Importance of Utilizing Spreadsheets for Budget Management

Spreadsheets are an indispensable tool when constructing a proposal budget. Their utility goes beyond mere tabulation; they enable dynamic and real-time calculations that can profoundly streamline the budget preparation and adjustment process. By integrating spreadsheets into your budgeting practice, you not only save time but also enhance the accuracy and reliability of your budget. This approach aligns particularly well when adapting your budget to match evolving project objectives or funder expectations. Consider these compelling reasons to use spreadsheets:

➤ **Easily Updated:** Spreadsheets allow you to adjust individual items quickly and easily, thereby automatically updating the total budget.

➤ **Use of Constants:** Constants, such as fringe and indirect cost rates, can be defined in single cells. These constants can then be used in formulas throughout the spreadsheet, ensuring consistency and ease of adjustment.

➤ **Error Minimization:** The automated nature of spreadsheet calculations minimizes the risk of human error, especially when dealing with complex computations.

➤ **Scenario Analysis:** Spreadsheets enable you to conduct what-if scenarios. You can quickly understand how changes affect the overall budget by adjusting key variables, which can help you make more informed decisions.

➤ **Automatic Salary and Inflation Adjustments:** By integrating the level of effort and inflation formulas into your spreadsheet, your budget will be more accurate and easier to update. This speeds up the budgeting process and ensures that you are planning for realistic costs across the project's life.

➤ **Dynamic Formulas:** The key to using a spreadsheet is formulas whereby you can automatically calculate (and recalculate) critical items like salaries, fringe benefits, indirect costs, and MTDC. This feature eliminates the need for manual calculations. In many proposals, personnel costs are dictated by the effort expected from each team member. Formulas can automate the calculation of these salaries. For example, you might use the following formula to calculate a team member's annual cost:

$$Personal\ cost = (Annual\ Salary * Percent\ Level\ of\ Effort) \tag{8.7}$$

Where Annual Salary is the full annual salary for the team member, and Level of Effort is the percentage of time they will dedicate to the project. You can also use hourly rates and convert between the two using the figure of 2,080 work hours per year.

For multi-year projects, accounting for inflation is crucial when estimating future costs. A spreadsheet can automatically adjust each year's budget based on an inflation rate. A sample formula might be:

$$Year2ItemCost = Year1ItemCost * (1 + \frac{InflationRate}{100}) \tag{8.8}$$

Where *Year1ItemCost* is the cost for the previous year, and *InflationRate* is the expected inflation rate for that class of items:

There are some tips and caveats to be aware of when using spreadsheets for proposal budgets. The call-for-proposal for many proposals will specify a budget format and many will provide spreadsheets. Unfortunately, many proposing organizations' internal spreadsheets differ from the proposer's format, and thus, one has to deliver two: one for internal use and one for external. Some organizations support the conversion; others leave that to the proposal writers. Linking the formula between the spreadsheets can be much easier and ensure consistency when there are changes. Almost all organizations will have a deadline for proposal documents, especially the budget, days or weeks before the final proposal submission. That is another reason to do the budget early—so check on those requirements and get the budget in with time for adjustments before the deadlines.

8.4.8   The Value of Work Breakdown Structures and Budget Mapping

Certain organizations require an elaborate Work Breakdown Structure (WBS) that meticulously maps each task to a budget line item and labor category. This level of granularity can appear tedious but serves multiple critical functions. Planning at the meticulous level the WBS requires helps to not only meet but exceed proposal commitments, thereby increasing the project's chances for successful execution and subsequent renewals. Adopting this approach can benefit your team and the project even if the funding agency or client does not require such detailed mapping.

Popular tools for this project management task include high-end, fully integrated tools like monday.com, Parallax, Wrike, or Jira that integrate with timekeeping, billing, and other project management tools. Simpler WBS commercial solutions like Microsoft Project and open-source options like ProjectLibre or GanttProject exist. One can even do a reasonable job of proposal planning with a spreadsheet template.

➣ **Budget-to-Task Accountability:** Having a detailed WBS tied to budget items makes it easier to hold specific teams or individuals accountable for their part of the project and clarifies where the budget is being spent. Some proposals require this level so they can better understand the impact of suggested budget cuts.

➣ **Resource Allocation:** The detailed mapping ensures that every resource is judiciously allocated, minimizing resource waste. Large projects will often have WBS with the proposal including breakdowns per task per labor category per month, see Fig. 8.2 and Fig. 8.3. Tools with built-in budgeting features can automate this process, making your budget allocations accurate and efficient.

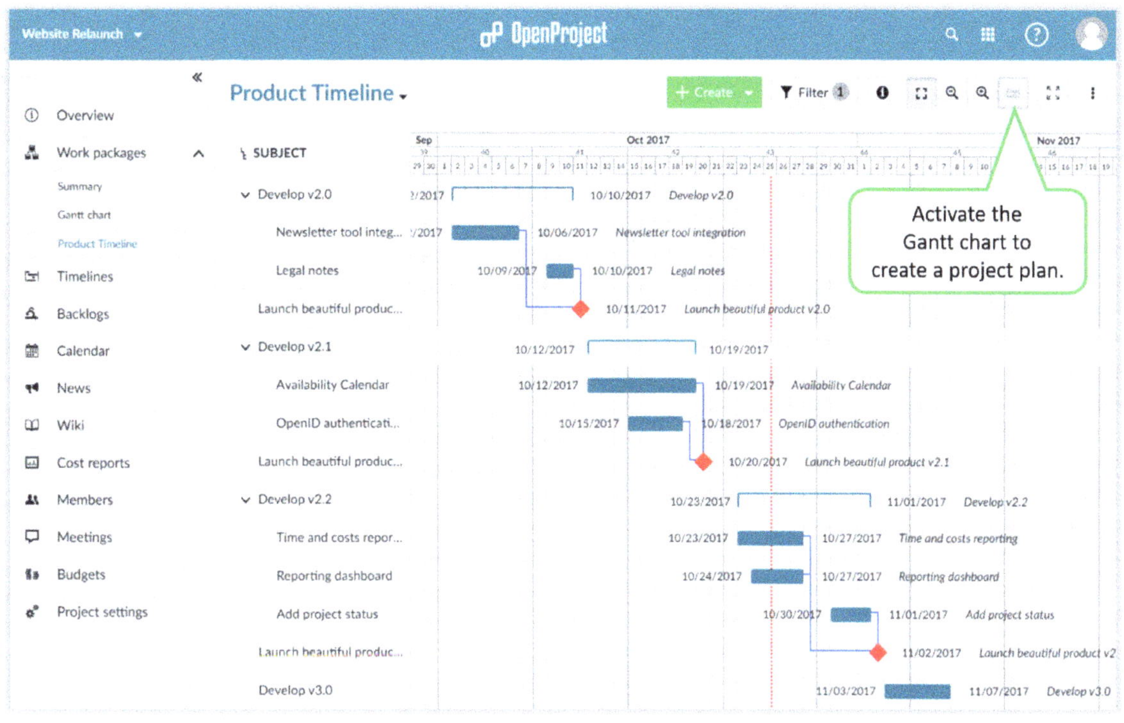

Direct Labor

Labor Hours

SOW Task #	Employee Name/LCAT	Organization	GFY POP	GFY22 Feb-22	GFY22 Mar-22	GFY22 Apr-22	GFY22 May-22	GFY22 Jun-22	GFY22 Jul-22	GFY22 Aug-22	GFY22 Sep-22	GFY23 Oct-22	GFY23 Nov-22	GFY23 Dec-22	GFY23 Jan-23	Totals
1.1.1	T.Boult	UCCS	8/1/2021 - 1/1/2023													4.00
1.1.1	PostDoc	UCCS	8/1/2021 - 1/1/2023					5.00				5.00			5.00	37.00
1.1.2	T.Boult	UCCS	9/1/2021 - 1/1/2023	1.00	1.00	1.00	1.00	1.00	1.00	2.00	2.00	2.00	2.00	2.00	2.00	28.00
1.1.2	PostDoc	UCCS	9/1/2021 - 1/1/2023	77.00	80.00	80.00	80.00	65.00	70.00	70.00	70.00	65.00	70.00	70.00	65.00	1,262.00
1.2.1	T.Boult	UCCS	9/1/2021 - 1/1/2023	1.00	1.00	1.00	1.00	1.00	1.00	2.00	2.00	2.00	2.00	2.00	2.00	28.00
1.2.1	PostDoc	UCCS	9/1/2021 - 1/1/2023	20.00	20.00	20.00	20.00	20.00	20.00	20.00	20.00	20.00	20.00	20.00	20.00	481.00
1.3.3	T.Boult	UCCS	9/1/2021 - 1/31/2023	8.00	5.00	5.00	3.00	3.00	3.00	3.00	3.00	3.00	3.00	3.00	2.00	60.00
1.3.3	PostDoc	UCCS	9/1/2021 - 1/31/2023	50.00	52.00	52.00	52.00	52.00	62.00	62.00	62.00	62.00	62.00	62.00	62.00	789.00
1.4.1.1	T.Boult	UCCS	8/1/2021 - 5/1/2022			4.00										17.00
1.4.1.1	Student	UCCS	8/1/2021 - 5/1/2022													30.00
1.4.2	T.Boult	UCCS	9/1/2021 - 1/31/2023													2.00
1.4.2	Student	UCCS	9/1/2021 - 1/31/2023	10.00	10.00	5.00	5.00	5.00	5.00							130.00
1.4.3	T.Boult	UCCS	9/1/2021 - 9/1/2022	1.00	1.00	1.00	1.00	1.00	1.00	1.00						28.00
1.4.3	Student	UCCS	9/1/2021 - 9/1/2022	30.00	30.00	30.00	30.00	30.00	30.00	50.00	50.00	50.00	50.00	50.00	50.00	740.00
1.6.2	T.Boult	UCCS	8/1/2021 - 1/1/2023													-
1.6.2	PostDoc	UCCS	8/1/2021 - 1/1/2023													-
1.7	T.Boult	UCCS	8/1/2021 - 1/31/2023	3.00	3.00	3.00	3.00	3.00	3.00	16.00	2.00	2.00	3.00	16.00	8.00	95.00
1.7	PostDoc	UCCS	8/1/2021 - 1/31/2023	8.00	8.00	8.00	8.00	23.00	8.00	8.00	8.00	8.00	8.00	8.00	8.00	151.00

Labor Rates

SOW Task #	Employee Name/LCAT	Organization	GFY POP
1.1.1	T.Boult	UCCS	8/1/2021 - 1/1/2023
1.1.1	PostDoc	UCCS	8/1/2021 - 1/1/2023
1.1.2	T.Boult	UCCS	9/1/2021 - 1/1/2023
1.1.2	PostDoc	UCCS	9/1/2021 - 1/1/2023
1.2.1	T.Boult	UCCS	9/1/2021 - 1/1/2023
1.2.1	PostDoc	UCCS	9/1/2021 - 1/1/2023
1.3.3	T.Boult	UCCS	9/1/2021 - 1/31/2023
1.3.3	PostDoc	UCCS	9/1/2021 - 1/31/2023
1.4.1.1	T.Boult	UCCS	8/1/2021 - 5/1/2022
1.4.1.1	Student	UCCS	8/1/2021 - 5/1/2022
1.4.2	T.Boult	UCCS	9/1/2021 - 1/31/2023
1.4.2	Student	UCCS	9/1/2021 - 1/31/2023
1.4.3	T.Boult	UCCS	9/1/2021 - 9/1/2022
1.4.3	Student	UCCS	9/1/2021 - 9/1/2022
1.6.2	T.Boult	UCCS	8/1/2021 - 1/1/2023
1.6.2	PostDoc	UCCS	8/1/2021 - 1/1/2023
1.7	T.Boult	UCCS	8/1/2021 - 1/31/2023
1.7	PostDoc	UCCS	8/1/2021 - 1/31/2023

Labor Cost

SOW Task #	Employee Name/LCAT	Organization	GFY POP	Totals
1.1.1	T.Boult	UCCS	8/1/2021 - 1/1/2023	688
1.1.1	PostDoc	UCCS	8/1/2021 - 1/1/2023	1,664
1.1.2	T.Boult	UCCS	9/1/2021 - 1/1/2023	4,836
1.1.2	PostDoc	UCCS	9/1/2021 - 1/1/2023	56,793
1.2.1	T.Boult	UCCS	9/1/2021 - 1/1/2023	4,836
1.2.1	PostDoc	UCCS	9/1/2021 - 1/1/2023	21,630

Figure 8.1: *Example of a Work Break Downstrucure (WBS) and Gantt chart from OpenProject. The lines are different tasks/subtasks with start and end dates. The thick dark blue regions are "time on task", with start/end dates show. The thin blue lines show dependencies, and the red diamonds are milestones. If one date is changed or a task slips, the system can automatically update the dependencies.*

Figure 8.2: *Example of a budget sheet with WBS-based task breakdown by labor category by hour. The top shows the hours, the middle is the per-hour rate, and the bottom is the total cost.*

> **Contingency Planning:** A comprehensive WBS linked to the budget allows for more effective contingency planning. The tools mentioned above provide robust features to facilitate this process.

> **Streamlined Reporting:** When tasks and budgets are mapped clearly and integrated with personal time reporting or accounting, reporting progress to stakeholders becomes more straightforward.

> **Project Success:** Detailed planning is the cornerstone of project success. The rigorous planning embodied by a comprehensive WBS and budget mapping, facilitated by proprietary and open-source tools, enhances project management and ensures alignment with objectives and increases the likelihood of project success.

8.4.9 Understanding and Demonstrating Cost Realism

Cost realism is not just about ensuring you have accounted for all possible expenses; it is about ensuring your proposal is not implausible. A well-calibrated, realistic budget conveys that you understand the scope of work and are prepared to manage the project effectively and deliver it. While underestimating costs might initially make your proposal more attractive, it can also undermine your credibility and possibly lead to rejection. A budget that is too low or otherwise unrealistic may lead reviewers to conclude that the team will not be able to deliver on the project's objectives. Consider carefully the following tips for navigating common pitfalls related to budgeting with cost realism in mind:

> **Avoid the "Too Good to Be True" Impression:** Offering a budget that seems like "too good of a deal" may raise flags for reviewers. They could interpret this as a sign that the proposing team is inexperienced and does not understand the complexities and challenges associated with fulfilling the project's objectives.

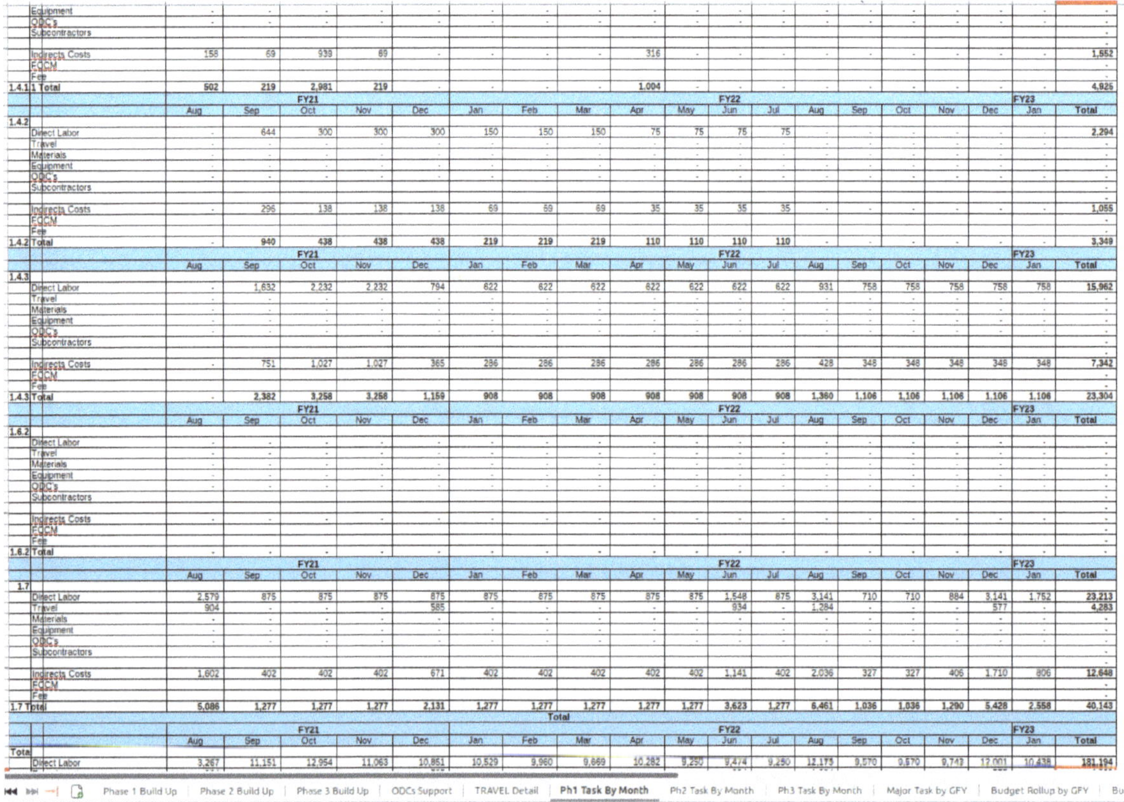

In the month columns below, fiscal years group the months as: **FY21** = Aug–Dec, **FY22** = Jan–Dec, **FY23** = Jan.

1.4.1.1

WBS	Category	Aug	Sep	Oct	Nov	Dec	Jan	Feb	Mar	Apr	May	Jun	Jul	Aug	Sep	Oct	Nov	Dec	Jan	Total
	Equipment	-	-	-	-	-	-	-	-	-	-	-	-	-	-	-	-	-	-	-
	ODC's	-	-	-	-	-	-	-	-	-	-	-	-	-	-	-	-	-	-	-
	Subcontractors																			
	Indirects Costs	158	69	939	69	-	-	-	-	316	-	-	-	-	-	-	-	-	-	1,552
	FCCM																			
	Fee																			
1.4.1.1	Total	502	219	2,981	219	-	-	-	-	1,004	-	-	-	-	-	-	-	-	-	4,925

1.4.2

WBS	Category	Aug	Sep	Oct	Nov	Dec	Jan	Feb	Mar	Apr	May	Jun	Jul	Aug	Sep	Oct	Nov	Dec	Jan	Total
	Direct Labor	-	644	300	300	300	150	150	150	75	75	75	75	-	-	-	-	-	-	2,294
	Travel	-	-	-	-	-	-	-	-	-	-	-	-	-	-	-	-	-	-	-
	Materials	-	-	-	-	-	-	-	-	-	-	-	-	-	-	-	-	-	-	-
	Equipment	-	-	-	-	-	-	-	-	-	-	-	-	-	-	-	-	-	-	-
	ODC's	-	-	-	-	-	-	-	-	-	-	-	-	-	-	-	-	-	-	-
	Subcontractors																			
	Indirects Costs	-	296	138	138	138	69	69	69	35	35	35	35	-	-	-	-	-	-	1,055
	FCCM																			
	Fee																			
1.4.2	Total	-	940	438	438	438	219	219	219	110	110	110	110	-	-	-	-	-	-	3,349

1.4.3

WBS	Category	Aug	Sep	Oct	Nov	Dec	Jan	Feb	Mar	Apr	May	Jun	Jul	Aug	Sep	Oct	Nov	Dec	Jan	Total
	Direct Labor	-	1,632	2,232	2,232	794	622	622	622	622	622	622	622	931	758	758	758	758	758	15,962
	Travel	-	-	-	-	-	-	-	-	-	-	-	-	-	-	-	-	-	-	-
	Materials	-	-	-	-	-	-	-	-	-	-	-	-	-	-	-	-	-	-	-
	Equipment	-	-	-	-	-	-	-	-	-	-	-	-	-	-	-	-	-	-	-
	ODC's	-	-	-	-	-	-	-	-	-	-	-	-	-	-	-	-	-	-	-
	Subcontractors																			
	Indirects Costs	-	751	1,027	1,027	365	286	286	286	286	286	286	286	428	348	348	348	348	348	7,342
	FCCM																			
	Fee																			
1.4.3	Total	-	2,382	3,258	3,258	1,159	908	908	908	908	908	908	908	1,360	1,106	1,106	1,106	1,106	1,106	23,304

1.6.2

WBS	Category	Aug	Sep	Oct	Nov	Dec	Jan	Feb	Mar	Apr	May	Jun	Jul	Aug	Sep	Oct	Nov	Dec	Jan	Total
	Direct Labor	-	-	-	-	-	-	-	-	-	-	-	-	-	-	-	-	-	-	-
	Travel	-	-	-	-	-	-	-	-	-	-	-	-	-	-	-	-	-	-	-
	Materials	-	-	-	-	-	-	-	-	-	-	-	-	-	-	-	-	-	-	-
	Equipment	-	-	-	-	-	-	-	-	-	-	-	-	-	-	-	-	-	-	-
	ODC's	-	-	-	-	-	-	-	-	-	-	-	-	-	-	-	-	-	-	-
	Subcontractors																			
	Indirects Costs	-	-	-	-	-	-	-	-	-	-	-	-	-	-	-	-	-	-	-
	FCCM																			
	Fee																			
1.6.2	Total	-	-	-	-	-	-	-	-	-	-	-	-	-	-	-	-	-	-	-

1.7

WBS	Category	Aug	Sep	Oct	Nov	Dec	Jan	Feb	Mar	Apr	May	Jun	Jul	Aug	Sep	Oct	Nov	Dec	Jan	Total
	Direct Labor	2,579	875	875	875	875	875	875	875	875	875	1,548	875	3,141	710	710	884	3,141	1,752	23,213
	Travel	904	-	-	-	585	-	-	-	-	-	934	-	1,284	-	-	-	577	-	4,283
	Materials	-	-	-	-	-	-	-	-	-	-	-	-	-	-	-	-	-	-	-
	Equipment	-	-	-	-	-	-	-	-	-	-	-	-	-	-	-	-	-	-	-
	ODC's	-	-	-	-	-	-	-	-	-	-	-	-	-	-	-	-	-	-	-
	Subcontractors																			
	Indirects Costs	1,602	402	402	402	671	402	402	402	402	402	1,141	402	2,036	327	327	406	1,710	806	12,648
	FCCM																			
	Fee																			
1.7	Total	5,086	1,277	1,277	1,277	2,131	1,277	1,277	1,277	1,277	1,277	3,623	1,277	6,461	1,036	1,036	1,290	5,428	2,558	40,143

Total

Category	Aug	Sep	Oct	Nov	Dec	Jan	Feb	Mar	Apr	May	Jun	Jul	Aug	Sep	Oct	Nov	Dec	Jan	Total
Direct Labor	3,267	11,151	12,954	11,063	10,851	10,529	9,960	9,669	10,282	9,250	9,474	9,250	12,175	9,570	9,570	9,749	12,001	10,438	181,194

Phase 1 Build Up | Phase 2 Build Up | Phase 3 Build Up | ODCs Support | TRAVEL Detail | **Ph1 Task By Month** | Ph2 Task By Month | Ph3 Task By Month | Major Task by GFY | Budget Rollup by GFY | Buc

Figure 8.3: *Example of a budget sheet with WBS-based task breakdown by high-level category by task by*

month. Each block shows the major budget categories (Direct Labor, Materials, Travel, etc..) per task per month. This level of breakdown tends to be required in multi-million dollar proposals

➤ **Align with Market Rates:** Make sure that salaries, subcontracting costs, material costs, and other direct costs align with current market rates. This lends credibility to your cost estimates and reduces the chances of your proposal being perceived as unrealistic.

➤ **Do Not Appear Unqualified:** Teams with a proven track record in the proposal domain are more likely to produce realistic and trustworthy budgets. If your team lacks direct experience, counterbalance this by demonstrating thorough research into the real-world costs associated with the tasks you propose.

➤ **Cost-Share or Matching Funds:** If the proposal requires or allows for cost-sharing or matching funds, be realistic about your ability to provide these resources. Over-committing may make your proposal look ambitious but could introduce significant risk and under-committing might make the proposal less appealing to reviewers. Make sure that any cost-share or matching commitments align with the project's objectives and the funder's expectations.

➤ **Validate Assumptions:** Clearly state and justify any assumptions you have made while preparing the budget including labor rates, overhead, and anticipated price changes for materials. Validation will add credibility to your cost estimates. Capital equipment, often anything over $5,000, may require quotes. Do not try to do "too much" work for "too little money," and do not just make up round numbers—nothing screams "made up" like budget items with round numbers like $10,000. Real items rarely round to nice numbers but rounding to whole dollars is normally fine.

➤ **Compliance with Federal and Sponsor Guidelines:** Any requests for financial support, especially from U.S. federal agencies, must align with the specific rules outlined in 2 CFR 200 or the sponsor's guidelines, whichever is more restrictive. This ensures that the costs you include are realistic and allowable. For instance, although postage is not normally an allowable cost, specific cases may warrant its inclusion if explicitly justified.

➤ **Understanding Direct vs Indirect Costs:** Be mindful of what costs are reimbursable under facilities and administrative costs (indirect costs). These will not usually be allowable as direct costs in a federal proposal. Understanding the delineation between direct and indirect costs is crucial for maintaining cost realism and compliance.

➤ **Do Not Leave Money on the Table:** Some grants have very explicit maximum requests. Particularly in smaller commercialization-focused grants such as SBIR, it is critical to request the full funding available under the grant guidelines if it can be utilized effectively. Under-asking might be interpreted as a lack of ambition, commercialization experience, and/or a limited scope for your project. Use every funding category permitted to adequately support your commercialization plan, from R&D to market research and customer acquisition. Show that you can allocate the funds to maximize the commercial potential and, thus, the ROI for the funder.

➤ **Best Value vs Cost-Efficiency:** While some business proposals are evaluated on "lowest cost," most cost-sensitive proposals are evaluated on a "best value" basis. The "best value" focus is not solely on cost but on factors such as technical excellence, risk-reward, time to delivery, and long-term sustainability. However, most proposals, especially those that do not specify "best value" as a review criterion, are evaluated based on overall project effectiveness. In such cases, cost efficiency, while important, is not the central focus. Thus, a well-justified higher budget that promises superior results may be more favorable than a lower budget that compromises the project's objectives.

➢ **Integrating Tactical Story Elements in Justification Documents:** Your budget justification serves a dual purpose: a detailed financial breakdown and a narrative document that should weave seamlessly into your proposal's tactical story. While most proposals have strict length limits on the main proposal, most do not limit the budget justification. So the budget justification is an opportunity to reinforce your story with minimal "space cost."

When outlining costs for personnel, be sure to highlight their roles within the project's story. Are they the lead researchers driving key innovations? Perhaps they are skilled technicians who ensure the operational efficiency of a critical process? Do they have unique experiences to help them relate to the people with whom the project will work? When hiring new people, the budget justification can emphasize skills that fit into the story and show that you are thinking about successful delivery.

Each line item concerning personnel should mention their role and explain how their involvement is crucial to achieving the project's objectives or milestones. Similarly, non-personnel costs like equipment or travel should be justified in the context of the tactical story, showing how they enable the team to accomplish their goals. This level of detailed storytelling around each budget item underscores the realism and strategic thought that has gone into your cost estimates, instilling greater confidence in the reviewers.

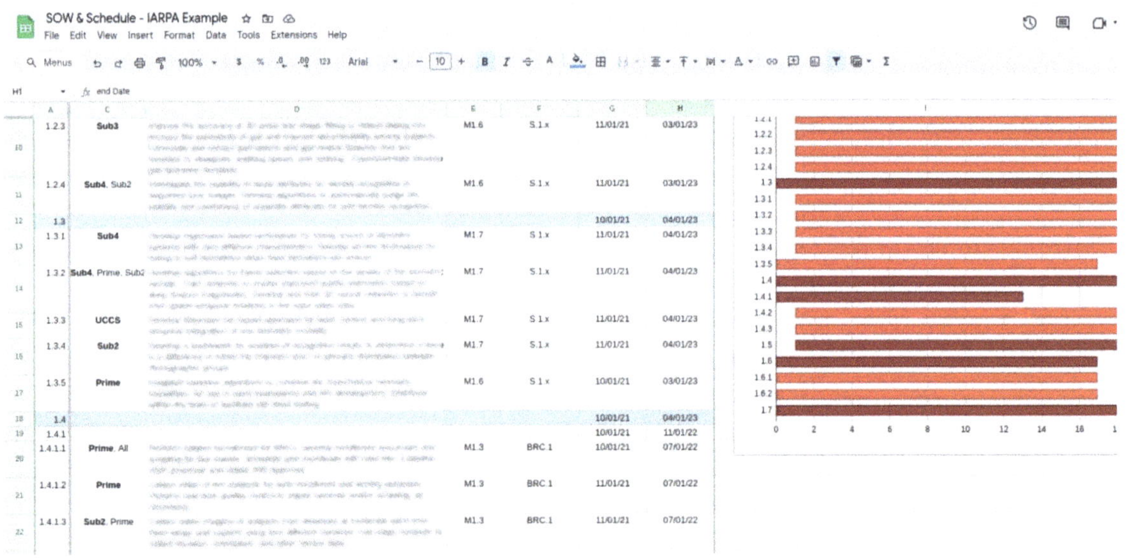

Figure 8.4: *Example of an SOW generated from the WBS-based task breakdown, with the task numbering in the first column, the resource committed in the second column, a description (blurred out), the Milestone it feeds into, the deliverable it feeds into and starts and end dates. The far right shows a simple Gantt chart (without dependencies).*

8.5 The Role of a Statement of Work (SOW) in Subcontracting Scenarios

After establishing a robust budget, the next step is to craft a comprehensive Statement of Work (SOW). The SOW provides a clear description of the scope and details the tasks required to accomplish the work the project proposes. Make no mistake, the SOW is not merely a to-do list. It evolves naturally from the budget and outlines your proposal's scope, objectives, and deliverables. Moreover, a well-defined SOW will set the boundaries of what is *not* part of the project, thereby offering protection from scope creep and potential misunderstandings in the future.

8.5.1 Role of the SOW in Subcontracting

The SOW assumes a pivotal role in subcontracting contexts for both the primary contractor or a subcontractor. It serves as the core of the contract between the primary contractor and the subcontractor, specifying the tasks, deliverables, timelines, and financial arrangements.

➤ **Task Definition:** The SOW clearly defines the tasks the subcontractor is responsible for, ensuring alignment with the overall project objectives and budget.

➤ **Risk Mitigation:** A well-defined SOW protects against scope creep and misunderstandings, providing a solid basis for dispute resolution.

➤ **Alignment with Main Proposal:** The SOW for the subcontractor must be congruent with the primary proposal's objectives, schedule, and especially the budget to maintain coherence and integrity across all project components.

8.5.2 Generating a SOW

Creating a robust SOW involves multiple steps and careful consideration. If one has a WBS, it often starts deriving the SOW, but with or without it, the SOW will list tasks, some timing, and deliverables. Tasks are at the core of the Statement Of Work (SOW) document, and it is not uncommon for the SOW to be a bit of text around a WBS chart, especially when the budget is based on the WBS task breakdown, see Fig. 8.4. However, the SOW will also have text describing the project's process. Here are some key elements to consider:

➤ **Introduction:** State the document's purpose, identify the parties involved, and outline the overall goals.

➤ **Scope of Work:** Describe in detail the tasks to be completed by the subcontractor. These tasks should align with those in the primary proposal's budget and schedule.

➤ **Performance Metrics and Timeline:** Identify quantifiable metrics and milestones to assess the subcontractor's progress and the timeline for each milestone.

➤ **Terms and Conditions:** Include legal and compliance considerations, payment terms, and other contractual obligations. If the project includes progress payments, that schedule should be clear.

➤ **Appendices:** Attach any supplementary documents that can clarify or add context to the SOW, such as GANTT charts, Work Breakdown Structure (WBS), or additional specifications.

Ensuring Budget-SOW Coherence

It is crucial that the tasks and associated costs outlined in the SOW directly correspond with those in the budget. Utilize widely-used tools like Microsoft Project or open-source alternatives such as GanttProject to create a WBS to explicitly map the budget and tasks. This meticulous planning is essential for ensuring a successful project and can be invaluable even if the final budget does not require that level of detail.

8.6 Developing a Project Schedule

A well-crafted schedule is indispensable for a successful project. It serves as the timeline that guides the project from inception to completion and is a vital tool for maintaining team coordination and instilling confidence in stakeholders. To ensure a coherent proposal, the schedule must perfectly harmonize with the budget and Statement of Work (SOW). If well-conceived and presented, the schedule reflects your team's deep understanding of the task, enhancing your credibility. Furthermore, a schedule helps address the program manager's need for projects to be delivered as expected and on time. Hence, the schedule needs to show your organization's ability to have the ideas and organizational skills to report them in an understandable fashion and deliver on them.

8.6.1   Graphic Representation of the Schedule

Graphic tools such as GANTT charts visually represent the timeline, tasks, and dependencies. These graphics provide an easy-to-read format that can quickly inform team members and stakeholders of the project's current status. Effective schedule graphics reveal pertinent project schedule data such as:

➤ **Task Duration:** Each task is represented as a horizontal bar, the length of which corresponds to the task's duration.

➤ **Dependencies:** Arrows or lines between tasks show dependencies, helping to identify potential bottlenecks.

➤ **Progress Indicator:** Many GANTT charts include a progress indicator to track completed tasks.

8.6.2   Important Milestones

Milestones are specific points along a project timeline that indicate a phase completion or a noteworthy accomplishment. In your schedule, define the following milestones carefully:

➤ **Kick-off:** When the project officially begins.

➤ **Interim Reviews:** Scheduled times for assessing progress toward objectives.

➤ **Critical Deliverables:** Points at which major components are completed.

➤ **External Milestones:** Dates where external dependencies, e.g., subcontractor deliverables, must be met.

➤ **Project Completion:** The date when all tasks are finished and the project is closed.

8.6.3   The Role of Work Breakdown Structure (WBS) Tools

WBS tools can play a pivotal role in generating a coherent schedule. While proprietary tools such as Microsoft Project or open-source alternatives such as OpenProject or GanttProject are available for this purpose, the choice of tool often depends on the complexity of your project and the level of detail required in your schedule. Some agencies will have higher expectations for very formal project management and expect more advanced tools where WBS is used during execution. A WBS that appears to be from Microsoft Project or OpenProject would be a minimal expectation for these organizations. Other agencies will be fine with a GANTT chart/schedule by coloring in cells in a spreadsheet to show the time allotted for each task. WBS tools are helpful for:

➤ **Task Decomposition:** WBS tools help break down tasks into sub-tasks, making it easier to allocate resources and time.

➤ **Task-to-Task Mapping:** These tools can link tasks and sub-tasks to visually represent dependencies.

- ➤ **Budget Integration:** WBS tools often allow for budget integration, helping to ensure that the schedule aligns with available financial resources.

- ➤ **Resource Allocation:** Allocate human and material resources to specific tasks visually.

- ➤ **Milestone Tracking:** Use the WBS tool to effectively mark and track project milestones.

8.7 Supplementary Forms and Elements for Government Proposals

While the core components of a proposal— objectives, Statement of Work (SOW), schedule, and budget— are crucial, government agencies often require additional forms and elements in order to evaluate a proposal's merit and feasibility. Often these forms have required formats that are specified in the proposal guidelines. In addition, many other diverse elements may need to be included in the proposal. It may come as a surprise that most of the additional required forms and elements are about something other than writing your story. Instead, they are about organizing and reporting required information in whatever form the funder requires to unify and simplify their review process. Yet compliance with these elements is unavoidable.

8.7.1 Importance of Government Registrations

Before even considering submitting a proposal to any federal agency, it is crucial to officially register with the U.S. federal government's System for Award Management (SAM), accessible at sam.gov. Here is why this step is indispensable:

- ➤ **Eligibility:** Many agencies will not accept proposals from organizations that are not registered in SAM. It is a basic eligibility criterion. Because the registration can take weeks to process, this task must be addressed early in the proposal process. Sometimes one can partner as a subcontractor to an already registered organization to work around this requirement.

- ➤ **Identity Verification:** Registering with SAM is a verification process for your organization's identity. It ensures you are a legitimate entity capable of entering into a legally binding contract.

- ➤ **Payment Setup:** SAM contains information for setting up payments should you win the grant, including EFT (Electronic Funds Transfer) details.

- ➤ **Faster Processing:** Being pre-registered can expedite the processing time for your proposal and subsequent award administration since the basic organization data need not be re-entered.

- ➤ **Universal Recognition:** Once registered on SAM, your organization becomes universally recognizable across various federal agencies, which can ease the submission process for future proposals.

Please note that SAM registration must be renewed annually, and it is a good practice to ensure that your details are up-to-date before submitting any new proposal.

8.7.2 Biographical Sketches

You may be required to provide a short biographical sketch of key personnel. The NSF and NIH have specific guidelines on the format and content, while DoD often expects a paragraph or two to be integrated into the proposal text. In each case, the sketch should be explicitly tailored to the story and project—electing to not tailor the sketch sends a message of lack of focus on the project. Biographical sketches should include:

- **Education and Training:** Outline the educational background of key team members.

- **Relevant Experience:** List pertinent work experience and roles in prior projects.

- **Publications:** Include recent publications, if applicable.

- **Collaborators and Other Affiliations:** Detail any potential conflicts of interest or important collaborations.

- **Synergistic Activities:** Explain how the individual's expertise will contribute to the project.

8.7.3 Current and Pending Support

This form details all ongoing and pending projects in which key personnel are involved. This information is, in part, used to identify potential overlap on projects. The proposal needs to explain why the related project is synergistic and not just an overlap. Sometimes that synergistic explanation can be in the biographical sketch, at other times it is in the main proposal.

- **Project Title:** Clearly state the title of each ongoing or pending project.

- **Funding Agency:** Name the agency supporting each project.

- **Project Duration:** Mention the project's time frame.

- **Overlaps:** Identify any overlap in resources or time with the proposed project.

- **Role of Key Personnel:** Describe the involvement level of each key member.

8.7.4 Data Management Plan

Many agencies require a plan that details how data will be managed and shared during and after the project. The plan often needs to address security and privacy aspects.

- **Data Types:** Enumerate the types of data that will be generated.

- **Storage:** Describe where and how the data will be stored securely.

- **Sharing and Access:** Outline policies for data sharing and public access.

- **Retention:** Mention how long the data will be retained.

- **Responsibilities:** Assign roles for data management tasks.

8.7.5 Facilities and Equipment

Describe the facilities and equipment available for the project. For some DOD proposals, this is just showing you have the needed esoteric equipment, e.g., Dr. Boult's lab might show it has the necessary infrared camera but would not get into basic computers or GPUs. For others, like NSF, it is expected to be a pretty complete list of all equipment that might be relevant, so it would include all the desktop computers and GPUs the lab owns. It also includes space and other parts of the facilities. It's critical that any proposed equipment to be purchased is justified, and the lack of it shows in the existing facilities. It should also list the actual size of the space and any special security offered.

- **On-site Resources:** List available labs, computers, and other facilities.

- **Off-site Resources:** Note any collaborative sites or shared resources.

- **Specialized Equipment:** Enumerate any specialized tools required.

- **Accessibility:** Discuss how key personnel will access these resources.

- **Constraints:** Mention any potential limitations or bottlenecks.

8.7.6 Letters of Commitment

Some proposals require letters from collaborators or end-users who are committing to certain roles or contributions to the project. These should be started early because they often take time to receive. Always offer to draft the letter or include a draft when you make the request. Organizations often have specific requirements in what must be, and sometimes what cannot be, in a letter. This letter is often a place to bring in management and get them to commit to getting these letters at least one to two days before proposal submission. If the letters are missing, parts of the proposal will need to be redone. Letters from the identified sources require the following affirmations and commitments:

- **Stakeholder Commitment:** Obtain letters that affirm stakeholder buy-in.

- **Subcontractor Roles:** Confirm the roles of subcontractors, if applicable.

- **Resource Allocations:** Have letters that confirm resource commitments.

- **Timeline Acknowledgment:** Get acknowledgments that collaborators know about the project timeline.

In addition to the general federal guidelines already covered, specialized proposals such as those for SBIR, NIH, and DARPA have unique requirements. Understanding and adhering to these agency-specific elements can make a critical difference in the evaluation of your proposal.

8.7.7 Small Business Innovation Research (SBIR) Proposals

Small Business Innovation Research (SBIR) proposals have a strong commercialization focus, as do some state-run programs. Below are elements unique to commercialization-oriented proposals:

- **Commercialization Plan:** Outline how the innovation will be brought to market.

- **Company Qualifications:** Establish the business credibility of your small business.

- **Letters of Support from Stakeholders:** Include commitments from potential customers or strategic partners.

- **Preliminary Data:** Provide any data supporting the feasibility of your innovation.

- **Budget Justification for Subcontractors:** Provide a detailed rationale for subcontracted work.

8.7.8 National Institutes of Health (NIH) Proposals

National Institutes of Health (NIH) proposals and some National Science Foundation proposals require a focus on research methodology and human subjects. These often require added sections, including:

➤ **Research Strategy:** An in-depth methodology section including preliminary data.

➤ **Human Subjects Section:** Detailed plans for recruiting and protecting human subjects.

➤ **Vertebrate Animals:** Justification for using vertebrate animals in the research, if applicable.

➤ **Bio-hazards:** Description and mitigation plans for any bio-hazardous materials used.

➤ **Multiple P.I. Leadership Plan:** If applicable, a plan outlining roles when multiple principal investigators are involved.

➤ **Modular Grants:** Some NIH grants have a formal modular structure requiring *modular budgets* with specialized requirements.

8.7.9   DARPA/DoD Proposals

DARPA and DoD proposals often require a strong focus on innovation technology and readiness levels for technology transition to military applications.

➤ **Technology Readiness Level (TRL):** Justify the TRL of your innovation and your plans to advance it.

➤ **Quad Chart:** A one-page visual summary of the proposal is often required.

➤ **Security Considerations:** Outline any national security implications and plans for secure data handling.

➤ **Transition Plan:** Plans for technology transition to the military or commercial sector.

➤ **Milestones and Metrics:** Specific measurable goals and performance indicators.

Checklist

Develop a specific checklist based on the proposal guidelines provided by the funding agency. This will ensure that your submission includes all required sections and elements.

Personal Story: Those Detailed and Annoying WBS, Budgets, and Plans.

You may have noticed that proposals are a big part of my approach to tactical writing and are the subject of many of my personal stories. Some of you, having read the previous sections on Work Breakdown Structures (WBS) and detailed budgets, might be wondering if all this detail is really necessary. The answer, from personal experience, is that it depends.

Early in my career, my first funded proposals were from the National Science Foundation, which is more of a granting agency than a contracting agency. As such, the budgets and work schedules were simple. However, when I started working with companies like Siemens, I encountered very large, detailed budgets. Initially, I didn't appreciate the complexity and thought it was a waste of time, but I went along with it because that was their process. I did not, however, adopt the process personally at that time. In retrospect, that might have explained some of my unsuccessful large DARPA proposals between then and when I finally adopted very detailed project management processes.

When I started my second company, where we taught our clients to do proposals, I had follow-up meetings with the funding agency regarding some of our unfunded proposals. From these meetings, I learned the importance of WBS and detailed budgets. I can't remember an exact quote, but the gist was that our job in writing proposals was to make their job of funding and managing the project easier. They explained that the high level of detail was required by their bosses, who had learned that when companies propose large projects without sufficient detailed planning and clear project management processes, they tended to underestimate costs, which led to failed projects or cost overruns.

From the agency's point of view, it wasn't the exact work breakdown structure that made the difference. Rather, the difference resulted from the effort we, as proposal writers, had put into the analysis and thorough planning. It is also worth noting that formal project management tools produce WBS and detailed budgets that are easily identifiable just from the form/charts, so the agency can generally tell who has done the work and who is just winging it.

Following this revelation, we revisited one of our clients whose first proposal had been unsuccessful. We worked with them to use MS project to expand the level of detail and ensure all required documentation was included. We showed a serious level of effort in planning and analysis, which led to a successful grant on the subsequent attempt. From that time forward, I understood that the value of detailed planning depends on the specific requirements of the proposal and the agency's overall practices. For contracts, especially large ones, expect to do more to justify the spending. If the agency handles large contracts, they will likely hold you to a high standard, even for smaller projects.

Two important phrases often used within military organizations are "no plan survives first contact with the enemy" and "plans are nothing; planning is everything." I've seen these sayings play out repeatedly in projects. Even if you expect your plan or proposal details to change, don't write that in the proposal. Write up a solid plan and include contingencies but give the agency what they are looking for. It's not the plan itself that matters as much as what the planning process produces.

8.8 Unique Aspects and Strategies for Philanthropic Grants

Unlike government-funded grants, philanthropic grants often come from private foundations or individual donors. These entities have unique criteria, priorities, and administrative structures, which makes them a different ball game altogether. Do not be fooled by the lack of formal structure and requirements frequently encountered for such proposals. This ambiguity makes it all the more important for you to make sure you have the critical items in the proposal. Even with limited guidance, it is up to you to craft an effective tactical story and make it easy for the funder to access the decision-making information they need. Consider how to address the following unique aspects and strategies when preparing a proposal for a philanthropic grant. If you tailor your proposal to align with the organization's expectations and preferences, you will increase your chances of submitting a successful proposal.

8.8.1　Ensure Mission Alignment

➤ **Understanding Values:** Take time to understand the philanthropic organization's mission, values, and priorities. Tailor your proposal to align closely with these elements.

➤ **Emotional Appeal:** Unlike scientific grants, philanthropic grants often allow a more emotional or narrative style. Use compelling stories or case studies to create a deeper, more meaningful impact.

➤ **Direct Engagement:** Many philanthropic organizations appreciate direct engagement before the formal proposal is submitted. This contact may include preliminary discussions or letters of intent.

➤ **Restrictions:** Many philanthropic organizations have geographic restrictions, and most will have restrictions on the types of organizations they fund. Some will require verification of non-profit status and financials, e.g., a copy of the IRS 501(c)(3) tax determination letter, IRS 990s, and two years of audited financial statements.

8.8.2 Meet Budgeting and Financial Transparency Expectations

➤ **Flexible Budgets:** Philanthropic grants may offer more budgetary flexibility than government grants, but this flexibility comes with the expectation of financial transparency.

➤ **In-Kind Contributions:** Unlike most government grants, philanthropic grants may consider in-kind contributions as part of your financial commitment. Make sure you understand the rules they use for in-kind contributions.

➤ **Multi-Year Funding:** Some philanthropic grants can be structured as multi-year commitments, for which they will require a detailed, long-term budget.

8.8.3 Establish Measurable Outcomes

➤ **Impact Metrics:** Philanthropic organizations often require different reporting and success metrics that focus more on social impact than scientific output. They may not specify what to measure, so you may need to be creative in figuring out what you will measure, how you will measure it, and how you will relate the outcomes to the organization's objectives.

➤ **Periodic Reporting:** The schedule for project updates or milestone reports can vary greatly, requiring close attention to grant stipulations.

➤ **Publicity and Recognition:** Many philanthropic grants require or offer avenues for public recognition, including co-branding opportunities or public announcements.

8.8.4 Adapt to Timelines and Deadlines

➤ **Rolling Deadlines:** Some philanthropic grants have rolling application deadlines that provide a broader window of opportunity for submissions.

➤ **Quick Turnaround:** Some, but not all, private foundations process applications and disburse funds much more quickly than governmental agencies.

➤ **Pilot Phases:** Given their flexibility, philanthropic grants often allow for pilot phases of projects before committing to full-scale implementation.

This chapter has focused on the application of the tactical writing process to creating successful proposals. It has shown how the art of crafting a compelling proposal is much like crafting a compelling story. Tactical storytelling serves as the proposal's backbone, guiding the narrative and influencing every operational element, from aligning objectives with funder goals to creating a financially and operationally sound budget.

As you endeavor to write your proposal, remember that each section is a chapter in your tactical story. The most compelling stories are well-written and well-executed, and the same holds for successful proposals. Your attention to detail, from the granularity of task-allocation budgeting to the specificity in your Statement of Work, contributes to a cohesive, compelling narrative that stands a strong chance of winning not just the hearts but also the confidence and resources of your intended audience.

8.9 Key Terms

1) **Proposal:** *A formal offer to undertake a project or provide a service, typically made in response to a*

request from a potential client or funding agency.

2) **Mission Alignment:** *The process of ensuring that a project's goals and values align with those of the funding organization.*

3) **Work Breakdown Structure (WBS):** *A project management tool that breaks down a project into smaller, more manageable components or tasks.*

4) **Statement of Work (SOW):** *A document that outlines the tasks, deliverables, and timelines for a project, particularly in subcontracting scenarios.*

5) **Budget:** *A financial plan that estimates the resources needed to complete a project including costs for personnel, materials, travel, and indirect expenses.*

6) **Fringe Benefits:** *Additional benefits provided to employees beyond their salaries, such as health insurance and retirement contributions.*

7) **Modified Total Direct Costs (MTDC):** *The base for calculating indirect costs is usually total direct costs minus certain exclusions like equipment and large subcontracts.*

8) **Indirect Costs:** *Overhead costs that are not directly linked to a specific project but are necessary for its completion, such as administrative expenses.*

9) **Cost Realism:** *The practice of ensuring that cost estimates are realistic, plausible, and reflect the true expenses required to complete a project.*

10) **Biographical Sketch:** *A brief summary of an individual's professional background, often required in grant proposals to highlight relevant experience and qualifications.*

11) **Terms and Conditions:** *Legal and compliance considerations, payment terms, and other contractual obligations, including progress payment schedules.*

12) **GANTT Chart:** *A graphical tool that visually represents the timeline, tasks, and dependencies in a project, often used in project management.*

13) **Milestones:** *Specific points along a project timeline that indicate phase completion or noteworthy accomplishments.*

14) **Current and Pending Support:** *A form detailing all ongoing and pending projects in which key personnel are involved, used to identify potential overlaps with the proposed project.*

15) **Philanthropic Grant:** *Funding provided by private foundations or individual donors, often with a focus on social impact rather than scientific output.*

8.10   Other Terms

1) **National Science Foundation (NSF):** *A U.S. government agency that supports fundamental research and education in all the non-medical fields of science and engineering.*

2) **National Institutes of Health (NIH):** *A U.S. government agency responsible for biomedical and public health research.*

3) **Department of Defense (DoD):** *A U.S. government agency responsible for military operations and national defense.*

4) **Defense Advanced Research Projects Agency (DARPA):** *An agency of the U.S. Department of Defense responsible for the development of emerging technologies for use by the military.*

5) **Small Business Innovation Research (SBIR):** *A U.S. government program that provides funding to small businesses for research and development projects with the potential for commercialization.*

6) **Commercialization Plan:** *A strategy for bringing a new product or technology to market, often required in SBIR and similar proposals.*

7) **Technology Readiness Level (TRL):** *A scale used to assess the maturity of a particular technology, often used in defense and aerospace industries.*

8) **System for Award Management (SAM):** *A U.S. government system that consolidates the capabilities of multiple federal procurement systems and the Catalog of Federal Domestic Assistance.*

9) **Data Management Plan:** *A document outlining how data will be handled during and after a project including storage, sharing, and retention policies.*

10) **Facilities and Equipment:** *Resources available for a project including laboratories, specialized tools, and collaborative sites.*

11) **Letters of Commitment:** *Documents from collaborators or stakeholders affirming their roles and contributions to a project.*

12) **In-Kind Contributions:** *Some government grants and many philanthropic grants may consider in-kind contributions as part of your financial commitment and cost-share; and you should make sure you understand the rules they use for in-kind contributions.*

13) **Multi-Year Funding:** *Some contacts and grants, can be structured as multi-year commitments, requiring a detailed, long-term budget.*

14) **Impact Metrics:** *Philanthropic organizations often require different reporting and success metrics, focusing more on social impact than scientific output. They may not specify what to measure, so you may need to be creative in determining what you will measure and how you will relate that to the objectives.*

15) **Periodic Reporting:** *The schedule for project updates or milestone reports can vary greatly, requiring close attention to grant stipulations.*

16) **Publicity and Recognition:** *Many philanthropic grants require or offer avenues for public recognition, including co-branding opportunities or public announcements.*

17) **Rolling Deadlines:** *Some philanthropic grants have rolling application deadlines, providing a broader window of opportunity for submissions.*

18) **Pilot Phases:** *Given their flexibility, philanthropic grants often allow for pilot phases before committing to full-scale implementation.*

19) **Coherence:** *Ensuring that the tasks and associated costs outlined in the SOW directly correspond with those in the budget.*

20) **Task Duration:** *The length of time each task takes, represented as a horizontal bar in a GANTT chart.*

21) **Dependencies:** *Arrows or lines between tasks that show dependencies, helping to identify potential bottlenecks in a GANTT chart.*

22) **Progress Indicator:** *A feature in GANTT charts that tracks the completion of tasks.*

23) **Quad Chart:** *A one-page visual summary of a proposal often required by DARPA and DoD.*

9   Tactical Business Storytelling

"The most powerful person in the world is the storyteller. The storyteller sets the vision, values, and agenda of an entire generation that is to come."

-Steve Jobs, Apple

In the world of business today, effective communication is not just a skill; it is a weapon. When told effectively, a business story has the power to forge a deep and personal connection between the storyteller and the audience. The right business story can reshape opinions, inspire individuals to achieve seemingly insurmountable goals, and illuminate paths toward positive change. A sharply written memo or a strategically constructed email can pave the way for success, while a poorly crafted one can become a stumbling block—or worse —close the door on a prized opportunity.

Successful leaders have learned to use the power of stories as potent tools to engage their teams and captivate their customers. If your goal is to motivate others effectively, then mastering the art of storytelling is essential. Whether you are writing memos and emails or preparing for oral communication such as speeches or presentations, storytelling is a critical skill. So buckle up as we unpack these tools, reveal actionable insights, and present applicable techniques that will arm you with the skills needed to tell business stories that do not simply inform but also persuade and motivate.

9.1 Understanding the Power of Business Storytelling

Unlike traditional stories designed for entertainment, business stories are a unique genre. To communicate successfully, they must be crafted with clear objectives, goals, or desired outcomes in mind. Whether we are writing memos, emails, protocols, or proposals or preparing for oral communication such as presentations or speeches, tactical business storytelling is a critical skill that applies to the full scope of business communication. TWWIST is a set of techniques used to connect and communicate with various audiences, including employees, customers, colleagues, partners, suppliers, and the media. As we delve into the practical application of TWWIST in business communication we will explore.

➤ **The Power of Tactical Innovation in Storytelling** - From crafting the opening line to the closing statements, we will use common structures for business storytelling that make it effective and actionable. We will provide examples and practical advice.

➤ **Structural Styles of Innovation and Business Stories** - While business stories can utilize almost any storytelling structure, we will review some of the classic business story structures so you can leverage the well-known patterns that likely already exist in the minds of your audience.

➤ **Decoding the Audience** - Understanding your audience dictates not only what you say but also how you say it. Businesses often have multiple audiences, and the inherent power dynamics that are not factors in other types of storytelling can change how you interact with your audience.

➤ **Applications: Memos, Email, Messaging, and Marketing** - While we emphasize storytelling in the TWWIST approach, not all tactical business writing really needs, or even does well, using storytelling. We will provide practical tips illustrating the dos and don'ts of tactical business writing for memos and emails. We then get into micro-case studies on storytelling for marketing.

➤ **Language and Tone** - Choose your words wisely; they are the bricks and mortar of your memo, email, presentation, or proposal. We will discuss the appropriate language and tone for different business scenarios.

9.2 Decoding Your Audience

Understanding your audience is pivotal for effective communication in any setting. But in business communication it is a strategic necessity. While the chapter on audience, Chapter 4, previously provided general techniques for audience analysis, business communication requires a more thorough understanding. Audience analysis in business communications differs from traditional settings because of the significance of long-term interactions with your audience and the unique considerations for writing up, down, or across the management chain. Knowing your audience sets the stage for every strategic decision you will make in creating a tactical business story.

9.2.1   Why Business Audience Analysis Is Different

In academic or casual communications, the audience often serves as a passive recipient with whom the author will not regularly interact. But business communication demands more of the relationship. The audience for all business communications becomes an active participant in the corporate ecosystem, and they will be in that role again tomorrow and the next day for as long as the business relationship continues.

While the primary goal of academic writing or casual conversations is to inform or entertain, the dynamics of business communications, whether they be written or oral, are considerably different. The business communication audience is not just a passive recipient but often is a key player in the decision-making process. Communication with the audience almost always requires action on their part. Furthermore, the stakes of your communication can be very high, making the need for a nuanced understanding of your audience paramount.

Consider power dynamics, for instance. While this is not usually a significant consideration in traditional settings, it becomes crucial in business. Your audience's position in the corporate hierarchy impacts not just the tone of your communication but also its content. A message to a subordinate might be instructive and direct, while the same information may need to be framed as a recommendation or suggestion when communicating upward in the hierarchy.

The decision-making role of your audience cannot be overstated. If you are writing to someone who has the authority to enact changes based on your communication, your message should be persuasive as well as informative. Facts are not enough; you must present them in a way that guides the decision-maker toward the outcome you desire.

Your audience's prior knowledge and expectations significantly influence your communication as well. An audience that is well-versed in the subject matter will have little patience for unnecessary details or gratuitous background information. Conversely, if you are communicating complex information to an audience unfamiliar with the topic, skipping over the basics can lead to confusion or misinterpretation.

In order to accommodate the diverse needs of your audience, consider the following five elements when writing business communications:

- **Objectives:** Clearly state the purpose of your communication. Whether you aim to inform, persuade, or instruct, align this objective with what you know about your audience's role and interests in the corporate structure.

- **Power Dynamics:** Your audience's position within the hierarchy will significantly affect both the tone and the content of your email or memo.

➤ **Decision-Making:** Consider the decision-making power of your audience and frame your arguments or information in a way that guides them toward the outcome you desire.

➤ **Prior Knowledge:** Be mindful of what the audience already knows about the topic. This will help you avoid unnecessary repetition or, conversely, glossing over crucial details.

➤ **Storytelling:** Use anecdotes or short stories to make your message more relatable and compelling. Storytelling elements can make complex business problems more accessible.

9.2.2   Making the Most of Long-Term Audience Interaction

Business communications are rarely isolated events or one-off interactions. More often than not, they are part of a larger series of interactions that contribute to ongoing projects, relationships, or objectives. As such they are part of a dynamic, unfolding story that shapes your professional relationships and outcomes.

Understanding the implications of long-term interactions with your audience is essential for effective communication. One of the great advantages is the shared context that comes from long-term interactions. On the other hand, one of the great disadvantages is that errors and miscommunication become embedded in that shared context and the fallout is hard to escape.

Credibility is a crucial factor that is built or eroded over time. It can take years to build up a reputation and just seconds to destroy it. Each meeting, memo, or email contributes to a broader perception of your competency, reliability, and worth. Consistency in your communication, therefore, is not just a stylistic choice but a strategic one. It helps you build a reliable persona that your audience can trust, which is invaluable in long-term business relationships.

Feedback loops also play a significant role in long-term interactions. If your audience has reacted positively or negatively to past communications, this feedback must inform your future messages. Ignoring such feedback is a missed opportunity for improvement. In addition, it might signal a lack of attentiveness or respect toward your audience's needs or concerns.

Your communication should be agile enough to adapt to the evolving business landscape and its impact on your audience and your business relationship. Strategies shift, projects pivot, and objectives change. Your presentations, meeting memos, and emails should reflect these dynamic elements, serving not just as static pieces of communication but as living documents that evolve within the broader business context.

Storytelling also has a role in promoting long-term interaction with your audience. A well-told story can serve as a memory anchor, making your messages more memorable and impactful in the long term. You can invoke that story later by exercising parts of the shared context while exercising other parts by omission or direct contradiction. Personal stories can also help build personal connections and improve relations, but do not get overly fixated on your personal views and experience as the primary source of information.

To summarize, the key elements to consider in fostering successful interaction with a long-term audience are:

➤ **Objectives:** In the long term, your communications should aim to build trust and establish credibility. Ensure each message contributes positively to these overarching objectives.

➤ **Credibility:** Each memo or email is an opportunity to build or erode trust. Consistency in tone, content, and quality is essential for building a credible persona.

- **Feedback Loops:** Incorporate feedback from previous communications to improve and fine-tune your messages.

- **Adapting to a Changing Landscape:** Keep your communications agile to adapt to shifts in company strategies or objectives.

- **Storytelling**: Allows you to help shape the way you and your objectives are viewed by your audience.

9.2.3   Writing Up, Down, or Across the Management Chain

The direction of communication within the corporate hierarchy significantly impacts how you craft your message. It shapes both the style and substance of your writing. For instance, when communicating with superiors in the management chain, the focus should be on brevity and impact. Executives and higher-ups are usually time-constrained and prefer communications that get straight to the point while highlighting the most critical issues. In such cases, the emphasis should be on providing key insights, summarizing value, and outlining the implications of the information presented.

When writing down the chain to subordinates, the emphasis often shifts to clarity and comprehensiveness. Junior employees or team members look to their supervisors and higher-ups for direction. Memos and emails should, therefore, serve as guideposts that offer both clear instructions and sufficient context for understanding the bigger picture.

Peer-to-peer communications, or those that go across the management chain, present yet another unique challenge. Here, the tone can be more collegial, but professionalism should still be the mainstay. Communications across the chain often involve coordination, delegation, or collaboration. Therefore, the focus should be on clearly outlining responsibilities and action items, setting expectations, and specifying any dependencies that may exist.

By understanding these dynamics, you can craft memos, emails, and other communications that not only serve their immediate purpose but also contribute to broader strategic goals. Below is a summary of key elements to consider in light of the management chain positioning of the writer and recipient:

- **Objectives:** When writing up the chain, your objective may be to influence or inform; when writing down, it may be to instruct or guide; and when writing across, it may be to collaborate or coordinate.

- **Brevity vs Comprehensiveness:** Executives value brevity, while subordinates may prefer detailed instructions. Peers usually fall somewhere in between.

- **Clarity and Context:** The level of clarity and context needed will vary depending on your audience's familiarity with the topic.

- **Professionalism:** Regardless of the direction, maintaining a professional tone is paramount.

- **Storytelling:** Stories can be used to highlight the significance of a project, illustrate a problem, or showcase a solution. The way you tell these stories should be tailored to your audience's position and role.

By paying heed to these elements about understanding a business audience, your communication efforts— whether they be written memos or oral presentations— will be more effective and resonate better with your audience to help you achieve your tactical objectives.

Used effectively, tactical business storytelling is a powerful organizational management tool. Once you have identified and decoded your audience, the recipients of your communication, you have many different opportunities to apply tactical business storytelling techniques to communicate your message. Consider the top ten applications for internal and external business storytelling.

9.3.1 Top Ten Applications of Internal Business Storytelling

Storytelling within an organization can be a potent tool for strengthening company culture, fostering collaboration, conveying values, inspiring employees, and resolving conflicts. It is pivotal in enhancing internal communication and guiding organizations through change. Here are the top ten applications for internal business storytelling:

1) **Motivating Teams:** Inspire and motivate your teams by sharing stories that reinforce your organization's vision and mission. Leaders can use narratives to set expectations, boost morale, and emphasize the significance of their work.

2) **Navigating Change:** During periods of change, use stories to communicate new strategies or directions. Stories can help ease concerns, instill confidence, and guide employees through transitions.

3) **Fostering Company Culture:** Share stories that exemplify the desired company culture. These stories can illustrate core values, work ethics, and expected behaviors, contributing to a cohesive and positive workplace environment.

4) **Onboarding and Training:** Accelerate the onboarding process and facilitate training by using stories to convey essential information and best practices. Stories make learning more engaging and memorable.

5) **Resolving Conflicts:** Storytelling can be an effective tool for resolving conflicts. Share narratives highlighting shared goals and common ground to bridge gaps and facilitate conflict resolution.

6) **Celebrating Success:** Recognize and celebrate achievements within your organization by sharing success stories. These narratives inspire employees, instill a sense of pride, and encourage ongoing excellence.

7) **Building Leadership Skills:** Developing leadership skills can be enhanced through storytelling. Encourage leaders to share personal leadership stories that demonstrate key principles and practices.

8) **Enhancing Communication:** Storytelling improves internal communication. Use stories to make complex information more accessible and relatable to employees, which will facilitate better understanding.

9) **Innovation and Problem-Solving:** Foster creativity and innovation by encouraging employees to share stories of innovative solutions to challenges. These stories can inspire creative problem-solving.

10) **Creating a Collaborative Environment:** Stories of successful collaborations and teamwork can encourage employees to work together effectively, fostering a culture of collaboration.

9.3.2 Top Ten Applications of External Business Storytelling

Business storytelling aimed at external audiences is a compelling tool for marketing, building brand identity, and engaging customers. It creates an emotional connection with your audience and sets your brand apart in a competitive landscape. Here are the top ten applications of external business storytelling:

1) **Influencing Decision-Makers:** Compelling stories can influence stakeholders, board members, or investors. Stories make complex information more digestible and relatable, aiding in securing support and funding.

2) **Developing and Growing Your Business Image:** Use business stories to craft your brand's image. Your story can shape marketing campaigns, website design, and social media posts, providing a cohesive foundation for your business.

3) **Creating a Memorable Brand:** In a competitive market, a compelling business story helps your brand stand out, fostering customer loyalty and providing a competitive advantage.

4) **Humanizing Your Brand:** Stories bridge the gap between businesses and individuals, helping people connect with your brand on an emotional level that will enhance sales strategies.

5) **Brand Advocacy:** Encourage customers to become brand advocates by sharing their stories about your products or services. These narratives build trust and encourage word-of-mouth referrals.

6) **Differentiating Your Brand:** In a crowded marketplace, your unique business story can set you apart from competitors, helping you to establish a distinctive position that will stand out from the pack.

7) **Effective Sales Strategies:** Sales professionals use storytelling to create emotional connections with potential customers. These stories demonstrate the value of products or services, making them more relatable and enticing.

8) **Fostering Customer Loyalty:** Customer loyalty is strengthened when customers connect with your brand. Business stories create this connection, leading to customer retention and word-of-mouth marketing.

9) **Customer Engagement via Content Creation:** Continually engaging customers can be invaluable for your business. Business storytelling provides effective content for blogs, videos, and social media posts. Storytelling enhances your content strategy and keeps your audience engaged.

10) **Enhancing Marketing Strategies:** Business storytelling forms the essence of marketing. Narrate your business's origin, your founders' journey, or your customers' stories to create powerful marketing campaigns.

9.4 Structural Styles of Business Stories

Many of the story structures considered in chapter 6 section 6.5 can be used in business storytelling. Some classic structures, such as the well-known "Hero's Journey" are used frequently. Ultimately, the structural style chosen for a business story should be driven by the key goal of the story.

Some specific story styles are described by author Annette Simmons in her book, "Whoever Tells the Best Story Wins." Simmons [2015] Simmons identifies six powerful structural styles for crafting business stories that align with the tactical writing process and offer versatile tools for achieving specific objectives. Let us introduce each of Simmon's six storytelling structures and consider how they work in business.

9.4.1   "Who-I-Am" Stories

These stories reveal your personal identity and experiences. They encompass your dreams, goals, accomplishments, failures, motivations, values, and history. "Who-I-Am" stories serve a fundamental role in building trust and are particularly valuable when introducing yourself to a new team or establishing a connection with a stranger.

"Who-I-Am" stories create a sense of authenticity and relatability. They can include your professional journey, your core values, and your sources of inspiration. When you share your personal experiences, whether they are achievements or struggles, you humanize yourself. This humanization is key in business settings where trust and rapport are essential.

Furthermore, "Who-I-Am" stories establish common ground with your audience. By sharing your history, you might uncover shared experiences, interests, or values. This common ground helps form connections with colleagues, clients, or stakeholders.

In summary, "Who-I-Am" stories:

➤ Humanize Your Identity: They make the person behind the professional more relatable.

➤ Establish Common Ground: These stories reveal shared experiences or values that can forge stronger connections.

➤ Build Trust: Sharing your authentic self fosters trust and credibility, especially in new or unfamiliar situations.

9.4.2   "Why-I-Am-Here" Stories

"Why-I-Am-Here" stories articulate your purpose and intentions. They help to assure others that you have no hidden agenda and that both parties stand to benefit fairly from the situation. This clarity helps when transparency is paramount, such as in fundraising or sales.

People want to know not only what is in it for them but also what is in it for you. "Why-I-Am-Here" stories present a clear picture of your intentions, thereby replacing suspicion with trust. In these stories you communicate your passion, goals, and motivations. You also might share your personal connection to the mission or objectives at hand.

Additionally, these stories address the unspoken questions in your audience's minds. They clarify whether your involvement is financially driven or based on genuine commitment. By openly discussing your motivations, you foster an environment of trust and transparency.

In essence, "Why-I-Am-Here" stories:

➤ Clarify Intentions: These stories provide a transparent view of your goals and motivations.

➤ Address Unspoken Questions: They proactively answer concerns about hidden agendas or financial motivations.

➤ Promote Transparency: Openly sharing your reasons for being present cultivates trust and authenticity.

9.4.3   Vision Stories

Vision stories serve as inspirational narratives that evoke hope and happiness. They convince your audience that their hard work and sacrifice are worthwhile by linking their actions to a valuable, noble outcome. They emphasize the ultimate goal, highlighting its significance and the positive impact it can have.

In a business context, vision stories are motivational tools that urge individuals to persevere in the face of challenges. Effective vision stories connect the efforts of the present to the rewards of the future. They evoke emotions and encourage individuals to push through obstacles. They help to inspire teams, employees, or partners to work toward a shared objective. Vision stories are particularly useful in times of change, as they provide a sense of direction and purpose.

In essence, Vision Stories:

➣ Inspire and Motivate: These stories spark hope and happiness, encouraging individuals to overcome challenges.

➣ Connect Efforts to Outcomes: They establish a clear link between present actions and future rewards.

➣ Provide Direction and Purpose: Vision stories are valuable during periods of change, offering a sense of purpose and direction.

9.4.4 Values-in-Action Stories

Values-in-Action stories reinforce the values you want your audience to embody. These stories can be either positive or negative. They can exemplify virtues or caution against undesirable attitudes.

Values-in-Action stories are powerful tools for promoting a culture of integrity, compassion, and commitment. They demonstrate these values in action, making them more tangible for your audience. By narrating real-life examples of these values, you provide a road map for others to follow.

These stories can also be used to caution against negative attitudes. By highlighting the consequences of cynicism, indifference to quality, or a weak work ethic, you can steer your audience away from behaviors that are detrimental to your objectives. Values-in-Action stories play a critical role in shaping the values and culture of your organization.

In summary, Values-in-Action Stories:

➣ Promote Virtues: These stories exemplify the positive values you want your audience to adopt.

➣ Provide Guidance: They offer practical examples of values in action, guiding others to follow suit.

➣ Discourage Negative Behaviors: Values-in-Action stories caution against attitudes that are counterproductive to your goals.

9.4.5 "I-Know-What-You-Are-Thinking" Stories

"I-Know-What-You-Are-Thinking" stories allow you to address the audience's anticipated objections, suspicions, questions, or concerns before they voice them. By validating your audience's perspective, you show understanding and empathy, you build trust and rapport. These stories also allow you to control the narrative by the way in which you present and resolve the objections.

These stories are anticipatory in nature. They require you to put yourself in your audience's shoes and identify their potential objections or concerns. By addressing these issues proactively, you demonstrate empathy and a willingness to engage with your audience on their terms.

"I-Know-What-You-Are-Thinking" stories are particularly valuable in sales, negotiations, or presentations to key stakeholders. They help you establish common ground and build trust by showing that you understand your audience's viewpoint.

In summary, "I-Know-What-You-Are-Thinking" Stories:

➣ Anticipate Audience Concerns: These stories address potential objections or worries before they are raised.

➣ Demonstrate Empathy: By validating your audience's perspective, you show that you understand and respect their viewpoint.

➣ Build Trust and Rapport: These stories help establish common ground and trust in sales, negotiations, and key presentations.

9.4.6   Teaching Stories

Teaching stories are narratives that create transformative experiences for your audience. They demonstrate how changes in behavior, perspective, or skills can lead to meaningful results. These stories can also be employed to illustrate best- or worst-case scenarios and can be combined as substories in any of the previous five types.

Teaching stories are tools for facilitating learning and personal growth. They help your audience grasp complex concepts by presenting them in the form of relatable narratives. In the context of tactical writing, these stories are valuable for educating team members, clients, or partners about processes, techniques, or best practices.

These stories can also be used to present scenarios that serve as learning opportunities. By showcasing both successful and unsuccessful outcomes, you provide your audience with valuable insights into what does and does not work. Teaching stories often leave a lasting impression, as they enable the audience to internalize lessons through narrative experiences.

In summary, Teaching Stories:

➣ Facilitate Learning: These stories help audiences understand complex concepts and best practices.

➣ Present Scenarios: They illustrate real-life situations including successes and failures.

➣ Encourage Learning Through Experience: Teaching stories offer valuable lessons through narrative experiences.

Personal Story: Launching an Innovation Degree

My personal story for business is actually one you've already read. If you look at the preface, you'll see I told a story about how some of my experiences led to writing this book, to my being at the University of Colorado Colorado Springs, and to my overall journey. This is probably the single most told business story in my career, in part because I consider launching and growing the "Bachelor of Innovation" to be the most significant business or opportunity I've explored.

Rather than repeating yet another version of that story, I want you to go back and look at the different types of stories I just wrote about. Then analyze the preface and see how many of those different types of stories I actually worked into it. Here's a hint: I only missed one or two types of stories!

I've evolved my personal story over time, incorporating different techniques because I learned what worked when I talked to parents, clients, or legislators. Different people and audiences are looking for different things, so parts of my story will resonate with some much more than with others.

Telling a good, tactical business story requires a mixture of understanding your audience, understanding your business objective, and knowing how to tell a story. The preface is tactical story intended to get readers/teachers to want to read/use the book. But I tell almost the same story when parents visit or when I meet company representatives at networking events. When I tell the story in such settings, I often don't have time to dig into audience analysis. Parents show up at my door to talk about their son or daughter coming to UCCS, and I tell the whole story. I meet with someone at a networking event and I tell the whole story. Even in the preface, I don't know who the students/teachers reading this book will be, so I tell most of the story, putting in all of the parts, hoping that one or two of those parts will resonate with my readers.

To me, these are the core elements of a good personal business story. You'll see lots of personal elements in it, but you will also see a vision of the future, the kinds of problems being addressed, and how they are addressed.

9.4.7 Alternative Business Story Structures

Simmon's six are one way of looking at the objectives and structure of business stories, but not the only way. Her structure styles are more tactical "story" oriented. Another common story structure view is the one-word key "plot" element. Here are the seven "one-word story plot" structures and their primary value:

➤ **Origin Stories:** Explain the beginnings of your organization, including ideation, struggles, and early achievements.

➤ **Failure Stories:** Narrate instances of setbacks and how they were overcome, connecting with the human experience of failure.

➤ **Success Stories:** Share milestones and accomplishments, building trust and an emotional connection.

➤ **Customer Stories:** Use customer narratives to promote your business, demonstrating real-life benefits and credibility.

➤ **Product Stories:** Communicate the value and practical usage of your products or services, fostering engagement and loyalty.

➤ **Personal Stories:** Focus on people in the company and what they did to make it great. These stories support company morale and employee loyalty and also help humanize the company to customers and stakeholders.

➤ **Job Stories:** This story highlights the job-to-be-done that your company can provide. These stories are related to customer stories, but the focus is on the unique advantage the company has in addressing the problem that needs resolution.

Thought exercise Simmon's six storytelling structures are versatile tools that align with the tactical writing process and can be integrated with multiple styles and structures. They help craft narratives that resonate with your audience and drive specific objectives but are very flexible, so it is worth spending some time thinking about how to apply themand what actual storytelling structure you can use.
For each of the above seven one-word plot stories, think about the most closely related of Simmon's six storytelling structures and note the similarities and differences.

There are many effective approaches to business storytelling. Written documents and presentations have their place, but there is also a time and place for oral business storytelling. Whether you are hiring employees, fostering company culture, boosting sales, or managing teams, the art of oral storytelling can be an invaluable tool for conveying messages, engaging audiences, and driving desired outcomes.

Used well, tactical oral storytelling is a powerful communication tool that creates a lasting impact. The power of a story can engage employees and clients, bridge gaps, and inspire action in ways that other forms of communication cannot. To better understand the role of oral business storytelling, consider the following examples of business activities ways to use tactical storytelling in everyday business activities.

➤ **Hiring and Recruiting:** Oral storytelling in the context of hiring and recruitment is essential for attracting top talent. Compelling narratives showcase your company's values, mission, and vision. Stories about successful employees who have grown within the organization illustrate opportunities for professional development. For example, begin interviews with a story about the company's humble beginnings that highlights how employees' contributions have shaped its growth. Use the "Hero's Journey" structure to share anecdotes of past hires who have advanced within the company and to highlight a candidate's potential transformative experience within the company. Leverage anecdotes that convey your organization's commitment to inclusiveness and employee development.

➤ **Company Culture:** Oral storytelling is a potent tool for defining and maintaining company culture. By sharing stories that exemplify your organization's values and ethics, you can inspire employees to embrace and embody these principles.

During onboarding, for instance, you can tell stories about how employees across various roles have demonstrated the company's core values from integrity to innovation. Use metaphors and analogies to clarify cultural concepts. Share values-in-action stories to illustrate what it means to be part of the company culture. Use narratives of failure and success to demonstrate how these experiences align with the company's culture.

➤ **Sales:** In sales, oral storytelling can transform the way customers perceive your products or services. Weave narratives that highlight customer success stories, the evolution of your offerings, and the impact they can have on clients' lives or businesses. During a sales presentation you could share an "I Know What You Are Thinking" story of a client who faced a challenge similar to the prospect's and overcame it with your product. Structure stories to lead prospects from a problem to a solution, painting a vivid picture of success. Emphasize the transformation and results achieved. Craft narratives that tap into the prospect's emotions and aspirations.

➤ **Teamwork:** Oral storytelling can enhance teamwork by fostering a sense of belonging and shared purpose among team members. Use "Why I Am Here" stories to unite individuals, communicate objectives, and inspire collaboration.

In a team meeting, share a story that underscores the importance of collective effort in achieving a common goal. Highlight how each team member's unique contributions led to success. Craft stories that emphasize the team's shared mission and achievements. Personalize narratives to make individual team members feel valued.

➤ **Management:** As a manager, you can use oral storytelling to motivate, provide guidance, and lead by example. Share your personal experiences and challenges through "Who I Am" stories to connect with your team on a human level. Share stories that align with leadership principles. In a leadership meeting, tell a story about a significant leadership lesson you learned from a past mistake. Use anecdotes to provide clarity and context for strategic decisions, making them relatable to your team. Emphasize personal growth and how it shaped your managerial style.

➢ **Change and Change Management:** Change is a constant in the business world, and effective communication during transitions is vital. Use vision stories to explain the reasons behind changes, share success stories from the past, and provide a vision of the future.

When implementing a new software system, share a story of another organization's successful adoption, emphasizing the benefits and improved efficiency it brought. Employ the 'Before and After' storytelling structure, showcasing the current challenges and the promising future state.

➢ **Conflict Resolution:** In business, conflicts are inevitable. Storytelling can help resolve disputes by fostering under- standing and empathy among the parties involved. Narratives can clarify misunderstandings and create common ground for resolution.

During a conflict resolution meeting, tell a story about a past disagreement that was successfully resolved through compromise and communication. Use "Perspective Shifting" stories, which present the same event from different viewpoints, to encourage empathy and compromise.

➢ **Customer Service and Satisfaction:** Oral storytelling that highlights exceptional service, resolved issues, or ways your business goes the extra mile to meet customer needs is a potent tool for improving customer service and ensuring satisfaction.

In customer service training, tell a "Values in Action" story that recounts an incident when an employee's dedication and quick thinking resolved a challenging customer issue, resulting in a positive review. Employ "Success Stories" or "Customer Stories" that portray how your business's commitment to exceptional service results in satisfied customers and brand loyalty.

➢ **Innovation and Creativity:** Businesses thrive on innovation, and oral storytelling can fuel creativity within your organization. Share "Teaching Stories" of past innovations, creative problem-solving, or instances where employees brought fresh ideas to life.

During a brainstorming session, recount a story about a team member who came up with a unique solution to a longstanding problem, sparking innovation. Use "Creativity Chronicles" to take listeners through the creative process, from the initial spark of an idea to its successful implementation.

9.5.1   Tactical Oral Business Storytelling in Action

For each of the business activities identified above, oral storytelling can be a valuable tool to inspire, educate, and engage. By adopting storytelling techniques that align with the specific context, businesses can harness the power of narratives to achieve their goals. To better understand what effective business storytelling looks like and how it works, consider the following real-life short examples.

➢ **Storytelling for Building Trust and Team Dynamics:** Consider Chris, who was perceived as an outsider when he assumed leadership of a new team. He quickly recognized that trust within the team needed to be improved and put the power of storytelling to work. Chris used "Vulnerability Stories," opening up to the team about past experiences and challenges. He shared personal stories about his leadership experiences, explained his enthusiasm for the new role, and disclosed details about his upbringing and hobbies. This honesty and vulnerability made a genuine connection with the team members and transformed the team's perceptions. They began to view Chris as a real person rather than a stranger, which ultimately led to increased trust and collaboration.

➤ **Storytelling for Influencing Client Decisions:** Imagine Elise, a sales representative, meeting a potential client who had limited knowledge about her organization's offerings. To convey the value of her products effectively, she employed a "Success Story" approach, using a real-life example to showcase the practical benefits of her product. Elise narrated a story detailing how one of her products significantly reduced another client's supply costs by 20 percent. The potential client was impressed by the narrative and, convinced of the product's effectiveness, placed an order and became a client.

➤ **Storytelling for Convincing Teams of Necessary Actions:** Elsa encountered strong skepticism when she asked her team to attend a workplace safety class. Her team members questioned the importance of this training. To address their concerns, Elsa utilized "Warning Stories," thinking that a cautionary tale to highlight the potential risks and consequences might persuade her team to prioritize safety. She shared a story from a recent trade journal that described an employee at a rival organization who suffered a severe injury while using machinery similar to what her team used. Elsa was right. The story convinced her team that the safety class was vital for preventing similar incidents and ultimately secured their participation.

9.5.2   Business Storytelling for Branding

There are a few areas in business in which oral storytelling is far more extensive than is evident in the examples above. Branding, annual meetings, and pitching new programs often require team planning and effort. Storytelling, for instance, can be one of the most critical tools for shaping and reinforcing a company's brand identity. It allows organizations to convey their values, missions, and unique selling propositions in a compelling and memorable manner. Through a story they can say, "We are good people and do good things," without actually saying that explicitly. Here's how a company might utilize storytelling techniques to enhance its branding:

Imagine a tech startup named "InnovateTech." They want to establish a brand image that highlights their commitment to cutting-edge solutions and their vision of a brighter technological future. InnovateTech chooses to craft a compelling narrative that reflects this ethos. They share a story about one of their early employees, Sarah, who was passionate about pushing the boundaries of technology from a young age. Relating Sarah's journey, from her garage-based experiments to becoming a key leader in InnovateTech's research and development team, symbolizes the company's dedication to innovation and the opportunities for promotion. The narrative showcases how InnovateTech encourages employees to explore uncharted territories and empowers them to make significant technological advancements.

This story is not just about Sarah; it is about the entire company's identity. It is a tale of innovation, passion, and the relentless pursuit of progress. As InnovateTech consistently tells this story through various marketing channels and touchpoints, it establishes a brand synonymous with cutting-edge technology and progress. Business storytelling becomes a powerful vehicle for building and promoting the brand identity.

To female employees and customers, the story also shows that the company empowers and rewards its female employees. It can do that without mentioning the terms diversity, equity, and inclusion—terms that can be a double-edged sword in a highly polarized world. When it comes to DEI, stories can speak both louder and softer than words, depending on the audience's context.

In this example, InnovateTech utilized a "Hero's Journey" approach, narrating the story of an individual's transformation and aligning it with the company's commitment to innovation.

9.5.3   Business Storytelling for the Company Annual Meeting

Annual meetings are crucial events for organizations. They provide a platform to review past accomplishments, set future goals, and engage with stakeholders. Business storytelling can transform these gatherings from routine affairs into inspirational and memorable experiences. Here is how it can be used effectively. Consider a 15-year-old manufacturing company we will call "TechQuest." TechQuest's leadership wants to inspire its employees, investors, advisors, and partners, including Dr. Boult, at the annual meeting. They decide to harness the power of storytelling.

The CEO, Dave, takes the stage and shares a story from the company's early days. He starts with the more traditional presentation of revenue and employee growth. Then, he shifts to a storytelling model, telling how TechQuest faced a critical turning point when a major client doubted the company's capabilities. In response, the team, driven by determination and commitment, worked relentlessly to not only meet the client's expectations but to exceed them. They tell a story, including graphics of the products, of how the delivered product not only met the project requirements but also opened up new opportunities for the client with real-time feedback on their lasers. They also tell of the million-dollar drone crash where the million-dollar drone was totaled but where their product survived the crash — showing it not only did its job but that it was very rugged, adding even more value.

This story serves multiple purposes. First, it highlights TechQuest's core values of commitment and resilience. Second, it showcases the company's track record of not just meeting but surpassing requirements and overcoming challenges. Third, it sends a powerful message that TechQuest is more than just a manufacturing company; it is a team of passionate individuals who rise to the occasion and provide true value to their government and commercial clients.

Throughout the annual meeting, other employees share stories of overcoming challenges and making significant contributions. The meeting becomes a collective narrative of TechQuest's journey filled with resilience, innovation, and success. In this way, business storytelling transforms the annual meeting into a platform for not only reviewing financial reports but also celebrating the company's shared history, values, and aspirations. It becomes a powerful tool for uniting stakeholders in a common vision for the future.

In this example, TechQuest used a "Resilience and Triumph" story approach, narrating past challenges and victories to inspire and motivate stakeholders.

9.5.4   Pitching Internal Ideas for New Programs

In an organizational setting, pitching internal ideas for new programs/products is a crucial skill. While oral business storytelling is often unplanned and often cannot use significant preparation, formally pitching new ideas generally does. Business storytelling can be a powerful tool in this context. It helps individuals convey the value and potential impact of their ideas to decision-makers with different story elements for different personality types. Let us explore how this works through two examples featuring Terry, a university faculty member who aims to create the "Bachelor of Innovation" degree program—and these were successful.

Example 1: Character-Centric Storytelling Terry, a dedicated faculty member, believed in the potential of an interdisciplinary degree program that crosses disciplines using innovation, entrepreneurship, and teamwork as core skills. He recognized that this program had the power to prepare students for the modern workforce, which demands creativity, adaptability, and entrepreneurial thinking. His vision was quite different from normal university operations, so he needed stories to set the context and communicate the unique ideas.

To gain support for his innovative idea, Terry needed to communicate its value effectively to the university's diverse decision-makers. For the first part, he chose a character-centric storytelling approach. Terry shared a story about a fictitious student named Alex, who went through the various courses in the program until he embodied the qualities the Bachelor of Innovation program aimed to nurture and was successful in his career.

Alex's journey was a compelling narrative, starting with a diverse set of interests and talents and culminating in ground- breaking innovations that solved real-world problems for clients. The story vividly depicted how the program would provide students with the skills and mindset to thrive in a rapidly changing world, emphasizing adaptability, creativity, and entrepreneurship.

Example 2: Multi-modal/Visual Storytelling Another aspect of the presentation Terry aimed to emphasize was the Bachelor of Innovation story via visual elements and images that appeared as he was telling the story. Knowing that seeing is believing, he used a visual storytelling approach to make his pitch more convincing. He created a presentation that included images, infographics, and multimedia elements as well as graphs about financial and program growth.

Terry used these visuals to illustrate Alex's journey, starting from enrollment in the program to graduation. The graphics showed how students' skills would evolve, how they would collaborate on real-world projects, and the innovative solutions they would create. After Alex's story, the presentation included visuals and data on expected overall program growth and financial success, with data from surveys to back up the presentation.

As Terry presented his visual narrative, decision-makers could see the transformation that the program would bring about. Visual storytelling allowed them to grasp the concept quickly and appreciate its potential impact on students' lives.

Example Techniques

➤ **Character-Centric Storytelling**: Terry's first example focused on a relatable character, Alex, whose journey represented the program's intended outcomes. Using characters can make a narrative more engaging and relatable.

➤ **Visual Storytelling**: In the second example, Terry leveraged visuals, infographics, and multimedia to convey the program's impact. Visual storytelling can be highly effective when conveying complex ideas.

➤ **Problem-Solution Framework**: Consider highlighting the challenges your program addresses and how it provides solutions. This framework can be compelling when pitching new ideas.

➤ **Emphasize Transformation**: Terry's storytelling emphasized how the program would transform students' lives. Highlighting the transformative aspects of your idea can make it more appealing.

➤ **Keep It Personal**: Sharing personal anecdotes or using a personable tone can create a stronger connection with your audience.

Incorporating these storytelling techniques can significantly enhance your ability to pitch internal ideas for new programs, products, or initiatives within your organization.

9.6 Effective Communication Through Emails and Messaging

While storytelling is critical in many aspects of business communications, many day-to-day operations are more factual and do not need, or even support, as much storytelling. However, many of the tactical writing elements still apply to writing these documents effectively. It is still essential to establish a clear understanding of your objectives and your audience. And not all emails are created equal. Some can be handled quickly with the knowledge you have on hand, but for others doing your research will pay off.

9.6.1   Top Ten Tips for Writing Effective Business Emails

Significant business activity today is conducted through emails, so crafting effective business emails is an essential skill. When writing emails, you must convey your message clearly, maintain professionalism, and build positive working relationships. That can be a tall order to fill. To guide you in this endeavor, consider our top ten tips on business emails:

1) **Write a Meaningful Subject Line:** The subject line of your email is the first thing the recipient sees. As the email equivalent of a headline, the subject line plays a critical role in determining whether your email is opened or ignored. To be effective, a well-crafted subject line should provide a concise and accurate summary of the email's purpose and content. It should give the recipient a good idea of what to expect when they open the email. Ambiguity or overly generic subject lines can result in your email being passed over and buried in a crowded inbox.

An honest and relevant subject line sets the tone for the entire email, demonstrating professionalism and respect for the recipient's time and attention. The subject line should be to the point and encapsulate the key message of your email within six to eight words! Use clear and descriptive language so the recipient knows what to expect. While it is essential to make the subject engaging, avoid sensationalism or clickbait-like tactics that can lead to mistrust.

2) **Put the "Bottom Line on Top:"** In business email communication it is often beneficial to adopt a practice known as "bottom line on top." This means that you start your email with the most crucial information or request. This approach provides the recipient with immediate clarity regarding the purpose of the message. It also respects the recipient's time and attention, especially when they likely have a packed inbox.

Placing the primary message or request at the beginning of the email increases the likelihood that your recipient will grasp the key points without having to read through lengthy introductions or explanations. The "bottom line on top" strategy also aligns with the principle of brevity and conciseness. It reinforces the importance of getting to the point quickly. Even if the recipient does not read the entire email, they still receive the essential information.

When implementing this practice, it is essential to provide context and details in subsequent sections of the email, but starting with the "bottom line" gives your message a clear and impactful beginning. While there may be cases where a more gradual introduction is necessary, leading with the "bottom line" enhances the efficiency and effectiveness of most email communication.

3) **Keep the Message Focused:** Clarity and conciseness are key to effective communication via email. Your email recipients are often busy professionals, and they appreciate messages that get to the point. When crafting your emails avoid bundling multiple topics or numerous requests in one email. Each email should focus on one central message and ideally address a single subject or topic. Overloading an email with multiple subjects can lead to confusion. If multiple topics require attention, consider

sending separate emails for each. This approach allows the recipient to digest and respond to each issue more effectively.

Maintaining a professional tone and language in your email messages is critical. Clear, well-structured sentences enhance readability, and proper grammar, spelling, punctuation, and standard capitalization maintain a professional tone. Avoid the use of overly casual language or text-style abbreviations such as "thx 4 ur help 2day ur gr8," which can be perceived as unprofessional. These practices demonstrate your respect for the recipient and your commitment to effective communication.

4) **Avoid Attachments:** While attachments are useful for sharing documents and files, they can be cumbersome, especially when dealing with large files. To enhance the efficiency of your communication, consider extracting and embedding essential information from attachments directly within the email. This ensures that your key message is conveyed without reliance on attachments. If the recipient expresses interest in the complete document or additional documents or files, you can then provide the attachment. This approach allows for quicker viewing, minimizes the need to open additional files, and enhances the efficiency and security of your email communication.

Attachments, especially large ones, can consume considerable storage space and lead to challenges for both the sender and recipient. From the sender's perspective, there is often uncertainty about whether the attachment will reach the recipient's inbox without issues. On the recipient's end, opening attachments, particularly from unknown sources, can raise security concerns, leading some organizations to restrict access to incoming attachments. Furthermore, attachments may not be accessible on all devices, which can hinder the recipient's ability to review the content promptly. Many mail systems provide ways to use links to replace large attachments, but those can cause security concerns, so make sure you understand your organization's processes in this regard.

5) **Identify Yourself Clearly:** Keep in mind that business email is often the primary means of professional communication, and it is vital to make a clear and professional introduction of yourself from the moment your message is opened. The recipient should know who the email is from and why it is relevant to them. Failing to identify yourself clearly can lead to confusion and may even result in your email being overlooked or deleted.

A brief but comprehensive self-introduction should include your name, title, and any relevant affiliations or organizations. This introduction should appear within the first few lines of the email to ensure the recipient recognizes the sender's identity from the outset. If the email is part of an ongoing conversation or project, it is helpful to provide context by referring to previous discussions or shared documents. This contextual awareness helps the recipient understand the purpose of the email and facilitates a more efficient response.

The importance of clear identification extends to the sender's email address. Make sure your email address is professional and easily recognizable. Using an obscure or overly casual email address can undermine your credibility.

6) **Be Kind - Avoid Flaming:** In the digital realm, it is important to remember that your words have a significant impact. Emotions and tone are not always conveyed accurately by the text of emails and misunderstandings can occur easily. Emails serve as a written record of your communication, and unprofessional, unethical, or offensive content can harm your reputation and business relationships. Therefore, it is essential to maintain a courteous and respectful tone in all of your email communications. Treat your email recipients with the same level of professionalism and courtesy as

you would in-person discussions.

Writing emails when emotions are running high can lead to impulsive and regrettable content. If you find yourself feeling upset or angry while composing an email, step back and refrain from sending the message immediately. Or, draft your message as a form of personal catharsis that allows you to express your emotions and complaints without any intention of sending it.

After some time has passed, revisit or rewrite the email with a clear and objective mindset. As you compose your email, consider the recipient's perspective and practice empathy, respect, and restraint. Avoid using harsh or offensive language, as it can damage professional relationships and harm your reputation. By demonstrating understanding and respect for the recipient's viewpoint you can forge a path to more productive and positive interactions. Ensure that your communication always reflects professionalism and respect. Once an email is sent, it cannot be taken back.

In this regard, be careful not to use the "reply to all" button in error, as sending messages to unintended recipients can lead to confusion and irritation. Take a moment before selecting this option and carefully consider whether all recipients genuinely need the information in your response. Take the same precautions when forwarding emails. Whenever possible, respect the original sender's intent and seek permission before sharing their emails. This practice demonstrates professionalism and ethical conduct. When you are dealing with confidential or sensitive information, apply heightened discretion and ensure that the appropriate recipients are granted access. Remember, emails leave a lasting digital trail, so use them responsibly.

7) **Proofread Your Email:** Mistakes in your email can undermine your credibility and professionalism. Take time to review and proofread your email before sending it. Utilize built-in spell-checking tools to catch spelling and grammatical errors. However, these tools will not catch all mistakes, so manual proofreading is essential.

As you read through your email carefully, check for grammar, punctuation, spelling, and sentence structure. Ensure that your message is clear, coherent, and free of typos. Pay special attention to names, titles, and any data or figures you include in the email. Accuracy and attention to detail reflect positively on your communication skills.

It is beneficial to read your email aloud, as this can help identify awkward phrasing or structural issues. Additionally, reading the email from the recipient's perspective can reveal potential areas of confusion or ambiguity. By proofreading your email thoroughly, you demonstrate your commitment to quality and professionalism.

8) **Do Not Assume Privacy:** In the world of digital communication, privacy is not guaranteed. Emails can be forwarded, shared, or accidentally sent to unintended recipients. So avoid including sensitive or confidential information in your emails, as they could potentially be accessed by unintended parties. To ensure the privacy and security of your communication when discussing confidential matters, consider using secure messaging platforms or speaking in person.

Remember, too, that employers often have the ability to access and monitor employee emails. In a professional context, your emails may be subject to company policies and legal regulations. Exercise caution and use discretion when discussing sensitive topics via email.

Finally, be aware that email communications can have a lasting impact. Any content you send may be archived or remain accessible to others long after the initial exchange. Always operate under the assumption that your emails could be shared more widely than originally intended.

9) **Distinguish Between Formal and Informal Situations:** Business emails can vary in tone and formality depending on the recipient and context. The level of formality in an email should align with the recipient's relationship and your purpose. When communicating with colleagues and superiors, for example, a formal tone is often expected. When communicating with close coworkers or friends, a more relaxed tone can be used. It is up to you to learn to recognize when a formal tone is required and when a more casual tone is appropriate.

Effective communication includes adapting to the preferences and expectations of the recipient. So understanding the appropriate tone and language for each situation is essential. Failing to address a recipient with appropriate titles or neglecting to use professional language can lead to misunderstandings or damage professional relationships.

In cases where you are unsure about the level of formality, err on the side of professionalism. You can gradually adjust your tone based on the recipient's response and established rapport. By consistently adapting your tone to the situation, you demonstrate social intelligence and adaptability.

10) **Respond Promptly and Follow Up When Necessary:** Timely responses in business email communication are crucial. When someone sends you an email, they typically expect a reasonably quick reply. Whether it is a colleague, client, or partner, responding promptly demonstrates professionalism and respect for their time. However, what do you do when you have sent an important email and there is no response?

This is when follow-up comes into play. If you do not receive a reply within a reasonable time frame, it is essential to follow up with a polite reminder. Here's a suggested approach for responding and following up:

➤ **Initial Response:** When you receive an email that requires a response, try to reply as soon as possible. Even if you need more time to provide a detailed answer, the courtesy of a quick acknowledgment of receipt keeps the lines of communication open.

➤ **If There Is No Response:** If you have sent an important email and a reasonable amount of time has passed without a reply (the exact timing depends on the context but typically ranges from a few days to a week), it is time to send a follow-up email. This message should politely remind the recipient of your previous email and kindly request the information or action you need.

➤ **Follow-Up Email Tips:** In your follow-up email, be concise and specific about the previous email's subject. You might use a subject line like "Follow-Up: [Original Subject]." Begin by referencing the initial email, mentioning the key points, and reiterating your request or question. Politely express your hope for a response or clarification.

➤ **Give an Out:** In your follow-up, offer the recipient an opportunity to provide a reason for the delay such as a request for more time, or the need to delegate to someone else. Keep the tone professional and understanding, acknowledging the demands of a busy schedule.

➤ **Remain Persistent but Respectful:** If you still receive no response after the follow-up, you may need to send one or two additional reminders. However, it is essential to balance persistence with respect. If, after multiple attempts, there is still no response, it is best to evaluate whether alternative forms of communication are more appropriate.

This comprehensive approach ensures that you are prompt in both your initial response and tactful in your follow-up strategy. Always maintain a professional tone and persistence while respecting the recipient's time and circumstances. Remember that email is often used for time-sensitive matters, and delayed responses can hinder progress and decision-making relationships.

9.6.2   SMS, Text, Slack, Chat, and Other Rapid Communication Tools

While email is likely to remain a critical tool for many companies, rapid communication tools are growing in importance, including SMS text messaging on phones and chat tools like Slack or Microsoft Teams. In the companies I've worked with, many still maintain formal policies for email because it is a more permanent record. These companies keep copies of emails and it is encouraged for formal communication. However, almost all of them also support text messaging and other tools as essential for rapid communication. Phone calls also qualify as rapid communication but they are increasingly viewed as intrusive, so it is common to use a rapid tool to ask if it is a good time for a call or to schedule a call.

Much of what we've said about good business communication via email holds true for texting. It is crucial to remember that even though you're thinking about a topic and writing to a person, you must ensure clarity in your communication. Depending on who your recipient is, they might receive so many messages that they don't remember what you last said. So you must keep your texts in context and make your objective clear. Aim to keep text messages bottom-line-up-front or bottom-line-on-top (BLOT).

Many companies struggle with balancing an open, informal culture while keeping communications on track and in compliance with potential legal implications. What is said in communications could be subject to court records and could be taken out of context. Keep that possibility in mind when texting or using Slack or any other rapid communication tools.

One compelling aspect of these rapid communication tools is that they enable what is effectively a conversation, similar to a phone call, but in text form. This can be convenient because you can search through them later and find what was stated and share documents in real-time. All of this gives rapid communication tools a growing presence in business communication.

Keep in mind that brevity and rapid interaction do not mean that storytelling is irrelevant in these communication mechanisms, in fact, quite the opposite. Because the use of these tools is closer to oral communication, thinking about storytelling may be even more important. You need to be convincing, as though you were giving a speech or interacting orally. You have to keep this in mind because, unlike written documents, you can't always revise what you have sent.

Some tools allow you to edit previous posts, but often the other side may have already seen them. So, you have to make sure you're being precise, clear, and telling your story in real-time as you use the tool. Sometimes, before you engage in a conversation using one of these tools, especially with higher levels of management or a client, you should work out your communication goal. Think about your story, your tactical objective, and how you're going to analyze it. You get the real-time feedback and audience analysis by seeing how they react, similar to a phone call. You might even prepare with "what if" scenarios: "If they do this, I'll do that," and use that as part of your communication style. Your story might have multiple paths depending on how the person on the other end responds. But don't forget that you're communicating for a reason and underlying that should be a tactical story that you're trying to get across while understanding and interacting with your audience.

Another point, drawn from feedback I've received from clients and students in innovation teams, is to respect the preferred form of communication of your client or colleagues. If they tell you they prefer email, then stick to email; don't text them unless they're open to it. Remember, many people have busy schedules, and while you might expect an immediate response to a text, it could take up to 24 hours. Understand the communication frequency within your organization. In security areas, for example, phones often aren't allowed, or they may not work well due to building shielding. In such cases, systems that use online chat like Slack or Microsoft Teams might be preferred because they're more accessible within the building.

Finally, remember the principles we discussed for writing email. Understand the hierarchy and who you're communicating with. You might be used to texting friends with shorthand and emojis, but when interacting with upper management or clients, your messages need to be more formal. Few people will complain about you being overly formal, but some will quietly hold it against you if you're too informal.

If you are unsure, err on the side of formality in your texts unless they explicitly tell you otherwise. Once you start receiving informal messages from them, you can ask if it's okay to be informal. But remember, they might still expect formality from you, even if they are informal with you. Navigate formality carefully as you get a feel for their preferences. Most people who expect strong formality will continue to expect it in return, regardless of their informal approach.

9.7 The Art of Writing an Effective Business Memo

Writing a business memo is a valuable skill in the corporate world. Memos serve as concise, internal documents used to communicate important information, make decisions, and provide recommendations. We provide the following guidance to help you grasp the art of writing a business memo.

9.7.1 Understanding the Purpose of a Business Memo

In the professional realm, business memos have a specific purpose: to convey detailed information or instructions efficiently within an organization. Memos are instrumental in addressing various issues such as sharing updates, seeking decisions, proposing solutions, or communicating policy changes.

Understanding your audience is crucial for tailoring your memo message effectively. Before you begin writing, make sure you have clearly identified your target audience. Who is the memo intended for? Is it your immediate supervisor? Your colleagues? Your subordinates? Or other departments?

You must also identify the specific focus of the memo content. Unlike emails or casual communication, memos are meant to convey substantial content. They often address complex issues such as project updates, strategic plans, financial data, or procedural changes. Therefore, clarity, precision, and relevance are key.

9.7.2 Business Memos for Personal Actions and Legal Implications

While business memos are primarily used for official communication within organizations, they can also play a role in addressing the personal actions and behaviors of employees. However, there are legal ramifications and formalities that must be considered when writing memos for such purposes.

When business memos are employed to address personal actions or behaviors of employees that impact the workplace, the issues might include:

➢ **Code of Conduct Violations:** Memos detailing the specific violation and potential consequences can be issued to employees who violate the company's code of conduct.

➢ **Performance Issues:** Memos may address issues related to an employee's performance, such as consistently missing deadlines, poor quality work, or disruptive behavior.

➢ **Attendance Problems:** Memos can be used to address excessive absenteeism, tardiness, or unauthorized leave.

- **Policy Violations:** Employees who violate company policies, such as data security or workplace safety regulations, may receive a memo outlining the breach.

In order to maintain formality and professionalism when addressing personal actions in memos, it is essential to follow specific guidelines:

- **Clear and Specific Language:** Memos should use clear, specific language to describe the personal action or behavior in question. Accurate and complete information is critical—this is one place *NOT* to tell or embellish stories. Avoid vague or ambiguous terms.

- **Consistency:** Memos should follow a consistent format, including headings for "TO," "FROM," "DATE," and "RE" (regarding or reference). This format ensures clarity and professionalism.

- **Legal Review:** In situations with potential legal implications, it is advisable for legal counsel to review the memo to ensure compliance with applicable laws.

- **Maintain Respect:** Even when addressing personal actions, maintain a respectful and professional tone in the memo. Avoid using derogatory language or personal attacks.

Whenever organizations use memos to address personal actions, they must be aware of the legal implications and ensure that appropriate practices are followed. These include:

- **Documentation:** Memos serve as a form of documentation, and they may be used as evidence in legal proceedings. Therefore, they must be accurate, clear, and factual.

- **Legal Compliance:** Memos must comply with employment laws and regulations, ensuring that employees' rights are protected. For example, memos related to disciplinary actions must adhere to due process requirements.

- **Confidentiality:** Personal actions discussed in memos often involve sensitive information. Maintaining the confidentiality of these memos is essential to protect employee privacy and minimize legal risks.

9.7.3   Structuring Your Business Memo

A well-structured memo makes it easier for readers to grasp the content. The key elements are in the example below.

Business Memo Structure Example

Heading: A memo heading is made up of the sender, the recipient, a subject line, and the date. For modern memos sent via email, many of these components are already baked in. However, for clarity, you may choose to include an introductory phrase (typically bracketed and capitalized) in the email subject line, which makes it clear that an emailed memo is not a regular email, e.g.

Subject: *[ALL OFFICE] An Amendment to Our Dog-Friendly Office Policy*

Introduction: The introduction paragraph highlights key information. It should explain the purpose of the memo and emphasize why employees should read it. In the case of an amendment to an office policy, you might write: "We have decided to amend our dog-friendly office policy to clarify that we will no longer allow dogs on the second floor."

Body: The body of the memo should provide context for the information supplied in the introduction. If the introduction states a new company policy, the body of the memo might go into detail about the factors that informed the decision. The writer of the dog policy memo might use this section to explain that there have been employee concerns around noise—specifically barking—in the office, so there needs to be one area that is entirely dog-free.

Action Items: A memo should clearly call out any actions or behavioral changes that employees should make. Use bullet points or bold text to make action items stand out to anyone who may be skimming the memo, especially if it is sent via email. You might summarize the dog policy changes and format them as follows:

To ensure our office remains a productive environment for all employees, please follow these protocols if you bring your dog into the office:

- Keep your dog on a leash.

- If your dog disturbs others, e.g., by barking, you may lose your pet's privileges.

- Do not allow any dogs to drink from the office water fountains.

- Do not visit the second floor or the kitchen area with your dog.

Signoff: A memo concludes with a brief signoff that includes the sender's name and provides a resource for follow-up questions. It may anticipate and address potential staff concerns—for example, you might reassure the team that dog treats will still be available in the office kitchen, but you should take them back to your desk to give to your dog.

[Your Name]

For Further Questions, Contact [Contact Information]

9.7.4   Memo Stylistic Guidelines

When writing a business memo, certain stylistic guidelines should be followed:

- **Conciseness:** Memos should be brief and to the point. Every sentence should serve a purpose. Avoid unnecessary elaboration and jargon.

- **Use of Headings:** Headings and subheadings help structure your memo and guide the reader. They also make it easier to locate specific information.

- **Grammar and Language:** Maintain a professional tone and use correct grammar and punctuation. Avoid casual language and abbreviations, just as you would when writing an email.

- **Visual Aids:** If necessary, include visual aids such as charts, graphs, or tables to support your points. Label these exhibits clearly and reference them in the text.

- **Proofreading:** Before finalizing your memo, thoroughly proofread it for spelling and grammatical errors. A well-edited memo reflects professionalism; a memo with errors does not.

9.7.5   Ensuring Effective Delivery

Once your memo is ready, consider how it will be disseminated and received:

➤ **Distribution:** Determine the most appropriate distribution method for your memo. Some may be delivered electronically, while others could be printed and distributed in hard copy.

➤ **Acknowledgment:** If you are seeking feedback, responses, or actions from recipients, ensure you clearly state expectations and deadlines. Mention whether recipients should acknowledge receipt.

➤ **Follow-Up:** After the memo is delivered, particularly if it is a critical issue, consider following up with the recipients to ensure they have read and understood the content.

In conclusion, mastering the art of writing a business memo is a valuable skill in the corporate world. Effective memos facilitate clear communication within an organization, enabling the dissemination of important information, decision- making, and problem-solving. Adhering to the guidelines and principles outlined in this section will help you craft concise, informative, and impactful business memos that connect with your intended audience.

9.8 Email vs. Memo: Pros and Cons

Corporate communication is an essential business activity and choosing the right medium for conveying specific information so that the objectives are achieved is crucial. While email and memos are both widely used for internal communication within businesses, each has its advantages and drawbacks. Let's examine the pros and cons of using email and traditional memos in a business context.

9.8.1   Email Pros and Cons

Pros

➤ **Speed and Accessibility:** Email allows for almost instantaneous communication, making it a valuable tool for quick exchanges of information. In addition, emails are accessible from anywhere with an internet connection, facilitating remote work.

➤ **Cost-Efficient:** Email is cost-effective, eliminating the need for paper, printing, and physical distribution. This can lead to significant savings in large organizations.

➤ **Multimedia Integration:** Emails enable the inclusion of various multimedia elements, such as attachments, links, and embedded images. This versatility makes it easier to convey complex information.

➤ **Archiving and Search:** Emails are automatically archived and can be easily searched, simplifying the retrieval of past communications and reference materials.

➤ **Interactivity:** Email allows for real-time interactions, making it suitable for discussions, feedback, and collaboration among team members.

Cons

➤ **Information Overload:** Email inboxes can become overloaded and cluttered, leading to missed messages, too much

information to review, and decreased productivity.

➤ **Lack of Formality:** The informality of email can lead to misunderstandings, as tone and context may be challenging to discern. In a business context, this can lead to miscommunication and disruption.

➤ **Security Concerns:** Email is susceptible to security threats, such as phishing attacks and data breaches. Businesses must invest in cybersecurity measures to protect sensitive information.

➤ **Privacy Issues:** Confidential information may be inadvertently shared, forwarded, or exposed to unauthorized individuals due to the ease of forwarding and reply-all functions.

9.8.2 Memo Pros and Cons

Pros

➤ **Formality and Clarity:** Memos offer a formal and structured format, reducing the potential for misinterpretation. They are suitable for conveying official announcements, policies, and directives.

➤ **Documentation:** Memos provide a documented record of communication within the organization. This can be valuable for legal and compliance purposes. For this reason, many organizations have formal rules about what must be in a memo so it can go into HR paper records.

➤ **Focused Communication:** Memos are typically single-topic and focused, ensuring that the main message is clear and not lost among unrelated information.

Cons

➤ **Time-Consuming:** Creating, printing, and distributing physical memos can be time-consuming. In a fast-paced business environment, this delay can be a drawback.

➤ **Costs:** Memos incur costs related to paper, printing, and distribution. In large organizations, these expenses add up.

➤ **Limited Interactivity:** Memos lack the interactivity of emails. They are typically one-way communication and do not facilitate real-time discussions.

➤ **Environmental Impact:** Using paper for memos has environmental implications, contributing to paper waste and the consumption of natural resources.

In summary, the choice between email and memos in a business context depends on the specific communication needs, desired objective, and organizational culture. While email offers speed and flexibility, memos provide a formal, documented approach. Businesses often find it beneficial to use both mediums depending on the nature of the message and the target audience.

9.9 Writing Marketing Stories with TWWIST

In the dynamic sphere of business communication, marketing stands out as a unique and complex field. It artfully combines elements of persuasion, psychology, and strategic communication, all aiming to resonate with and influence the target audience. The TWWIST methodology—Tactical Writing With Impactful Storytelling Techniques—serves as a powerful approach that elevates standard marketing communications into compelling narratives that engage, persuade, and drive action. Although marketing communication is a complex topic worthy of a course or two on its own, we have included a very short overview of how to use the TWWIST approach for developing marketing stories.

9.9.1 Understanding the Marketing Context

Marketing is not just about selling products or services; it is about creating stories that people connect with on an emotional level. It is the emotional connection that transforms potential customers into loyal brand advocates. TWWIST in marketing means crafting messages that are not only informative but also emotionally resonant. This emotional connection helps to ensure that each campaign is more than just a transactional interaction: it is also a transformational step toward building a long-term relationship with the audience.

Furthermore, in the world of digital marketing, where consumers are bombarded with endless content streams, standing out from a crowded field is more important than ever. TWWIST provides a framework for creating unique, memorable marketing messages that cut through the noise. By weaving strategic storytelling into every aspect of marketing communication, businesses can capture the attention of their audience more effectively and leave a lasting impression.

9.9.2 The Role of TWWIST in Marketing

The essence of TWWIST is to align the storytelling with the core values and objectives of the brand. This means going beyond the surface-level features of a product or service and delving into the "why" behind the brand. It is about creating narratives that reflect the brand's identity, mission, and vision, thereby forging a deeper connection with the audience. This approach transcends traditional approaches by embedding strategic storytelling into the heart of communication efforts. The TWWIST technique intertwines the art of storytelling with tactical writing, ensuring that every marketing message is both captivating and purpose-driven.

TWWIST empowers marketers to craft stories that are not just one-way communications but are interactive and engaging. This interactive approach encourages audience participation, making them feel like a part of the brand's story. By engaging the audience in this way, TWWIST transforms passive consumers into active participants, creating a more dynamic and impactful marketing experience.

Equally significant for today's consumers, TWWIST emphasizes the importance of authenticity in storytelling. In an age when consumers are increasingly skeptical of advertising, authentic stories stand out. They build trust and credibility, which are essential for establishing a strong brand presence and customer loyalty.

9.9.3 Analyzing Marketing Objectives

Identifying and articulating clear marketing objectives is paramount to success in marketing. It is essential that you understand the specific actions you want your audience to take and tailor your message to guide them toward your goals. The first step in this process is setting clear, measurable objectives:

- What does success look like?

- Is it increased brand awareness and more website traffic?

- Is it higher sales, or improved customer loyalty?

By defining these objectives upfront, marketers can ensure that every element of their storytelling is aligned with these goals.

Once the objectives are set, the next step is to understand how these objectives resonate with the target audience. This requires not just identifying demographic information but also understanding the motivations, pain points, and desires. TWWIST advocates for a deep dive into the audience's psyche, enabling marketers to craft messages that are not just seen but are also felt.

Last, it is crucial to continually measure and refine these objectives. The world of marketing is ever-changing, and so are audience preferences and behaviors. Regularly revisiting and adjusting the marketing objectives in line with audience feedback and market trends ensures that the storytelling remains relevant and effective.

9.9.4 Audience-Centric Storytelling

The essence of successful marketing lies in a deep understanding of the audience. With *TWWIST*, marketers delve into the psyche of their target demographic, crafting messages that resonate on a person. Tailoring your marketing message to these different segments while also maintaining a coherent overall brand narrative is key to effective audience-centric storytelling, lives, challenges, aspirations, and what truly matters to them. This deep understanding allows the creation of stories that are not only relevant but also deeply impactful.

Different segments of your audience may have different needs and respond to different types of storytelling. And TWWIST encourages marketers to view their audience as diverse and multifaceted. Tailoring your marketing message to these different segments, while also maintaining a coherent overall brand narrative, is key to effective audience-centric storytelling.

In addition, audience-centric storytelling is about creating a two-way dialogue. It is not just about telling your audience about your brand; it is also about listening to them, understanding their feedback, and incorporating that into your ongoing narrative. This dynamic approach fosters a more engaging and meaningful connection with the audience.

9.9.5 The Power of Narrative in Marketing

At its core, the marketing narrative is about connecting the dots between the brand, the product, and the consumer. It is about weaving a story that encapsulates the essence of the brand and highlights how the product or service fits into the lives of the consumers. A well-crafted narrative that accomplishes these objectives is the heartbeat of effective marketing. It transforms products or services from mere commodities into elements of a larger, emotionally resonant story. This connection makes the narrative powerful and memorable. It builds brand loyalty and encourages consumer engagement.

It is important to remember that a good narrative is not static; it evolves. As the brand grows and the market changes, so should the narrative. This evolution keeps the story fresh and relevant, maintaining the interest and engagement of the audience.

A strong narrative transcends the product or service itself; it taps into the consumer's larger aspirations and values. By aligning the brand's narrative with these higher-level concepts, marketers can create a deeper emotional resonance with their audience.

9.9.6 Leveraging Data and Research

Research-backed stories have the power to influence perception and drive decision-making. Data and research provide the foundation for a credible and convincing narrative. They offer concrete evidence to support the story. By incorporating data-driven insights into your storytelling, you enrich and add weight to the narrative, making it more credible, persuasive and compelling.

Moreover, data-driven storytelling allows for personalization. By leveraging data insights about the audience, marketers can tailor their stories to be more relevant and engaging for different audience segments. This personalized approach increases the narrative's effectiveness. Additionally, continuous research and data analysis help keep the narrative up-to-date with the latest trends and consumer behaviors. In a rapidly changing market, staying informed and agile is key to maintaining relevance and impact.

9.9.7 Top Ten Tips for Effective Marketing via Storytelling

This list provides a TWWIST-based structured approach to enhancing your marketing strategies through effective storytelling. By following these tips, you can create stories that not only captivate your audience but also drive tangible results for your brand.

➤ **Know Your Audience:** Tailor your story to resonate with the interests, values, and experiences of your audience. Understanding the demographic, psychographic, and behavioral traits of your audience is crucial for crafting a compelling narrative.

➤ **Define Clear Objectives:** Establish what you aim to achieve with your storytelling. Objectives could range from increasing brand awareness and enhancing customer engagement to driving sales.

➤ **Emphasize Authenticity:** Authentic stories create deeper connections with the audience. Share genuine narratives that reflect your brand's values and mission.

➤ **Incorporate Emotional Elements:** Emotions drive engagement. Craft your story to evoke emotions such as happiness, inspiration, empathy, or even nostalgia to create a lasting impact.

➤ **Keep It Simple and Relatable:** Avoid complex jargon and keep the story straightforward and relatable. A simple, well-told story often has more impact than a complicated one.

➤ **Be Consistent Across Channels:** Ensure your storytelling is consistent across all marketing channels. Consistency reinforces your brand message and identity.

➤ **Leverage Visuals and Multimedia:** Enhance your story with compelling visuals or multimedia elements. This can include images, videos, infographics, or interactive content.

➤ **Encourage Audience Participation:** Make your storytelling interactive. By encouraging your audience to share their experiences and stories, you foster a sense of community.

➤ **Measure and Adapt:** Continuously measure the impact of your storytelling efforts and be ready to adapt. Use audience feedback and analytics to refine your approach.

➤ **Integrate a Call-to-Action:** Conclude your story with a clear call-to-action. Guide your audience on what to do next, whether it is visiting a website, signing up for a newsletter, or making a purchase.

9.10 Case Studies in Marketing with Impact

As we have discovered in this brief overview, TWWIST in marketing is about crafting narratives that do more than just inform; they transform. It is about building bridges between brands and audiences through stories that are not only heard but felt. This approach ensures that marketing efforts are not viewed as mere advertisements but as meaningful connections to the brand's journey. By crafting compelling stories that resonate on a personal level, campaigns can achieve more than just brand visibility; they can create emotional connections, foster community, and adapt to changing market landscapes, exemplifying the power of storytelling in contemporary marketing. Consider the following micro case studies of successful marketing that demonstrate TWWIST in action.

9.10.1   Apple's "Think Different" Campaign

➢ **The Campaign Narrative:** Apple's "Think Different" campaign is a quintessential example of TWWIST in action. Launched in 1997, the campaign was more than just an advertisement for Apple products; it was a declaration of Apple's brand identity and values. The campaign celebrated the rebels, the misfits, the ones who see things differently - aligning these qualities with the Apple brand.

➢ **Audience Engagement:** The campaign resonated deeply with Apple's target audience - creative, innovative individuals who value thinking outside the box. It created a strong emotional connection with this audience, positioning Apple not just as a technology company but as a symbol of creativity and innovation.

➢ **Impact and Legacy:** The "Think Different" campaign had a profound impact, not just on Apple's sales and brand perception but on advertising as a whole. It showcased the power of narrative in marketing and how a well-crafted story can elevate a brand to iconic status.

9.10.2   Nike's "Just Do It" Slogan

➢ **Creating an Empowering Narrative:** Nike's "Just Do It" slogan is another excellent example of TWWIST in marketing. Launched in 1988, the slogan and the accompanying campaign narratives have inspired millions. It is a call to action, an affirmation, and a testament to the human spirit's resilience and determination.

➢ **Audience Connection:** The slogan and its narratives connect deeply with Nike's audience - athletes and individuals aspiring to push their limits. It speaks to their inner drive, their desire to overcome challenges, and their pursuit of excellence.

➢ **Sustained Brand Identity:** The "Just Do It" narrative has become synonymous with Nike's brand identity. It has sustained its relevance over decades, adapting to different generations and continuing to inspire and motivate.

9.10.3   Coca-Cola's "Share a Coke" Campaign

➢ **Personalized Storytelling:** Coca-Cola's "Share a Coke" campaign is a prime example of personalized narrative marketing. Launched in 2011, the campaign featured Coke bottles with people's names, inviting consumers to share a Coke with someone special.

➢ **Engaging the Audience:** This personal touch transformed the simple act of buying a Coke into a personal and shareable experience. It encouraged customer interaction and created a buzz on social media, with people sharing stories of finding bottles with their names or the names of their loved ones.

➢ **Enhanced Brand Connection:** The campaign not only boosted sales but also strengthened Coca-Cola's brand as a symbol of sharing and togetherness. It showcased how a personalized narrative can create a powerful and lasting connection with the audience.

9.10.4 Spotify's "Wrapped" Campaign

➤ **Personalized Year-in-Review:** Spotify's "Wrapped" campaign, an innovative annual feature introduced in 2019, revolutionizes user engagement by offering a personalized recap of their listening habits. This data-driven storytelling creates a unique narrative for each user, weaving their year's musical journey with Spotify's brand story.

➤ **Enhancing User Engagement and Sharing:** The personalized nature of "Wrapped" not only strengthens the bond between the user and Spotify but transforms each user into a brand storyteller. As users share their "Wrapped" stats on social media, they extend Spotify's narrative into diverse personal networks, showcasing the brand's reach and impact.

➤ **Long-Term Brand Connection:** This campaign transcends traditional marketing as it evolves into a cultural phenomenon eagerly anticipated by users annually. It reinforces Spotify's brand image as a platform deeply integrated into the user's personal and emotional landscape, further cementing its market position.

9.10.5 Peloton's "Together We Go Far"

➤ **Building Community Through Fitness:** Peloton's "Together We Go Far" campaign is a masterclass in community-building storytelling. By featuring real stories of Peloton members, it transforms the individual fitness journey into a collective narrative, enhancing the emotional and motivational appeal of joining the Peloton community.

➤ **Emotional Resonance and Encouragement:** The campaign's narrative artfully connects with potential customers by showcasing the power of shared fitness experiences. It taps into the audience's aspirations for personal growth and community belonging, making Peloton not just a fitness product but a symbol of collective resilience and support.

➤ **Strengthening Brand Loyalty:** This focus on real and relatable community stories elevates Peloton's brand from a

mere exercise equipment company to a lifestyle emblem that fosters social connection, personal achievement, and loyalty among its users.

9.10.6 Airbnb's "Go Near" Campaign

➤ **Adapting to New Travel Norms:** Airbnb's "Go Near" campaign, introduced in 2020, adeptly adapts to the new travel context brought on by the COVID-19 pandemic. The campaign shifts the travel narrative from global exploration to discovering local treasures, resonating with the emerging trend of staycations and regional travel.

➤ **Highlighting Local Experiences:** The "Go Near" narrative skillfully encourages users to engage with their immediate surroundings, uncovering hidden local gems. This pivot not only aligns with the changing travel dynamics but also creates a new story of exploration and appreciation for local cultures and experiences.

➤ **Reinforcing Brand Flexibility and Relevance:** This strategic narrative shift showcases Airbnb's adaptability and understanding of its audience's needs during challenging times. It enhances the brand's relevance and connection with its audience, reinforcing its position as a flexible and responsive player in the travel industry.

9.11 Language and Tone in Business Storytelling

Most of us recognize that language and tone are critical aspects of effective, face-to-face communication. We may not realize, however, that language and tone are equally important in all forms of business storytelling. Language and tone set the stage for how your story is perceived and can greatly influence the impact of your message on your audience. Here we explore the significance of language and tone in business stories and provide examples of different approaches.

9.11.1 General Business Storytelling

In general business storytelling, your choice of language and tone affects how your story connects with your audience. Consider when and how you might use these techniques:

➤ **Inspirational Tone:** Use an inspirational tone to motivate your team or stakeholders. Share stories of individuals or teams that overcome challenges to achieve success. Highlight the values that drive your organization's vision. Use powerful and emotionally charged language to convey a sense of purpose and determination.

➤ **Informative and Educational Tone:** An informative and educational tone is effective when you want to convey expertise and provide insights. Share stories that illustrate complex concepts or best practices within your industry. Use clear and concise language to educate your audience and keep them engaged.

➤ **Humorous and Light-Hearted Tone:** Inject humor and light-heartedness into your stories when appropriate. This can be particularly effective in team-building or internal communications. Share amusing anecdotes or stories that showcase your organization's culture, creating a positive and enjoyable atmosphere.

➤ **Thought-Provoking and Contemplative Tone:** Engage your audience with thought-provoking and contemplative stories. Share narratives that challenge conventional thinking or pose ethical questions. Use language that encourages reflection and discussion among your audience.

➤ **Empathetic Tone:** An empathetic tone is essential when addressing sensitive topics or challenges. Use stories that convey understanding and empathy for the experiences of your audience. Choose words that resonate with their emotions and experiences, showing that you genuinely care.

➤ **Assertive and Persuasive Tone:** In situations where you need to drive action or make a compelling argument, adopt an assertive and persuasive tone. Share stories that highlight the urgency of your message and use confident and assertive language to persuade your audience to take action.

9.11.2 Tone in Emails and Memos

In email and memo communication, the tone can significantly influence how your message is received. Here are two examples of different tones in emails and two examples of different tones in memos:

➤ **Email - Formal Tone:** A formal tone is appropriate when writing to a client or addressing a higher-level executive. Use polite language, proper salutations, and a respectful tone to convey professionalism and respect.

➤ **Email - Friendly and Casual Tone:** A friendly and casual tone is suitable for internal team communications. Use conversational language, informal salutations, and a warm tone to build rapport and a sense of camaraderie.

➢ **Memo - Authoritative Tone:** In a memo outlining a change in company policies, adopt an authoritative tone. Use clear and confident language to convey the seriousness of the topic and the importance of compliance.

➢ **Memo - Supportive and Collaborative Tone:** When sending a memo to employees about a new project, use a supportive and collaborative tone. Encourage teamwork and engagement by using inclusive language and expressing a willingness to work together.

9.11.3   Language and Tone in Marketing

In marketing, the language and tone used in storytelling are crucial in defining the brand's voice and influencing how the audience perceives and interacts with the brand. The right choice of words and tone can significantly enhance the effectiveness of marketing campaigns, while choices that miss the mark can derail a campaign. Here are some examples:

➢ **Aspirational Language:** Use aspirational language to inspire and uplift your audience. This approach is effective in luxury branding or lifestyle marketing where the goal is to position products or services as not just *purchases* but as *gateways* to a better, more desirable lifestyle.

Marketing Example: A luxury car brand might use language that evokes a sense of sophistication and achievement, appealing to the aspirations of its audience.

➢ **Conversational and Relatable Tone:** Adopt a conversational and relatable tone in scenarios where building a personal connection with the audience is key. This tone is especially effective in social media marketing and influencer campaigns.

Marketing Example: A lifestyle brand might use a casual and friendly tone in their social media campaigns to create a sense of familiarity and approachability.

➢ **Urgent and Direct Language:** Use urgent and direct language in promotional campaigns where the goal is to drive immediate action, such as limited-time offers or flash sales.

Marketing Example: An e-commerce site might use language that creates a sense of urgency, like "Limited offer" or "Sale ends soon," to encourage quick purchases.

➢ **Professional and Informative Tone:** In B2B marketing or in industries where trust and expertise are paramount, use a professional and informative tone. This approach is crucial for brands that want to establish themselves as authoritative voices in their field.

Marketing Example: A financial services company might use a professional and informative tone in their marketing materials to convey expertise and reliability.

➢ **Empowering and Motivational Language:** Empowering and motivational language can be highly effective in campaigns that aim to inspire action, especially in cause-related marketing or health and wellness sectors.

Marketing Example: A fitness brand might use empowering language in their campaigns to motivate their audience to embrace a healthier lifestyle.

➢ **Story-Driven and Narrative Tone:** Using a story-driven and narrative tone helps in creating brand stories that are memorable and emotionally engaging. This approach is effective across various marketing channels, from TV commercials to online content.

Marketing Example: A travel company might use narrative storytelling in their advertisements to take the audience on a journey, highlighting the experiences and emotions associated with travel.

Mastering language and tone in business storytelling is essential for creating a lasting impact on your audience. Whether you are sharing stories in general business contexts or through emails and memos, your choice of language and tone can enhance or hinder the effectiveness of your communication.

9.12   Key Terms

1) **Tactical Business Storytelling:** *A strategic method of using storytelling to connect and communicate with various business audiences, enhancing the effectiveness of business communication.*

2) **Internal Business Storytelling:** *Using storytelling within an organization to foster collaboration, convey values, and inspire employees.*

3) **External Business Storytelling:** *Using storytelling for marketing, building brand identity, and engaging customers.*

4) **Brand Advocacy:** *Encouraging customers to share their stories about products or services to build trust and encourage referrals.*

5) **Fostering Customer Loyalty:** *Creating a connection through business stories that lead to customer retention and word-of-mouth marketing.*

6) **Hiring and Recruiting Stories:** *Using oral storytelling to attract top talent by showcasing company values, mission, and opportunities for professional development.*

7) **Sales Stories:** *Using oral storytelling to transform how customers perceive products or services by highlighting success stories and their impact on clients.*

8) **Management Stories:** *Using oral storytelling to motivate, provide guidance, and lead by example.*

9) **Conflict Resolution Stories:** *Using storytelling to resolve disputes by fostering understanding and empathy.*

10) **Customer Service and Satisfaction Stories:** *Using oral storytelling to improve customer service by highlighting exceptional service and resolving issues.*

11) **Simmon's Six Storytelling Structures:** *Six powerful storytelling styles identified by Annette Simmons for crafting business stories: Who-I-Am, Why-I-Am-Here, Vision, Values-in-Action, I-Know-What-You-Are-Thinking, and Teaching stories.*

12) **Writing Up, Down, or Across the Management Chain:** *Crafting messages differently based on whether the communication is directed upwards, downwards, or across the corporate hierarchy.*

13) **Empathy in Email Communication:** *Practicing empathy and considering the recipient's perspective to maintain professionalism and uphold ethical standards in email communications.*

1) **The Power of Tactical Innovation Storytelling:** *The use of common structures for business storytelling to make it effective and actionable, focusing on crafting opening lines and closing statements.*

2) **Structural Styles of Innovation and Business Stories:** *Classic business story structures that can be leveraged to align with audience expectations and enhance storytelling effectiveness.*

3) **Decoding the Audience:** *Understanding the audience's needs and preferences to tailor the communication approach effectively, considering power dynamics and multiple audiences in business.*

4) **Language and Tone:** *The appropriate choice of words and tone for different business scenarios to ensure effective communication.*

5) **Motivating Teams:** *Sharing stories that reinforce the organization's vision and mission to inspire and motivate teams.*

6) **Navigating Change and Change Management:** *Using stories to communicate new strategies or directions during periods of change to ease concerns and guide employees by explaining the reasons behind changes and provide a vision of the future.*

7) **Fostering Company Culture:** *Sharing stories that exemplify the desired company culture to contribute to a positive workplace environment.*

8) **Onboarding and Training:** *Using stories to convey essential information and best practices, making learning more engaging and memorable.*

9) **Customer Engagement via Content Creation:** *Using storytelling to provide effective content for blogs, videos, and social media posts.*

10) **Vulnerability Stories:** *Stories where leaders share personal experiences and challenges to make a genuine connection with their team members.*

11) **Success Story:** *A narrative that highlights real-life examples of how a product or service benefited a client, used to convince potential customers.*

12) **Warning Stories:** *Narratives that highlight potential risks and consequences to persuade an audience to prioritize safety or other critical actions.*

13) **Resolving Conflicts:** *Using storytelling to highlight shared goals and facilitate conflict resolution.*

14) **Celebrating Success:** *Recognizing and celebrating achievements within the organization by sharing success stories.*

15) **Building Leadership Skills:** *Enhancing leadership skills through storytelling by sharing personal leadership stories.*

16) **Enhancing Communication:** *Using stories to make complex information more accessible and relatable to employees.*

17) **Creating a Collaborative Environment:** *Encouraging teamwork through stories of successful collaborations.*

18) **Influencing Decision-Makers:** *Using compelling stories to influence stakeholders, board members, or*

investors.

19) **Developing and Growing Your Business Image:** *Using business stories to craft and shape the brand's image.*

20) **Creating a Memorable Brand:** *Using compelling business stories to foster customer loyalty and stand out in the market.*

21) **Humanizing Your Brand:** *Using stories to bridge the gap between businesses and individuals, enhancing sales strategies.*

22) **Differentiating Your Brand:** *Using unique business stories to set the brand apart from competitors.*

23) **Enhancing Marketing Strategies:** *Using storytelling to narrate the business's origin, founders' journey, or customers' stories for powerful marketing campaigns.*

24) **Oral Business Storytelling:** *The use of oral storytelling to convey messages, engage audiences, and drive desired outcomes in various business contexts.*

25) **Innovation and Creativity Stories:** *Using oral storytelling to fuel creativity and share stories of past innovations and problem-solving.*

26) **Company Culture:** *Using oral storytelling to define and maintain company culture by sharing stories that exemplify the organization's values and ethics.*

27) **Convincing Teams of Necessary Actions:** *Using warning stories to emphasize the importance of certain actions, such as safety training, by sharing cautionary tales.*

28) **Brand Origin Stories:** *Narratives that reveal the inspiration and values driving a company's products and marketing campaigns.*

29) **Hero's Journey:** *A storytelling approach where an individual's transformation is used to align with and highlight a company's commitment to innovation.*

30) **Business Storytelling for the Company Annual Meeting:** *Using storytelling during annual meetings to inspire and motivate employees, investors, and partners by sharing past challenges and victories.*

31) **Resilience and Triumph Stories:** *Narratives that highlight past challenges and victories to inspire and motivate stakeholders.*

32) **Character-Centric Storytelling:** *A storytelling approach that focuses on a relatable character whose journey represents the intended outcomes of a program or initiative.*

33) **Visual Storytelling:** *Using images, infographics, and multimedia to convey the impact of a program or idea.*

34) **Problem-Solution Framework:** *Highlighting challenges and how a proposed program or idea provides solutions.*

35) **Transformation Emphasis:** *Focusing on how a program or idea will transform lives or situations to make the pitch more appealing.*

36) **Who-I-Am Stories:** *Stories that reveal personal identity and experiences to build trust and establish connections.*

37) **Why-I-Am-Here Stories:** *Stories that articulate purpose and intentions to replace suspicion with trust.*

38) **Vision Stories:** *Inspirational narratives that evoke hope and happiness by linking actions to a valuable outcome.*

39) **Values-in-Action Stories:** *Stories that reinforce the values you want your audience to embody by exemplifying virtues or cautioning against undesirable attitudes.*

40) **I-Know-What-You-Are-Thinking Stories:** *Stories that address anticipated audience objections, suspicions, or concerns to demonstrate understanding and empathy.*

41) **Teaching Stories:** *Narratives that create transformative experiences by demonstrating changes in behavior, perspective, or skills.*

42) **Origin Stories:** *Narratives explaining the beginnings of an organization, including ideation, struggles, and early achievements.*

43) **Failure Stories:** *Narratives that highlight instances of setbacks and how they were overcome, connecting with the human experience of failure.*

44) **Customer Stories:** *Narratives that use customer experiences to promote a business, demonstrating real-life benefits and credibility.*

45) **Product Stories:** *Stories that communicate the value and practical usage of products or services, fostering engagement and loyalty.*

46) **Personal Stories:** *Stories about the people in the company and their contributions, helping to build morale and humanize the company to customers and stakeholders.*

47) **Job-to-be-Done Stories:** *Stories focusing on the problems a company can uniquely address, related to customer stories but centered on the problem and solution.*

48) **Timely Email Responses:** *Responding promptly to business emails to demonstrate professionalism and respect for the recipient's time.*

49) **Follow-Up Emails:** *Sending follow-up emails when there is no response to an important email, using a polite and respectful tone.*

50) **Business Memos:** *Concise, internal documents used to communicate important information, make decisions, and provide recommendations within an organization.*

51) **Personal Actions in Memos:** *Addressing personal actions or behaviors of employees in business memos while considering legal implications and maintaining professionalism.*

52) **Data-Driven Storytelling:** *Incorporating data-driven insights into marketing storytelling to enhance credibility and personalization.*

53) **Inspirational Tone:** *Using emotionally charged language to convey a sense of purpose and determination in business stories.*

54) **Informative and Educational Tone:** *Using clear and concise language to educate the audience while keeping them engaged.*

55) **Humorous and Light-Hearted Tone:** *Injecting humor and light-heartedness into stories to create a positive atmosphere.*

56) **Thought-Provoking Tone:** *Using language that encourages reflection and discussion by challenging conventional thinking.*

57) **Empathetic Tone:** *Conveying understanding and empathy in stories to resonate with the audience's emotions and experiences.*

58) **Assertive and Persuasive Tone:** *Using confident and assertive language to drive action and make compelling arguments.*

59) **Formal Tone in Emails:** *Using polite language, proper salutations, and a respectful tone when addressing clients or higher-level executives.*

60) **Friendly and Casual Tone in Emails:** *Using conversational language and a warm tone in internal team communications to build rapport.*

61) **Authoritative Tone in Memos:** *Using clear and confident language in memos to convey the seriousness of topics such as policy changes.*

62) **Aspirational Language:** *Using language that inspires and uplifts the audience in marketing messages, often in luxury or lifestyle branding.*

63) **Conversational Tone in Marketing:** *Using a casual and friendly tone in social media marketing and influencer campaigns to create familiarity.*

64) **Urgent Language in Marketing:** *Using language that creates a sense of urgency in promotional campaigns to drive immediate action.*

65) **Professional Tone in Marketing:** *Using a professional and informative tone in B2B marketing to convey expertise and reliability.*

66) **Empowering Language in Marketing:** *Using motivational language in cause-related marketing or health and wellness sectors to inspire action.*

67) **Story-Driven Tone in Marketing:** *Using narrative storytelling in marketing to create memorable and emotionally engaging brand stories.*

10 Applying TWWIST to Speech Writing and Presentations

"If I went back to college again, I'd concentrate on two areas: learning to write and to speak before an audience. Nothing in life is more important than the ability to communicate effectively."

-Gerald R. Ford, 38th American President

Audiences may marvel at the delivery of a speech yet fail to realize that its effectiveness is rooted in careful writing and preparation. A well-written speech enhanced by thorough preparation that ensures a quality delivery is the backbone of a powerful verbal presentation. In this chapter, we will address the commonly overlooked but integral role of writing in crafting speeches and presentations. We will show how to use rhetoric, storytelling, meticulous writing, and practice effectively in order to deliver memorable verbal messages. We will explore the art of transforming ideas into eloquent and impactful public speaking through the TWWIST approach.

10.1   Master the Art of Speech Writing Through Tactical Writing Techniques

Speech writing is a distinct and nuanced form of communication, differing significantly from traditional text writing. In contrast to written text, where readers have the liberty to process information at their own pace, speeches require immediate comprehension and retention. So speech writing demands a unique blend of clarity, engagement, and memorability that are essential to captivating an audience and leaving a lasting impact.

Recognizing the essential role of tactical writing in verbal communication, we will use the TWWIST approach, with its emphasis on tactical objectives and SMART goals, to explore effective strategies for speech writing. We will delve into the complexities of verbal, visual, and physical storytelling, and dissect the differences between speeches and presentations, providing insights for crafting speeches that resonate with and influence their intended audience.

10.1.1   Verbal Storytelling in Speeches and Presentations

Verbal storytelling is the cornerstone of effective speeches and presentations, the apex where the power of words and the art of narration come together to create a compelling experience. Unlike writing that is intended to be read, where the subtleties of language can be pondered at the reader's convenience, speech writing requires immediate comprehension and connection with the audience. The TWWIST approach to speech writing emphasizes aligning the verbal story with the objectives of the speech to ensure that the message is not only clear but engaging and memorable. By incorporating the following writing techniques in your speech writing, you can enhance the effectiveness of your verbal storytelling and leave a lasting impact on your audience.

➤ **Story Structure:** A well-structured story is pivotal. Open with a strong beginning that captures attention, proceed with a clear and logical development of ideas, and end with a powerful conclusion that reinforces the message.

➤ **Language Use:** Choose words that resonate with the audience. Utilize metaphors, similes, analogies, and other rhetorical devices to clarify complex ideas and make your message more relatable.

➤ **Engagement Techniques:** Employ rhetorical questions, anecdotes, and humor to maintain audience interest and facilitate a connection.

➣ **Memorability:** Craft key phrases or "sound bites" that are easy to remember and likely to be repeated to ensure that your message lingers in the minds of your audience.

10.1.2   Physical Aspects of Storytelling in Speeches and Presentations

The physical aspects of storytelling encompass non-verbal cues such as body language, gestures, and overall stage presence. These cues are essential in bringing a speech or presentation to life. They can significantly influence how the audience perceives and connects with the speaker and message. The TWWIST methodology stresses the importance of harmonizing these physical elements with the verbal and visual components of the presentation. Mastering these physical aspects of physical storytelling can transform a presentation from the mere delivery of content into an engaging, persuasive, and memorable experience for the audience.

➣ **Purposeful Body Language:** Use controlled movement —gestures and postures that align with your message to highlight key points or to transition between topics.

➣ **Facial Expressions:** Use facial expressions to convey emotions and reactions and establish a deeper connection with the audience.

➣ **Effective Use of Space:** To make your presentation feel more dynamic and inclusive, move around the stage or presentation area in a way that engages different parts of the audience.

➣ **Eye Contact:** Eye contact with various members of the audience is essential for creating a sense of connection and ensuring that your message is received effectively.

These physical aspects seem to come naturally to some speakers, but most of us have to work on them and even write them into our script. Many professionals admit it takes a lot of practice to make non-verbal cues seem natural. So do not try to deliver your speech/presentation and critique your physical aspects at the same time. Practice with a camera and a coach/mentor who can provide effective feedback. As an added plus, be aware that many of these physical cues also can be worked into everyday conversations, which will make you a more dynamic conversationalist.

10.1.3   Visual Storytelling in Presentations

Effective visual storytelling is often the biggest difference between a speech and a presentation. The integration of visual elements with verbal content in presentations not only aids in conveying information but can significantly elevate the audience's understanding and engagement. Visual storytelling also enhances the overall aesthetic appeal of a presentation, making it more memorable and impactful. In the TWWIST approach, the visual storytelling aspect involves carefully selecting and designing visuals that align with the speech's objectives and complement the verbal narrative.

➣ **Complement the Verbal Message:** Choose visuals that directly support and reinforce your spoken content. This could include graphs to illustrate statistics or images that evoke the emotions you are discussing.

➣ **Simplify Complex Information:** Use diagrams, infographics, and charts to break down complex ideas into understandable and memorable images.

➣ **Engage the Audience:** Incorporate dynamic elements like videos or interactive slides to maintain audience interest and encourage participation.

➤ **Consistency in Design:** Provide a cohesive visual experience by ensuring that all visual elements follow a consistent design theme including color schemes, graphic features, and typography.

10.1.4   Understanding the Differences Between Speeches and Presentations

While speeches and presentations are both essential communication tools, they differ in various aspects. Recognizing these differences is crucial for choosing the appropriate format and style for a given situation.

➤ **Primary Focus:** Speeches often emphasize the spoken word and delivery, while presentations integrate spoken content with visual aids like slides or charts.

➤ **Interactivity:** Presentations tend to be more interactive, often involving Q&A sessions, while speeches are usually unidirectional.

➤ **Purpose:** Speeches often aim to inform, persuade, or entertain with a focus on rhetoric, whereas presentations are typically geared toward instruction, explanation, or reporting.

➤ **Setting:** Speeches are commonly delivered in formal settings like ceremonies or large gatherings, whereas presentations are more common in educational, business, or collaborative environments.

➤ **Duration:** Speeches generally have a set duration with little flexibility, whereas presentations might be more adaptable in length, depending on audience engagement and interaction.

➤ **Preparation:** Speech preparation focuses heavily on memorization and delivery, while presentation preparation involves significant work on visual aids and anticipating audience interaction.

➤ **Style and Tone:** The style and tone of speeches often lean towards formality and eloquence, whereas presentations might adopt a more conversational and pragmatic tone.

➤ **Audience Expectation:** Audiences typically expect speeches to be more polished and oratorical, while presentations are expected to be informative, clear, and sometimes, hands-on.

Understanding these differences aids in tailoring the content, delivery, and style to suit either a speech or a presentation, ensuring effective and appropriate communication for the intended purpose.

10.1.5   Writing a Personal Speech vs. Writing a Speech for Others

When crafting your own speech, you know your content intimately. You likely share some common interests, educational background, or professional experiences with your audience. And you inherently understand your speaking style, strengths, and nuances. All of these factors allow you to tailor the speech to your comfort level, your audience, and your manner of expression, which allows for a more personalized and authentic delivery. In contrast, writing a speech for a third party is an entirely different challenge.

Writing for a third party necessitates a deep understanding of their unique message, speaking style, and audience expectations. When writing a speech for someone else that will be authentic, engaging, and impactful, it is crucial to engage with them using the TWWIST methodology. It will help you to develop the preliminary story and secure the speaker's buy-in early in the process. This collaborative approach ensures that the speech reflects their persona so that the words and delivery will appear natural and credible when they present it.

When practicing the speech with a third party, it is important to rehearse together, fine-tuning delivery and making needed adjustments. This practice is vital for the speaker to become comfortable with the content and flow of the speech. However, if the individual for whom the speech is written has limited time for practice, an alternative approach is to practice and record the speech yourself. This recording can then be shared for their review, providing them with an opportunity to familiarize themselves with the speech's rhythm, pace, and tone. This method also allows them to provide feedback or request changes, ensuring that the final speech aligns with their preferences and speaking style.

10.2   Classical Approaches to Speech Writing

The classical methods for speech writing, although ancient in origin, continue to profoundly influence and shape the art of speech writing today. The speech writing steps established over the centuries are deeply rooted in principles dating back to the ancient Greek rhetoricians. These timeless techniques, articulated in seminal works such as Aristotle's *Rhetoric*, Cope [1867], and Quintilian's *Institutio Oratoria*, Quintilianus [1854], Watson et al. [1892] formed the foundation of modern speech writing.

These classic works emphasize a structured approach to speech writing that begins with identifying the purpose and understanding of the audience, akin to Aristotle's emphasis on ethos, pathos, and logos for effective persuasion. This is followed by meticulous content gathering and organization that mirrors the ancient Greek emphasis on well-structured arguments. The speech is then tailored to the audience, a concept that resonates with the sophistic emphasis on the power of adaptability in oration. Subsequent steps include drafting and revising for clarity and impact, which are reminiscent of the meticulous methods advocated by Cicero. Finally, the preparation for delivery, a key aspect highlighted in Quintilian's teachings, involves not just memorization but also understanding the nuances of delivery, including tone, gesture, and pacing.

Not surprisingly, the TWWIST approach aligns closely with the classic speech writing steps outlined above—the steps to effective persuasion. By incorporating the TWWIST approach into speech writing and presentations we are able to elevate the impact and effectiveness of public speaking.

10.2.1   The Relationship Between the TWWIST Technique and Classic Speech Writing Steps

Let's now review the classic speech writing steps and how each TWWIST step maps onto classic speech writing. As we have already covered the key steps, you should be in a good position to directly apply TWWIST to speech writing.

➤ **Analyzing Objectives and Opportunities vs Classic Step: Defining Purpose and Audience:** The initial TWWIST step of analyzing objectives and opportunities corresponds with the classic speech writing step of defining the purpose and understanding the audience. Both methods involve identifying the main message of the speech and understanding who the audience is, what they care about, and what the speaker aims to achieve.

➤ **Research vs Classic Step: Gathering Content and Supporting Data:** Research in the TWWIST approach is akin to the content-gathering stage in traditional speech writing. This step involves collecting relevant data, anecdotes, statistics, and any other information that supports the main message of the speech, ensuring the content is both credible and engaging.

➤ **Audience Analysis vs Classic Step: Tailoring the Message to the Audience:** Audience analysis in TWWIST is about tailoring the message to the audience's interests and level of understanding. This mirrors the classic speech writing step of customizing the speech content and style to resonate with the audience, ensuring it is appropriate and compelling.

➤ **Review Processes vs Classic Step: Editing and Refinement:** The review processes in TWWIST, which include both internal and audience reviews, correspond to the editing and refinement phase in classic speech writing. This involves revising the speech for clarity, coherence, and impact and refining it based on feedback.

➤ **Team Writing Processes vs Classic Step: Collaboration and Feedback:** Team writing processes in TWWIST align with the collaboration and feedback step in traditional speech writing. This stage involves working with co-writers, advisors, and others to brainstorm ideas, refine the message, and ensure the speech is effective and polished.

➤ **Storytelling Techniques vs Classic Step: Structuring the Speech:** The use of storytelling techniques in TWWIST maps onto structuring the speech in classic speech writing. This involves organizing the speech in a way that is engaging and easy to follow and using narrative elements to make the speech more memorable and impactful.

➤ **Timing and Effort Allocation vs Classic Step: Practice and Delivery Preparation:** The final TWWIST step of allocating timing and effort corresponds with allocation for writing then practicing and preparing for the speech delivery in traditional speech writing. This step is crucial for ensuring the speaker is comfortable with the content, timing, and delivery of the speech.

A wise man speaks because he has something to say; a fool speaks because he has to say something. Plato

10.3   The Five Canons of Rhetoric and Their Relation to Storytelling Techniques

The Five Canons of Rhetoric established by Cicero and expounded by Quintilian, provide a powerful framework for crafting and delivering effective, persuasive speeches. The Five Canons of Rhetoric are pivotal in the art of crafting powerful speeches and have been the foundation of rhetorical theory and practice. They have influenced generations of speakers and writers in the art of eloquent and effective communication.

Assembled and organized by the eminent Roman orator Cicero in his treatise *De Inventione,* around 50 BC, these canons were later explored in depth by the Roman rhetorician Quintilian in his landmark 12-volume textbook on rhetoric, *Institutio Oratoria,* in 95 AD. Quintilian's comprehensive work, along with Cicero's foundational concepts, established the Five Canons of Rhetoric as the cornerstone of rhetorical education, a status they maintained well into the medieval Renaissance period and beyond.

1) **_Inventio_ (Invention)**: *Inventio* is the process of developing arguments and discovering persuasive strategies. It involves identifying and formulating the core message of the speech, including establishing ethos (credibility), logos (logical reasoning), and pathos (emotional appeal). *Inventio* is critical in determining the substance of the speech, laying the groundwork for effective persuasion and argumentation.

2) **_Dispositio_ (Arrangement)**: *Dispositio* refers to the organization and structuring of the speech. This canon guides the arrangement of the material in a logical and coherent order to enhance the persuasive impact. It encompasses various parts of the speech: the introduction (*exordium*), statement of facts (*narratio*), division (*partitio*), proof (*confirmatio*), refutation (*refutatio*), and conclusion (*peroratio*). The effectiveness of *dispositio* lies in presenting the argument in a clear, concise, and engaging manner.

3) **_Elocutio_ (Style)**: *Elocutio* concerns the stylistic choices made in the speech, including the use of language, figures of speech, vocabulary, and overall level of formality. This canon emphasizes the

importance of adapting the style to suit the subject matter, audience, and speaker's personality. *Elocutio* is about crafting the speech in a way that is not only persuasive but also memorable and impactful.

4) ***Memoria* (Memory)**: *Memoria*, historically, involved techniques for memorizing speeches, an essential skill in a time before printed materials were widely available. In modern contexts, it pertains to the speaker's familiarity with the content and structure of the speech, enabling confident and effective delivery. *Memoria* involves internalizing the speech to the extent that it can be delivered naturally and with conviction.

5) ***Pronuntiatio* (Delivery)**: *Pronuntiatio* is the final canon, focusing on the actual presentation of the speech. It involves aspects such as voice modulation, gestures, eye contact, and overall body language. *Pronuntiatio* is crucial in bringing the speech to life, ensuring that the delivery is engaging, dynamic, and persuasive, thereby maximizing the impact on the audience.

10.3.1 Relating Rhetorical Canons to The Science of Story

When integrated with insights from Kendall Haven's works "Story Proof" and "Story Smart," Haven [2007, 2014] the Canons of Rhetoric provide a deep foundation for effective storytelling and provide modern scientific support for these ancient techniques. The relationship between the rhetorical canons with Haven's story science is not an accident. Haven's exploration of story science complements the rhetorical canons by elucidating the neurological and cognitive underpinnings of how stories impact audiences. Learning how to give effective and persuasive speeches evolved over time to match what works because of human evolution and environment. Combining these techniques provides a powerful framework for crafting and delivering speeches that are not only structurally sound but also cognitively and emotionally resonant, ensuring a powerful and lasting impact on the audience.

1) ***Inventio* and Cognitive Engagement:** In line with Haven's insights, *Inventio* is not just about creating content but also about engaging the audience's cognitive processes. Haven suggests that stories resonate when they align with the audience's experiences and worldviews. This step involves crafting narratives that connect with the audience's values and beliefs, making the story relatable and memorable.

2) ***Dispositio* and Narrative Coherence:** Haven's research underscores the importance of a coherent narrative structure, aligning with the *Dispositio* canon. A well-structured story, with a clear beginning, middle, and end, facilitates cognitive processing and emotional engagement. This structure helps the audience follow the narrative logically and become emotionally invested in the story.

3) ***Elocutio* and Linguistic Effectiveness:** Consistent with Haven's findings, *Elocutio* involves using language that is not only stylistically appropriate but also effective in triggering emotional and cognitive responses. Haven emphasizes that the choice of words and language patterns can significantly impact how the story is received and processed by the audience.

4) ***Memoria* and Story-Enhanced Memories:** Haven's research into how stories are remembered and retold aligns with the *Memoria* canon. A deep understanding of the story enhances the storyteller's ability to convey it effectively, making it more likely for the story to be internalized and remembered by the audience.

5) ***Pronuntiatio* and Engaging Delivery:** Haven's research on the impact of delivery in storytelling parallels the *Pronuntiatio* canon. His research on storytelling effectiveness suggests that the way a story is presented — including vocal modulation, body language, and emotional expression — plays a crucial role in how the audience perceives and engages with the story.

10.3.2 Relating the Classical Rhetorical Triangle to the Tactical Storytelling Tetrahedron

The rhetorical triangle is a foundational concept in the field of communication and rhetoric. It traces its origins to Aristotle in ancient Greece who first introduced this model in his work *Rhetoric*, written around 350 B.C. It has been fundamental in shaping rhetorical theory and practice since that time.

The triangle consists of three key elements: *ethos, pathos,* and *logos. Ethos* relates to the speaker's credibility and character, *pathos* to the emotional connection with the audience, and *logos* to the logical argument or reasoning. Aristotle's concep- tualization of these elements laid the groundwork for effective persuasion and communication strategies that emphasize the importance of balancing all three components in order to create compelling arguments. The rhetorical triangle is still used today as an essential tool for understanding and developing effective communication in contexts as varied as public speaking, writing, marketing, and media.

Rhetoric then may be defined as the faculty of discovering the possible means of persuasion in reference to any subject whatever.

-Aristotle, Rhetoric

In chapter 6, we discussed the storytelling triangle and expanded it to the Tactical Storytelling Tetrahedron. The connection between the classical rhetorical triangle and the tactical storytelling tetrahedron supports its use as a framework for effective communication. The analysis that follows underscores the synergy between the classical elements of rhetoric and the components of the tactical storytelling tetrahedron. It highlights their combined effectiveness in creating impactful and purposeful communication. Consider the ways in which ethos, pathos, logos, and the tactical objective from the tetrahedron relate to each other.

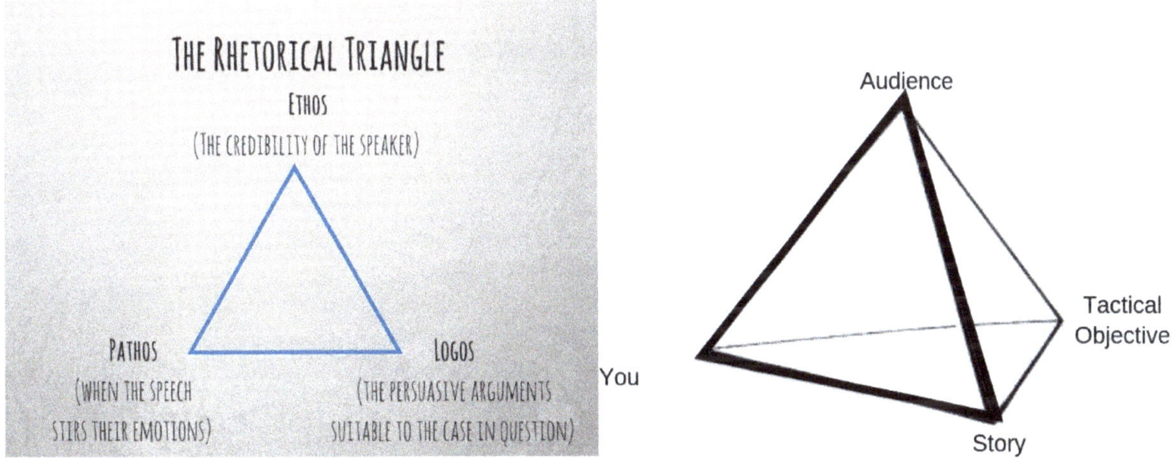

Figure 10.1: *Left shows the classical rhetorical triangle; right is the tactical story tetrahedron.*

- **Ethos and the Author:** Ethos, in the rhetorical triangle, pertains to the credibility and ethics of the speaker or writer. In the storytelling tetrahedron, this corresponds to you, the author, highlighting the importance of your credibility and authority in storytelling in crafting a compelling narrative.

- **Pathos and the Audience:** Pathos involves the emotional connection with the audience, a key aspect of the rhetorical triangle. In the tetrahedron, this aligns with the audience. It emphasizes the need for the story to resonate emotionally with the audience, influencing how they receive and interpret the narrative.

- **Logos and the Story:** Logos is the logical and structured argument in the rhetorical triangle. In the storytelling tetrahedron, this is mirrored by the story. It involves creating a coherent, logical narrative that effectively conveys the intended message.

➤ **The Tactical Objective:** The Tactical Objective is the strategic purpose or goal in the storytelling tetrahedron, an element that extends beyond the classical triangle. It guides the narrative's development, influences how the author crafts the story, and shapes the audience's understanding and engagement, ensuring that the story achieves its intended purpose.

"90% of how well the talk will go is determined before the speaker steps on the platform."

-Somers White

10.4   The TWWIST Strategy for Achieving Common Goals in Speeches

Speeches can have varied objectives, and each speech goal necessitates a distinct approach to ensure effectiveness. For example, informative speeches thrive on clarity and factual content, persuasive speeches hinge on emotional resonance and logical arguments, and entertaining speeches rely on engaging narratives and humor. Understanding these nuances enables the speaker to tailor their speech effectively to the desired outcome.

By applying the TWWIST approach to our understanding that the primary goals of speeches are to inform, persuade, or entertain, it is possible to achieve diverse, high-level goals in speeches. TWWIST's focus on tactical objectives and then looping to refine them into SMART goals ensures that each speech is not only aligned with a high-level goal like informing, persuading, or entertaining but also meets specific, measurable, achievable, relevant, and time-bound refined objectives. This process results in a message that not only reaches the audience but also resonates and inspires the desired response.

Let's explore some of the practical considerations for achieving common goals in speeches:

➤ **To Inform:** The primary aim is to educate the audience.

➤ *Clear and Logical Structure:* Organize content in a coherent sequence that is easy to follow.

➤ *Use of Visual Aids:* Incorporate charts, diagrams, or slides to clarify complex points.

➤ *Simplicity in Language:* Utilize straightforward language to enhance understanding.

➤ *Factual and Accurate Information:* Ensure all data and statistics presented are accurate and up-to-date.

➤ **To Persuade:** The focus is on influencing the audience's beliefs or actions.

➤ *Emotional Appeal:* Use narratives that resonate emotionally with the audience.

➤ *Speaker Credibility:* Establish trustworthiness and expertise in the subject matter.

➤ *Strong Evidence:* Support arguments with credible and compelling evidence.

➤ *Addressing Counterarguments:* Preemptively tackle potential objections to strengthen the argument.

➤ **To Entertain:** Aim at engaging and amusing the audience.

➤ *Incorporation of Humor:* Use light-hearted jokes or anecdotes to maintain a fun atmosphere.

- *Engaging Storytelling:* Employ captivating stories to keep the audience interested.

- *Dynamic Delivery:* Utilize an expressive and animated speaking style.

- *Audience Interaction:* Engage the audience through direct interaction to enhance entertainment value.

10.5 Applying Linguistic and Rhetorical Devices in Storytelling and Speech Writing

More so than in written text, linguistic and rhetorical devices play a crucial role in speeches and presentations. In live communication, the audience does not have the luxury of processing information at their own pace or revisiting previous material for clarity. This constraint elevates the importance of crafting memorable, impactful "sound bites" in storytelling for speeches. Effective use of rhetorical tools such as anaphora, antithesis, and parallelism can create memorable moments that ensure the message not only hits home but also sticks in the audience's memory.

Linguistic and rhetorical devices add rhythm, emphasis, and clarity, making complex ideas more digestible and retainable in real-time. In essence, they transform the transient nature of spoken words into lasting impressions that are essential for the effectiveness and longevity of the message. Below are examples of effective linguistic devices and rhetorical tools from literature, speeches, and famous works that illustrate ways they can be used to captivate your audience in storytelling, writing, and speeches. You may not remember the formal terms when we are done, but you will remember many of the examples and know how to use them.

- **Alliteration:** The repetition of initial consonant sounds in adjacent or closely connected words.

  - *In Storytelling:* "The fair breeze blew, the white foam flew." - *The Rime of the Ancient Mariner, Samuel Taylor Coleridge*

  - *In Writing:* "Doubting, dreaming dreams no mortal ever dared to dream" *The Raven, Edgar Allen Poe*

  - *In Speeches:* "Let us go forth to lead the land we love." - *Inaugural Address, J. F. Kennedy, 1961*

- **Anadiplosis:** Repetition of the last word of a clause at the beginning of the next.

  - *In Storytelling:* "Fear leads to anger. Anger leads to hate. Hate leads to suffering." - *Star Wars, George Lucas*

  - *In Writing:* "Injustice anywhere is a threat to justice everywhere." - *Letter from Birmingham Jail, Martin Luther King Jr., 1963*

  - *In Speeches:* "Strength through unity, unity through faith." - *V for Vendetta, 2006*

- **Antimetabole:** Repeating a phrase in reverse order.

  - *In Storytelling:* "When the going gets tough, the tough get going." - *Popular Saying*

  - *In Writing:* "Ask not what your country can do for you – ask what you can do for your country." - *Inaugural Address, J. F. Kennedy, 1961*

➤ *In Speeches:* "It's not the size of the dog in the fight, it's the size of the fight in the dog." - *Mark Twain*

➤ **Antithesis:** Juxtaposing contrasting ideas in balanced phrases.

➤ *In Storytelling:* "It was the best of times, it was the worst of times." - *A Tale of Two Cities, Charles Dickens*

➤ *In Writing:* "To err is human; to forgive, divine." - *An Essay on Criticism, Alexander Pope*

➤ *In Speeches:* "We must learn to live together as brothers or perish together as fools." - *Martin Luther King Jr.*

➤ **Metaphor:** A figure of speech that implies a comparison. When using extended metaphors or similes, guard against losing the principal subject in the image. Avoid using two or more metaphors in a single sentence or thought.

➤ *In Storytelling:* "All the world's a stage, and all the men and women merely players." - *As You Like It, William Shakespeare*

➤ *In Writing:* "Time is a thief."

➤ *In Speeches:* "The torch has been passed to a new generation." - *Inaugural Address, J. F. Kennedy, 1961*

➤ **Simile:** Comparing two different things using 'like' or 'as.'

➤ *In Storytelling:* "Brave as a lion, he faced his enemy."

➤ *In Writing:* "She was as brave as a lion in that situation."

➤ *In Speeches:* "Our soldiers fought like lions on the battlefield."

➤ **Asyndeton:** Omission of conjunctions to create a concise, impactful statement.

➤ *In Storytelling:* "I came, I saw, I conquered." - *Julius Caesar*

➤ *In Writing:* "He provided the vision, the design, the implementation."

➤ *In Speeches:* "Government of the people, by the people, for the people." - *Gettysburg Address, Abraham Lincoln, 1863*

➤ **Paralipsis:** The technique of drawing attention to something by claiming not to mention it.

➤ *In Storytelling:* Used to create intrigue or highlight a point indirectly. Example: "Not to mention the secret passage in the old mansion."

➤ *In Writing:* Adds information with a layer of ironic emphasis. Example: "I will not speak of his failures, which are many."

➤ *In Speeches:* Draws attention to a point by professing to omit it.

Example: "Not that I loved Caesar less, but that I loved Rome more." - *Julius Caesar, William Shakespeare*

➤ **Aristotelian Rhetoric:** The use of ethos, pathos, and logos as persuasive strategies.

➤ *In Storytelling:* Balances character credibility (ethos), emotional engagement (pathos), and logical development plot (logos).

➤ *In Writing:* Ensures a well-rounded argument or narrative with credibility, emotional appeal, and logical reasoning: "As a doctor (ethos), I understand the pain you feel (pathos), and here is the solution (logos)."

➤ *In Speeches:* Uses the speaker's credibility, appeals to the audience's emotions, and employs logical arguments. "We do not want war (ethos). The mothers of America who sent their sons to war do not want war (pathos). And I have not spoken to a man who fought in war who wants it again (logos)." - *Attack on the Welfare State, Ronald Reagan, 1964*

➤ **Rhetorical Questions:** Questions posed for effect rather than to elicit an answer.

➤ *In Storytelling:* Used to engage the reader or to prompt introspection. "What would you do if you found a hidden treasure?"

➤ *In Writing:* Provokes thought or emphasizes a point. "Is this not what we all strive for?" or "Who among us can say they have never faced adversity?"

➤ *In Speeches:* Engages the audience and highlights key points. "How long? Not long, because no lie can live forever." -

Our God Is Marching On!, Martin Luther King Jr., 1965 or "Will you join in that historic effort?" - *Inaugural Address, John F. Kennedy, 1961*

When effectively utilized in speech writing, these rhetorical devices elevate the orator's message and enhance engagement, depth, and memorability of the communication.

10.5.1 Impactful Linguistic Forms in Speech Writing

Speech writing benefits greatly from various linguistic forms that add emphasis, clarity, and engagement. When adeptly incorporated into speech writing, linguistic tools serve to make the speech more engaging and memorable, enhancing its impact and effectiveness. The utilization of such devices has been demonstrated time and time again in some of the most iconic speeches throughout history. Consider the following examples of some less classical linguistic techniques that are effectively used in speeches:

➤ **Hyperbole:** Exaggerated statements used for emphasis.

➤ "So first of all, let me assert my firm belief that the only thing we have to fear is fear itself." - *Franklin D. Roosevelt, First Inaugural Address, 1933*

➤ **Irony:** Using language that signifies the opposite for humorous or emphatic effect.

➤ "Democracy is a precious thing – especially to a dictator."

➤ **Parallelism:** Similarity of structure in a series of related words, phrases, or clauses.

  ➤ "To err is human; to forgive, divine." - *Alexander Pope, "An Essay on Criticism," 1711*

➤ **Chiasmus:** A reversal in the order of words in two otherwise parallel phrases.

  ➤ "Ask not what your country can do for you – ask what you can do for your country." - *John F. Kennedy, Inaugural Address, 1961*

➤ **Anaphora:** Repetition of a word or phrase at the beginning of successive clauses.

  ➤ "We shall not flag nor fail. We shall go on to the end. We shall fight in France and on the seas and oceans; we shall fight with growing confidence and growing strength in the air. We shall defend our island whatever the cost may be; we shall fight on beaches, landing grounds, in fields, in streets and on the hills. We shall never surrender and ..." - *Winston Churchill, "We Shall Fight on the Beaches" speech, 1940*

➤ **Repetition of phrase:** Repetition of a phrase multiple times with slight variations of visualization

  ➤ Martin Luther King's "I have a dream" speech was a striking example of this technique, using that phrase to introduce a series of his visions for a better future.

10.6   Mastering Speech Presentation

Every speech, even a very well-written speech, is not fully prepared for presentation until it is practiced. Writing the speech is the beginning step that prepares the content; practicing the delivery of the speech is what makes the content resonate with the audience. A well-practiced delivery can elevate a speech to a transformational experience.

10.6.1   Preparation and Practice

It can be tempting to minimize the importance of thorough preparation and practice for a speech presentation. If we use the TWWIST process in writing our speech, we know our message and anticipate how the audience will receive it. Even so, practice is essential to a successful speech delivery. Practice helps us seamlessly refine our engagement with the audience so that our message becomes as meaningful to them as it is to us. Here are several strategies to enhance this process:

➤ **Camera Recording:** Record practice sessions to analyze your performance, including voice modulation, body language, and overall delivery.

➤ **Video Self-Critique:** Review your recordings to identify areas for improvement, paying attention to your gestures, expressions, and clarity.

➤ **Iterative Improvement:** Use feedback from each recording to refine your speech, focusing on different aspects each time.

➤ **Audio Review:** Regularly listen to your recordings to familiarize yourself with your speech's rhythm and pace.

➤ **Peer Review:** Present your speech to friends or colleagues and ask for constructive feedback.

➤ **Fine-Tuning Content:** Adjust the content of your speech based on practice sessions to ensure clear and concise delivery.

➤ **Mock Presentations:** Conduct full dress rehearsals in an environment similar to the actual speaking venue.

10.6.2 Auto-Timed Presentations

Speeches with strict time constraints can be particularly nerve-wracking. Not only do you need to practice content delivery, you must be certain that you can deliver it consistently within the time constraints. The following strategies can ensure precise timing:

➤ **Timing Practice:** Repeatedly practice your speech with a timer to ensure it fits within the allotted time.

➤ **Slide Timing in Presentations:** If you are using PowerPoint or similar tools, select automated slide timing and transitions to help you regulate your pace.

➤ **Script Editing for Brevity:** Edit your speech to remove unnecessary parts and limit your focus to key messages.

➤ **Contingency Planning:** Prepare for possible interruptions or questions by timing sections of your speech.

➤ **Cue Cards:** Use cue cards with time indicators to stay on track during the speech.

➤ **Dry Runs:** Conduct several full-length practices to get comfortable with the timing.

➤ **Rehearse with an Audience:** Practice in front of a small audience to simulate real-time constraints.

10.6.3 Reading the Audience

Written stories are crafted with an audience in mind that is based on anticipated reactions and preferences. Live speeches, in contrast, allow for direct observation of the audience's reactions— body language and facial expressions. These real-time observations provide the speaker with an immediate and dynamic interpretation of the audience's responses. The speaker's challenge, then, is to adjust the delivery accordingly. Consider the following methods for enhancing your awareness of and response to a live speech audience.

➤ **Body Language Analysis:** Pay attention to audience reactions, movements, and facial expressions, adjusting your delivery accordingly.

➤ **Interactive Elements:** Incorporate questions or polls to gauge and maintain audience interest.

➤ **Adaptability:** Be ready to change the tone, pace, or even content in response to audience cues.

➤ **Feedback Incorporation:** Utilize live feedback, both verbal and non-verbal, to refine your speech on the fly.

➤ **Audience Engagement Techniques:** Use rhetorical questions, anecdotes, or humor to connect with the audience.

➤ **Eye Contact:** Maintain eye contact with different audience segments to create a personal connection.

➤ **Post-Speech Interaction:** Engage with audience members after the speech for direct feedback and questions.

Practicing Reading the Audience

The interactive nature of speeches demands a more flexible and responsive approach to audience engagement that is not required when communicating via written stories. Understanding and adapting to your audience in real-time is a pivotal skill that ensures the effectiveness of your speech delivery. Skillful application of real-time adaptations is learned and perfected by practice. By investing time in implementing the following strategies, you can significantly enhance your speech delivery, making the experience more memorable and engaging.

➤ Developing the skill to read an audience effectively is crucial for speakers. It requires practice and experience to interpret non-verbal cues accurately.

➤ Working with a coach/mentor skilled in audience analysis can provide invaluable insights. A coach can observe your speech, compare your interpretations with theirs, and offer guidance on how to better read and respond to your audience.

➤ Post-speech analysis with a coach can reveal discrepancies between your perception and the audience's actual reactions, leading to improved skills in audience engagement.

10.7   Techniques for Overcoming the Fear of Public Speaking

If you are afraid of speaking in public, you are not alone. Public speaking is a common source of anxiety for many individuals. In fact, the fear of public speaking is so well known it has a scientific name—glossophobia. The National Social Anxiety Center (NSAC) says "the fear of public speaking is the most common phobia ahead of death." The mental health website, PSYCOM, adds that up to 75 percent of the population may suffer from a fear of public speaking. For some, public speaking may cause some anxious moments, but for others the idea of speaking in front of a crowd of as little as 25 attendees or as large as 1,000 can be overwhelming and downright terrifying.

Personal Story: Face Your Fears

I grew up in a rural area where the nearest person my age lived a mile away, so I was not very comfortable in groups and was very afraid of public speaking. I had struggled to read aloud in class in middle school, and the other kids made fun of me. Yet when I realized I wanted to become a professor, I knew I needed to overcome that fear.

I first joined the debate team, where my ability to study the material, face a smaller audience, and practice, practice, practice made the fear more manageable. Then I joined the high school theater groups but was too afraid and, as a dyslexic, too insecure at reading out loud to manage a speaking role. The solution? I played Toto and Igor. At first, just being on stage was terrifying enough! But after a few rehearsals, I did not even think about the audience anymore. That is, I did not worry until we actually did the show. Then the laughter as I barked out my only line, a Toto, barking out "Ro-ra-thy Ro-ra-thy," had them laughing and me very self-conscious.

Through the years, I personally have used many of the techniques that follow to overcome the fear of speaking in public. Other techniques I learned as I studied how to become better, even if I did not use them myself. I still generally avoid talking to large crowds and get a few butterflies if I am talking to a new and large group, but I believe that facing our fears is the best way to overcome them.

Facing fear is part of Bandura's theory of self-efficacy, Bandura [1977], where mastery builds your skills and reduces your fear. This happens even if you are not confident you can do it as long as you approach it as a learning experience. So start small, and continue at that level until the fear is manageable and you have mastered it. Then move up to the next level of fear and do it again and again.

10.7.1   Understand and Address the Fear

While many first-time speakers who have been tasked with the responsibility of presenting in front of an audience experience some fear, overcoming that fear is crucial for a successful speech delivery. Overcoming the fear of speaking in public also enhances effective communication and confidence in various professional and personal contexts. The following strategies can help you conquer the fear of public speaking.

➢ **Identify the Source:** Recognize which aspects of public speaking are causing the fear. Is it fear of judgment, making mistakes, or something else?

➢ **Positive Visualization:** In order to build confidence and reduce anxiety, practice visualizing a successful speaking experience.

➢ **Cognitive Reframing:** Shift your mindset from viewing public speaking as a threat to seeing it as an opportunity to share knowledge and connect with others.

➢ **View It as a Learning Opportunity:** Very few speaking opportunities are actually going to make or break your career or life. Even if things go wrong, you can learn from any mistakes you make.

10.7.2   Prepare and Familiarize

"Prepare and practice" are as important to an engaging and impactful speech delivery as "set your objectives and know your audience" is to write that speech. Fear dissipates when you are in familiar surroundings. The more familiar you are with your speech delivery and the environment in which you will speak, the more comfortable you will be. Consider the steps you can take to build your confidence through preparation.

➢ **Thorough Preparation:** Know your topic inside out. Being well-prepared with your material significantly reduces anxiety.

➢ **Familiarize with the Venue:** If possible, visit the venue beforehand to get comfortable with the environment.

➢ **Practice Sessions:** Practice your speech repeatedly in a safe environment, alone or with a supportive audience. After a few times, practice with a friendly audience or family members. Ask them to toss things at you while you speak (which you need to catch, by the way) to further improve your comfort and ability to flow with the audience.

➢ **Practice Like You Will Perform:** Practice your speech under conditions similar to the actual performance. Avoid "practicing in your head" or while seated, especially if you will be standing during the presentation. Practice using the same energy and volume you intend to use, and in a similar space if possible. This approach will increase your comfort with the physical and vocal demands of your speech.

10.7.3   Relax and Breathe

Some people naturally experience more anxiety and fear than others. Even those who are well prepared and practiced or who normally are not fearful may still have some last-minute public speaking anxiety. Here are some practical ways to reduce that stress.

➢ **Deep Breathing:** Practice deep breathing exercises to calm nerves before and during your speech.

➢ **Progressive Muscle Relaxation:** Use this technique to relieve physical tension that may accompany anxiety.

➢ **Mindfulness Meditation:** Mindfulness can help manage stress and improve focus and composure.

10.7.4　Seek Professional Help

➢ **Public Speaking Coaches:** A coach can provide personalized guidance and feedback to improve your speaking skills. If you have fears, take a course; taking one really helped me.

➢ **Therapeutic Support:** For those with severe anxiety, professional therapy, such as cognitive-behavioral therapy, can be beneficial.

➢ **Feedback Mechanisms:** Regularly seek constructive feedback to understand your strengths and discover areas for improvement.

10.7.5　Build Confidence Through Small Steps

Incremental steps are key to building confidence in public speaking. These expanded strategies can gradually enhance your comfort level and skill in addressing an audience:

➢ **Start with Smaller Groups:** Begin your public speaking journey by addressing small, familiar groups. This helps to build confidence in a less intimidating environment.

➢ **Join a Speaking Group:** Participate in groups like Toastmasters, where you can practice public speaking and receive constructive feedback in a supportive setting.

➢ **Continuous Learning:** To gain valuable skills and insights and boost your confidence, engage in workshops or courses focused on public speaking.

➢ **Karaoke Practice:** Karaoke can be an effective and enjoyable way to practice public presentation skills. Choose songs you are familiar with and focus on aspects like dynamic speaking, maintaining energy, making eye contact, and engaging with your audience. It is a unique opportunity to practice presentation skills in a fun setting. Performing karaoke when sober is advisable, as it allows you to remember and learn from the experience more effectively.

➢ **Record and Review:** Record your practice sessions or small group presentations. Review these recordings to help identify areas for improvement and track your progress over time.

➢ **Feedback Mechanisms:** Actively seek feedback from your audience, mentors, or peers. Constructive criticism is invaluable for understanding your strengths and identifying areas needing improvement.

➢ **Gradual Exposure:** Slowly increase your audience size as your confidence grows. This gradual exposure can help ease the transition to larger and more diverse audiences.

➤ **Take Public-Facing Roles:** Engage in public-facing roles such as a sales job or customer service, especially in areas where you are not known. This provides real-world practice in speaking and presenting to strangers, helping you to build confidence and adaptability in your speaking style without the pressure of familiar audiences.

10.7.6 Speaking Journals

Developing confidence in public speaking is a gradual process that can be significantly enhanced by incorporating journaling into your public speaking practice. Journaling will provide a structured way to reflect, learn, and grow and will contribute significantly to building confidence and enhancing your speaking capabilities. Here are ways to maintain a journal of your speaking experiences:

➤ **Journal Your Speaking Events:** After each speaking event, document what went well, what challenges you faced, and how you felt before, during, and after the presentation. This reflective practice helps in recognizing progress and identifying areas for improvement.

➤ **Pre-Event Review:** Before a future speaking engagement, review your journal entries. Reminders of your past successes and lessons learned can help alleviate anxiety. Your journal serves as a personal guide, highlighting strategies that worked and areas where you have grown, reinforcing your confidence and ability to handle various speaking scenarios.

➤ **Continuous Learning:** Use your journal as a learning tool. Over time it will accumulate valuable insights and personal growth milestones, offering a tangible record of your development as a speaker.

➤ **Personal Feedback Loop:** Treat your journal as a feedback mechanism. Regular review and reflection of your entries function like a personalized feedback loop from which you can continue to refine your speaking skills.

➤ **Setting Goals:** Use your journal to set specific, achievable goals for future presentations that are based on your reflections and learning points.

➤ **Celebrating Progress:** Recognize and celebrate the progress documented in your journal. Acknowledging your achievements, no matter how small, can boost confidence and motivation.

10.7.7 Beyond Reading: Memorization and Talking Points

Relying solely on reading a script to deliver your message can diminish the impact of your speech. Here are strategies to avoid this pitfall:

➤ **Know Your Content:** Internalize your speech as much as possible. Familiarity with your content allows for a more natural and engaging delivery.

➤ **Use Key Talking Points:** Instead of a full script, use key points or bullet points to guide your speech. This approach allows for more flexibility and spontaneity in your delivery.

➤ **Leverage Visual Aids:** Use slides or other visual aids not just as a presentation tool but as prompts for your talking points.

➤ **Practice to Video for Memory and Timing:** Recording and reviewing your practice sessions can significantly help you memorize your content and refine your timing. This method also allows you to observe your body language and improve your stage presence.

➤ **Regular Reviews:** Regularly review your key points and the structure of your speech. This habit will reinforce your memory and confidence in the material.

10.8   Learning to Excel in Extemporaneous Speaking

Extemporaneous speaking involves delivering a speech in a seemingly impromptu manner. It requires quick thinking and adaptability. It stands apart from prepared speeches due to its spontaneous nature, although some degree of preparation is typically involved. When practiced and honed, extemporaneous speaking is a skill that can significantly enhance your ability to communicate effectively in a wide range of settings. It requires a blend of preparation, adaptability, and the ability to read and respond to an audience. Acquiring the skills for extemporaneous speaking is an invaluable asset to have in many professional and personal communication scenarios. It can also be a small step in building confidence in public speaking.

10.8.1   How Extemporaneous Speeches Differ from Prepared Speeches

➤ **Interactive/Flexible:** Unlike the fixed content of prepared speeches, many extemporaneous speeches are interactive and allow for adaptation based on audience feedback.

➤ **Spontaneity:** Extemporaneous speeches rely on the speaker's quick thinking and adaptability, which provide a dynamic and engaging experience.

➤ **Audience Interaction:** A higher level of audience engagement requires the speaker to be attentive and responsive. Understanding and responding to audience cues is vital in extemporaneous speaking. The speaker must interpret body language and verbal feedback to make real-time adjustments. For example, a speaker may notice disengagement and immediately shift to a more interactive discussion format.

➤ **When Speaking Is Optional:** Engage in extemporaneous speaking when you have sufficient confidence in your knowledge of the material. In many corporate settings, opportunities for such speaking are abundant, making it crucial to be well-prepared and informed. An example might be a project manager who gives an impromptu update on project status during an unplanned executive visit.

10.8.2   Preparing for Extemporaneous Speaking

Preparation is crucial for extemporaneous speaking, as it provides the confidence and foundation necessary for an effective delivery.

➤ **Topic Mastery:** Deep understanding of your subject allows you to speak confidently without a script. A marketing executive, for instance, might discuss industry trends in an impromptu meeting.

➤ **Improvisational Practice:** Participate in activities like debate clubs or improv workshops to sharpen your quick- thinking skills.

➤ **Mental Structuring:** Develop a flexible mental framework of your speech with key points and transitions. An entrepreneur might mentally outline their pitch before an unexpected investor meeting.

➤ **Staying Informed:** Keep abreast of current developments in your field so that you may speak authoritatively at any time. For example, a tech professional regularly reads industry news in order to discuss the latest technologies spontaneously.

➤ **Reflective Learning:** Analyze past speaking engagements to identify areas for improvement.

➤ **Seize Opportunities:** Engage in extemporaneous speaking in less formal settings, such as at a community event or workplace meeting, to build your experience.

10.9   Key Terms

1) **Verbal Storytelling:** *The use of words and narration to create a compelling experience in speeches and presentations*

2) **Physical Storytelling:** *The use of body language, gestures, and stage presence to enhance a speech or presentation*

3) **Visual Storytelling:** *The integration of visual elements with verbal content to enhance audience understanding and engagement*

4) **Ethos:** *Credibility and character of the speaker or writer*

5) **Pathos:** *Emotional connection with the audience*

6) **Logos:** *Logical argument or reasoning in a speech or writing*

7) **Alliteration:** *The repetition of initial consonant sounds in adjacent or closely connected words*

8) **Antithesis:** *Juxtaposing contrasting ideas in balanced phrases*

9) **Metaphor:** *A figure of speech that implies a comparison*

10) **Simile:** *Comparing two different things using 'like' or 'as'*

11) **Paralipsis:** *The technique of drawing attention to something by claiming not to mention it*

12) **Aristotelian Rhetoric:** *The use of ethos, pathos, and logos as persuasive strategies*

13) **Rhetorical Questions:** *Questions posed for effect rather than to elicit an answer*

14) **Hyperbole:** *Exaggerated statements used for emphasis*

15) **Irony:** *Using language that signifies the opposite for humorous or emphatic effect*

16) **Parallelism:** *Similarity of structure in a series of related words, phrases, or clauses*

17) **Extemporaneous Speaking:** *Delivering a speech in a seemingly impromptu manner, requiring quick thinking and adaptability*

18) **Spontaneity:** *Reliance on the speaker's quick thinking and adaptability to provide a dynamic and engaging experience*

19) **Audience Interaction:** *Engagement with the audience, requiring attentiveness and responsiveness to cues*

20) **Improvisational Practice:** *Participation in activities like debate clubs or improv workshops to sharpen quick-thinking skills*

21) **Mental Structuring:** *Developing a flexible mental framework with key points and transitions for a speech*

1) **Inventio (Invention):** *The process of developing arguments and discovering persuasive strategies*

2) **Dispositio (Arrangement):** *The organization and structuring of a speech*

3) **Elocutio (Style):** *The stylistic choices made in a speech, including language and figures of speech*

4) **Memoria (Memory):** *The techniques for memorizing and familiarizing with a speech's content and structure*

5) **Pronuntiatio (Delivery):** *The actual presentation of a speech, including voice modulation and body language*

6) **Anadiplosis:** *Repetition of the last word of a clause at the beginning of the next*

7) **Antimetabole:** *Repeating a phrase in reverse order*

8) **Asyndeton:** *Omission of conjunctions to create a concise, impactful statement*

9) **Chiasmus:** *A reversal in the order of words in two otherwise parallel phrases*

10) **Anaphora:** *Repetition of a word or phrase at the beginning of successive clauses*

11) **Interactive/Flexibility:** *The ability of extemporaneous speeches to adapt based on audience feedback*

12) **Topic Mastery:** *Deep understanding of the subject, allowing confident speech without a script*

13) **Staying Informed:** *Keeping abreast of current developments in the field to speak authoritatively*

14) **Reflective Learning:** *Analyzing past speaking engagements to identify areas for improvement*

15) **Seize Opportunities:** *Engaging in extemporaneous speaking in less formal settings to build experience*

11 The Final Step: Rewriting/Editing

"My writing is a process of rewriting, of going back and changing and filling in. In the rewriting process, you discover what's going on, and you go back and bring it up to that point."

-Joan Didion

Welcome to the final chapter—**editing and rewriting** – where good writing is chiseled into greatness. It is a tedious step that you may be tempted to get through as quickly and with as little work as possible. But don't take the shortcuts. A rigorous and thoughtful editing process will result in a rewarding end product.

The rewriting/editing journey is about far more than correcting grammar or pruning words, although that is part of the process. Rewriting is the process by which the tactical aspects of your writing transform, aligning precisely with your SMART (Specific, Measurable, Achievable, Relevant, Time-bound) objectives. In this chapter, we will delve into the nuances of editing and rewriting — the alchemy of turning the initial draft into clear, concise, and compelling communication.

Only you can tell your story, but automated tools can help with many editing tasks, especially with smaller chunks of text. However, you need to guard against the overall tone and voice changes that can occur with ChatGPT by independently editing smaller chunks. Make sure to use a consistent role and have a voice specified in your ChatGPT custom instructions or the prompt. ChatGPT has a "writing coach" mode, which can be a good pre-defined role. Throughout this chapter, we will give examples, but these tools are changing rapidly, so keep up to date on their usage; some of the suggestions may be quickly supplanted by new advances.

11.1 Strategies for Critical Analysis While Editing and Rewriting

Critical analysis, by which the initial draft is scrutinized to enhance its clarity, effectiveness, and alignment with the intended goals, is a vital step in the editing and rewriting phase. The following five key strategies and examples provide a framework for conducting a detailed critical analysis of your drafts. Each of these strategies contributes to a rigorous examination of your writing. By systematically applying them, you can transform your initial drafts into refined, impactful pieces of writing that effectively convey your intended message and meet your strategic objectives.

11.1.1 Strategies for Critical Analysis

➤ **Evaluate Argument Strength:** Are your arguments robust and logically sound? Are they well-supported with evidence? When assessing a persuasive essay on renewable energy, for example, be sure you have backed up each claim about its benefits with relevant research and statistics.

➤ **Check for Consistency:** Ensure that your writing aligns with the target audience and purpose and maintains a consistent tone, style, and voice throughout. For example, when editing a technical report, maintain a formal tone and consistent use of technical terminology.

➤ **Identify Redundancies:** Look for and eliminate repetitive or unnecessary information that does not contribute to the main message or purpose. For instance, you will want to remove repeated mentions of the same benefits or features in a business proposal in order to make the document more concise.

➤ **Analyze Structure and Organization:** Assess whether the structure of your writing effectively presents the information and whether it follows a logical sequence. In an academic article, you will want to check that each section logically follows from the introduction to the conclusion with clear, well-organized arguments.

➤ **Examine Clarity and Precision:** Use precise language and avoid vague terms in order to ensure that your writing clearly conveys the intended message without ambiguity. In a policy brief, for example, it is essential to use specific language when describing policy recommendations and avoid using generalizations or vague terms.

11.2 Detachment and Objective Review

Detachment-based analytics is essential in aligning writing with strategic objectives, particularly in the TWWIST framework. This method involves reviewing one's work objectively, as if through a fresh pair of eyes, to evaluate its alignment with set goals. It allows writers to critically assess argument strength, tone consistency, and message effectiveness. By identifying and rectifying any divergences from intended objectives, writers can make revisions that enhance clarity and impact. This approach ensures that each element of the writing directly contributes to the overarching strategic purpose, resulting in more effective and goal-focused communication.

11.2.1 Achieving Detachment

➤ **Take Time Away:** Distancing yourself from your work can provide a fresh outlook upon return.

➤ **Read from Another Person's Perspective:** Pretend to be someone else, like a boss or a family member, and consider how they would interpret your writing. This method can reveal biases or assumptions in your work.

➤ **Read Aloud:** Reading aloud helps to spot issues in flow and structure that may be missed when reading silently.

➤ **Change Your Physical Environment:** Sometimes, reviewing your work in a different setting can offer new perspectives and insights.

➤ **Seek External Feedback:** Getting feedback from others can provide an objective viewpoint, especially from those who may not be familiar with the topic.

➤ **Use ChatGPT for Objective Review:** Tools like ChatGPT can provide an unbiased analysis of your writing, offering insights into areas such as clarity, coherence, and grammar. Submit a section of your writing to ChatGPT and ask for an analysis of its coherence and style. Use the feedback to refine your writing. Utilizing AI tools like ChatGPT for objective feedback can be significantly enhanced by framing detailed and specific prompts.

➤ **Targeted Feedback:** Detailed prompts help in receiving focused and relevant feedback for your specific needs ask for feedback such as "Correct errors and give feedback on this text for understandability for those with less than high-school education:"

➤ **Role Assignment:** Assigning ChatGPT a specific role, like an experienced editor or a particular type of reviewer, can yield insights tailored to that perspective.

➤ **Comprehensive Analysis:** A well-structured prompt encourages a thorough and holistic review of your writing.

- **Example of a Role-Specific Prompt:** "As an NSF reviewer, please assess this section of my proposal based on NSF proposal review criteria. Offer feedback and suggestions for improvement, particularly focusing on the intellectual merit and broader impacts of the proposed work."

- **Breaking Down the Proposal:** When seeking feedback on larger documents like proposals, breaking them into smaller sections can be beneficial. ChatGPT's responses are optimized for shorter text inputs, allowing for more focused and accurate feedback on each part of the proposal. You can do this manually or use tools like ChatGPT splitter.

- **Detailed NSF Review Prompt:** "Imagine you are reviewing a proposal section for NSF. Prompt for input of sections until I say DONE. For each section, explain how well it meets the NSF merit criterion, considering both the new input and the previous sections reviewed. For each input, rate it on a scale of 1-10 and provide specific suggestions for enhancing its impact and clarity."

11.3 Validate and Improve Message Impact

Editing and rewriting are not only about correcting errors but also about validating and enhancing your message's impact. This section focuses on analyzing the effectiveness of your message and refining it, considering the balance between perfecting the content and adhering to time constraints.

11.3.1 Prompts for Assessing Writing Effectiveness

The following prompts are designed to validate and improve the impact of a message in various types of writing. They are suitable for both human reviewers and AI tools like ChatGPT. The goal is to ensure that the writing effectively communicates its intended message and resonates with the audience. After receiving the analysis based on these prompts, use the feedback to make targeted improvements in the text.

- **Policy Advocacy Article:** "Evaluate whether this policy advocacy article effectively persuades the reader to support the new policy on renewable energy. Provide specific suggestions for enhancing its persuasive elements, focusing on argument strength, emotional appeal, and call-to-action."

- **Scientific Discovery Article:** "Analyze this article on a recent discovery in quantum physics. Assess its clarity and accessibility for a general audience. Offer recommendations to improve clarity and simplify complex concepts without compromising accuracy."

- **Company Memo for Employee Motivation:** "Review this company memo intended to motivate employees during a restructuring phase. Does it effectively boost morale and convey a positive outlook? Suggest changes to enhance motivational aspects and ensure a tone of empathy and encouragement."

- **Public Health Advisory:** "Assess this public health advisory for its effectiveness in educating readers about new health guidelines. Check for clarity, accessibility of language, and the inclusion of actionable steps. Provide feedback on how to make it more engaging and easy to follow for the general public."

- **Environmental Project Grant Proposal:** "Review this grant proposal for an environmental project. Evaluate its alignment with the funding agency's criteria, focusing on the clarity of objectives, the feasibility of the proposed methods, and the potential impact. Advise on improvements to increase its chances of success."

- **Marketing Content for a Tech Gadget:** "Examine this marketing content for a new tech gadget. Does it effectively highlight the product's unique features and appeal to the target demographic? Offer suggestions to enhance its persuasiveness and appeal, particularly in the product description and user benefits sections."

➤ **Performance Review Feedback:** "Analyze this draft of a performance review. Does it provide balanced and constructive feedback while maintaining a positive and encouraging tone? Recommend ways to ensure it is clear, specific, and helpful for the employee's professional development."

11.3.2   Make Necessary Changes According to Analysis

Armed with a strong and comprehensive impact analysis, it is time to focus your efforts on areas identified as needing enhancement, such as clarity, argument strength, emotional appeal, or specificity. Revise the text to address these areas, ensuring that the revised version aligns more closely with the intended message and impact. Regularly review and iterate the text based on ongoing feedback to continually refine and improve its effectiveness.

➤ **Evaluate Effectiveness:** Determine if each part of your writing effectively communicates its intended message and resonates with the audience.

➤ **Example of Change (Time Constraint):** In a business proposal due shortly, if feedback indicates that the benefits are not clearly highlighted, promptly revise those sections for clarity.

➤ **Example of Change (No Time Constraint):** For a comprehensive report, if sections are found to be lacking in detail, take the time to conduct further research and elaborate.

➤ **ChatGPT Prompt:** "Analyze this section for clarity and impact. If under a tight deadline, suggest quick enhancements. If time allows, recommend more in-depth revisions."

➤ **Feedback Incorporation:** Actively incorporate feedback, especially from target audience representatives. But don't blindly incorporate all feedback – it's your story, so find the balance between when to accept and when to reject feedback.

➤ **Example of Accepting Feedback:** Lots of the feedback will be easy to just accept – if it does not change your story or tone, it is often best to take someone else's point of view as important. Things that may strongly impact your intended audience must be seriously considered, especially if you are not from that audience segment.

➤ **Example of Maintaining Original Content (Time Constraint):** For an urgent press release, maintain the core message if it is well-received, despite minor subjective preferences for stylistic changes.

➤ **Example of Maintaining Original Content (No Time Constraint):** In a story, keep the well-received narrative style and character development, even if some readers suggest stylistic changes.

➤ **ChatGPT Prompt:** "Based on feedback, identify elements in this document to maintain under both time-constrained and relaxed scenarios and which are critical to change."

11.3.3   Balancing Refinement with Timeliness

Balancing the refinement of your message with timing considerations is crucial. This approach ensures that your commu- nication is not just effective but also delivered in a timely manner. Whether under time constraints or not, the goal is to produce a message that achieves its intended impact while respecting practicality and deadlines.

➤ **Weighing the Need for Further Edits:** Decide whether additional edits are necessary against the importance of timely dissemination.

➤ **Example:** In a time-sensitive project update, prioritize conveying essential updates over perfecting language.

➤ **ChatGPT Prompt:** "Evaluate the importance of timeliness versus further language refinement in this project update."

➤ **Understanding the Time Cost of Revisions:** Recognize that each round of reviews and edits adds time to the writing process.

➤ **Example (Time Constraint):** For an upcoming presentation, focus on major impactful edits and forego minor stylistic changes.

➤ **Example (No Time Constraint):** For a manuscript submission, thoroughly review and revise all sections, even if it extends the process.

➤ **ChatGPT Prompt:** "Advise on prioritizing revisions for this document, considering time constraints and the impact of potential changes."

➤ **Deciding When to Finalize:** Establish a point at which the document meets objectives and deadlines.

➤ **Example (Time Constraint):** Finalize a grant application after addressing all major feedback, ignoring minor improvements.

➤ **Example (No Time Constraint):** For a book manuscript, continue refining until the narrative meets your artistic standards, regardless of time.

➤ **ChatGPT Prompt:** "Review this document and advise whether it is ready for submission, considering both time-sensitive and open-ended scenarios."

11.4   Alignment with Tactical Objectives

Aligning your writing with tactical objectives is a critical step in ensuring that your communication is not just effective but also strategically impactful. However, maintaining a consistent tone and message throughout the piece while also staying in alignment with tactical objectives can be a challenge. Writers often struggle to keep their content focused and may inadvertently drift into tangents that dilute the main objective. Alignment requires a careful balancing act that ensures your writing addresses each of your SMART objectives and does so logically, stylistically, and persuasively.

11.4.1   Refining Strategies for Alignment

To overcome the trap of losing focus and diluting the impact of the message, writers must regularly and critically review their writing against the established tactical objectives. This requires writers to refer to their objectives frequently and refine each section to ensure it contributes directly to its specific goals. In addition, seeking external feedback can provide a fresh perspective and may identify misalignment that is not immediately apparent to the writer. The following steps serve as a guide to aligning your writing to the tactical objectives.

➤ **Review SMART Objectives:** Revisit your objectives to ensure they are clear and SMART. Does your writing address these objectives both in content and intent? Assess each part of your writing and ask how it contributes to your objectives. Is there a direct connection between your words and your goals?

➤ **Message Consistency:** To ensure that your writing maintains a consistent message and supports your objectives, avoid diverging into tangents that do not serve your purpose.

➤ **Logical Alignment:** Does the writing logically support and progress toward your objectives? Are the arguments and information structured in a way that guides the reader to your intended conclusion?

➤ **Targeted Language and Tone:** Match your language and tone to the requirements of your objective. Persuasive writing requires a different lexicon compared to informative writing.

➤ **Using Persuasive Techniques:** If your objective is to persuade or inspire, analyze how well you use rhetorical techniques such as storytelling, emotional appeal, and compelling arguments and make improvements where needed.

➤ **Stylistic Consistency:** Ensure that the style and tone of your writing complement your objectives. A persuasive piece should have a different style compared to an informative one.

➤ **Effective Call to Action:** If your objective includes prompting action, ensure that your writing clearly articulates what action is desired and why it is important.

➤ **Comprehensive Analysis:** Regularly step back to analyze if each section of your writing contributes to your overall objectives, making adjustments as needed.

11.4.2　　Expanded Examples of Objective Alignment

Through meticulous alignment with tactical objectives, your writing becomes more than just words on a page; it becomes a strategic tool designed to inform, persuade, and inspire—effectively achieving your intended goals. Consider the following examples of objective alignment and how it relates to the impact of specific writing objectives.

➤ **For Persuasive Writing:** In a persuasive article that advocates for environmental conservation, each paragraph must weave compelling facts with emotional appeals that culminate in a strong call-to-action for engagement in sustainable practices.

➤ **For Informative Writing:** An informative blog post on blockchain technology logically presents facts and figures using clear, accessible language that aligns with the objective of educating readers who have little prior knowledge of the subject.

➤ **For Proposal Writing:** In a research proposal to seek funding, each section must meticulously address the objectives by outlining the research's significance, methodologies, expected outcomes, and alignment with the funding body's goals.

➤ **For Business Memos:** A business memo announcing a new company policy starts with a clear statement of purpose followed by a concise explanation of the policy, its relevance to the employees, and steps for implementation, all of which align with the objective of clear and direct internal communication.

➤ **For Motivational Speeches:** A motivational speech for a sales team aligns with the objective of boosting morale by using an engaging narrative, highlighting success stories, addressing challenges, and ending with a rallying call for collective effort and goal achievement.

11.5 Editing for Content

Editing for content is a crucial aspect of the rewriting process. Through meticulous content editing, you can refine your work into a coherent, concise, and clear piece of writing that effectively addresses its intended purpose and makes a lasting impact on the audience. Consider what to look for when editing content.

- **Clarity of Purpose:** Make the purpose of your writing immediately clear. Avoid a build-up that delays understanding. For example, in an executive summary, state key findings and recommendations upfront instead of revealing them gradually.

- **Subject Limitation:** Keep each section focused on content that relates directly to the main theme. If writing a review article, for instance, ensure that each section includes only literature relevant to the specific topic being discussed.

- **Inclusion of Major Points:** Include all significant points and information necessary for the reader's understanding. For instance, a research proposal must clearly state the objectives, hypothesis, and significance of the study.

- **Adequate Supporting Details:** Ensure that adequate details and evidence support each topic or argument. Support each claim in a technical report with data, research findings, or specific examples.

- **Detail Overload:** Avoid including more details than necessary for the context. An overabundance of details can lead to information overload. For a project plan provide details essential for understanding the project scope but avoid excessively technical specifics that may not be relevant for all readers.

- **Organizational Flow:** Ensure the organization of your writing is logical and use headings to make it easy to follow. In an academic essay, for example, organize content logically with clear introductions, body paragraphs, and conclusions for each section.

- **Address Key Questions:** Answer "Who, What, When, Where, Why, and How" to provide a comprehensive view of your topic. When writing a case study, thoroughly cover all these aspects to give a complete case overview.

- **Implications and Contribution:** Discuss the implications of your work and its contribution to the field. For example, conclude an academic research paper with how your findings add to existing knowledge and their practical applications.

11.6 Editing for Paragraph Strength, Brevity, and Clarity

When refined by editing for paragraph strength, brevity, and clarity, your writing becomes more than a message. It becomes a strategic vehicle that drives the audience toward your objectives with precision and effectiveness. By careful editing, your paragraphs will be strong enough to carry the weight of your message and your words will engage your audience to understand and respond as your message intends.

11.6.1 Editing for Paragraph Strength

In the TWWIST framework, paragraphs are the building blocks of your narrative. To fulfill its role and convey your message effectively, each paragraph must be robust, clear, and succinct. The following editing guidelines demonstrated through well-written and not-so-well-written examples, will help to ensure that each paragraph has a clear topic and sticks to its foundation.

➤ **Focus on Topic Sentence and Unity:**

➤ *Well-Written Example:* "Whales are among the most intelligent creatures..." followed by details exclusively about whale intelligence.

➤ *Poorly Executed Example:* A paragraph on whale intelligence sidetracks into their feeding habits, diluting the focus.

➤ **ChatGPT Prompt (Voice: Critical Analyst):** "Analyze this paragraph on whale intelligence, ensuring each sentence supports the main idea; identify any off-topic content."

➤ **Support the Main Idea:**

➤ *Well-Written Example:* "Employees should receive pay raises..." with a logical explanation of rising living costs.

➤ *Poorly Executed Example:* Including unrelated information about company profits in a paragraph about employee pay raises.

➤ **ChatGPT Prompt (Voice: Logical Reviewer):** "Please evaluate this paragraph's support for its main idea about employee pay raises, highlighting any irrelevant details."

➤ **Logical Development and Transitions:**

➤ *Well-Written Example:* "Renewable energy is economically viable..." with a natural progression from general benefits to specific economic statistics.

➤ *Poorly Executed Example:* Jumping from renewable energy's environmental impact to its economic benefits without a logical transition.

➤ **ChatGPT Prompt (Voice: Flow Inspector):** "Critically assess the flow of this paragraph on renewable energy, focusing on the transitions between environmental and economic aspects."

11.6.2 Editing for Brevity, Clarity and Sensitivity

Brevity, clarity, and sensitivity in the TWWIST framework are not just stylistic choices; they are strategic imperatives. When editing for brevity and clarity, each sentence should be purged of extraneous words, and every term should be as concrete and clear as possible. It is also important to be sensitive to potential wording that could alienate part of your audience. Consider the practices demonstrated through negative and positive examples that will ensure your writing communicates the intended message as efficiently and effectively as possible.

➤ **Streamline Wordy Phrases:**

➤ *Negative Example:* "The study serves to bring to light the significant importance of intervening at an early stage..."

➤ *Positive Example:* "The study highlights the significance of early intervention."

- **ChatGPT Prompt:** "Review this paragraph and suggest alternatives for any overly wordy phrases, aiming for concise yet powerful expressions."

➣ **Eliminate Redundant Phrases:**

- *Negative Example:* "The end result of the report is that it presents a full and complete account..."

- *Positive Example:* "The report presents a full account of the project's outcome."

- **ChatGPT Prompt (Voice: Conciseness Coach):** "Review this paragraph and suggest where redundant phrases can be condensed for clarity and conciseness."

➣ **Remove Unnecessary Qualifiers:**

- *Negative Example:* "The results were actually quite significant."

- *Positive Example:* "The results were significant."

- **ChatGPT Prompt:** "Examine this text for unnecessary qualifiers and recommend edits for greater precision and directness."

➣ **Avoid Repetition:**

- *Negative Example:* "The budget was insufficient and inadequate for the project's needs."

- *Positive Example:* "The budget was insufficient for the project's needs."

- **ChatGPT Prompt:** "Identify and eliminate repetitive words or phrases in this paragraph to enhance its clarity and effectiveness."

➣ **Use Active Voice:**

- *Negative Example:* "Groundbreaking results were achieved by the team."

- *Positive Example:* "The team achieved groundbreaking results."

- **ChatGPT Prompt:** "Rewrite sentences in this paragraph using active voice to make them more dynamic and engaging."

➣ **Choose Precise Vocabulary:**

- *Negative Example:* "The experiment did not succeed."

- *Positive Example:* "The experiment failed."

- **ChatGPT Prompt:** "Provide suggestions to replace indirect or vague language in this paragraph with precise and impactful vocabulary."

➣ **Use Gender-Neutral Language:**

- *Example 1:* Replace "chairman" with "chairperson" in official documents.

Example 2: Use "they" as a singular pronoun instead of "he/she" in a company policy document.

ChatGPT Prompt: "Please review this business document and suggest changes to make the language more gender- neutral."

Avoid Cultural Stereotypes:

Example 1: Refrain from using clichéd cultural references in a marketing proposal.

Example 2: Ensure examples in a training manual are culturally diverse.

ChatGPT Prompt: "Examine this marketing proposal for any cultural stereotypes or generalizations and recommend more inclusive language."

Respect Original Ideas:

Example 1: Preserve the core message of a colleague's report during editing.

Example 2: Edit a team member's proposal input without altering their fundamental ideas.

ChatGPT Prompt: "Review this co-authored article and provide suggestions for edits that respect the original ideas of each author."

Transparency in Changes:

Example 1: Inform a co-author if their section in a joint paper is significantly modified.

Example 2: Discuss major revisions with the team before finalizing a collaborative document.

ChatGPT Prompt: "Assess these edits made to a collaborative document and provide feedback on whether they maintain the integrity of the original ideas."

11.7   Structural Edits

Structural editing focuses on the overall organization and flow of the document, ensuring that it logically and coherently presents the information. Structural edits are essential in making your document reader-friendly and help to ensure that your message is delivered effectively. Even if you have a good story, if the structure is in the way, the reader may get lost, give up, and skip the material, which reduces your impact. Good structure can also help readers understand transitions between topics when you are transitioning between topics. They can also add visual appeal by breaking up "walls of text." This can all be done by you or peer reviewers by asking for a specific assessment of the structure. We also show examples of using tools like ChatGPT to get structural analysis.

11.7.1   Evaluating Overall Structure

Logical Flow: Ensure the document follows a logical progression from introduction to conclusion.

Example: A proposal that begins with an overview, moves through the problem statement and the proposed methodology and ends with expected outcomes.

ChatGPT Prompt: "Review the structure of this proposal and suggest improvements to enhance its logical flow from introduction to conclusion."

➤ **Cohesion and Coherence:** Check if all document parts are well-connected and collectively present a unified argument or story.

➤ *Example:* In a business report, each section should build upon the previous one to support the overall conclusion.

➤ **ChatGPT Prompt:** "Analyze the cohesion and coherence of this business report, identifying sections that may seem disjointed or unrelated."

11.7.2   Improving Paragraph Structure

➤ **Strong Opening/Topic Sentences:** Check that each paragraph begins with a strong opening sentence. You may use a clear topic sentence that sets the tone for the content. Or, you may use a connection/transition sentence that motivates the reader to keep going in the paragraph. Note not every sentence needs to have this, sometimes you want to add details that follow on to previous material, but you should at least be doing that as a conscious choice.

➤ *Example:* The first sentence of each paragraph in a marketing strategy document clearly motivates the reader or provides that paragraph's focus.

➤ **ChatGPT Prompt:** "Evaluate the first sentence of each paragraph in this marketing strategy document and suggest improvements for clarity and focus."

➤ **Paragraph Length:** Check for paragraphs that are too long or too short. Maintain an appropriate length and balance to ensure readability within the context of your document.

➤ *Example:* Adjusting paragraph lengths in a policy brief to ensure they convey complete ideas without overwhelming the reader.

➤ **ChatGPT Prompt:** "Review the paragraph lengths in this policy brief for optimal readability and suggest adjustments where necessary."

11.7.3   Enhancing Section Transitions

➤ **Transition Signals:** Use transition words and phrases to guide readers from one section to the next smoothly.

➤ *Example:* Implementing transitional phrases in a research paper to connect various sections logically.

➤ **ChatGPT Prompt:** "Identify sections in this research paper that require smoother transitions and recommend appropriate transitional phrases."

➤ **Recap and Preview:** At the end of each major section, provide a brief recap and a preview of what is coming next.

➤ *Example:* Summarizing key points at the end of a section in a training manual and introducing the next topic

➤ **ChatGPT Prompt:** "Suggest ways to recap and preview content at the end of each major section in this training manual for better reader engagement."

Rhythm and cadence play a crucial role in the readability and impact of your writing. Line edits focused on these aspects ensure your writing has a pleasing flow that maintains the reader's interest. Consider the following techniques and tools for improving the rhythm and cadence, which will enhance audience engagement.

11.8.1   Techniques for Refining Rhythm and Cadence

➤ **Vary Sentence Length:** Mixing short and long sentences helps maintain reader engagement.

➤ *Example:* "The project was a success. Our team worked tirelessly over several months, overcoming challenges with creativity and determination."

➤ **ChatGPT Prompt:** "Review this paragraph for sentence length variety and suggest changes to improve rhythm."

➤ **Use of Pacing:** Adjust the pacing to match the tone and action of the content.

➤ *Example:* "The chase was on. Heart racing, feet pounding the pavement, she sprinted through the crowded streets."

➤ **ChatGPT Prompt:** "Analyze the pacing in this chase scene and recommend adjustments for enhanced impact."

➤ **Employing Literary Devices:** Tools like alliteration and assonance can add musicality to your writing.

➤ *Example:* "The whispering winds wove through the willows."

➤ **ChatGPT Prompt:** "Identify and enhance the use of alliteration in this sentence for rhythmic effect."

11.8.2   Automated Tools for Rhythm and Cadence

Apart from manual editing, several automated tools can assist in refining the rhythm and cadence of your writing.

➤ **Grammarly:** For checking grammar and punctuation, which indirectly affects rhythm. The paid version has significantly more suggestions.

➤ **ProWritingAid:** Offers reports on sentence length and variety.

➤ **Hemingway Editor:** Highlights complex sentences for simplification.

➤ **Text-to-Speech Software:** Helps identify awkward phrasing when heard aloud.

➤ **Slick Write:** Analyzes style and rhythm issues in your writing.

11.8.3   Example of Rhythm and Cadence Enhancement

➤ *Before Editing:* "The team worked hard. The project was completed successfully. The results were satisfactory."

➤ *After Editing:* "After months of relentless effort, the team triumphed, delivering a project marked by stellar outcomes and resounding success."

➤ **ChatGPT Prompt:** "Revise the original sentences to improve rhythm and cadence, focusing on sentence variety and flow."

11.9   Key Terms

1) **Editing and Rewriting:** *The process of refining a piece of writing by correcting errors, improving clarity, and ensuring alignment with specific objectives.*

2) **Critical Analysis:** *The process of examining and evaluating the clarity, effectiveness, and alignment of a piece of writing with its intended goals.*

3) **Detachment-Based Analytics:** *A method of objectively reviewing one's work to evaluate its alignment with strategic objectives by assessing argument strength, tone consistency, and message effectiveness.*

4) **Objective Review:** *Reviewing work from an unbiased perspective to identify areas of improvement in clarity, coherence, and overall effectiveness.*

5) **Content Editing:** *Editing focused on ensuring that the writing is concise, clear, and effectively conveys the intended message.*

6) **Brevity and Clarity:** *The strategic imperative to ensure each sentence in writing is free of extraneous words and every*

7) **Redundant Phrases:** *Unnecessary repetitions that do not add value to the content and should be eliminated for clarity.*

8) **Active Voice:** *A sentence structure where the subject performs the action, making the writing more dynamic and engaging.*

9) **Precise Vocabulary:** *The use of specific and impactful words to convey meaning clearly and effectively.*

10) **Structural Editing:** *The process of refining the overall organization and flow of a document to ensure logical and coherent information presentation.*

11) **Logical Flow:** *Ensuring that a document progresses in a logical sequence from introduction to conclusion.*

12) **Cohesion and Coherence:** *The unity and consistency of a document's parts, making sure they collectively present a unified argument or story.*

13) **Paragraph Structure:** *Ensuring that each paragraph begins with a clear topic sentence and maintains an appropriate length for readability.*

14) **Recap and Preview:** *Summarizing key points at the end of each major section and introducing the next topic for better reader engagement.*

11.10   Other Terms

1) **Alignment with Tactical Objectives:** *Ensuring that writing logically, stylistically, and persuasively addresses specific strategic goals.*

2) **Paragraph Strength:** *Ensuring that each paragraph has a clear topic, supports the main idea, and maintains logical development and transitions.*

3) **Rhythm and Cadence:** *The flow and readability of writing are achieved through varying sentence length, adjusting pacing, and employing literary devices.*

4) **Automated Tools for Editing:** *Software and applications like Grammarly, ProWritingAid, and Hemingway Editor that assist in refining writing by checking grammar, style, and readability.*

5) **Streamlining Wordy Phrases:** *The process of reducing lengthy phrases to more concise and powerful expressions.*

6) **Unnecessary Qualifiers:** *Words that do not contribute to the overall meaning and can be removed to make the writing more precise.*

7) **Repetition:** *The recurrence of words or phrases that can dilute the clarity and impact of the writing. However, repetition can also be used intentionally to enhance memorability.*

8) **Gender-Neutral Language:** *Using terms and pronouns that do not specify a particular gender to promote inclusivity.*

9) **Cultural Stereotypes:** *Generalizations about cultural groups that should be avoided to ensure inclusive and respectful language.*

10) **Respecting Original Ideas:** *Maintaining the core message and fundamental ideas of a colleague's or team member's input during editing.*

11) **Section Transitions:** *Using transition words and phrases to guide readers smoothly from one section to the next.*

12) **Transparency in Changes:** *Informing collaborators about significant modifications made to their contributions to maintain integrity and collaboration.*

Bibliography

John R Anderson, Daniel Bothell, Michael D Byrne, Scott Douglass, Christian Lebiere, and Yulin Qin. An integrated theory of the mind. *Psychological review*, 111(4):1036, 2004.

Bonnie B Armbruster. The problem of "inconsiderate text.". *Comprehension instruction: Perspectives and suggestions*, pages 202–217, 1984.

Bonnie B Armbruster, Thomas H Anderson, and Joyce Ostertag. Does text structure/summarization instruction facilitate learning from expository text? *Reading research quarterly*, pages 331–346, 1987.

Elisa Bandini, Alba Motes-Rodrigo, Matthew P Steele, Christian Rutz, and Claudio Tennie. Examining the mechanisms underlying the acquisition of animal tool behaviour. *Biology Letters*, 16(6):20200122, 2020.

Albert Bandura. Self-efficacy: toward a unifying theory of behavioral change. *Psychological review*, 84(2):191, 1977. Jerrold E Barnett. Facilitating retention through instruction about text structure. *Journal of Reading Behavior*, 16(1):1–13, 1984.

Mina Beigi, Jamie Callahan, and Christopher Michaelson. A critical plot twist: Changing characters and foreshadowing the future of organizational storytelling. *International Journal of Management Reviews*, 21(4):447–465, 2019.

Tony Bingham and Marcia Conner. *The new social learning: A guide to transforming organizations through social media.*

Berrett-Koehler Publishers, 2010.

Ken Blanchard, Jane Ripley, and Eunice Parisi-Carew. *Collaboration begins with you: be a silo buster*. Berrett-Koehler Publishers, 2015.

Mary E Boyce. Organizational story and storytelling: a critical review. *Journal of organizational change management*, 9(5): 5–26, 1996.

John H Bradley and Frederic J Hebert. The effect of personality type on team performance. *Journal of Management Development*, 16(5):337–353, 1997.

John D Bransford and Barry S Stein. *The IDEAL problem solver*. Centers for Teaching Excellence - Book Library. 46., 1993.

John D Bransford, Ann L Brown, Rodney R Cocking, et al. *How people learn*, volume 11. Washington, DC: National academy press, 2000.

Jerome Seymour Bruner. *Acts of meaning: Four lectures on mind and culture*, volume 3. Harvard university press, 1990.

Lin Chen, Shaowu Zhang, and Mandyam V Srinivasan. Global perception in small brains: Topological pattern recognition in honey bees. *Proceedings of the National Academy of Sciences*, 100(11):6884–6889, 2003.

Michael P Clough. The story behind the science: Bringing science and scientists to life in post-secondary science education.

Science & Education, 20:701–717, 2011.

Edward Meredith Cope. *An introduction to Aristotle's rhetoric: with analysis, notes and appendices.* Macmillan, 1867. Michele Crossley. *Introducing narrative psychology.* McGraw-Hill Education (UK), 2000.

Frans De Waal. *Are we smart enough to know how smart animals are?* WW Norton & Company, 2016.

11 Bibliography

Merlin Donald. *Origins of the modern mind: Three stages in the evolution of culture and cognition.* Harvard University Press, 1991.

Vanessa Urch Druskat and Jane V Wheeler. How to lead a self-managing team. *MIT Sloan Management Review*, 2004. Nancy Duarte. *Resonate: Present visual stories that transform audiences.* John Wiley & Sons, 2013.

Lisa S Ede and Andrea A Lunsford. *Singular texts/plural authors: Perspectives on collaborative writing.* SIU Press, 1992. Joshua Foer. *Moonwalking with Einstein: The art and science of remembering everything.* Penguin, 2012.

Howard E Gardner. *Leading minds: An anatomy of leadership.* Basic Books, 2011.

Stephen D Gladis. *WriteType, Personality Types and Writing Styles.* Human Resource Development, 1993.

Narasimhaiah Gorla and Yan Wah Lam. Who should work with whom? building effective software project teams. *Commu- nications of the ACM*, 47(6):79–82, 2004.

Kendall Haven. *StoryProof: The Science Behind the Startling Power of Story.* Bloomsbury Publishing USA, 2007.

Kendall Haven. *Story smart: Using the science of story to persuade, influence, inspire, and teach.* Bloomsbury Publishing USA, 2014.

Chip Heath and Dan Heath. *Made to stick: Why some ideas survive and others die.* Random House, 2007. Jerome Kagan. *Surprise, uncertainty, and mental structures.* Harvard University Press, 2002.

Joshua Klayman. Varieties of confirmation bias. *Psychology of learning and motivation*, 32:385–418, 1995.

Lorelei Lingard. Collaborative writing: Strategies and activities for writing productively together. *Perspectives on Medical Education*, 10(3):163–166, 2021.

Robert R McCrae and Paul T Costa Jr. Reinterpreting the myers-briggs type indicator from the perspective of the five-factor model of personality. *Journal of personality*, 57(1):17–40, 1989.

Bonnie JF Meyer, Carole J Young, and Brendan J Bartlett. *Memory improved: Reading and memory enhancement across the life span through strategic text structures.* Psychology Press, 2014.

Isabel Briggs Myers, Mary H McCaulley, and Robert Most. *Manual: A guide to the development and use of the Myers-Briggs Type Indicator.* Consulting Psychologists Press, 1985.

Katherine Nelson and Robyn Fivush. The emergence of autobiographical memory: a social cultural developmental theory.

Psychological review, 111(2):486, 2004.

Ram Nidumolu, Jib Ellison, John Whalen, and Erin Billman. The collaboration imperative. *Harvard business review*, 92(4): 76–84, 2014.

Ivan P Pavlov. Conditioned reflexes: An investigation of the physiological activity of the cerebral cortex., 1927. Translated and edited by Anrep, GV.

Marcus Fabius Quintilianus. *De institutio oratoria*, volume 2. Teubner, 1854. Philippe Rochat. *The self in infancy: Theory and research*. Elsevier, 1995.

Theodore R Sarbin. Believed-in imaginings: A narrative approach. In *Believed-in imaginings: The narrative construction of reality.*, pages 15–30. American Psychological Association, 1998.

11 Bibliography

Simone G Shamay-Tsoory. Brains that fire together wire together: interbrain plasticity underlies learning in social interactions.

The Neuroscientist, 28(6):543–551, 2022.

Robert W Shumaker, Kristina R Walkup, and Benjamin B Beck. *Animal tool behavior: the use and manufacture of tools by animals*. JHU Press, 2011.

Annette Simmons. *Whoever tells the best story wins: How to use your own stories to communicate with power and impact.*

Amacom, 2015.

Stephen J Skripak, Anastasia Cortes, and Anita Walz. Teamwork in business. *Fundamentals of Business*, 2018.

Perry W Thorndyke and Frank R Yekovich. A critique of schema-based theories of human story memory. *Poetics*, 9(1-3): 23–49, 1980.

John Selby Watson et al. *Quintilian's Institutes of Oratory: or, Education of an Orator*, volume 2. Bell, 1892.

Douglass J Wilde. *Teamology: the construction and organization of effective teams*. Springer Science & Business Media, 2008. R Yuste. Cells that fire together, wire together. *Journal of NIH Research*, 4:60–60, 1992.

www.ingramcontent.com/pod-product-compliance
Lightning Source LLC
Chambersburg PA
CBHW041139300726
48978CB00016B/1322

* 9 7 9 8 8 9 7 9 5 4 5 8 2 *